"The Coordination Computer," Finesse argued, "just happens to be the only instrument capable of organizing the incredible variety of physical and mental mutations that space travel has brought to the human species. There are millions of people settling thousands of worlds scattered through billions of stars. If it were not for the computer's ability to match specific mutants to specific habitats, and direct them there, there would be no human colonization of the galaxy at all."

"Regardless," answered Knot "it makes the Coordination Computer the *de facto* ruler of mankind. I distrust and fear that power, and do not want to be associated with it. I value my freedom, and I am loyal to my own kind. You are a normal, representing the galactic government I detest."

"CC knows everything about everyone it is interested in. And now CC is ready to recruit you. You are the one selected."

Other Avon Books by
Piers Anthony

BATTLE CIRCLE
CHAINING THE LADY
CLUSTER
KIRLIAN QUEST
MACROSCOPE
OMNIVORE
ORN
OX
RINGS OF ICE
THOUSANDSTAR

MUTE

PIERS
ANTHONY

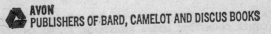

AVON
PUBLISHERS OF BARD, CAMELOT AND DISCUS BOOKS

MUTE is an original publication of Avon Books. This work has never before appeared in book form.

AVON BOOKS
A division of
The Hearst Corporation
959 Eighth Avenue
New York, New York 10019

Copyright © 1981 by Piers Anthony
Published by arrangement with the author
Library of Congress Catalog Card Number: 80-69936
ISBN: 0-380-77578-6

All rights reserved, which includes the right
to reproduce this book or portions thereof in
any form whatsover. For information address
Blassingame, McCauley & Wood, 60 East 42nd Street,
New York, New York 100017

First Avon Printing, April, 1981

AVON TRADEMARK REG. U.S. PAT. OFF. AND IN
OTHER COUNTRIES, MARCA REGISTRADA, HECHO EN
U.S.A.

Printed in the U.S.A.

Part 1

MUTATION

CHAPTER 1

Knot always slept on his left side. Early in life he had tried to vary it, but long ago had given that up as futile. Normal, symmetrical repose was for normal, symmetrical people.

He put his right foot over the edge of the hammock, ready to get up. He paused, as he always did, to look at it. It was a fine, big, healthy foot, with six well-formed toes. The foot of a minimally mutant human being.

He set it on down to the floor, doing a slow barrel-roll emergence from the web. He stood and stretched. His left foot was smaller, stunted, with only four toes, but it served. His legs differed in length, but he had learned to compensate, walking with his right knee chronically bent so that he hardly bumped at all when he traveled. His hands differed from each other similarly, and his ears; it was as though nature had run out of raw material before completing him. Often he had wished for a redistribution: a finger moved from this hand to that one, some muscle and bone shifted from one side to the other. But he always had to remind himself that as physical mutancy went, his case was marginal. He could, with proper clothing and effort, pass for normal.

Here at the enclave, he didn't bother; his condition was really an asset that he tried to make more obvious. The *real* mutants were better able to accept him that way.

Knot dug out his clothing, which was tailored to his physique. The enclave had excellent handcraftsmen: a source of personal pride to him. It was Knot's job to make the employment assignments, and this was no casual matter. This enclave had an excellent record, and this was due in large part to Knot's professional skill.

He set out for the mess hall. The dawning day outside his bunk-cube was lovely; the blue sun of Planet Nelson was striking through the green morning cloud layer, starting the strong updraft that would soon clear the sky. In the evening the process would reverse, with a visible downdraft and closure by vapor. Knot, like most residents, was fascinated by these natural color shows. No two were quite alike; the patterns and colors shifted with countless minor variables, and the shows were useful for entertainment, divination, artistic inspiration, and wagering. Holographs of them were exported commercially.

But he could not dawdle, this time; his slot for breakfast was upon him, and the mess-chief became surly when the normal flow was disrupted.

The mess-guard had four eyes. All of them focused on Knot as the man frowned. "Have you checked in at the office?" He spoke with a certain awkwardness, for he also had two tongues.

"I have," Knot said, standing so that his suit exaggerated his imbalance. No one could mistake him for a normal now. "Here is my card."

The guard perused the card. "Very well. Go in and take your ration from the counter and sit down at a green table. You do have color perception?"

"Yes—in the right eye," Knot said. "Monochrome in the left—"

"Once you get established, you'll be assigned to a compatible group at a red or blue table," the guard said. "But newcomers have to eat alone, until we get to know them. We have a lot of variation here, but we're the top enclave in this region of space, and we don't like trouble."

"I understand," Knot said with due humility. "I'll try to conduct myself properly."

He went on in, smiling privately. He had gone through this ritual with this guard for the past year, every morning—and with the predecessor-guard for two years before that. Knot would be alarmed if the man ever recognized him.

MUTE

Breakfast was a leaf of leanfruit, the succulent foliage that was a meal in itself. An enterprising mutant had discovered how to detoxify it, at one swoop ameliorating the enclave's problem of nourishment. Knot felt pride in that, too; he had selected that mutant for that research. The man had been blind and scrawny, with reverse joints on his fingers, unable to do much useful work, but had an insatiable appetite. At another enclave he would have been a useless burden destined for an untimely accident—such accidents were common in such situations—but Knot had told him he could eat all he wanted if he could figure out how to avoid being poisoned by what was most available. The man had proceeded with a will, noting that no native animals died, though many consumed leanfruit. An enzyme in their saliva did the trick. Now that enzyme was routinely included in the salad dressing. The mutant had become a hero, while Knot was forgotten—and that was the way it had to be.

Actually, the leanfruit breakthrough had not helped everyone. Some mutants could consume grass, wood shavings, or paper refuse; others were unable to digest any natural food. But the breakthrough had helped the majority, and enhanced the status of the enclave. The hero had been awarded a silver medal on a chain—which was typical of the bureaucracy, since he happened to be allergic to that metal.

Knot glanced around the hall. There were twenty tables, half of them occupied. This was a small mess, its service extended efficiently by its continuous shifts of operation. There were several others, to allow reasonable segregation among mutants. These ones were minimal: extra digits, or distorted portions of the body, or superfluous appendages of not too gross a nature. Some did not show, as with the woman who had three livers and an extra lung; she would have been much in demand among enclave males had she not also had three reasons opposing any friendly approach.

Some of those present looked at Knot with mild curiosity, not recognizing him. He knew them all, of course, but made no show of familiarity.

After the meal Knot repaired to his office. The outdoor color show was over by this time, as it generally was. One

5

day he was going to pull a string to get his breakfast slot shifted, so that he could enjoy the show as most others did. But it was hard to pull strings when no one remembered him.

His secretary was already bustling about. Her name was York, and she looked impressively normal. It took a second glance for newcomers to realize that her bosom was composed of three breasts. Knot wondered whether she was any relation to the woman with three livers, but decided against; there was no physical resemblance, and in any event mutations were not hereditary. Not in that sense.

But that superficial normality could be a problem. Once York had been challenged by a surly arrival who hated normals and refused to deal with her. In a fit of pique York had ripped off her own blouse and triple halter and silenced him most effectively. There were no normals in this enclave.

"Two routine and one special," York announced with a smile. She was moderately pretty, and more than moderately smart. He wondered at times why she didn't apply for cosmetic surgery to enable her to join the normals without onus. It was permitted. Mutants, on the few occasions they conceived, gave birth to normal babies; there were no breeding restrictions, and many mutants did go under the knife so they could pass. Yet the majority did not, and this was not merely a matter of economics. A person who had been raised a mutant, identified with mutants for the rest of his life. Probably it was York's pride of the flesh; she did not *want* to be normal.

Actually, Knot thought, it would be a shame to mastectomize such a beautiful breast. She was a true mutant, not a genetic freak; her extra breast was directly between the other two and of equal size and configuration, except it was somewhat squeezed. She had quite a double cleavage, when she cared to show it! When nonmutant females had extra breasts, in contrast, they tended to be below the regular ones, like the teats on an animal, in parallel lines down the torso.

She caught him looking. "Did we do something last night?" she inquired brightly. "I have no note of it—"

"No, no, my mind was drifting," Knot said quickly.

"That was evident, as was its direction of drift. Maybe tonight, then—?"

"I'll take the two routines first, then the special," Knot said. "Make notes as usual."

"Of course." She knew exactly what he meant. She would listen in on the intercom and transcribe a summary of each interview for the file. She was very good at this. Her summaries were complete almost before each interview ended. If she didn't have a note on a given event, it probably hadn't happened. Which was the case with their conjectured liaison of the prior night.

The first client was a large man, whitish of skin, with reddish splotches, whose head rose into a blank and hairless dome. The ears were mere holes, the nose a double slit, and there were no eyes at all. Only the mouth was normal.

"Salutation," Knot said. "You can hear?" York's preliminary note, on the desk before him, indicated that the man could perceive sound, but it was better to establish this openly. Mutants could be sensitive about their handicaps, even among other mutants. The attitudes engendered by life among callous normals could take time to abate.

"I can hear," the man said clearly. "I am Flas, from Planet Jeen."

"Excellent! I've heard good things of Jeen."

Of course the man challenged this, suspiciously. "What do you know of it?"

Knot was prepared; he had an excellent geographic memory, which he cultivated for just this reason. Clients were much easier to put at ease when their home worlds were complimented. "The crystal dunes on the north continent there are among the prettiest sights in the galaxy. If I ever can afford a vacation, that is where I'd go." Knot paused, artfully. "Um, I did not mean to refer to a sense you lack. My apology."

"Who are you?" the mutant demanded gruffly, satisfied. He was not, as Knot had surmised, sensitive about his blindness, and now he knew that Knot was indeed familiar with his home planet.

"I am Knot, the placement officer of Enclave MM58 on Planet Nelson."

The lofty forehead wrinkled. "If you are not he, why do you address me now?"

"Knot, with a sounded K, one syllable," Knot said patiently. He had been through this, too, many times before, and rather enjoyed it. "My name."

The mutant smiled. "Knot," he repeated, pronouncing the K. "Apology." He was now fairly well relaxed.

"Accepted. It is a common misapprehension. Some claim my name has suffered more mutation than my body. May I shake your hand?"

The mutant put forth his large right hand. Knot met it with his equally large hand. The mutant's grip was gentle, though he was obviously quite strong.

"You are larger than you sound," Flas said. "And mutant," he added, feeling the sixth finger.

"We are all mutant here," Knot assured him. That was why he had shaken hands; otherwise the blind mutant could have been in doubt about Knot's status, despite his hint about it. "We don't like to have normals interfering. We are all like you: min-mutes and mod-mutes, of human-norm intellect or above, able to function independently. This enclave is self-supporting; we export as much as we import. We have pride."

"Pride," Flas echoed wistfully. "I have known little of that. Even the lobos have higher social status than my type, on Jeen."

Which was evidently the major reason Flas had come here. "Lobos are surgically normal people, of no special significance," Knot said warmly. "Mutants are the catalyst of modern human society." This message, too, he had repeated many times, but it always buoyed him: the justification of his kind. "Without us, there would be no space travel, no colonization of inclement planets or habitats. Without us, in fact, the human empire would collapse and the Coordination Computer would be junk."

"You speak as if you believe."

"I *do* believe! And you will believe too, or you will not fit in well here. We have the pride of the flesh. Normals are largely restricted to the surfaces of Earth-type planets; the future of the species lies with the mutants."

"The psi-mutes, maybe," Flas said. "Not with our kind."

"The phys-mutes too! Today Enclave MM58 is self-supporting; ultimately we may become a creditor entity, with our own representative in the Galactic Concord. Because of the loyalty and application of specially skilled mutants like you."

"Pep talk," Flas said. "I have heard it before."

"You will perceive new meaning in it. This is not a junkyard enclave; this is a viable economic society. What are your skills?"

Despite his superficial reserve, Flas smiled, responding to Knot's enthusiasm. "I am good with my hands. I have made hundreds of baskets in my day."

"A basket case!" Knot snorted. "Where is the future in baskets?"

The mutant shrugged. "When I asked them that, they sent me here."

"You have a questioning mind and an independent spirit. They don't like that in some places. We do like it here." Knot considered. "It is my job to find the ideal situation for you considering your physical, mental and social propensities. You will not be assigned anywhere against your will; if you don't like what I suggest, I'll look for something else. Sometimes I get too innovative and miss the mark embarrassingly. Sometimes something sounds good, but doesn't work out in practice. If there were not such problems, there would be no point in my job, would there?"

"You're working up to something awkward," Flas said.

"Astute observation. We have a local animal we call the snird, a kind of cross between a snake and a bird in the Earth-book listing. It lays eggs in the dark, and these eggs contain a chemical of value in stellar photography. The elevated radiation of space interferes with conventional processes, as we mutants well know, but this chemical is resistant. The problem is that in the raw state it is hypersensitive to light. Even an instant's exposure ruins it. So we must collect the eggs in complete darkness. Unfortunately the snirds are protective of their eggs, and their bite is poisonous."

"Take the eggs with pincers, or wearing gauntlets," Flas suggested, interested.

"The eggs are extremely delicate, and of odd shapes and sizes. Careless or mechanical handling breaks them. They must be kept warm and intact until brought to the laboratory. In addition, they must be harvested at the right moment; only a 'ripe' egg, distinguished by a slightly hardened surface, possesses the necessary quality. A green one is useless. Only an expert human touch suffices to distinguish between them—but for some reason most of our sighted people are reluctant."

The mutant laughed. "I can well believe!"

"We have elevated the incentive bonus, to no avail. A good snird-egg harvester can arrange his own hours of work, has a 20 percent extra food ration, and a generous personal-expense allowance. It is possible to develop a comfortable savings account that permits early retirement."

"If he survives that long!"

"Yet the snird gives fair warning. A faint buzz before striking—" Knot paused. "How good is your hearing?"

"Excellent. And my courage. How bad is a snird strike?"

"Not fatal, if treated in time. We do have excellent treatment facilities, and an alert, attractive and solicitous nurse. But it is better to avoid it—which an experienced harvester can normally do."

"You figure I'll rise to the challenge?"

"You do strike me as that sort of man."

"You play me like a violin," Flas said. Then he decided. "I'll give it a try."

"Excellent." Knot activated the intercom. This was a redundant gesture, as it was already on, but he preferred not to advertise that fact. "Have a courier conduct Mutant Flas to the Foraging Unit, and notify them that he will essay the egg harvesting, snird division."

"He's got nerve," York remarked.

"The women of MM58 appreciate nerve," Knot told Flas. "I believe you will like it here. The Foraging foreman will brief you thoroughly, of course."

The courier entered the office. She was a young lady whose arms were linked together by fused hands; she could move them only as a unit. They could not be surgically separated because the bones were merged, palm to palm; she would have to have both hands on one arm, and nothing on the other, and the hand would not have functioned well enough to be worthwhile.

10

Flas stood, tracking her by the sound. "This way, Mutant," the girl said. Her voice was dulcet, and her pronunciation of "mutant" made it sound like a badge of honor.

Knot relaxed. He had put together a good crew here, trained to make clients respond positively and feel welcome. Nevertheless, there was always a certain tension, and the first interview of the day was the worst. This one had gone very well. The Foraging Unit had been bugging him for another harvester for some time.

The next client entered. This was an older woman. She had large bright eyes, but instead of ears her head sprouted a stout pair of horns. The lower part of her face projected forward, like the muzzle of a sheep, and her mouth was obviously unsuitable for human speech. She wore a rather voluminous robe that concealed any other mutations she might have, except for hands that were callused and hooflike.

Knot held up his right fist in the clubfoot signal of greeting. A number of mutants had problems with their extremities, so this sublanguage was useful. Knot was familiar with a great many forms of communication.

The woman perked up when she recognized the gesture. She brought up her own fist.

Knot introduced himself, speaking aloud at the same time as he signaled, so York could transcribe it. "I am Knot, the placement officer of MM58." There was no problem with the pronunciation of the name in sign language. "You are"—he read the signals she returned—"Greta, transferred here at your request because"—he smiled warmly—"because you received news of our stature and wanted to participate." He made an expansive gesture. "That is a very positive attitude, Greta. What do you have in mind to do here?"

Now Greta was doubtful. She had been employed before as a water carrier, but had not been very efficient because it was hard for her to pick up the buckets. Also, there had been no need for the service, since water was pumped in to central locations of that enclave. Thus it had been mere make-work, useless. She preferred to find better employment before she met with a UA—Untimely Accident—but did not know what that might be. Yet she had heard that MM58 seemed to be charmed that way, with everyone there finding good jobs.

Knot pondered briefly. She had paid him a considerable compliment, unknowingly—but it also showed the challenge. He had a high level to maintain, and not every mutant could be made useful. His chief skill was the ability to align mutants with employments no one else would have thought of, but a certain amount of luck was important.

"Most of our tasks are menial, but they are necessary to our best functioning as an enclave," Knot said/signaled. "You don't object to routine physical labor, so long as you know it is productive?"

Greta agreed with a forceful motion of her hoofed fist.

"Let me see your foot," Knot said.

Surprised, she showed her feet. Her legs were human, and fairly good ones at that, but the extremities were indeed like hooves. They were cloven in three or four places, marking where the toes should be, but the nails were so gross as to dominate the entire digits.

"We have a local winery," Knot said/signaled. "We don't like the tax burden on imported beverages, but we have to process all our water anyway, and we do like our relaxation. So we do for ourselves. Perhaps some year MM58 vintage will be renowned in the galaxy. But since at the moment the authorities governing the good planet of Nelson frown on such activity, we operate quietly. We use no power equipment, no foreign additives. We just press the grapes—they're not really grapes, but we like to call them that—we press them in ancient and time-honored fashion. We—"

"Trample out the vintage?" she asked, catching on.

"Your feet would seem to be admirably suited to the labor. Our grapes have small spines that make it difficult for ordinary human feet to press them properly, and of course we don't use footwear for this. So if you don't find it offensive or morally objectionable—"

"I'm thrilled!" she signaled. "It's much better than carrying buckets of water nowhere!"

Knot tapped the intercom. He had made another good placement. "After a day's hard work, our men grow lusty and thirsty," he concluded. "They like anything associated with their drink."

Greta, obviously starved for male companionship, seemed to be considering the prospects as she left. Knot never neglected the social angle; here where every person was mutant, deformities and differences that were prohibitive elsewhere became negligible. In general, the more closely a person approached human norm, the more attractive he or she was considered to be—but there was an extremely broad middle ground, and almost anyone could find a partner if he or she really wanted to.

"CC Knot scores again," York murmured over the intercom in the moment Knot was alone. It was a standing joke between them. CC was the abbreviation of the Coordination Computer, which fitted mutants to specialized positions on a galactic scale. Knot did it only for this enclave. But there was a similarity between their jobs. York teased him because she knew he did not like the Coordination Computer.

The third client was indeed special. She was young and pretty and so completely normal in appearance that he was startled. But there were many nonapparent forms of mutation. She could have an exotic chemical imbalance that prevented her from functioning normally. She might have eyeballs in her belly, concealed by her clothing. She might have brain tissue in her chest and a spleen in her head. York had no note on any such thing, but York was not infallible. He would simply have to fathom her mutancy for himself, by observation and careful questioning, and proceed from there.

Knot started his routine introduction, but the girl leaned forward and turned off his intercom. In the process her blouse separated from her torso in the fashion blouses had been designed to do for thousands of years, showing that there were certainly no eyeballs or brain tissue in that portion of her anatomy. Her breasts were fully as firm and shapely as York's, and there were only two, so that there was no undue crowding.

Knot forced his attention back to business. He started to protest her action, though he really would not have minded if she had leaned forward similarly ten more times.

But before he spoke, she brought out a printed card. It said AUDITOR.

Oh no! A surprise audit of the enclave! And he had just placed a client in a quasilegal position, making moonshine wine. Also, more insidious: This meant this woman was in fact a normal, so that all of her visible and suggested attributes were genuine. That provided a retroactive luster to his recent glimpse, exciting him and embarrassing him simultaneously.

The woman watched him with calm amusement. She had certainly turned the tables on him! Knot nodded with rueful resignation. He activated his intercom. "York, this client poses special problems. I'll have to take her on a tour of the premises before I can make a placement."

"Understood," the secretary answered. Her tone was disapproving; she was evidently suspicious that he wanted to get an especially attractive min-mute into a truly private nook for a seduction. His office made such things feasible, for those mutants who did not get suitably placed were not permitted to remain in the enclave beyond a reasonable grace period. Knot wished York's suspicion were true; he did have an eye for the woman. He knew that York felt that if he wanted to seduce anyone today, she should be first in line. But now, not only did he have no chance with this luscious client, he would incur York's wrath anyway. It would be hard to convince her of the truth.

"We can't be overheard outside," Knot murmured as they emerged from the office. The sky was now completely clear; day was well established. "Do you want the full tour, or shall I fill you in on the enclave indiscretions at the outset and save us both time?"

She smiled. Knot, accustomed to the efforts of mutants who often had strange faces, was surprised again; she was beautiful. Even after allowing for the fact of her normalcy, the humanoid ideal. Normals differed from each other less than mutants did, but this one had to be close to the positive extreme. "Show me the leadmuter."

Knot grimaced, surprised a third time. "You have a better source of information than we thought."

"Much better," she agreed with a smugness that would

have been objectionable in anyone else. She held out her petite, five-digited hand. "My name is Finesse."

He shrugged and took the hand in his huge right. She drew him in toward her, leaning forward to plant a light kiss on his cheek. She smelled refreshingly of pine needles.

"Finesse," he said. "Is that literal or allegorical?"

"Yes." She shifted to his small left hand, neatly interlocking her four fingers with his three and capturing his thumb with her own, and walked beside him. The mutants that they passed glanced enviously, not recognizing either of them but wishing they did.

"I presume this is a friendly audit," Knot said. "Or are you merely making sure I cannot slip away?" He gave his hand a token shake, as though hefting shackles. He did not care to admit how exciting it was to have a lovely normal turn on to him as if he were attractive to her. She had an ulterior motive, of course—but what was it? She could have required the leadmuter information of him without ever touching his hand.

"Never trust an auditor," she said, squeezing his hand. She had to have noticed his disparity of fingers, but gave no sign of aversion. "Every one of them will deceive you."

Fair warning! But she really hadn't provided any information yet, straight or deceiving. It seemed he would have to wait on her convenience.

"The leadmuter is separate from the main enclave," he said. "In an isolated region, with a difficult approach. Not suitable for clothing like yours."

"You wish me to remove it?"

Yes! he thought. And said aloud: "I was hinting that you might prefer to come back at another time, dressed for the occasion. Boots, leather breeches, outdoor gloves—"

"During which period of delay the exhibit would disappear?" she asked, smiling to disarm the charge.

Knot essayed a gesture of denial—and found he could not, for she still held his hand captive. The enclave had been audited before, many times, for the powers that existed on the planetary level were suspicious of success.

But never an audit like this! Knot became reluctantly more suspicious. "May I see your credentials?"

"You perused them pretty well in your office." But she finally let go his hand and fished in her bosom, bringing out an ID disk on a neck chain. She faced him so as to bring the disk close to him, and held it up beside her face. The illumination came on, showing the holograph of her head, with her name, code and position. She was a legitimate Coordination Computer auditor.

"CC?" he exclaimed, distracted from the physical credentials that were again in view below the legal ones. "You're from offworld?"

"Naturally. Did you think I was a backplanet girl?"

This was a new dimension. He had assumed she was a Planet Nelson representative. Yet it was hardly possible to counterfeit such IDs; only the Computer staff commanded the authority and technology. In addition, he noticed now, she had the forearm tattoo pattern of a space traveler. This was a galactic audit!

"Satisfied?" Finesse inquired with another sunny smile.

"No. Since when does a galactic auditor hold hands with the auditee?"

"Was I holding hands with the whole enclave?" she asked with mock alarm.

"The enclave is innocent of this particular crime. I represent the enclave administration, and that is what you are auditing, I presume. But you hardly need to play up to me; you can have me fired if I do not cooperate with you in every way."

"True," she agreed sweetly, taking his hand again. "Why do you resist?"

Why, indeed? he thought. *You are begging for seduction, and unless you are a nymphomaniac, this is too suspicious to be accepted.* And he almost imagined he heard an answer: *Smart man!*

"I am not so naïve as to believe that an attractive normal woman representing CC itself prefers to dally with a mutant."

"Some normals have perverse tastes."

She said it lightly, but the remark chilled him. Some normals did indeed have abnormal inclinations. They had a twisted fascination for deformity. The strange aspects of mutants turned these normal people on sexually. Yet many mutants were so eager for the attention of normals that they would put up with the most extreme indignities for it. If Finesse were a person of power with the taste for perversion, she could make things extremely difficult for him. He did not like perversion—but his enclave was hostage for his behavior, and he would have to do whatever she demanded.

This was, of course, exactly the sort of leverage he exerted against incoming mutant females who attracted him. Knot could appreciate the irony of it, that a woman he had at first taken for a mutant was now putting him in this position. No doubt he deserved it. Fortunately, he had a special resource. He could manage.

"A penny for your thoughts," she said.

"A genuine Earth-type ancient bronze coin?"

"Of course not. They're collector's items. Rarity has made them appreciate so inordinately in value that they are now actually worth their face amount. Would you accept another kiss instead?"

What *was* this? "Do I have a choice?"

"You're avoiding the issue."

"You play with fire. How do you know I won't take you into the wilderness, rape you, and drop your body in a bog, never to be found again?"

"What, never?"

"Once a body is mired, it can remain for millennia. Old Earthly fossils, dinosaurs, were found—"

"No decent bogs here, according to the geography I checked."

"There are things here that the geography does not dream of." All too true, as she must know.

"Then I suppose I should answer your question." She brought out another disk. "I have an alarm bleeper. You would not be too thrilled if I set it off before you were through."

Knot nodded soberly. Actually, any threat to an auditor would create enormous mischief. His question had been an expression of petulance rather than any real threat, and she knew it. She could play with him as she wished, with virtual impunity. That was exactly what she seemed inclined to do.

"You can have it," she said, handing him the disk.

Yes, she was playing with him. She was cocksure. Bye and bye, in his own fashion, he would play with her. She was not dealing with an ordinary patsy, this time. Her experience on other worlds gave her confidence that was not necessarily warranted.

The route, as he had warned, was devious and difficult. The leadmuter was supposed to be an enclave secret, and was hidden well out of the way. They had to climb a rocky escarpment, wedge through a thick tangle of brush, and wade through a cold stream.

"You're right," Finesse said. "I would have been better off without clothes."

"Except for the brambles," he agreed. "It grows easier once we pass the brushland. Then you may take off your clothes if you wish to."

"I may. Is this terrain comfortable for the leadmuter?"

"No. Fortunately he doesn't have to experience it. He works in a cave."

"I didn't know this was cave country."

"It isn't, according to your geography."

"You rather fascinate me."

"Mutual, I'm sure."

She turned her sweetly tousled face toward him, brushing a tress out of her eyes. "I have given you every opportunity, but you haven't taken advantage of me yet. Are you normally this slow, or are you unconscionably shy?"

"I wouldn't want that alarm to bleep."

"You have charge of it!" she protested, her bosom heaving enticingly.

"A voice-activated device keyed to your voice? I only hold it; I don't control it."

"But you left it the other side of the river."

Knot patted his pockets. "I must have dropped it!"

"That was the most gentle drop I ever watched. Were you afraid of breaking it?"

She was one hideously perceptive female! He had not spied her watching him. "Some of these things go off when broken," he admitted. "That could have been awkward."

"So you were setting me up—but you haven't made your move. Or did I miss it?"

"These things do take time."

"You must have remarkably easygoing reflexes."

"The flesh is willing, but the spirit is cautious."

"You don't trust me," she complained.

"Well, you did warn me about auditors."

She laughed. "So I did. I didn't mean you to take it so to heart."

"I trust you to do your business. I'm not sure what that business is."

"You have a microscopic memory. I'm an auditor."

Knot felt a chill. Why her reference to memory? "Fortunately, I'm *not* an auditor. I don't need to entrap anyone."

She drew on his arm. "Did I offend you? I apologize and offer to make delicious amends."

"No offense," he said quickly. He had the growing feeling that he was fencing with someone of greater skill than his own.

"But you reacted." She turned a beautifully innocent gaze on him. "Knot, I don't want it to be negative between us. What did I say to hurt you?"

"We mutants can be very sensitive about our abnormalities, in the presence of normals." That wasn't it, but he was most concerned that she not catch on to his real worry.

"Six-four fingers? That's hardly enough to notice. I'm sure *I* haven't noticed."

"Obviously." He had to smile, relaxing. She was on the wrong track. "Here is the cave."

"Already? We were just getting warmed up."

"There's always the return trip. I know a longer, more scenic route."

"Oh? I thought you distrusted my motive."

"I do. So I had better ascertain what it is before letting you go."

"That's more like it." She peered into the cave. "Is it safe?"

"Should be. It has endured for thousands of minutes."

"You hollowed out a whole cave, just to hide your project?"

"Well, it isn't easy to hollow out half a cave."

She delivered a reproving glance. She was so cute it was

hard for him to keep properly in mind that she was extremely hazardous to his welfare. "The leadmuter did it, before we tuned him in to lead. He changed the rock to lead because the metal was denser and occupied less space than ordinary material. He hollowed out quite a chamber, entertaining himself."

"I don't understand. You said he did this before he learned about lead, yet—"

"He turned ordinary rock to lead, at first. Then it occurred to us that if he could do that, he might in turn convert the lead to something even more dense. So we persuaded him to change his lead to gold, almost twice as compact. That pleased him, because it gave him more room in his cave with less debris. Then we started using the gold for our artwork—the enclave has a number of fine sculptors and other artisans—so we did him the additional favor of hauling the gold out of his way. That keeps his cave entirely clean, so he's happy. We tuned him into lead as a raw material, instead of as a product."

"Lead transmuted into gold," Finesse murmured. "No wonder your enclave is self-sufficient."

"Oh, we don't sell much of the gold," Knot hastened to assure her. "We do trade some of it for other things we need."

"Barter," she agreed. "Avoiding discovery and taxation."

"Until now," he agreed glumly.

"Not to mention the matter of concealing a viable psi-mute in an enclave allocated for phys-mutes."

"Not to mention," he agreed again. This was real trouble. Fortunately, he had his way to alleviate it—provided he were able to play his trump effectively.

They entered the cave. They rounded a bend in it, and the passage opened into a pleasant chamber. There was none of the moisture or dirt associated with a natural cave; this was even and clean and dry. A normal-seeming man sat on a crude throne made of solid gold, concentrating on an ingot of lead before him. He gave no sign of being aware of the intruders.

"He is almost deaf and blind," Knot said. "And feeble-minded. He was not very happy until we arranged this occupation. Now all his needs are provided for, and he is left alone most of the time. He lives for his work; he gets a thrill from a challenging transmutation. But all he knows now is lead, as origin or product. It would be a shame to take him away from this. He really doesn't belong in psi-mute facilities."

"I can appreciate that," Finesse said dryly. She walked around the cave as though about to move into it as an apartment, her eyes taking note of the crude blocks of lead at one side, the crude blocks of gold at the other. A compact, sturdy cart stood on a steel track in an alcove. "What's this?"

Knot walked across. He put his arms around the nearest block of gold and heaved it up, his right arm doing three quarters of the work. It was about the size of a four-liter container, called a gallon locally, but it weighed as much as Knot himself did. He took one staggering step and eased it into the cart, slowly extricating his pinched fingers.

The weight started the cart on its way. "That will roll to our metalshop; it's downhill from here," he said, flexing his arms to alleviate the cramp caused by the effort. He could have handled the weight more readily, had both arms been of equal size and strength; but he wasn't really sure his build was a disadvantage. Most normals were right-handed, too; it just wasn't as extreme.

"You do have a notion what a gallon of gold is worth?" Finesse asked. "Maybe seventy kilograms in that one block—"

"The earnings of a normal's lifetime," Knot said. "But you have to understand, it takes our leadmuter several hours to convert that amount, and he is tired afterward."

"Tired!" she snorted. She looked at the man again. He had not moved. His head was supported by his hands, and a small string of drool dangled from his flaccid lips. The block of metal before him seemed smaller than before; it was changing to gold.

"Can he transmute anything to anything?" she asked. "I mean, were he trained appropriately?"

"We don't know. He prefers the heavier metals, and it is not easy to change his program. It took several months to shift him from lead-as-product to lead-as-origin. The gold is worth enough to stay with, I think."

"It is not for you to decide. The leadmuter must be registered with the Coordination Computer."

"Who will take him away from us, to no advantage to him, us or CC."

"The law is the law," she said firmly.

Knot sighed. "Do you realize the removal of this source of income will put our enclave into the red?"

"Surely an executive of your ability will find ways to make up the difference. Most mutant enclaves operate in the red, after all; it is no colossal shame."

"But we're the best enclave, no burden on the economy of our planet. We want to stay that way."

"Solvency that is attained by illegal means is much the same as thievery." She looked again at the little set of tracks. "I don't suppose we could take the cart back?"

"Unsafe," Knot assured her. "Besides, we must pick up your alarm bleeper before it gets lonely and sets itself off."

"It's a dummy." But she moved toward the exit passage.

He followed her out. Obviously she was still teasing him—but why? She had verified what she had come for: the presence of an unregistered mental mutant. There would be hell to pay, for the enclave's concealment of this asset was a crime against the Coordination Computer, which was the effective executive branch of the human government of the galaxy. She could reasonably expect to face a desperate man in Knot. Why should she leave herself open to persuasion or threat?

Knot distrusted this, but decided he had better play along. He needed to know what this too-attractive and too-devious auditor was really up to. Naturally she had sufficient means of self-defense; there would be no physical coercion possible, even if that happened to be his style. It was *not* his style, not by a parsec. It was time he let her reel him in.

"You mean I could have laid hands on you any time with impunity?" he asked, as though none of his private thoughts had occurred.

"That depends." She selected a hummock and sat down on it. She reached into a pocket and brought out what seemed to be a small ball. "This is Mit," she said, holding it in the palm of her hand. "Hold him."

Knot took Mit. Mit was an ornate shell, of the kind found in oceans, curled into a tightening spiral of nacreous hue, with a shiny pink lip around the opening. "A very pretty conch," he said. "I like it. Is the ocean audible?" He lifted it toward his ear.

Then a greenish claw emerged from the shell. Knot paused, startled. The claw was small, but could have taken a nasty nip from his lobe.

"Mit is a hermit crab," Finesse said as two hesitant eye-stalks appeared. "Very shy around strangers."

"A crab—out of water?"

"He keeps a reserve in his shell, and he's modified. He can remain indefinitely on land."

Knot was fascinated, knowing she was not showing him this as an idle curiosity. This might relate to whatever she was hiding from him. "So he's more than a shell. I still like him. Come on out, Mit; I would be the last one to hurt you. I like animals."

Mit came out. His right claw was comparatively large and strong, while his left was small. He peered up at Knot with coalescing confidence. He tapped his claw against the rim of his shell, once.

"That's a click of approval," Finesse said. "He likes you."

"He should. He is built like me. Is Mit a mutant too?"

"It is normal for crabs to have one claw larger than the other."

"I'm not sure you answered my question."

"You are not as slow as you look. You are right. Mit is mutant."

"Ah. Mental rather than physical? Does he have psi?"

"Yes. He is probably the best psi-crab in existence. He is clairvoyant and precognitive."

Knot laughed, pleased. "He *knows* there is no danger!"

"Precisely. No danger to him or to you. When I carry him, I know when there is any threat to me. He hides in his shell and chatters his teeth."

"Chatters his teeth!" Knot knew she spoke figuratively. "Did you say he has a double psi talent? I thought that was impossible."

"Extremely rare, but it happens. Even triple talents are theoretically possible. One chance in a hundred billion or so, I believe—and since there are not nearly that many mutant births in a century, we really don't need to let the prospect concern us unduly. CC is very interested in such combinations, and collects all the dual-mutes it finds."

Knot felt another chill. He covered it with a smile. "No wonder I couldn't bluff you. You know all my secrets."

She nodded smugly. "Mit knows, at any rate. Tangible things, mainly; intangibles become too complex for his comprehension."

Intangibles were beyond the crab's limited power. Knot allowed himself more hope. "I find myself liking you, Finesse. Let me be blunt, while I have the clairvoyance in my hand. You've been coming on to me from the outset, but you're a normal, and not an ugly or stupid one. What is on your mind? You can't find me physically attractive."

"Men don't have to be physically attractive." She squinted at him appraisingly. "Actually, there is a certain appealing quality to you. Were your proportions normal, you would be a handsome man, and even as it is—"

"You're avoiding the issue again. There is no visible reason why you should play up to me, especially on business time. You've gotten your information; you verified the power of the leadmuter. You caught our enclave cheating the planetary government and hiding a psi-mutant from CC. It makes most sense for you to scoot the hell home to the machine and make your devastating report. Instead you're acting as though I'm of more interest than—" He paused, glancing down at the hermit crab. "Mit, did she come to investigate *me*?"

"Won't work, Knot," she said. "He's only a crab, with the mind of a crab. Even if he could grasp the complexities of human subterfuge, he can neither comprehend your speech nor reply in kind. He tunes in on danger to himself and to those nearest him, without defining it. At least, not in our terms. Were you telepathic, you could converse with him and obtain more specific information; otherwise the best you can do is tap questions on his shell and get yes-no answers. Since I mean you no mischief of a tangible kind, he feels secure. You'll learn nothing from him you can use."

"Getting me fired or transferred to an inclement enclave or lobotomized as a criminal would not be completely intangible by my reckoning," Knot said. "You don't have to club me on the head to hurt me."

"Oh, such things are not beyond Mit's ken. He might not understand them, but he can precog your future grief. And he would inform you by clicking on his shell. But my plans for you are a good deal more devious, and I really do not mean you any harm, Knot. I do rather like you, despite your ornery ways, though I will not pretend you are any rival to a normal or any model of integrity."

She was really working him over—but she still had not caught on to his secret, he judged. Best not even to think about that. "And if I take you in my arms and do with you what you're obviously made for—?"

"In due course. I'm not an amateur in that respect. But first there is one other thing I must show you." She reached into another pocket and drew out a small, slender, long animal with a little round, whiskered face. "This is Hermine, the weasel. She's a mutant too."

Knot accepted the weasel in his left hand. She was warm, with sleek fur, and had the secure footing and litheness of a healthy predator. Knot liked all animals other than household pests, but he found himself liking this one in quite a strong, specific way. "And what is your talent, Hermine?" he asked, not expecting an answer.

Nice man. Like you.

Knot started, almost dropping the crab in the forgotten hand. "Broadcast telepathy!" he exclaimed. "And near-human intelligence. Mental verbalization. Isn't that at least a double mutation?"

"Double mutations of a beneficial nature are prohibitively rare," Finesse said. "Usually they'll be a physical-mental combination, such as a minimal body abnormality and a substantial mental one, or vice versa."

Did she know? Knot was suddenly nervous again.

She knows you are a double mutant, Hermine projected.

And you are a transceiver telepath! Knot thought back. *You can read minds, and you can project your own* thoughts. **You must be one of the most potent telepaths in the human galaxy.**

I'm not human! the weasel retorted.

I didn't think you were. But you are in the human galaxy.

The weasel galaxy!

Do weasels build spaceships?

You are too smart for me.

But you've got my number, you cute little huntress. Aloud he said: "Hermine does seem pretty smart. If she's not a double mute—telepathy and intelligence—what is she?"

"She's a full telepath—receive and transmit. A single mutation, but a potent one. Most telepaths are partial, being either readers or senders, with varying degrees of proficiency. In range of a human mind—her range is three or four meters, the power varying inversely with distance—she draws on the intelligence of that human mind, much as we draw on the abilities of computers. By herself, she is ordinary weasel intelligence."

"Fascinating. Did you pick up our mental conversation just now?"

No.

"No," Finesse echoed. "She transmits on a narrow band, mind-to-mind. Close up she can send to anyone; from a distance she must target a particular mind, one she knows well. She can receive from a familiar mind at greater distances. But the other party has to be consciously projecting, and Hermine has to work at it. Right now she's in touch with you, not me; I have no idea what secrets you two are exchanging."

Is that true, Hermine?

Half true, Knot. She isn't receiving, but she's guessing.

I don't want her to know my secret, Knot thought with a mental picture of a human face with a closed zipper in lieu of the mouth.

Nice man. Funny man. I won't tell. But she will know. She's very smart. Her thoughts are like the teeth of a carnosaur.

"I don't need to be a telepath to figure that out," Finesse said, frowning prettily. "You're making a deal to hide your paranormal power from me. But I'll have it anyway."

"So Hermine tells me. But you already have the lead-muter, who is potentially far more valuable to you than I could ever be. Can't you settle for that?"

"Let the animals play," she said. "They'll be all right."

Mit feels no threat, Hermine agreed. Put us on the ground.

Knot put his hands to the ground, and both weasel and crab moved into the grass.

Now Finesse leaned forward, treating him once more to a glimpse of her frontal charms. Her eyes were large and green, the prettiest Knot had seen in a long time. She was a marvel of appearance, and obviously knew it, and used her physical attributes to sway his mind. Knot was aware of all this, yet felt the impact. She was deliberately making him want her, and the strategy was working.

"I am here to interview you," she said. "The lead-muter was only a pretext. I'm not really an auditor; I'm a scout. The Coordination Computer is looking for someone, and suspects you may be that one."

"How did CC catch on that I have mental mutancy? I thought I had escaped detection."

"You are the son of a man who traveled in space within a year before you were born. That made you a potential mutant. The sperm of the male is affected by the radiation of deep space, so that for up to three months thereafter, until the affected reservoir is used up, the offspring—"

"And I *am* a mutant, as is plainly evident," Knot said. He put his hands together, making obvious the disparity in their sizes and configurations. "Here I am working in a mutant enclave, doing a satisfactory job—"

"More than satisfactory," she said. "Enclave MM58 is, as you surmised, No. 1 on the index for client adjustment. That points right to the placement officer."

"So I'm doing a good job, then. An excellent job. A superlative job—whatever you will. I happen to have empathy, a feel for the needs of mutants, and I like my work. I like helping people. This is no psi-power; it is just personality and inclination and effort. And luck. Next year some other enclave will be No. 1, when one of its gardeners discovers a diamond mine in the barren soil and it can suddenly afford to cater to all its outré whims, and its placement officer will seem suddenly more talented—while simultaneously our own enclave has to make do without our illicit income from transmuted gold. A great fat huge lot that will prove!"

Finesse was watching him, smiling. That only spurred him to further commitment. "I empathize with mutants because I *am* one, and I work hard to make my clients comfortable. Had you been a client, I would have worked just as hard for you, to place you where you would do best and be happiest. This is the one job I am really fitted for. Why should CC want to take me away?"

"You're beautiful when you're earnest," Finesse said, stroking the side of his face. "Maybe your psi-talent is not useful elsewhere in the galaxy. Why don't you just tell me what it is and let me form an opinion? I can't make the decision, of course, but I *am* a trained interviewer, just as you are, and I might be able to provide some hint how CC will react."

There was a kind of exhilaration he obtained from fencing with another person in his specialty. Knot interviewed physical mutants and placed them compatibly; she did the same for mental mutants. But this time he was the subject, and he did not want to be placed. "Why don't you just kiss me and slap me and go home in a huff?"

"I'll try," she agreed. She stood, kissed him on the lips, slapped him lightly on the cheek—and remained blithely looking at him. "Give me a nudge. I haven't quite mastered the third action yet."

Is she really as seduceable as she seems? Knot thought fiercely at the weasel, not certain whether the little animal remained in range.

"Of course I am," Finesse said.

He started. "Oh—Hermine broadcast to you instead of to me?"

"She knows me better. She decided I would want to make that particular decision for myself. Most females do, regardless of what they profess openly, and she's one of us. Not that I needed any telepathy to grasp that particular thought."

"You have encountered it before?" He felt jealous.

"Many times. That's par for the course. I hardly even

need to work at it anymore; the signals come naturally. But what I really want at the moment is your secret— and Hermine, a pox on her secretive little heart, has not vouchsafed that to me."

"Suppose I ask her to report to me on *your* questions?"

"Be my guest."

Knot concentrated, seeking contact with the weasel. Finesse seemed to be doing the same. They were outside Hermine's immediate range, but within her general range.

Knot laughed, receiving the telepathic message. "Right now!" he said, and took Finesse in his arms.

Ellipsis, Hermine thought, and went back to the vole she was stalking.

CHAPTER 2

In the afternoon Knot called on Hlet, the enclave supervisor. Hlet was proportioned like a normal, but he had two faces—one on each side of his head. This was hardly noticeable until he walked away—and he preferred to sit at his desk, his back to the wall. Knot wondered whether the backface got bored staring at the blankness, or whether it merely slept.

Hlet blinked. "I don't believe I know you."

"I'm the new placement officer," Knot said. "You can verify it with my secretary."

"Perhaps I'd better." No one bluffed Hlet. He made the call. "York—do you have a new man, name of Knot?"

"Yes, sir," she replied smoothly. "Did I forget to notify you? I'm sorry; we've been so busy. He's been with us several days. He's a min-mutant, right-handed—"

"Thank you." Hlet cut the connection. "Never can get anything straight around here. How can I help you?"

York had covered for him, as she always did. They had it down to a routine, and played this scene for someone almost every day. York was not immune to Knot's psi, but she remembered the routine so well that the slightest nudge sufficed. "I was audited this morning," Knot said. "A normal from CC—"

"Oh, yes. They do check us out periodically. They don't really care about things like our winery or untaxed artifacts. You'll get used to it. Did you brush her off?"

30

"Not exactly. She asked about the leadmuter—"

"You didn't show him to her!" Hlet exclaimed, aghast. "We don't admit to any outsider that—"

"I had no choice. She already knew of him, somehow; a lie would have been disaster. But I hope she will downgrade his performance in her report."

"A CC auditor? They squeeze blood from stones!"

"And are interested in squeezing gold from lead. But it seems she considered me, ah, attractive as mutants go. So I saw no alternative except to—"

Hlet's eyes widened appreciatively. He had the good of the enclave at heart, and was not scrupulous about how that good was achieved. "You romanced a normal?"

"I thought if she had an emotional attachment, she might be less inclined to—to damage the enclave."

"You rogue! You may have real potential in your office. Let's hope it works. We need the leadmuter, not to mention the penalties we could suffer for—"

"Yes. Nothing is certain, but it is my understanding that she will go easy on us. Perhaps only a reprimand, and we will not lose the leadmuter."

"Keep up the good work, Knot. You should do well here. Your predecessor did an excellent job. I forget his name—"

"Thank you, sir. I'll strive to fill his shoes." Knot departed. He had fulfilled the letter of his duty.

"You're a sly one," his secretary, York, said. "You used you-know-what on you-know-who, didn't you!"

"I have no idea what you mean," Knot said, smiling. "Anything I did was purely in the line of business."

"But some business is sweeter than others. Just watch it doesn't backfire one day. Suppose one of those floozies you seduce catches on?"

"*You* never catch on, do you?"

"Of course I catch on. Usually. I think. But I don't count. I'm not a floozie. And I have my notes. Been some time since I made a note, though."

"I'll update your notebook shortly. What could she prove, anyway?"

"If she bribed me, she could prove a lot."

"I've already counterbribed you." He stretched, his

right hand almost brushing the ceiling while his left fell far short. "What's the tote, today?"

"Routine." Then her phone buzzed. Knot waited while she answered it. Her lips pursed. "Finesse? Certainly; he will be ready." She disconnected.

"She's coming back?" Knot asked, surprised.

"It seems she forgot to ask a question or two, last time."

"Didn't you give her the literature?"

"Of course I did! You think I have a death wish? But she's a CC auditor; she's clever despite her appearance. A pretty face can mask a viciously cunning mind. I think you're in trouble, Knot."

"No doubt. But I've been in trouble before. Maybe she merely hankers after the same medicine she got before."

"Especially if she's pregnant," York said with irony. "We shall see, all too soon."

Finesse arrived on schedule. She was just as pretty as before. Knot knew he could not afford to see much more of her, lest he get emotionally hooked.

Knot had cleared the hour, knowing he had to employ a deft touch on this case. "So good to see you again, Auditor! I understand there was some item we neglected to cover?"

She squinted at him as if trying to remember him. That was reassuring; it meant his psi had worked, and that she remembered nothing of their private walk. Her recollection would encompass York and the enclave and the literature she had been given—literature carefully crafted to conceal the enclave's secrets—and she would know that someone had shown her about, and that he must have been the one, so she had to play along, pretending to remember him. "Yes. I had intended to clarify the matter of the leadmuter, but I fear I forgot."

Knot considered. "Leadmuter?" he asked as though perplexed.

"I think it would be best if I could actually see this mutant. I realize that the name is more suggestive than the reality, but as long as there is any question—I'm sure you understand."

He certainly did! She had fallen into his trap, and all

her clever exposure of his secrets had come to nothing. Now, like the good scout she was, she was trying to remedy her seeming neglect. It would be easier to fool her the second time, now that he knew she was susceptible to his psi. "Oh, of course. We must have complete accuracy for CC! I'll take you there now."

"That is most kind of you," she said with a certain edge. How much did she suspect? Ordinary people could be fooled easily, but to a trained observer the discrepancies of memory and experience became upsetting.

Soon they were outside, following the same trail as before. Finesse had not dressed properly this time, either, which was another encouraging evidence of her loss of memory. She wore a green jumper-dress that deepened the green of her eyes and showed her fine calves to advantage. Her shirt, however, fit more closely about her neck, permitting no "accidental" exposures there. Ah well, he thought; chance gave and chance took away; today was a leg-admiring day. Unless he managed to seduce her again; then he might get to see it all. That was chancy; women had ways of remembering seductions when they forgot routine things. York was a good example; she had uncanny ability to fathom what he had or had not done with her the night before, and generally let him know. He would be safest to keep his hands off Finesse, despite considerable temptation.

"I really should have done this the first time," Finesse said, pausing to unhook her skirt from a tenacious bramble, in the process showing as nice a knee as Knot could recall. "I can't think why I didn't. I don't recall raising the issue at all."

Yes, indeed. "Well, the leadmuter is only one of several hundred mutants here," Knot said. "I dare say you overlooked him in the confusion. He's just an old man who likes to work with old lead, trying to make things from it. Harmless hobby."

"I suppose so. Your literature does make that clear. But it still seems odd I didn't check it out directly."

"By no means. You must be very busy."

He helped her negotiate a steep bank, bracing himself while she put one hand on his shoulder for steadiness while she climbed. Then she stood at the top, her feet at

33

the level of his head, waiting for him to climb. Oh, my, those legs!

"Even more confusing is the discrepancy between my memory of the occasion and the holosonic recording I made."

Oh no! Knot thought, caught in midadmiration of her limbs. *The utter bitch!*

He scrambled up the bank while he wrestled with it in his mind. How was he going to deal with this? His psi did not work on machines. Finesse had been playing with him all this time, letting him lay himself deeper into the hole, and now he was fairly trapped. Had he not been so absorbed by her anatomy, he might have caught on in time to prepare a countermove—as she surely was aware. Why did he keep having to bite at the bait she proffered?

Well, at least he could survey the extent of the damage before proceeding further. *Are you with us, Hermine?* he thought.

There was a ripple of surprise. *You know me?*

I think you're the prettiest weasel I know, with wonderful psi power. How is Mit?

How can you know me when I do not know you? Mit is fine.

We met before. You forgot. You can read it in my memory. What is Finesse up to?

She is very angry with you.

"Are you all right, Knot?" Finesse inquired solicitously.

"Uh, just startled. I'm not sure I know what you mean by 'recording.'"

She is absolutely furious. She knows you're lying.

Finesse smiled angelically as she lightly brushed the dirt off his clothing. "I'll be happy to clarify it, Knot."

Please don't tell her anything, Hermine. Let me play my game. Mit will tell you I mean no harm to Finesse or to you.

I know that, Knot. Mit does not read thoughts; he reacts empirically. Finesse is ready to cut you into bite-sized pieces with blood dripping. The weasel paused, reflecting. *Oh, that looks delicious!*

"Are you sure you're well, Knot?" Finesse's voice was soft, her eyes filled with innocent concern. What an actress she was!

34

"At the moment." Or was the weasel having fun with him? Finesse gave absolutely no evidence of ill favor. Yet if she really had a holograph of their prior encounter . . . "Somehow I have the impression you're piqued with me."

"You have been thinking with Hermine. She always did have too free a mind."

"Yes. Why did you introduce me to these animals? You could have trapped me much more effectively if I had never known of them or their abilities. As it is, I like Hermine, and I believe she likes me. That compromises your main weapon."

"That was part of the interview. We had to know how well you related to the animals. Hermine, especially, has trouble communicating with minds she doesn't like."

Yes, the weasel agreed. **With you it's easy, naughty man.**

"Perhaps it is time we turned our cards faceup," he said.

"High time!"

She is putting the pieces through a meat grinder.

"I am very curious to know the nature of your interest in me."

Her voice was dulcet. "Do you customarily provide auditors with faked data to buttress their lapses of memory?"

She is grinding the pieces into jelly, Hermine thought gleefully.

"Do you customarily seduce your auditees?" Knot responded.

"That's my job!" At least her temper was showing now.

"Women of that profession do not normally represent themselves as representatives of the Coordination Computer."

Oh, naughty man! You've done it now! She is burning the jelly into noxious smoke.

"You know very well what I mean," Finesse said with a mild frown. "It is my job to ascertain how a prospective CC recruit reacts to people and situations."

"Well, it's my job to protect the interests of my enclave."

Good shot. She respects that attitude.

"You have the power to erase memories," Finesse said.

35

"You used it on me. Had I not verified my experience with the recording, I would have been sadly confused."

"You were not intended to remember. You would have gone on to your next assignment, and Enclave Min-Mute 58 would have proceeded undisturbed, no harm done."

"It is not my business to be deceived!" Increasingly, her ire was showing, as it worked its way out of her system in the manner of a deep bruise, discoloring the surface only as the healing process advanced.

"You recorded everything?"

"Of course. It is standard CC policy in such cases. Machines are immune to most mind-affecting psi, since machines do not have subjective perception. I now remember the full interview—via that holographic reminder. And you were quite ready to lie to cover it up."

"You lied to me first," he protested. "You claimed to be auditing the leadmuter." He was getting angry himself.

She's cooling, Hermine announced. **She understands this sort of dealing.**

"I was auditing the leadmuter—*and* you," Finesse said hotly. "To determine whether CC can use you."

"I refuse to be used by CC."

She likes your independence, grudgingly.

What a marvelous little lie-detector! No wonder Finesse had managed him so well, before. Fortunately she and Hermine had underestimated the potency of his psi, and been overcome by it. Now if only he could find a way to get rid of that holo—

Naughty man! You never give up.

Don't tell on me!

I wouldn't think of it. It's so much fun watching you operate. The weasel's admiration for his villainy infused her thoughts.

"It could be very important," Finesse was saying. "I had to be sure you were right for the position."

"I'm right for my present position, and wrong for CC, I assure you. I don't like big government."

"CC is not government at all," she argued. They had come to the field where they had made love before, and here she paused. The grass remained flattened where they had lain, mute vindication of the holograph's account. "The Coordination Computer just happens to be the only instrument capable of organizing the incredible variety of physical and mental mutations that space travel has brought to the human species. There are millions of people settling thousands of worlds scattered through billions of stars; the mere job of locating a known planet in the immensity of space is a colossal calculation with a prohibitively small margin for error. If it were not for the computer's ability to match specific mutants to specific habitats, and direct them there, there would be no human colonization of the galaxy at all."

"I am familiar with the rationale," Knot said dryly. How could she stand there, looking at the flattened grass, while spouting CC propaganda? "Some mutants can breathe only methane-dominated atmosphere, so they are matched with methane worlds. Some can survive only in quarter gravity, so they are sent to low-gee worlds. All this may be good and necessary, if we set aside the fact that mutancy is impermanent; mutants breed normals, not more mutants of their type, on the rare occasions when they manage to breed at all. So if normals cannot survive on those frontier planets, the colonists can never raise families. There will never be self-sustaining human communities there. Regardless, it makes the Coordination Computer the *de facto* ruler of mankind. I distrust and fear that power, and do not want to be associated with it."

She is getting to like you, Hermine thought. **Now you are not deceiving her, you are speaking from the heart. And you like her, because she is very pretty. Are you going to copulate again?**

Go chase a fat vole! he thought violently, and the weasel made a ripple of humor.

To Finesse he said: "Something tells me I had better get the hell away from you before you talk me into something I don't like."

"You seemed to like it well enough last time!" Finesse snapped, glancing again at the place where they had lain. "Not that I remember how *I* felt." How cleverly her manner deviated from her mood!

"Just how much detail did that recording show? If you had a bug hidden on your person, it could not have picked up a great deal of detail of that sort."

"See for yourself," she said, smiling grimly. She brought

out a sphere, holding it in her hand. In a moment a haze formed around it. A larger sphere of image developed, obliterating her hand and her arm to the elbow. It showed Knot and Finesse in quarter size, standing together, kissing, and proceeded in full-color animation from there.

Knot watched, spellbound. There was no doubt about it: This was a genuine recording, not a re-creation. He remembered the episode vividly. Now, as voyeur, he became strongly excited. There were details he could perceive now that he had been unable to see while in action, pornographically complete, and they—

He saw Finesse's eyes beyond the spherical image, bearing on him. She was watching this too! How could a man properly appreciate a stag film when its object was watching the subject? Yet that instant of embarrassment, of realization only increased his reaction. He wanted her again, with a craving much greater than before. The first time, there had been great promise; this time there was confirmation.

But he controlled himself. "You were angry because I made you forget this," he said. "Because you had to learn it from the recording."

"Wouldn't you be angry? You robbed me of my most intimate experience! And you did it deliberately!"

"Involuntarily," he said. "I don't control my psi. Everyone forgets me, within an hour of separation from me. Sometimes much sooner. My own enclave supervisor meets me for the first time every few days. I always eat in the newcomer section of the mess hall. The people I interview and place in compatible positions never remember who did that favor for them, and no one reminds them. I am the original forgotten man. So I live for the present, taking my joys on an immediate basis, knowing memories count for nothing. I couldn't have let you retain that experience anyway."

"What about your secretary, Pork? *She* knows."

"Her name is York. She transcribes my interviews from a distance, so is not affected. She remembers what she needs to, and more important, remembers that everyone else forgets. She covers for me all the time. But when I seduce her, she too forgets. She knows it has happened because she makes notes on everything, but she can't remember it personally. It's a great frustration to her. She always hopes one day she'll find the key and retain a memory. It's a game we play."

You are holding something back, Hermine thought. **It is in your background mind. There is a way to retain memory—**

Keep the secret! Knot thought.

"And I, a top-notch investigative interviewer, with the assistance of clairvoyance, precognition and telepathy— you made a complete, utter and thorough fool of me! My report was at absolute variance with my recording. CC must have laughed its circuits loose!"

She's working into another fit, Hermine thought. **I haven't perceived a show like this in months!**

"I'm sorry," Knot said. "We all do what we must do. You were playing cruel games with me, so I played back my trump. I love this enclave, I like the work I do, I value my freedom, and I am loyal to my own kind. You are a normal, representing the galactic government I detest. I had to put you off."

She's going to destroy you!

"At least you could have warned me," Finesse said sweetly.

"And had the warning recorded on your holograph, for all the galaxy to know! My secret is virtually worthless if it isn't secret." He was still watching the image, fascinated. At the time of his performance, he had been under the impression that he was doing the doing and she the acquiescing, but from this vantage it was evident that she had keyed in many of his doings, leading him from one exploit to another. She was certainly no amateur! "Where was the pickup?"

"In my hair. It's a heat reader. CC interprets the variance patterns and renders them back into a visual representation. It is independent of line-of-sight. I still think you could have made your point without humiliating me."

"There would have been no humiliation for anyone without that recording. I never intended anyone to know about my ability, apart from necessary individuals like York. I would be much happier if you just forgot the whole matter."

"Which I shall surely do—until I review the current recording."

"CC already knows?" That was rhetorical. Since CC had processed the recording and assimilated her contrasting report, that was a foregone conclusion. The net was drawing tight, and Knot had not yet found a way to slip free. For one thing, CC would have a copy of the recording on file, now.

"CC always did know, I'm sure. CC knows everything about everyone it is interested in."

"Even you? Why did it select a normal for this mission?"

"CC surely knows more about me than I know about myself! I was a foundling, a bastard baby sired by a spaceman; CC arranged for my care. It was only natural that I should grow up to work for CC."

"A spaceman? They only have short planet-leaves. You should have been a mutant."

"Well obviously I wasn't!" she flared. "Probably CC took me in with the hope that I would manifest psi, since I had no physical mutation. I must have been a disappointment. But by the time that was evident, too much was invested in my education. Now you know more than you deserve to know about me. And now CC is ready to recruit you."

"Why didn't CC just come flat-out and *ask* me, then?"

"Because a number of prospects are under consideration, and CC must select only the best one, and needs further data. My first interview with you provided that. You were the cleverest, smoothest, slipperiest, least ethical scoundrel who remained true to his basic loyalties and knew what they were, and you very nearly foiled the investigation itself. That, it seems, was what CC was looking for. You are the one selected."

"Selected for what?" Knot decided not to make an issue of the personal description; it was accurate enough.

"For whatever mission CC has in mind. That's its job, you know—to match the mutants to their best situations. I'm only an interviewer."

"Yeah, sure," he muttered. "Tell CC to go ram a disrupter electrode up its tubing sidewise."

She looked at him obliquely. "Most people are flattered

to be chosen for special assignments by the Coordination Computer. It means they are the very best for the position. The best in the galaxy."

"I told you: I don't like CC or approve of the system. I refuse—"

Alert! Alert! Hermine broadcast. **Mit says a bad act of nature forms.**

"Oh come on," Knot muttered. "I'm not going to rape her."

"Shut up," Finesse said. "Hermine never jokes about a thing like this."

Apparently at this range it was possible for the weasel to send to two minds simultaneously, because Finesse had reacted at the same time Knot picked up the thought. "Storm?" she asked now, evidently thinking it at the weasel too.

Not water. Strange.

"We have very sudden, fierce tempests at erratic intervals," Knot said. "Some are wet, some dry. We'd better get under cover in a hurry—if Mit's clairvoyance is to be trusted." Knot looked at the sky. "Though I see no sign of a storm."

"Mit's precognition has its limits, but is to be trusted," Finesse said. "He may not be able to define properly what is coming up, but it is surely dangerous. We've never been able to define his ability precisely; it seems to be a unified perception embracing present and future. Clairvoyance with a temporal dimension."

Not storm, Hermine repeated. **Something else.**

"We'd best use the leadmuter's cave," Knot decided.

They hurried forward. But it took several minutes to near the cave, and the threat coalesced before they arrived. The trees began to move strangely, aligning their leaves along common planes or lines of cleavage, none touching others. Grass stood erect, similarly aligned. Finesse's hair began to rise.

"An electric charge!" Knot cried, feeling his own hair extend. "Rare, but bad. Keep moving!"

The charge intensified. Now Finesse's hair radiated out like an anemone helmet, and even her eyebrows bushed out. Knot's skin tingled; all the hairs of his body were straightening. Where was the charge coming from,

41

and where was it going? Knot had supposed the wild stories about this effect were exaggerated. Now he wasn't sure.

My fur is sprung! Hermine thought, alarmed.

"It is discharging the electricity," Knot explained, for weasel and woman. "A harmless effect—for the moment. But if sparks start jumping—"

There was a crackling. Jags of light struck upward from the trees. At first the displays were small and faint, but they soon grew more spectacular.

"I don't like this!" Finesse exclaimed, trying to pat her standing hair in place. A little aura of light showed where her hand approached her head. She resembled a remarkably cute witch with an uncharacteristic halo. "I'm sure it's playing havoc with my recording."

"That so?" Knot asked, not at all disgruntled by the news. "You mean you'll have no way to remember what is happening now?"

Oh ho! Hermine thought, projecting a fleeting vision of a predator closing in on prey.

Knot was startled. "Hermine sends pictures, too!"

"Of course she does," Finesse snapped, giving up on her hair. "Where is this cover we're headed for?"

"Just coming into sight ahead."

They ran on, each person radiating fat sparks. The whole landscape was blazing with the electrical discharges, and small lightning forks were jumping from the trees high into the sky before petering out in umbrellalike spreads. Knot was a good deal more alarmed than he cared to admit.

Me too, the weasel thought. **But Mit says we'll make it. The cave is safe.**

They did make it. They bundled into the cave mouth as if taking shelter from hail.

No farther! Hermine warned. **Mit says it is safe only here at the edge.**

"Thanks," Knot said aloud. It was easier to focus his thoughts when he engaged the vocalizing mechanism, and it let Finesse know what he was thinking too. Though he had no doubt he could learn readily enough to project without vocalizing or subvocalizing, at such time as he needed to. "The leadmuter gets excited by storms and things and tries to transmute other substances—such as people—into lead. Doesn't work, but it's not too healthy either—for him or the subjects."

Finesse looked out at the electrical display, then into the passage leading to the leadmuter. She shuddered. "I'm not used to this sort of danger."

She's pretending, Hermine thought mischievously. *She's tough as rats.*

You're helping me against her? Knot thought, managing to avoid vocalization nicely.

It doesn't matter. There is no help for you.

Hmm. "If I understand the situation correctly, there's no danger as long as we heed Mit," he said, uncertain himself.

"Yes, we must stay right here," she agreed.

"Of course—until the threat passes. But you know, it is hardly in my interest to keep you safe. What you have already recorded is enough to damn me."

"I didn't come here to damn you!" she protested. "CC needs your help."

What is her real interest? Knot asked Hermine, who had now climbed from Finesse's pocket and was prowling the cave.

She means to seduce you into joining CC.

Just as he thought. Finesse's first visit had been exploratory. The second was recruitment, and she had an obvious weapon. He recognized that, but remained vulnerable. She was really his enemy, but he would do a lot to obtain her goodwill. *Ask Mit whether she will succeed.*

Knot expected no direct answer to that. He was wrong. *She will succeed.*

The seduction or the conversion to CC?

Both.

Don't I have anything to say about it? Knot demanded.

Nothing.

Nothing?

It has been determined. Mit knows.

Knot experienced a sudden firm resolve. He would see about that! He had little faith in precognition, especially as it might relate to himself. A storm might be predicted accurately enough; it had no free will. A man was different.

Finesse was making herself comfortable, arranging her limbs attractively, setting up for her effort. Knot tried to ignore her.

Other psi powers were remarkable but basically sensible. They merely accomplished by mental means what could also be done by physical means. His own talent was an example: There were drugs and treatments that could cause people to forget recent events, temporarily or permanently. They interfered with the intermediate process of memory fixation, so that the short-term memories never made the necessary transition to long-term memories. Electric currents applied to certain sections of the brain could erase established memories. The leadmuter's ability was another example. Transmutation of substances could be accomplished in the laboratory, with extraordinary effort and expense; this was not worthwhile economically, but it was possible. Clairvoyance was merely the awareness of surrounding landscapes and events, and extension of the normal perceptions. Telepathy was like a built-in intercom.

But precognition—that was essentially fortune-telling. It was inherently paradoxical, since the future was mutable. Tell a man he was about to step into a hole and hurt himself, and he would avoid that hole, rendering that prediction inaccurate. Thus true precognition could not exist—at least, not if what it showed were told to the subject.

There are rats who don't believe weasels can kill them, Hermine thought.

I'm a rat, all right.

"Dollar for your thoughts," Finesse said, smiling at him. He almost felt the warmth penetrating his skin, compelling his body to react. She was so infernally pretty; it was her weapon, and she used it well.

"A genuine archaic hundred-cent note?"

"Or equivalent in service. Women have been known to do a lot for a dollar."

Don't try to fence with that predator; she'll eat you up, Hermine warned.

"Hermine thinks I'm a rat and you're a weasel."

Finesse stretched, elbows bent, breasts flattening under

the cloth of shirt and jumper. "Some rats are attractive enough."

"And some weasels." But he had a challenge to rise to: the proof or disproof of precognition. "What's to stop me from just walking out of here, now, a rat that slips the trap?"

She gestured at the effects continuing beyond the mouth of the cave. "That."

The electrical display was at its height. Every tree radiated streams of light, illuminating the landscape so brightly it was difficult to watch. Knot was not sure what such a flow of current would do to his body and brain, and did not care to experiment. On the other hand, he knew it was not safe at this time to approach the lead-muter. To that extent the precognition was correct. He would have to remain here.

But he did not have to be seduced into anything! Finesse was lovely, and she was a normal, and his memory of his last engagement with her—and the timely and graphic reminder of it she had provided via the holograph —fired his imagination and desire. But he had willpower, and he could not sell his conscience for sex.

Yes you will, Hermine thought. *Her net is closing over you already. She obtained a distance precog about the storm, and timed this visit to coincide. You never had a chance.*

Shall we make a wager?

No. I never take easy prey. You cannot win. Mit knows.

Mit cannot know. A storm he can predict; it has no self-will. I am a man. My fate is not predetermined.

It is in this respect.

"Whatever are you two thinking about that distracts you from the immediate prospect?" Finesse murmured, self-assured and twinkling.

"Free will or not free will."

She smiled, and again he felt the impact. Oh, she knew how to use her assets! "As William Ernest Henley put it in 'Invictus': 'It matters not how strait the gate, How charged with punishment the scroll; I am the master of my fate; I am the captain of my Soul!' "

Knot considered her curiously. "Which side are you on?"

"I'm on your side, Knot. And on CC's. I know what's

best for you. That's why I must work to reconcile the two of you; you belong together."

"I have no use for CC! I refuse to join it. My free will will not permit it."

"So you prefer to argue with Mit? This is futile."

"I defend my right to pursue my own destiny!"

"Your unconquerable Soul," Finesse agreed. "I like it."

"You really believe in this stuff, don't you! You think everything will come out exactly as the crab predicts."

"I *know* it will. But that doesn't mean you are in any way under duress."

"This is a contradiction!"

"Not at all. It simply means that your free will will bring you to CC."

"I could knock you out and toss you into the electricity. Neither your faded memory nor your fouled-up recording would ever betray the truth. You cannot force me to join!"

Finesse put her hands on his shoulders. In the flickering electric light her face was animated despite its stillness, the shadows leaping across nose, lips and brows. She was eerily beautiful. "Knock me out. Throw me away."

Of course he could not. "Pointless. Your memory and recording will be washed out anyway, by my psi and the storm. But CC has the prior recording anyway. I can't hide any longer. But I still don't have to join."

Finesse smirked knowingly. Knot threw his arms about her, bore her back against the rock, and kissed her savagely. She offered no resistance.

He drew back. "No! This is how you're doing it! Seducing me. You showed me how good it could be, with your sophisticated subtle expertise, getting me hooked; then you carefully reminded me with the holo, making sure that hook was tight; now you're putting your price on it. You figure I'm already addicted. You think I'll throw away my conscience for your favors."

"I wouldn't respect you if you did."

"So it's all right with you if we just lie here awhile, wait out the storm, then go back to the main enclave?"

"It's all right with me if you try to do that. But I would be deceiving you if I said I thought you'd succeed.

You will join CC before we leave here, or at least make a sufficient commitment."

"I submit I will not—and that you will not remember any of this, and this time will have no recording to remind you. You will either have to turn me in for hiding the leadmuter, or let me go entirely. I have beaten you, this time."

Fool, Hermine thought, as Finesse smiled complacently.

Knot plowed on heedlessly. "You're all locked into your brainwashed belief in the machine, in nonsensical psi. Well, you may have nabbed the leadmuter, but not me."

"You're repeating yourself," Finesse said. "Next, you're supposed to plead the welfare of your enclave."

"Though why you want to take the leadmuter away from his only joy, to the detriment of our fine enclave—" Knot broke off, realizing that he was proceeding exactly as she predicted. The precognitive crab was probably keying her in. The very thing he was trying to disprove, mocking him!

"That I can answer in a manner you can understand," Finesse said, adjusting herself on the rock for greater comfort. Knot realized that he was still halfway embracing her, and drew back farther. "You are evidently using this mutant to produce gold, a metal of unquestionable value for sculpture and coinage and the plating of assorted objects and the illumination of fancy manuscripts. Has it occurred to you that he might as readily produce platinum, which is more valuable than gold, or iridium, which is several times as valuable as platinum? With proper management, the value of his metallic output might be multiplied tenfold, with no inconvenience to him. He might even like iridium better."

"Well—"

"CC is aware of that prospect. That's CC's job—to coordinate mutant talents, to the best advantage of humanity. You are largely wasting the gold you have here, in the interest of secrecy. Suppose we tuned the leadmuter to something really precious, like crystallized carbon—diamond—and granted your enclave a percentage of the proceeds? You could have more profit from that than from all your present gold, and the leadmuter would be happy, and it would all be legal. The leadmuter would not even have to move from his cave. CC expediters would be provided to attend to all his needs. He could be much better off than he is now."

Knot looked at her cynically. "CC is offering that?"

"Not necessarily. I'm merely making the point that CC takes good care of mutants, especially the ones with special psionic powers. If you really care about the welfare of the leadmuter—"

She was becoming uncomfortably persuasive. He *did* care about the leadmuter, and knew that what she offered was probably the best possible situation for the old mutant—and for the enclave. To keep all that they had now, plus the intangible benefit of legitimacy . . . "What assurance do I have that CC would honor such a commitment?"

"Practicality. On bucolic worlds like Nelson, the best bovine milkers are the ones who are the most pampered. The most productive hens—"

"And this is the hen with the gold eggs," he agreed. "All right, I bow to expedience. If CC will make a formal royalty commitment, and eschew recriminations, penalties—"

"I have no doubt it will—if you acquaint it with the facts I will have forgotten."

"Making me an agent of CC! Is *that* what Mit means?"

"A hint of it. You will have to do what you feel is best for the interests you serve—in this case, the leadmuter and the mutant enclave. You aren't going to hurt a number of mutants just to spite CC."

"Why do I have the sinking feeling that all is fore-ordained?" he grumbled rhetorically.

"Because it is."

He had walked right into that one! "*My* service isn't! The leadmuter is one thing, but—"

"An analogy, if you will," Finesse said, adjusting her skirt to show a trifle more leg. His eye was of course drawn to it. The flickering light made the shadow between her thighs jump forward and back, as though beckoning. He wished he could run his hand into that shadow, and knew that he could—which was why he could not. The moment the fish did more than nibble at the lure . . .

"You think of the leadmuter in terms of precious metals or stones," Finesse continued, as if blithely unaware of the lure of leg and shadow. "But he may be wasted in that capacity. Did you ever think what transmutation of substance entails?"

"It is an exercise in futility to speculate how a mutant performs," Knot said. "The processes of the brain are in many respects too complex for the brain itself to comprehend. Somehow it taps into a source of power no machine can even detect, and uses it to do things no machine can do as readily. If laboratories could duplicate any portion of true psi, they would have done so long ago."

"I was not referring to the mutant, but to the effect." She switched a muscle in her thigh, and Knot finally had to look away, lest his battle be lost right here. "Do you know how nature produces lead?"

Knot focused on that as though grasping a lifeline. "Never thought of it. Isn't it one of the elements, the basic forms of matter from which all others are made? Created in a supernova by heat and compression and whatnot? As with copper, silver and gold? I do know it is one of the four most used metals of the Industrial Age, or used to be."

"Start with the radioactive element thorium 232," she said briskly. "It has a half-life—you know what half-life is?"

"What I have here."

She did not smile. "It is the time it takes for a substance to lose half its radioactivity."

"Why not double it and take the whole life?"

"Because it is not a linear progression. It's a percentage loss. It takes just as long to halve the remaining radiation as it did the first time, and as long to halve it again. A theoretically endless progression. So for convenience—"

"I get it. What does this have to do with lead? I understood lead was not radioactive."

"Thorium 232 has a half-life of close to fourteen billion years. As it—"

"Fourteen billion years!" he exclaimed. "That's longer than they used to think the universe existed! Who was standing there with a stopwatch, timing it?"

"Rates of decay are calculable. Now stop playing the ignoramus and let me get on with—"

"The seduction?"

"In my fashion. If the physical appeal is not immediately effective, the intellectual one may be. Unless you have some other approach to recommend?"

"No, I'm sort of interested. I've never been intellectually seduced before."

"As the thorium breaks down, it transmutes naturally into radium 228, with a half-life of a scant seven years. Then into actinium 228—actually the radioactive elements have different names, but I'm simplifying for convenience—"

"How nice. Simplify some more."

"With a half-life of about six hours."

"That's simplifying almost too rapidly. From fourteen billion years to six hours?"

"Then into thorium 228 for two years, and radium 224 for three and a half days, and radon 220 for one minute—"

"That's certainly speeding up! From six hours to one minute. But—"

"And polonium 216 for sixteen one-hundredths of a second—"

"Haven't we gone about as far—or fast—as we can go?" His eyes had drifted to her thighs again, refuge from the sudden complexity of her listing.

"And lead 212—"

"At last I see the relevance!" he cried with relief.

"Which has a half-life of ten and a half hours."

"Now wait a minute—or maybe ten and a half hours! I thought lead was the end of the line!"

"Some lead is radioactive. After that it becomes astatine for three ten-thousandths of a second, and bismuth for an hour, and polonium 212 for three ten-millionths of a second. I'm speaking in round figures, of course."

"Of course," Knot agreed weakly, eyes locked to her legs. He had declined her physical round figure, so she was battering him with mathematical round figures. He should have known when he was well off.

You're learning, Hermine's thought came.

"Then into thallium 208 for three minutes," Finesse continued, as if unaware of the havoc she was wreaking in his mind. "And finally lead 208, which is stable. That's the thorium series; there's also the actinium series, which carries through its series of permutations to lead 209. It's a bit more complicated—"

"I'll take your word!"

"And the neptunium series, which goes to bismuth 209. And the uranium series, to lead 206. So my point is—"

"That lead in its various forms is the end product of a fantastic exercise of nature. And the leadmuter does it in a single step, in a matter of hours, thereby transcending time as well as matter."

"But he is not merely accelerating the processes of nature. He is bypassing them, creating lead from substances that are in none of these chains, that are not radioactive. In turn he is rendering stable lead into other substances—something that never occurs in nature. Lead is only a stage for him, not the end product. The significance of this ability—"

"I comprehend. This is more of a talent than we thought. We're just backwater planet mutes. But—"

"Suppose he learned how to transmute radioactive wastes into inert lead? That would solve a problem that has bedeviled man since the onset of the atomic age. That service could be worth more than any precious metals he might make."

"I hadn't thought of it that way," Knot admitted, cowed. He had indeed been simplistic in his handling of the leadmuter, relying on the age-old dream of transmuting lead into gold, not realizing that far broader horizons offered.

"CC thought of it, though. That's CC's job. To ascertain the maximum value of any mutant's talent it surveys. It may develop an entirely different use for your leadmuter—one you and I are not even capable of thinking of. None of us has the right to conceal such information from the Coordination Computer."

Knot was impressed. "I suppose not. But—"

"Now we come to your own psionic talent. Aren't you even curious what CC has in mind for you?"

"Not the disposition of radioactive wastes?"

"I have no idea. I doubt that forgetting about such wastes would be a good solution, though, so it probably isn't that. But if you don't join, you'll never know, will you?"

Now the electricity outside was abating, and with it the show of leg and shadow. He could depart. But Knot remained. "You think there is anything for me, anywhere close to the value of the transmutation of lead into diamond or whatever? Anything that my forgetting talent could accomplish?" The question was rhetorical; obviously the leadmuter was potentially the most important man in the galaxy.

"All I know is this: The leadmuter was only the pretext. It is you CC wants."

"But that implies—"

"That you are something extremely special. That is why I, one of CC's most able interviewers, was sent to you, instead of a routine enforcement squad."

"Is your head packed with all the knowledge of the universe?"

She laughed. "Impressed you, didn't I! No, after I saw my recording of the leadmuter, I did some research and memorization. I don't really understand what I'm talking about, in heavy metals or physics. CC thought this line of presentation would be effective with you."

"The big machine was right. It's an effective presentation. I'm impressed. But that doesn't mean I'll join CC. For one thing, I simply don't believe I'm that important."

"You don't have to believe. You just have to do what is required. CC pays well—in more currency than money. You can probably name your price."

"Such as the protection of the leadmuter and my enclave?"

"In addition to such things."

Despite himself, Knot was intrigued. How far would Finesse and CC go? "How about Mit and Hermine—?"

I thought you'd never ask! Hermine put in. *Mit says we've already been assigned to you.*

"And you," he finished, flicking his gaze from her thigh to her face.

"Wasn't that a foregone conclusion?" Finesse inquired. "Or am I losing my touch?"

"Was it? Ask Mit."

It was, the weasel assured them. *We already asked.*

"And you are willing?" he asked incredulously.

Finesse nodded soberly.

"You sell yourself?"

"If the price is correct."

"If CC orders you to."

"Yes." She seemed to feel no shame in this. She had been quite serious when she said she owed CC a lot.

"You give yourself to an asymmetrical mutant? You're a beautiful normal!" Knot was getting disgusted, but was also fatally intrigued.

"You understate the case," she said. "You are a minimum physical mutant, yes; that aspect of you hardly sweeps a girl off her normal feet, and I'm no fetishist. But I've dealt with many more grotesque mutants than you, and many much duller normals than you. You are not repulsive, taken as a whole. But your psi power—that is quite another matter. It is enormous, it is subtle, it is beautiful. It undercut me completely—and I have had experience with psi before. It is rare; there is no other like it in CC's files, which means it is probably unique. How much it is worth inherently I don't know, but there is considerable value in its rarity. For association with such psi I would sell my soul, let alone my mere body."

"You can't even remember my power!" Knot exclaimed, unreasonably flattered by her forceful statement.

"Yes I can. The same way York does. Once I have the recording, my memory is secure. Your power is primary, not secondary; the subject has to interact with you directly to be affected. So with the help of technology I can counter your power—but I remain dazzled by it. How I envy you psi-mutants!"

"*You envy me!*" Knot said in unfeigned wonder.

"But don't be naïve about price. When you join CC, you can specify any kind of company you want—or CC will provide a woman for you more exactly tailored to your tastes than you can now imagine. I am grossly imperfect for you, and so is your secretary, York; once you met her—"

"Am I going to ask for such a woman?"

No, Hermine thought. You're such an independent cuss,

you will refuse as a matter of foolish principle. Finesse has already netted you, even though you know better.

"You will preserve the semblance of self-determination by making your own flawed selection," Finesse said, frowning prettily. "You are guided more by appearance and personality and familiarity than by logic. Mit knows. Do you think for half an instant I would have broached the subject, otherwise?"

Yes, he thought, if she wanted to convert him without having to keep him. Bait and switch. But he hoped Hermine had not intercepted that thought.

Smart man, the weasel thought. But you still have power. She can't switch you unless you wish to be switched.

"And if I don't join CC?" Knot demanded. "How much of you would I see then?"

"That's academic. But speaking theoretically, I would say that in such a case I would be reassigned elsewhere and would not meet you again."

"So you *are* the carrot before the ass."

"Donkey," she corrected him. "And I prefer to think of myself as a plum. The symbolism is more conducive."

"I adhere to my terms. You are making me bray. I swore I would not join, yet here I am negotiating terms. Are you really ignorant why CC wants me?"

She is.

"Yes. But Mit might know. His range is limited, but sometimes when he orients on a particular person—"

Big awful threat, Hermine thought. Mit says something will destroy the empire. Many people and animals will die, and CC will be helpless. Only six people can stop it, and two are enemies of CC, and one is insane. Two are animals. You alone remain—and for you the chance of success is one in ten.

Finesse's eyes widened. "Oh, Knot—I read that too! I didn't know it was that bad!"

True? he thought at the weasel.

Half true. She suspected.

She would have to have suspected, he realized. If a person as valuable as the leadmuter was only a pretext to reach Knot, he would have to be virtually invaluable. But the whole thing could be a gross exaggeration to evoke his galactic patriotism. It was easier for him to believe that

CC would lie about his importance than to believe that he really was the most important man in the galaxy. How could he be important, when no one remembered him?

Awful smart man, Hermine thought. But Mit says that because you are the one who can do what CC needs done, you are most important to CC.

So he was the nail for the shoe for the horse for the messenger who could save the kingdom. That just might make sense. Circumstance could make little things important, on occasion.

"I don't know whether I really want to save CC," Knot said seriously. "But it sounds like one hell of a challenge."

"You do like challenges," she said.

"It's more that I feel compelled to rise to them. You come auditing my enclave, I'm turned off; you bring me a challenge that involves my hidden power, I'm hooked. Why didn't you mention the challenge at the outset?"

"My first visit was exploratory; I thought you understood that. I didn't know what your power was, only that you had one CC was interested in. CC is interested in lots of people; it is constantly gathering data and locating mutants. So it was my job to put you through your paces and make my report. I did that. CC was impressed. It seems it had an inkling of your power, despite—or because of—certain lapses of information, lacunae in the files, and such. It wanted to see if that power could deceive an interviewer who was not specifically braced for it. If it could fool a CC interviewer, it could fool almost anyone. It seems CC needs to fool someone. My second visit was to recruit you."

"I did my best to remain inconspicuous. But I think CC could have run me down years ago, had it really tried. Why didn't it act before?"

"I can only conjecture. I think it is to CC's advantage to keep some talents in reserve. Any agent it develops and uses is soon known to whatever enemies it has. So it must constantly recruit unknown ones, and do it in ways that do not betray its intent. When a special need arises, it draws on its reserves—and it seems the need has now arisen for a good psi memory-erasure specialist."

"I don't erase memories. I merely prevent the memory of me from registering in a person's permanent recollection. It is pretty specific, relating only to me and my actions. Like doctoring a photograph to remove one person, without leaving evidence of that doctoring."

"That can be quite a feat."

"Still, it is hardly on a par with transmuting lead to—"

"I know," she said, frowning prettily. "I admit it doesn't seem like much to save the galaxy with. But it must be an excellent power for a secret agent. At any rate, have you become resigned to your fate?"

"You are inquiring yet again whether I am joining CC? Seems to me I have made my attitude plain enough."

"Not whether you are joining; I know you are. I asked whether you are resigned to that fact. I'd rather have you satisfied than join unsatisfied."

"The answer, to whatever question, is no." Knot got up and walked out of the cave.

You can't do it, Mit warned through Hermine. *Your course is predetermined. You can only make it more difficult for yourself, forcing yourself to yield ungracefully.*

Like hell! he thought back.

"Why be difficult?" Finesse demanded, scrambling up after him. Whether she believed in predestination or not, her pride had obviously been stung. "Oh!"

Knot turned at her exclamation. She had tripped and sprawled. He hurried back to help her. "I didn't ask you to fall for me. Are you hurt?"

Naughty man! Is that a human pun? About falling?

"Oh, go away," Finesse said, pouting. "It's nothing." She touched one ankle and winced.

"You might have sprained an ankle," he said, not believing it. "Let me see."

Touch her and you are lost, Hermine warned.

Knot put his right hand on her ankle. It was an extremely nice ankle, smooth and warm, tapering into the kind of calf and leg only normals could generate.

"Give that back!" she cried, jerking her leg away. In the process she showed the upper portion of her leg, the inner thigh beneath her skirt, without the benefit of concealing shadow. The view was accidental, and therefore compelling. "It's not hurt."

"My touch offends you now?" he asked. "The lowly mute may not lay hands on the celestial normal?"

"You think I'm trying to vamp you with a fake injury!" she exclaimed.

Isn't she? he asked Hermine.

No. She meant to vamp you intellectually, this time. She feels that is more permanent. You're too smart for the straight physical approach. She took a spill, making herself look foolish. She is angry again. Her ankle hurts.

"I apologize for what I thought," Knot said.

Finesse melted. "No, you're only trying to help. I do not take gracefully to falls or other lapses of dignity."

"So Hermine told me. Did she also keep you posted about my thoughts?"

"Yes."

"She's a little tattletale."

"She enjoys it. You two get along very well."

"And did she tell you I saw up your leg?"

"Of course. She takes special glee in news like that."

"It's some leg."

"Nature worked very hard on it."

"Um."

"Men are fools. No woman would let the sight of a man's leg sway her from her ignorant determination."

"True."

No weasel either, Hermine put in.

"You really like my leg?"

"I like all of you."

"Even my temper?"

"That's the best part of you."

"Better than my leg?"

"Well—"

"The lightning has abated. My recorder is operating again."

He blinked. "What has that to do with what I'm thinking?"

"I don't want to forget a moment of this." She opened her arms to him.

"I'm not agreeing to join CC!" he protested.

"But you will allow me to complete my mission by bringing you in for a direct CC interview?"

"Direct offworld interview? Never!"

"To plead your case for the leadmuter's welfare. If you don't join, that remains in doubt. You need to convince

CC that your way is best, and you can only do that effectively in person. Anyone else would forget your message, unless you made a hologram, and that would further betray your nature."

"You're very clever."

"CC employs only the cleverest."

"All right," he said grudgingly. "One CC interview, on the subject of my choosing. I'll leave directly after that."

You will never leave, Hermine thought. **You touched her, you saw her leg. The point of decision has passed. Fool.**

"I am indeed a fool," Knot agreed, and swept Finesse in, kissing her hungrily. She was delicious.

CHAPTER 3

Finesse drove him to the spaceport. The vehicle was a summer sleigh, generating a layer of ice on its underside that slid across the road surface. It steered by changing the temperature of the ice on one side or the other, and braked by letting it melt too far. A jet of ice-fog provided the initial propulsion. This made a somewhat jerky ride, at times rather cold, but it was fast and fun. They sat close together, sharing a fluffy blanket: That was part of what made it fun.

Knot experienced nostalgia for this countryside, suspecting that despite his best intent and endeavor he would not see it again.

But maybe he didn't have to suffer false premonitions. He now had the services of a precog—for what that was worth. *Hermine—does Mit know? Will I return here?*

Mit does not know. His precognition is short-range, usually, like his clairvoyance. It is also more difficult to read strong mutants like you.

Even when their mutancy is not related to precognition? Or to telepathy?

Yes. There is a common bond between psi-mutants; we interact in devious ways that transcend the limits of species. We do not understand this; we only know it is so. Usually.

Makes sense, Knot decided. *Will you keep me company?*

The little weasel-face poked out of Finesse's purse. *Yes. Mit too.*

"May I?" Knot inquired aloud, extending his left hand toward the purse. The weasel came into it.

"Which is another reason I vamped you," Finesse said. "These are my friends. We've been together a long time, in terms of experience. You are taking them away from me."

"No, I have no intention of—" Knot protested.

"Damn you, I can't fight predestination any more than you can!" she snapped.

Knot looked at her, startled. Her lower lip was trembling despite her effort to firm it with her teeth. "I am precogged to take your friends away from you—and you knew that before you came to me?"

She knew it, Hermine thought. **She is only our caretaker. CC told her that from the start. You are to be our permanent associate.**

"I don't own them," Finesse said. "I'm not their kind."

"Not a psi-mutant," he agreed soberly, appreciating the enormous longing and frustration she felt. "Here I was jealous of your normal status, while you—"

"Can we drop the subject?"

"No! I don't want to do this to you!'

"You can't help it. You like animals, you have a way with them. Just as you do with phys-mutes. CC knew that too. You can work with disadvantaged creatures more effectively than I can, even though I have worked very well with them. Without them, I don't know how I'm going to interview—"

Disadvantaged creatures. She had the typical normal's arrogance toward nonnormals. No wonder she could not work as effectively with them as he could! She thought it was her lack of psi, but it was her fundamental attitude, even more of a liability because it was unconscious. She had been born to that attitude; it could not even be regarded as a fault in her. It was part of being what she was: the inherent pride of normal flesh. And he, possessed of the pride of mutant flesh, yet longed so hard for what could never be that her very arrogance became part of her appeal. Ironic, foolish, yet true.

"I won't be taking them from you," he said, "since I won't be working for CC."

"So you think," she sniffed.

And it was that pride, too, that prevented her from breaking down, bewailing her misfortune, or pleading for some change. She was in her fashion tough, even in her vulnerability. Knot had no doubt Finesse could produce a storm of tears if she thought that would forward her mission; but she would never let her emotions interfere with that mission.

Awful smart man, Hermine thought approvingly. **The smartest mind I've ever met, considering how foolish you are about to be.**

"Do you know I'm half in love with you already?" Knot inquired conversationally. The weasel had called the shot with telling accuracy.

Finesse almost steered the vehicle off the track. But her voice was firm. "You are intrigued by an attractive normal female. Most mutant males are. That's one of my prime qualifications for my position. Men don't slam any doors in my face, or throw me out of their domiciles. Good interviewers are commonplace, aesthetic ones less so."

"Yes, I am intrigued," he agreed. "You prime qualification worked like a charm on me. You're the first really attractive normal who ever took me seriously, and I have no adequate defense. I never interacted like this with a normal woman before, and not just because they forgot me. So—you are conquering me, just as you intended, and I do not want to hurt you. But you don't have to worry about my taking your friends and leaving you. I can appreciate that working with Hermine is very like being telepathic yourself, and losing her would be like getting lobotomized. Even if I intended to work for CC, I would not do it by depriving you of—"

She put her sweet five-fingered genuine-normal hand on his deformed four-fingered mutant hand. "Thank you, Knot. I know you mean it. It's not your fault that Mit foresees his own separation from me. You will be separated from your enclave, too."

"I thought Mit was unable to precog whether I would come back here."

"He gets occasional distance flashes of major events. But he cannot tell whether you will return to your enclave. He only knows that you will at some point be separated from it, in an important and significant manner—as I will be separated from him and Hermine. Take the psi-animals; they do belong with you, and they will be with you despite anything you or I can do, and I'd rather have them with you than with someone else."

"You forget that I'm only going to try for a compatible deal for my enclave and the leadmuter. Your friends belong with you and CC."

We belong with both of you and CC, Hermine thought. **But there are periods of opacity and separation and grief ahead that Mit cannot yet perceive clearly.**

Knot nodded, experiencing warm affirmation and cold misgiving. These were indeed his people. Finesse possessed, as she admitted, the lure of sex appeal—but the animals were psi. Never before had he had the chance to interact on a personal basis with psi-powers equivalent in magnitude, if not in type, to his own. He was quickly developing an addiction to it.

We understand, Hermine thought. **Finesse is a good woman, very good, but—**

CC had connived well when it sent this trio to fetch him: a woman to get his attention, the animals to show him what he had been missing in psi. CC had known that the bond of psi would transcend the bond of species. He might tell CC to go to hell, and find himself another woman; but without CC he would never find himself equivalent psi-mutants. CC pretty well controlled the market on psis. CC was like a monstrous spider, throwing loops of silk over him, each strand differing in type but just as strong. But he knew this was happening, and recognized the ploys; that gave him strength to oppose the net.

The sleigh slid into sight of the spaceport. The term was a misnomer; the true spaceport was in orbit about Planet Nelson, where the spaceships parked. To a considerable extent, the ships *were* the port. Shuttles connected them to the surface. Still, this shuttleport was impressive enough. It was one of several scattered about the planet, whose barges boosted freight to the main port. Each shuttle barge was a bullet-shaped unit set in the deep bore of a cannon pointed at the sky. Compressed gas launched the loads gently but forcefully. In fact, the shuttles' similarity to bullets was in more than their shape; they were shot from guns.

A shuttle was rising as the sleigh approached, the shuttle's massive vapor-jet marking the sky. Another was lowering, gliding in on spread wings; no sense wasting fuel in the descent. They were both very pretty, to his taste: galactic technology against a setting of planetary wilderness. Knot trusted the wilderness more than the technology, but certainly did not hate the latter. It was mechanized government he objected to, not the machines.

Finesse parked the sleigh and got out, limping slightly. Her ankle injury was not serious and would soon heal; in fact, she had mentioned that there was a psi-healer who worked for CC who would take care of it in an instant.

They rode a belt to the central office, where they proffered their left arms. Finesse's pattern print checked without any problem, but Knot's arm was bare. An alarm sounded, summoning a human attendant.

This was a normal male of advanced age. "First trip, eh, Mute?" the oldster said. "Have to register you with CC."

"There goes my freedom," Knot muttered.

"Eh?"

"He's nerovus about space," Finesse explained.

Isn't she a beautiful liar? Knot asked Hermine, smiling inwardly. Space was not his concern.

Needs a better pelt for true beauty, the weasel responded. **But she does lie well.**

"We shall need to verify your identity in due course," the man informed Knot. "Where is your residence and what is your employment?"

As if he didn't know where a mute lived. But Knot was used to this. "Enclave MM58. Ask for York for a reference."

"It is a formality," the man said. "Your CC pattern will be your definitive identifier henceforth. Have you relatives or associates with whom you prefer to be grouped?"

That would give people a better handle on him, betraying his nature when his associates could not remember him. Better a clean break. "No."

"Then you get the top number in the stack. Please put

your arm in the imprinter." The man indicated the maw of a squat machine.

"It doesn't hurt," Finesse assured him mischievously. "Much."

"About like your ankle?" He liked that analogy: a minor physical, but major emotional bruise.

Ooo, mean man!

"Touché," Finesse agreed, grimacing cutely. She could make the most negative expressions become positive.

With considerable anxiety and distaste, Knot inserted his arm into the forbidding hole. There was a sudden sting that seemed to penetrate right through to the bone. He yanked his arm out. "All done," the man said.

Knot looked at the smarting pattern on his arm. It was formed of dots and blanks, outlined by a square. Thirty-six positions, like a little map or a segment of a magnified print.

"That's all there is," Finesse assured him. "A tattoo pattern on your skin, indelible, and a similar one on the bone beneath, so you can't erase or forget it. You'd have to lose your whole arm to be anonymous to CC now."

"Trapped," Knot said lugubriously. It really was not a joke.

"You must memorize your number, just in case," she continued. "It's in binary code, twelve digits, each one delineated by three characters. So your first digit is a seven, and your full number is 710225430613."

"Just like that, she reads it," Knot muttered.

"I work for CC, remember? I need to communicate readily with the computer even when no voice adapter is present. I think you will want to too, just as you do with assorted mutants, each in his own mode. It's an advantage to be able to converse with anyone in his own style."

She had scored on a pet discipline. Knot had labored diligently to master every established system of linguistic communication. The human galaxy had a common language, thanks to its relatively recent colonization and the extent of individual travels within it, but many nonverbal variants of that language existed. He had just never thought of the computer's digital coding as such a language, though of course it was. His antipathy to CC had caused him to limit his education. "I'll work on it. Do you have a chart of numbers and letters?"

"Of course. Mit told me you would ask for it." She handed him a card.

"Thanks, Mit," he muttered.

The clerk checked the new number, nodded approvingly, and had Knot go through the travel-clearance line again. This time there was no alarm. Then Hermine and Mit went through; the weasel had a tiny pattern on her left front leg, and the hermit-crab a microscopic one on his left claw. The patterns did not have to be large enough for the human eye to read; that was merely for human convenience, not the machine's need.

"Your party is cleared for shuttle-lift," the clerk announced.

"That's all?" Knot asked, surprised. "No wearisome, pointless colored tape?"

"This is not the twentieth century," Finesse assured him.

"But don't we have to be checked to be sure we won't sabotage the ship in deep space, or hijack it to some pirate hideout?" Knot asked. He had never been to space before, fearing that a telepathic check would betray his nature to CC.

"A specialized distance precog at the orbiting station checks the complete hop," Finesse explained patiently. "He won't let the ship go until the reading is clear."

Precognition again: They certainly had a lot of faith in it! If Knot managed to prove that precognition wasn't valid, would he also prove that the security of space travel was an illusion? Maybe it *was* an illusion, and the news of lost ships was hushed up. With psi mind-affecting techniques, such a cover-up should be possible.

Finesse nudged him; he was hanging back. **If you don't move it, she'll stick you with a hatpin,** Hermine thought.

They boarded the shuttle and settled into the voluminous cushion seats reserved for them. Hermine and Mit took places separately. The object, Knot knew, was to have plenty of resilience to absorb the initial shock of launching. There would be a stasis field for the worst of it, but that could be maintained only a few seconds, lest it interfere with the life processes of the marginally healthy travelers.

They waited, while the mysterious mechanisms of the lift countdown proceeded. Knot's left arm itched, and there was an ache in his bone. Perhaps it was psychological. There were other passengers in other seats of the compartment, but he ignored them, distracted by the ache. Knot looked at the code card Finesse had given him, trying to take his mind off his arm.

The number code was quite simple: 0 was three blanks (- - -), 1 was blank-blank-dot (- - .), 2 was blank-dot-blank (- . -), 3 was blank-dot-dot (- . .), 4 was dot-blank-blank (. - -), 5 was dot-blank-dot (. - .), 6 was dot-dot-blank (. . -), and 7 was dot-dot-dot (. . .). The basic numbers were 1, 2 and 4, with the others being combinations of those: The number 3, for example, was a combination of 1 and 2; 5 was 4 and 1, 6 was 4 and 2, and 7 was 4 and 2 and 1.

His arm itched again. Now he contemplated the full pattern:

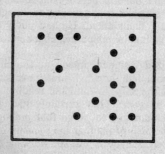

It didn't look like much; just sixteen dots in a neat square, forming little horizontal, vertical and oblique rows of one, two, three and four dots. But now, seeing it as a thirty-six-dot square, or as two numbers abreast, six lines deep, he developed the meaning: . . . was 7, followed by - - ., which was 1. Then the second line: - - - for 0 and - . - for 2. Thus, laboriously, through the whole number: 71 02 25 43 06 13, a twelve-digit number economically rendered by sixteen dots in a square. Then the alphabet of letters, rendered into numbers for general speech—

"Does it hurt?" Finesse inquired. "Let me kiss and make well." She took his arm, lifting it toward her face.

"Leave alone!" he snapped, shoving her away violently.

"Sorry." She drew as much apart from him as the seats permitted.

Immediately he regretted his impulsive reaction. He had acted just the way she had about her ankle, and for a similar reason. His pride was involved. The CC pattern was an obscene mark on him, a devil's signature he wished he could erase—and knew he could not. This devil proffered many things Knot wanted—at a price it galled him to pay. Yet he should not blame Finesse.

Does she hate me? he thought to Hermine.

No, she understands. She calls it imprinting trauma. We all went through it.

You too? You disliked being numbered?

There is freedom in anonymity. Even Mit was horrible right after. He pinched my tail with his big pincers.

Knot had to smile. *Tell Mit I understand.* And to Finesse: "I apologize."

"Only a person of no spirit can take imprinting without reaction," she said. "You have made a sacrifice."

Tell her I'm three quarters in love with her, he thought to Hermine.

I am not good at fractions.

Well, tell her—

She knows.

Finesse took his hand in hers. He wanted to kiss her, but suddenly he was unable to move. The stasis field had taken hold. The shuttle launched, accelerating at flesh-pulping level, like a shell in the barrel of the big gun it was. As they shot out of the muzzle the chemical rockets ignited, boosting it to yet higher velocity. Then the stasis field cut off; it had lasted perhaps five seconds. Knot was pressed into the cushion as though dropped on it from a high tower; now his mass was his own. Bad as it seemed, the acceleration was only two gravities and diminishing; the worst had been over before he felt it. That was of course the point of stasis.

Finesse squeezed his hand reassuringly. "One gets used to it," she assured him.

So it seemed. The acceleration eased, and finally they

were back at standard gravity. Then less, until it was virtually free-fall.

Then he wondered, belatedly: *Did she refer to the acceleration, or to the imprinting, when she said I would get used to it?*

Both, Hermine thought.

The shuttle drifted in semi-orbit, converging on the galactic vessel. There wasn't much to see, as the shuttle did not have windows, only a pseudo vid screen on which the positions of spaceship and shuttle were marked in glowing symbols. There was some maneuvering, as no shot was perfect; then the two bumped together, much as a dinghy might have bumped an ocean liner in the ancient days. Things never really changed much, he thought; the details merely became more sophisticated.

"You are gawking like a child," Finesse chided him. "Do you want the whole galaxy to know this is your first trip in space?"

Knot smiled, mildly intoxicated by free-fall and a rebound from his gloom of imprinting. "Hey, Galaxy!" he exclaimed loudly. "This is my first trip in space!" The other passengers looked away, embarrassed for him. "And hers!" he added, jabbing at Finesse with one thumb.

"You nebula-head!" Finesse swore, her color rising instantly.

"Don't worry," he said confidentially, "they won't remember I said it."

"But they'll remember *me!*"

He shrugged. "You're worth remembering."

She's thinking about kissing you or boiling you in oil, Hermine thought with weasel glee.

What's the difference? he thought back. He was still off-balanced, emotionally, at the high extreme of the pendulum release from his depression. He would soon swing back to the tensions of space baptism and his coming encounter with CC. But right now he was giddy, and he intended to make the most of it.

The oil is cooler. There was more animal mirth.

"I trust you mutants are enjoying yourselves?" Finesse inquired coolly.

"If you get mad again, I'll grab you and kiss you

violently in front of all these people. With a loud smacking sound."

"You wouldn't dare!" Then she listened to what Hermine was telling her. "Oh, no!"

"Mit says it's inevitable?" Knot asked, catching on. "Let's find out."

He grabbed her and kissed her. There was a chuckle elsewhere in the compartment. "Hermine is right," Knot said. "The oil is cooler."

"You haven't experienced it yet," Finesse said warningly.

The other passengers were leaving the shuttle, staring straight ahead as they pulled themselves along the free-fall hold-bars. All except for one elderly gentleman following a woman who looked like a harridan. The man winked. That was the extent of his rebellion.

But, oh, what he's thinking! Hermine thought. **He hoped you would go on to tear off her clothes and—**

Finesse made a little sniff of warning that must have had a mental component, because the weasel cut off the thought.

They got out of their cushions and joined the floating line. Soon they swam through the porthole into the larger ship. Here artificial gravity took over, providing orientation. They were in a low-ceilinged room with a slight concave curvature above, and a convex floor. Knot noticed that the people on one side of the chamber stood at a slight angle with respect to those on the other. "Down" was toward the center of the ship, and though it was much larger than the shuttle, it was minuscule compared to a planet. He could form a fair notion of its diameter by considering the visible rondure of the floor.

A holograph of a man in a dashing spacer uniform formed in a cubby ahead of them. "Welcome to space," the holo said. Had Knot not seen it form, he could not have told it from the original. It was life-size and perfectly reproduced, not at all ghostlike the way backplanet holos tended to be. "This is the galactic diskship *Starstep*. Enjoy your voyage."

"Thanks, I will," Knot answered.

Finesse elbowed him. "Must you be a complete boor?" she whispered. "That's just a recording."

The holograph man chuckled. "That's what you think, miss."

The elderly gentleman burst out laughing as Finesse blushed. "I can see this is going to be a fun journey," he said.

The harridan beside him glared. Evidently she did not approve of fun. Knot wondered how such couples ever got together, the fun-lovers with the fun-haters; he had seen such combinations even among mutants.

Didn't Finesse check with you about the holo? Knot asked Hermine. Already he was depending on the weasel for information and companionship.

She didn't bother. Usually the holos are recordings.

"We try to make up in camaraderie what a tub like this lacks in elegance," the holo-captain said. "Please take your assigned deck-seats for the precog-verification. After we weigh anchor you will have free run of the ship. Any questions?"

"Anchor?" Knot asked.

"Figuratively speaking," the captain said, smiling. "Till anon, then." He faded out.

Finesse grimly led Knot to their deck-seats in an adjacent chamber. The walls of this room were vision screens, showing what presumably would have been visible outside: heartgrabbingly deep space, with the local planet hanging hugely in the middle ground, all its clouds and land masses and oceans manifesting in compelling color. Knot was fascinated.

"Mutant," a voice behind Knot said.

Knot turned in his seat, remembering that he was among normals now, and so had become an object of curiosity. By law, mutants could not be segregated from normals physically, but socially certain barriers existed. "You address me, Normal?"

"I do." It was a nondescript man of middle age. "Please take no offense. My daughter is mutant. Has gills; she lives in an ocean. I just wanted to say it has been a pleasure to meet a mute with spirit and humor. Many lack these qualities."

Knot knew it well. But he was sure the same could be said of many normals. "Thanks," he said. He was privately irritated that the man saw him as a mutant, not as a person.

Finesse wants to know why that man remembers you, Hermine thought.

Because I'm still with him. Memory of me continues until separation or sleep; then it fades. Everyone on this ship should remember me until the voyage ends, with some lacunae for those who nap.

"If I had a girl like that," the other passenger continued, "I'd kiss her too."

"Be my guest," Knot said.

Finesse made an angry squeak of protest.

"Oh come on," Knot told her. "You're highly kissable, and there is nothing wrong with normals."

Naughty man! came the weasel's familiar thought.

"You rascal, you!" the man said.

"You complete oaf!" Finesse swore.

"Normals have feelings too," Knot reminded her. "Prick them, and they bleed. Green blood."

"Blue blood," the man behind corrected him.

"I don't kiss strange men!" Her color was rising again.

"You kissed me, and I'm as strange as they come."

"That's for sure!" she cried. But she was unable to maintain her anger.

You're fun! Hermine thought.

The captain formed in holo again, in front of the compartment. "Hello, passengers; long time no see. I am required to remind you that this is a transgalactic disk voyage. Males are subject to temporary mutation of their sperm that may affect their offspring conceived within thirty standard Earth days of their return to planetary residence, possibly even longer. Any males who wish to avoid this complication should not make this voyage, and may return now to the shuttle." He paused.

"I thought it was ninety days," Knot said.

"We have improved the shielding," the captain said. "Beyond thirty Earth days, the chances are prohibitively minor. Any other questions?" He paused again. "Sokay, now let's have the precog's formality."

There was a longer pause. Then the captain looked startled. "Oh-oh, folks. We have a technicality."

"Oh no," the passenger behind Knot lamented.

"I have been called many things," Knot said, "but this is the first time I've been called a technicality."

The holo-captain smiled. "Character, yes. Technicality, no. In this case, it seems our precog foresees a problem."

There was a general murmur of alarm.

"Now take it easy," the captain said. "It merely means there will be a delay until we get a clear reading. No ship ever takes off on a transdisk voyage without proper precog clearance. If it isn't safe, we don't go, period. All we have to do is hold off until we know it *is* safe. So there is absolutely no risk, just inconvenience. Could be a random meteor scheduled to knock out our guidance mechanism. A few minutes' delay will abate that."

"Doesn't your precog know what the threat is?" Knot asked.

"No, unfortunately. Distance precognition is not very specific on details. All we know is that we can't afford to head into deep space right now. Meanwhile, we'll call in the clairvoyant for a routine check."

"We're going to crash in space!" a woman cried.

"A manifest impossibility," the holo-captain snapped. "There is precious little to crash into, in space. That's one reason we travel outside the galactic disk; by definition, deep space is virtually empty. We could have a drive failure, however, or decompression."

"Oh!" the woman cried. "I'm going to be sick!"

"Save it for the decompression," the oldster said. "Easier to puke, then." There was a thud as the harridan kicked his leg.

"But we won't do any of these things," the captain continued firmly. "Because, as I said, we are able to read ahead. We do have excellent precogs, and if our voyage is slated for trouble, we simply won't go. There is no danger."

"Now I wonder about that," Knot said. "A precog told me I was going to do something, once, and I swore I wouldn't—but I think it came to pass anyway. If this ship is fated for trouble—"

"Oh!" the woman repeated, horrified.

"There's a bag on the seat ahead of you," the oldster said. "My grandpa called them barf—" He broke off as he fended off another kick.

"There are distinctions among precogs," the captain said, "and between the specific and the general. Our precog says, 'If you take off now, you will have trouble.' So we avoid trouble by postponing takeoff. We are shifting, as it were, to an alternate reality. Your precog may have given you a short-range, highly specific reading; much greater definition is possible when scope and time are limited. Beyond a few hours, there is no such thing as predestination; advance knowledge can always change it, with certain gross exceptions, such as supernovas and the temper tantrums of women."

"Thank you; that makes absolute sense," Knot said, appreciating Finesse's glare.

"I regret to advise you that our clairvoyant consultant reports that there is a person on this vessel who is apt to cause a mishap," the captain said. "It seems this is what is stymieing our precog clearance. We shall have to make a telepathic verification of passenger motives."

"You can't do that!" Finesse exclaimed. "Invasion of privacy."

"I'm afraid the welfare of the majority pre-empts personal privilege," the captain said. "I can quote the applicable clause of the spaceflight code if—"

"That depends." She fished a card from her purse and held it up where the holo-captain could see it. "My companions and I will be verified last. If you don't locate your culprit before reaching us, we'll leave the ship."

The captain looked at the card. "Of course," he said equably. "We'll start with clairvoyant analysis, and use the telepath in a second capacity." He faded out.

Knot nudged Finesse. "That's a magic card?"

"Yes," she said, showing it to him. Printed on it were the large letters CC, with a code pattern.

Your nature must not be known, Hermine explained.

Will it be discovered? Ask Mit.

Mit says no. Not here. Finesse has been able to keep the secret.

Even from the station clairvoyant?

Yes.

Knot shook his head in wonder. Clairvoyant versus precog, or vice versa, or whatever. How could one override the other?

He told you, Hermine thought. *The specific pre-empts the general. We are very specific.*

The holo-captain reappeared. "Please rise and file past my image separately," he said. "Our clairvoyant is with me now, and will halt the person who complicates our voyage. The faster we accomplish this identification, the faster we shall be on our way. I know none of you wishes to be delayed any longer than necessary."

"Oh, I don't mind," Knot said, before Finesse elbowed him in a rib.

"I haven't had this much adventure in years!" the man behind Knot said happily. "What a thrill if I'm the one!"

The people formed a crude line and began marching past the image. One little boy poked a finger at it. "No, there's nothing there," the captain said, smiling. "By law, I cannot mingle with passengers. That is one of the safety precautions CC enforces. Should I catch some loathsome disease and have my brain turn to jelly and steer the ship into a black hole, you passengers would be most unhappy with me. Especially if it hadn't been precogged."

There was a general chuckle, as the passengers adapted to the situation and felt more at home with the joking captain. Knot and Finesse took their places at the end of the line. "What if it *is* us?" Knot asked.

"It isn't. Hermine checked with Mit."

These were really useful animals! "Who is it, then?"

She turned her green eyes upon his in silent rebuke.

You talk too much, Hermine explained. *We don't want others to know our natures.*

Then tell me privately, because I don't care who knows our natures, at the moment. Who is it?

The woman in green. She doesn't know it yet.

Knot looked at the woman. She was young and fairly pretty, with her hair done in an elegant bouffant, and displayed a prominent bosom. *That should be interesting.*

No, it is mundane.

Any woman with a bust like that is interesting.

It is like that because she is pregnant.

That deflated him. The weasel was right: The woman was suddenly less interesting. Still, the situation intrigued him. He was seeing precognition in operation, and wanted to know to what extent it was valid. Maybe Mit's precog about him joining CC could be foiled, simply by a change in plan.

Knot waited as the other passengers were checked. Sure enough, when the green woman passed the holo-captain, he challenged her. "I regret to inform you, miss, that our clairvoyant indicates you are the focus of our problem."

"Me!" she exclaimed, shocked. "I'm just going to join my husband in System Fitzgerald. I take this ship to CCC, then transfer."

"You are fated not to arrive," the captain said with polite grimness. "I know you would not want anything untoward to happen. It's probably a perturbation, an anomaly that will clear in a few hours. Will you take the next ship?"

"No! This is the only ship that makes the connection to Fitzgerald this week. I can't wait."

"Then will you submit to telepathic probe?"

"Yes! I have nothing to hide. Your precog is wrong, that's all there is to it. I have no intention of doing anything rash. Far, far from it!"

"The queen protests too much, methinks," Finesse murmured.

"Excellent," the captain said. "If you will kindly step forward to the crew compartment—"

"Oh no! I'm not getting mixed up with the crew. I know why the law keeps you from mingling with the passengers! You horny spacemen get a girl in your cubby, you really go to work! I'm going to join my *husband!*"

"Madam, you misunderstand." The captain's patience was becoming strained. "I am married myself, as are most—"

"You married stags are the worst of all!" she flared. "You think that protects you from suspicion!"

"Oh, I love this gal," the man who had been behind Knot said. " 'Course, she's probably right—"

The captain did not seem to be enjoying himself, though. "We only want to protect your privacy in what may be a delicate matter—"

"I'll *bet!* I've met that kind of delicacy before! You men are all alike! You don't get *me* in that crew shack! Bring your telepath out here, where everybody can see him."

"Our telepath is not—"

"That's what I thought. You men trumped this whole thing up, just to get a girl in that room. Bring him out here, or admit your game!"

Now other passengers were murmuring assent. The woman had struck a nerve of suspicion that a number of people shared, including Knot. Who knew what tricks a bored crew might perform to gain access to attractive passengers they knew they would encounter only once? How could anyone challenge the information of precog or clairvoyant, or deal with a telepath who could read a person's real nature and intent?

Beneath that was a more fundamental suspicion: a general distrust of and aversion to the Coordination Computer itself. Did CC really have to have these psis checking out passengers, or was it gathering data for the aggrandizement of its own power? A machine ruled the galaxy; everybody knew that, though all officials denied it. But if it was awkward to challenge the insight of an individual psi-mute, how much more awkward was it to challenge the phenomenal organizational computer itself? So the undercurrent of hostility showed only obliquely, as Knot suspected was the case here.

"Very well," the captain said with an enigmatic smile.

Now comes the good part, Hermine thought. With all your complex thoughts, you have missed the obvious. Mit's laughing.

A middle-aged woman entered the passenger compartment. She wore a transparent facemask to protect her from possible contamination by passenger ailments, and translucent skintight gloves. "I am the telepath," she announced.

"A female peep!" the man behind Knot exclaimed. "It's indecent!"

The woman glanced at him. She was matronly, with smile lines around mouth and eyes. "I'm sure it would be, in your case," she said to the man. "Fortunately I read only with permission." She addressed the woman in green. "May I read you?"

Somewhat deflated, the young woman consented. "Of course."

The telepath stood before her, concentrating. "Please

think of this trip," she murmured. "Your expectations for the voyage, your concerns, fears——"

The woman in green screwed up her face, thinking. Knot was tempted to make a remark about the obvious effort and what it signified of her intelligence, but Finesse nudged him warningly before he got started. **And no comments about garbage burning, Finesse says,** Hermine thought. Knot had indeed been generating such a thought, too; the weasel must have read it, reported it to Finesse, and relayed the reply.

"It isn't working," the telepath said. "Like many people you do not focus your thoughts clearly unless you vocalize. Try talking to yourself, subvocalizing, so I can follow."

Rat twaddle! Hermine thought. **A good telepath can pick up images. This one is only a partial tele; she can perceive only what is directly broadcast, and she can't send at all.**

"Subvocalize?" the woman asked.

"Speaking in your mind."

"I can't do that! You think I'm queer?"

Knot had trouble following that. How could subvocalizing relate to oddity?

"The alternative," the telepath said patiently, "is to speak aloud, while I verify the accuracy of your presentation. You would not be able to distort the facts. I really think there should be a more private place to——"

The woman looked at the entrance to the crew's quarters. "Nuh-uh! I stay right here."

She's as difficult as I am! Knot thought to Hermine, intrigued.

"As you wish," the telepath agreed with resignation.

And will suffer similarly, the weasel warned.

"So you want me to say what I'm thinking aloud?" the woman asked. "Here goes. My name is Stenna, and this is my fourth disk trip, and I'm not worried at all about it, and I have absolutely no intention of blowing up this ship or derailing it or pulling out the bilge plug or whatever, so your precog or clair or whoever has a gear loose, or maybe he just wanted to get me in that crew room alone."

The telepath looked perplexed. She glanced at the holo-captain. "She's telling the truth, as she sees it. She has a limited intellect."

Hoo! Hermine thought. **They are fed up with that woman.**

"She may not know the truth," the captain said. "Keep working. If we get much farther behind schedule, we'll have to scrub this flight."

"Why are you making this trip?" the telepath asked.

"I told you," Stenna said, sounding irritated. "To rejoin my husband. He works for Nebula Chemical Company, researching new strains of organic catalysts, and he'll be there another six months or more. So I want to be with him. Why would I muss up the ship that's taking me there, even if I knew how?"

"A good question," Knot murmured. "I think the precog goofed."

"Your self-interest leads you to question the validity of precognition," Finesse replied.

And the precog is right, Hermine put in.

"Do you have any personal problems?" the telepath asked. "History of aberration?"

"Of course I don't!" Stenna said indignantly. "You think I'm a mutant freak or something?"

"Who are you calling a freak?" Knot demanded.

Stenna looked at him, her nervousness making her more carelessly assertive. "You, you freak! You shouldn't be allowed on board with normal people. You should be shipped in the cargo hold. You're probably the one causing the trouble, only your mute-loving girl friend is cozy with the captain so they have to fix the blame on someone else."

"Madam, please do not address a mutant in that manner," the captain said. "They are citizens of the galaxy too. Common courtesy requires—"

"You're talking just as if they're people," Stenna said with bravado. "They should all be locked in the enclaves where they belong, every last freak—and the freaklovers with them!"

The captain looked pained, and the telepath was hardly pleased, but they maintained their façade of politeness. Knot was under no such restraint. He ripped free of Finesse's cautioning hold and strode to confront Stenna. His light mood had now swung back to ponderosity, and he wanted to shove his burden of negation onto someone else.

"You uncompromising bigot!" he exclaimed. "Without mutants, you would not be able to join your normal-loving husband at all. Galactic travel would be impossible. Did you ever think of that?"

Stenna was too far gone to be cowed. Her normal eyes, which were green like Finesse's, fairly flashed. "I don't mean psi-powered people; they're a necessary evil. But you physical freaks—you're the failures that happened instead of psi-mutes. You should be thankful you even exist. If it were up to me, you *wouldn't* exist. Why don't you stay in your place. Look at you, with your lopsided body. You should be ashamed to show yourself in public."

"I'd be ashamed to show a mind like yours in public," Knot retorted. There was an element of awkwardness here, because she did have those green eyes and large bosom and was physically attractive. He would rather have fought with an ugly normal. But her bigotry, to his mind, was like a nest of maggots, eating out the substance of what could have been a lovely woman. "You've already inconvenienced this whole ship because of it."

"You think so? Prove that I'm going to do any damage whatever to this voyage!"

Knot studied her, bringing his square-pegs/round-holes alignment expertise into play. Suddenly it clicked. All he needed was the proper formulation of the problem. "You're pregnant," he said.

"What business of yours is that?"

That might have been a setup for a smart remark, but now he was more interested in establishing his devastating point. "Don't you know how the mutations occur?"

"Of course I know! I haven't been in space for a year, until now, and once conception has taken place it doesn't matter."

"It doesn't matter anyway, for the mother," Knot said. "Where was your husband the month before you conceived?"

"Right on Planet Vermiform with me!" she said.

"The whole month?"

"Thirty full days. I wouldn't let him touch me until I'd

checked the last one off on the calendar. So there's absolutely no chance of—"

"Two things," Knot said. "First, aren't you aware that
the clearance date is approximate, not absolute? The
good captain has explained that this particular ship has
improved shielding—but many other ships do not. Prospects of mutation decrease geometrically with the passage
of time, so that you are 90 percent safe after a month—
if you operate correctly. Only 50 percent safe if you play
it incorrectly."

Suddenly she was uncertain. "Incorrectly?"

"The problem is that the mutated sperm cells stored in
the male body do not clear automatically. One day after
a space flight ends, they number 50 percent to 99 percent of the total. As the body continuously generates new
ones, the ratio changes. But as long as there are any
mutant cells remaining, even 1 percent, you cannot be
sure. Since, as you put it, you did not let your husband
touch you—well, did he touch any other women in the
period?"

"Of course not! I wouldn't marry a philanderer!"

"Then the presumption is that he did not manage to
dispose of all of those tainted cells. It would have taken
them longer than a month to clear."

"No!" she exclaimed, horrified. "It can't be!"

"It can be. My own father was onplanet a month before—"

"You're stretching the case," the captain interjected.
"Most ships carry the improved shielding now, so that the
mutations lack viability. After a month, very few survive,
so even if they are not expelled from the body they
can't—"

"Can you guarantee that her husband's ship did have
that improved shielding?" Knot asked evenly.

The captain was silent.

Knot returned his attention to the woman. "As I was
saying, my parents used the same system. I was conceived thirty-five days after my father's excursion in
space, according to the records."

"And I was conceived twenty days after," Finesse
called, galled by this line of attack.

Stenna grabbed desperately at the proffered straw.

"And she's obviously normal! Freak chances happen, but the overwhelming probability—"

"Which brings up my second point," Knot said, getting set to close his trap. "How long is your day on Planet Vermiform?" He happened to have a notion, because he had once placed a mutant from that planet.

"A day is a day, dolt! What—"

"Not in terms of the human system. The galactic standard is the Earth day, but local standards conform to the cycles of their own planets. Some days are longer than Earth's; others—"

"No!" she cried again, stricken. "Vermiform has short days—"

"Which translates into less time per day. So your probability of bearing a mutant baby has just escalated again, because you did not really wait a full thirty Earth days. So—"

"Never!" she screamed, lunging at him. The lady telepath put her hands to her head.

Knot moved aside, and Stenna missed him. She grabbed at her own hair, suddenly drawing out a long, wicked hatpin. She turned on the captain, who stood closest, stabbing him. Of course the pin passed right through the holograph without resistance. There was another reason for the segregation of crew from passengers! Stenna collapsed, sobbing.

The man who had been behind Knot muttered: "You *are* a freak! But she asked for it. A pox on both."

"What's the matter with the telepath?" Finesse asked, going to the woman.

"It's all right, all right," the telepath said, still holding her head. Her facemask had become dislodged; she had become contaminated by interaction with the passengers. "An emotional overload—I was tuned to her mind when she exploded—oh, it hurts! I won't be able to function telepathically for days!"

"You are relieved from duty," the captain said, concerned. "Debark to the orbiting port and report to their med officer."

Finesse nodded as the telepath left. "Which explains what was scheduled to happen in space. Stenna was going to realize that her worst nightmare was coming true

—that she carried a freak fetus—and her reaction would wipe out the power of the telepath who was going to guide the ship to port. We would have been lost in space."

"But the woman has not conceived a mutant!" the captain protested. "Our clairvoyants check routinely for such things, to make sure no blame for mutancy is fixed unfairly."

"Perhaps you should have reassured her at the outset," Finesse said gently. "This small misunderstanding has delayed your flight, tormented one passenger, and knocked your telepath out of commission. It could have been much worse."

"Affirmative," the captain agreed, shaken.

Finesse returned to Stenna. "Your baby is normal," she said. "The clair checked it. The odds may have been against you, as they were against my own parents, but it is all right. Do you hear me?"

Stenna looked up at her. "N-normal?"

"Normal," Finesse repeated firmly. "It happens all the time. Some mutes are conceived after the 'safe' period, like Knot here—" She shot Knot a dark look. "But some normals are sired by spacefaring men well within the critical month, like me. As you can see, I'm completely normal, and so is your own baby."

"Normal . . ." Stenna repeated, hope returning. "The clair says . . . ?"

"Yes. Now you can rejoin your husband, secure in that knowledge."

Finesse stood and looked across at Knot again. "And you, you freak—"

Volcanoes! Novas! Planetbuster bombs! Hermine thought.

All I did was solve the riddle, Knot thought innocently.

It was the way you did it. You brutalized a normal.

I comeuppened a bigot.

"Now don't you start in, miss," the man behind Knot said. "Can't blame the man for not liking being called a freak. I called him that myself, but I shouldn't have. I didn't like it much when people made ignorant remarks about my daughter."

"The precog has now cleared this ship for travel," the

captain said. "A substitute telepath is boarding. Please take your seats."

They took their seats, subdued. Stenna was silent, not looking at Knot—and Finesse was the same. He was back in the mutant enclave. **Normals,** he complained to Hermine. **They're all alike.**

Yes, the weasel agreed, enjoying the byplay.

They don't object to mutants, so long as the freaks keep their places.

True.

And if a mutant ever has the temerity to talk back—Volcanoes! Novas! Explosions!

Right, freak!

Finesse looked straight ahead, refusing to acknowledge any of this, though Knot was sure Hermine was gleefully filling her in. Weasels did seem to have a predatory sort of humor.

The ship got under way at last. A stasis field encompassed them, and acceleration commenced at 100G, increasing as they cleared the immediate environs of Planet Nelson.

The holo-captain appeared. "This is a recording, this time, folks. I'm locked in stasis the same as you are, at the moment. The entire ship is in stasis; we wouldn't want anything to fall off, ha-ha! We are now clearing the local stellar system, advancing our acceleration smoothly to approximate one million gravities. Without the stasis field we would all be in sad shape. Stasis, as much as any other thing, is responsible for the development and maintenance of the galactic empire of man. You can put that in your next term paper on the history of life.

"It will take us about ten minutes to reach lightspeed. Don't worry, you can survive it; diskship stasis fields are carefully tailored to protect the life processes despite almost total immobility. After we achieve C—that's lightspeed—we shall use the tachyon drive to assume short-hop travel velocity. Sit tight; the stasis field will release when we go to tach-one." He smiled, as though making a small joke, but Knot did not fathom the humor and was sure most other passengers missed it also.

Implied pun on mach one, the speed of sound through Earth-type atmosphere, Hermine thought. **Finesse told me.**

Oh. That must have been a common term back when the velocity of sound through air seemed to be the absolute limit. No wonder he had missed the reference! Still, it showed how one became acclimatized to the contemporary state of the art.

Still, Knot was not yet used to transgalactic velocity. He had thought the acceleration of the planetary shuttle was fierce! This diskship's drive was of another magnitude. He wished he could look out the portals, but of course there were none, and if there had been, the stasis would have prevented him from looking, and had he surmounted that problem there still would have been nothing out there he could visually assimilate. Trans-lightspeed was a different universe.

"You may wonder at the strength of our propulsion," the holo-captain said. Knot could see him fuzzily, since Knot's eyes were aimed that way but could not focus. The stasis field did not seem to interfere with sound. He knew that the holo-recording was intended to distract and entertain the passengers, who might otherwise panic in the extended stasis and do themselves emotional harm. As it happened, he *had* just been wondering about the propulsion; he was a typical first-time passenger!

"We use a psionic drive," the recording continued. "The technical aspects are complex, so I'll use an analogy. The normal chemical propulsion is reactive; it is like firing a rocket with the exhaust being shoved back as the rocket shoves forward. This psionic drive is like climbing a ladder; no mass is expended. We are climbing very rapidly, of course, and the ladder we are using is the framework of space itself, in the region of our galaxy. It is the same ladder light uses—but we shall soon be leaving light behind. This drive is made possible by the efforts of psionic mutants, who create the fuel, relate to the framework, and orient telepathically on our destination. Yes, it is quite fair to say that this trip would be impossible without mutants."

And what did bigoted Stenna with the nonmute baby think of that? Knot asked himself smugly. She hated mutants, but was dependent on them. Was she closing her mind to the captain's canned message? No—she accepted mental mutation as a necessary evil; it was physical mutation that bothered her. Yet of course the two types occurred in equal numbers. So normals like her simply ignored or shut out the physicals, while accepting the largesse of the mentals. No doubt it had ever been thus.

The stasis released. "We are now in tach," the captain announced. "The normal interactions of mass no longer apply to this ship with respect to the galaxy. We shall maintain token artificial gravity of one-quarter norm until we depart the galactic disk. As far as conventional space-time is concerned, we no longer exist; but as far as *we're* concerned, the galaxy no longer exists. So we shall simply proceed as if we are the only people in the universe, and hope we all get along together. You may leave your seats and mingle freely."

Just as the normals preferred to ignore the mutants, the ship was ignoring the rest of the universe. Ah well; the universe would remanifest in due course.

The passengers got up and stretched. "I hate that stasis," the man behind Knot said, then glanced at him with mild surprise. "Hello, I don't believe we've met."

He had forgotten already? After only ten minutes? "I'm Knot," Knot said. "With a sounded K."

"I'm Manfred. Pleased to know you." The man moved on, mingling, satisfied with this one-minute depth of mutual knowledge. It occurred to Knot that wealthy normals probably traveled in space largely for the joy of socializing with others of their ilk, in the temporary isolation of deep space. Perhaps it helped them relinquish their inhibitions and opened a new universe of possibilities. Why should spouses be true to spouses when the universe no longer existed?

Finesse looked at Knot, startled. "You're here?"

"Where else?"

"But I don't remember——"

"I suspect the stasis served in lieu of separation," he murmured. Could his psi have more direct ties to the universe than he had supposed?

"I—it must have," she agreed, catching on. "The episode of the pregnant woman must have helped distract me. Good thing you weren't involved in that."

"Good thing," Knot agreed. His psi power sometimes acted in marvelous ways!

Oooo, naughty! Hermine chided him gleefully.

How come you remember?

Because I read your memory. Your mind is weasellike.

Oh, really not that good, he thought, chuckling mentally.

Knot was tempted to introduce himself to Stenna, but resisted. The passengers' memory of him should not yet be beyond recall. If he made an issue of it he could restore it. That would put him in bad repute, so seemed pointless. Of course, they would forget again when he left them at the conclusion of the voyage. Only by means of a key reminder from outside, such as Finesse's recorder, or a call from Knot himself, could the forgetting be reversed. Anonymity pursued him always.

Except for the CC record of his new number, he thought darkly. But CC had already known about him, he reminded himself; the CC number made no difference. It was merely symbolic. CC had sent Finesse to rout him out; he had been doomed from that moment. The fish had not been able to resist taking the bait.

"We are now approaching the first right-angle turnabout," the holo-captain announced. "Stasis will reestablish momentarily; no need to resume your seats."

There was a brief freeze and wrench. "All done. We are now in maindrive, proceeding across the face of the galaxy at approximately one thousand light-years per hour. This hop will last twenty hours. Please avail yourselves of the facilities aboard ship. We do not have tennis courts and a swimming pool the way the larger liners do, but our 'indoor' entertainments should suffice for a while."

Finesse glanced at Knot, startled. "You're here? I don't remember—"

"Ask Hermine," he murmured. No doubt about it: A few minutes of stasis had the same effect as a few hours of ordinary time, with respect to his own psi power. The brief flash of stasis just now had been enough to wipe out the few minutes' impression he had just made since the prior stasis. He would have to figure out ways to apply that effect to his benefit. Maybe if he obtained a portable stasis-unit—

"Ah yes," Finesse agreed, evidently in touch with the weasel. "You are very—interesting, Knot."

"I certainly am," he agreed.

The remainder of the voyage was uneventful, largely because Finesse did not have occasion to review her recording and refresh her memory on the initial episode with Stenna. They did avail themselves of the ship's facilities, and these were indeed adequate. There was a fine gaming room in which the passengers wagered against machines, setting the risk levels wherever they chose. There were private compartments with very soft floors, where men could dally with other men's women, or vice versa. There were also, as Mit warned, holo-pickups; for a price the neglected spouses could watch what their legal partners were doing in their supposed secrecy. It seemed the diskship had evolved very specialized tastes in amusement. The amazing thing was the way all this was accepted; Knot saw one woman observing her husband in action via the holo, and when he emerged from his endeavor she acted exactly as though nothing at all had happened.

Because she would have to confess to peeping, Hermine explained. She enjoyed the demonstration, but can't admit that. It is a convention; they must never speak of what they know.

Maybe telepathy had caused that convention to evolve. The uttering of something was a more grievous crime than the something itself! Maybe that was part of what had set Finesse off, when he had exposed Stenna. To be a bigot was all right; to expose someone as a bigot was not.

There are lots of human things that don't make much sense, Hermine agreed.

When he tired of speculating on the nuances of human interaction, Knot turned to the machine. He wondered what the Coordination Computer would be like. He understood that CC occupied an entire planet, with a huge bureaucracy of normals and psi-mutants serving it, and the galaxy's busiest spaceport and communications center. He pictured the myriad domes and towers and buildings scintillating in the sunlight, with brightly colored antigrav vehicles flitting from one landing site to another, and subway rockets plunging through the planet, and bubbles rising and falling through the waters of the ocean, carrying important passengers to the mer-domes.

But he really didn't know what to expect. He was only a backplanet lout, somewhat at a loss out here in mainstream civilization, as his experience during this voyage showed. Without Finesse and Hermine, he would have been in a sorry state.

They went back into stasis for the right-angle turn toward the galaxy, and plunged back into the disk at the slow speed of light, or reasonable multiple thereof. He kept losing his perspective; even the comparatively trifling distance of five thousand light-years would be prohibitive at lightspeed.

At any rate, soon he would see the center of civilization! He remained anti-CC, but could not help being impressed by the magnitude of the empire the computer governed.

"There will be a brief stop at a minor system for a fuel recharge," the holo-captain announced. "Please do not be concerned."

Finesse looked at Knot as they emerged from stasis, startled. "What—?"

Tell her, Hermine, he thought. *She has forgotten I'm here, again. Read the details in my mind and update her.* It had become a game, this memory-tag with stasis.

They went into stasis again for the final maneuvering and deceleration. Knot marveled that the diskships did not carry enough fuel for their full voyage, so that irregular pit stops like this were required. Was the fuel massive?

No, it is small, Hermine thought. *But strong. So it is kept on minor worlds in case of accident. Not on Coordination Computer Central.*

Can't the precogs anticipate accidents, as they do for the ships?

No. A planet is too big, too complex, and the time scale is too much. Also, there are a great many psis on CCC, interfering with clear perception of such things. By the time the precog knew there was fuel trouble, it would be too late to stop it.

Limitations of scale, Knot agreed, seeing it. *One hop by one ship is small; one century on one planet is big. A ship* is self-contained, almost immune from outside influences; a planet is the center of galactic interactions. I'm glad we're not staying long.

Your huge human brain can certainly generate strong thoughts, Hermine thought admiringly.

Knot issued a mental laugh. He formed a mental picture of a man picking a weasel up by the tail and shaking it.

Hermine retaliated with a picture of the weasel flipping its head up to nip the man's thumb. **We get off here.**

Knot froze—a natural reaction, since he was already in stasis. **Here at the pit-stop refueling planet? We're going to CCC!** he thought in protest.

The enemy watches CCC. If the enemy sees you come, he will know you are a CC agent.

I'm not a CC agent! I oppose CC!

Mit says—

To hell with Mit! My future is a complex planet, not a simple ship, and Mit is only a little crab.

Uh-huh, Hermine thought complacently.

All right. You've had your little joke. We're not really getting off at this rest-stop station, are we?

We really are. Along with the chickens. Hermine licked mental chops. **Delightful!**

Chickens?

Delicious.

The stasis lifted. "Do not wander far from your seats," the captain warned. "We shall be resuming travel in a few minutes. This is Planet Chicken Itza."

"Chicken Itza?" Knot asked.

"A pun on an archaeological site back on Earth," the captain explained. He had evidently gone through this routine many times before. "A former Mayan city in the continent of Latin America, Chichen Itza, with many fine old temples. When the colonists here went into chicken farming, some historically minded wag among them suggested this name, and it stuck. Many of our worlds have names at random, such as Fitzgerald, named after a writer, and Nelson, after a Navy person. Pretty foolish, don't you agree?"

"Uh, yes," Knot said, disgruntled. He had never realized that his home planet had been named for a sailor.

"He's the one who said, 'England expects that every

man will do his duty,'" the captain continued. "I rather like him. We ship handlers must stick together."

Obviously Knot had run afoul of a pet subject. He was silent. The captain probably had choice bits of information about every planet on his route.

Now Finesse turned to Knot, her eyes widening. But Hermine, who had never been out of contact with him, so had never forgotten, was already filling her in.

"Come on," Finesse said. "There's a port where we can see the rendezvous with the fueling shuttle. That should be interesting."

"Oh, fascinating," Manfred, the man behind Knot, muttered disdainfully. "Nothing like a routine docking for excitement."

The other passengers evinced similar disinterest. Knot agreed with them. "I don't care about—"

"She's asking you for one last liaison, idiot," someone in the group said *sotto voce*.

"Be my guest," Knot muttered back.

Move! Hermine thought. **This is where we get off. We don't want the other passengers to notice.**

Damned if I'll cooperate with this! I came to see CC, not some chicken outfit!

Finesse will think a nova at you, and I'll relay it, the weasel warned.

Knot laughed inwardly. **You females are all alike! Go ahead with your nova.**

Suddenly there was a terrible burst of light in his mind. Knot felt as if he were being flung violently through space, stunned, his extremities burning, melting, vaporizing.

CHAPTER 4

<hr/>

When Knot recovered, he was in a crate with several fat hens. "What—?" he asked, trying to stand. He banged his head; there was no room to stand. The hens squawked angrily.

Then the stasis came, holding him and the chickens firm.

You weren't kidding about that nova! he thought to Hermine.

The weasel was contrite. **I did warn you. You did ask for it.**

So you did. So I did. I thought it was a figure of thought. Can you do that to anyone?

No. I can't generate novas. I only relay them, and they hurt me too, some. And some people shield their minds against such overloads.

How do they do that?

It is hard to explain. They just—do.

Intriguing. What could be generated by an act of will could be blocked by another act of will. Had the ship's original telepath developed such a mind shield, she might not have suffered when Stenna exploded mentally. Maybe it was possible to bounce such attacks back to the sender. That would be a most fitting defense!

Knot resolved to work on a similar defense for his mind. Hermine was all right; he liked her, liked her well. But he didn't want stray telepaths peeping on his private processes.

Will you help me develop a mind shield? he inquired. *That would be fun!*

The stasis released. The chickens completed their squawking and fluttering. Feathers drifted in the crate. The shuttle was down.

Finesse emerged from the adjacent crate. She looked neat and composed, despite a strand of straw on her shoulder. She also wore the perplexed expression that had become so familiar recently—until the weasel updated her. "I have the feeling there will be some interesting material in my recording," she murmured. "Now let's get on to the farm."

"I just came from a bucolic world," Knot complained. "I wanted to see the high technology of CCC."

Finesse ignored him. *Mit thinks you will see some medium technology in a few months,* Hermine offered consolingly. *He isn't sure, though; it's too far for him to precog well.*

"Medium technology," Knot muttered, scowling.

The shuttleport opened. Outside was a small spaceport whose buildings resembled chicken coops. "This really *is* a chicken planet!" Knot exclaimed, not pleased. The air wafting in was redolent of bird manure.

"It really is," Finesse assured him. "But don't denigrate it. These are unique birds. Some lay eggs that are radiation-resistant. Others' eggs will store at ordinary temperatures virtually indefinitely. But the hens themselves are delicate, and need special conditions for laying. This planet is their ideal home. It has a broad temperate zone, and the soil and plant life and insects are all conducive to chicken raising."

"So they're breeding them here and shipping out the eggs?"

"Yes, mostly." She led him outside, where robot machinery was moving up to pick up the crates of birds.

"Then why are they shipping full-grown birds *in?*" he demanded. He hardly cared, but he was casting about for some way to express his irritation at being shanghaied down here.

"Because the mutations develop all over the galaxy, the same as with human beings," she said patiently. "The promising ones are shipped here for study and breeding, so that we can try to stabilize the best qualities. Some roosters are taken on space hops just to induce new mutations."

"But mutations don't breed true. Their offspring revert to normal, if they can breed at all. Most mutants are mules, unable to propagate despite having the reproductive drive." Which happened to be a sore spot with him, and with most mutants. To be normal was not merely to belong to the great central society, it was to be able to beget freely.

"Most revert," she agreed. "But in some few cases, the mutation affects the generative process. Then it is possible to come up with stable mutant breeds. Many generations, many trips in space—the chances increase. We have been developing fairly impressively here; we have many breeds of chicken that never existed before. Most new mutants are failures, of course, and must be destroyed; some are actually psi-mutes—useless in a chicken."

Hmph, Hermine thought. She knew psi-animals could be quite valuable!

"Some of the grown birds," Finesse continued blithely, "are shipped to planets where they may survive better than ordinary chickens could. There are generally a number of experimental breeds being shipped out at any given time; the galaxy is large."

Knot looked back at the shuttle. "What breed are those we were crated with? They looked ordinary to me."

"I think those are Moon Rocks. They're an egg-mutation. Irregular shapes to the shells, like stones, but very special flavor, much in demand."

"So they get hauled from their homeworlds to this . . . outfit," he said. "Just as I was."

She glanced at him in the way she had, obliquely. "Unique mutants, yes. You should feel right at home here."

"I understood I was going to chat with CC," he grumped.

"You are," she assured him.

"Is CC a big chicken, then?"

"Something like that."

He formed a mental picture of a huge robot chicken with shiny metal wings and geartooth eyes, clucking in binary-octal code, while the human galaxy scurried to obey the translated directives. Feathers flew when CC squawked. Hermine sent an appreciative thought.

They were walking to the nearest building. "You are speaking metaphorically?" he asked at last.

"I mean CC is wary of the ubiquitous enemy, so CC is very careful. In the ancient vernacular, that is termed chicken."

"I'm not too strong on ancient vernacular," Knot admitted. "So now CC has in effect abducted me by promising me an interview, while instead trapping me on this wayside planet with the other unfortunate birds. No wonder CC has enemies!"

"I thought you regarded yourself as an enemy."

"I thought CC was trying to convert me."

"Have we discussed this before? I don't remember what I've told you, and until I review my recordings—"

"No need for that! We agreed to go see CC so I could explain why I wasn't interested in being a CC agent, and work out some suitable compromise for my enclave and the leadmuter. Had I known you were going to haul me to this hen-party planet, I would not have come. It would have been much easier for you to leave me where I was. I admit I'm now trapped here on Chicken Itza, since I can't leave the planet without showing my new ID, and there's not much I can do to interfere with CC here. But I really hadn't been planning to mess with CC anyway. I was just minding my own business. Or had some precog discovered that I was about to do something obnoxious?"

"I don't think so," she admitted. "There was no indication you were going to be any trouble at all. I'm sure CC ran an intensive precog check on you, and that if left alone you just kept anonymously helping your enclave and making time with the local girls who never remember what advantage you've taken. No ripples at all. That must be why CC wants you."

Knot shook his head. "I must have missed something."

"It's very simple. CC needs agents the enemy doesn't know about. They are the only ones who can be effective. You are completely unknown."

"There's a whole galaxy of unknown people! Why not pick on someone else?"

"Didn't I tell you? Your infernal psi-power. It seems to have a unique position in the present and future scheme. There are only five or six entities that can materially improve the galactic picture. One of them is you, and two more are animals, and the others are committed enemies. Some ratio like that. CC does not confide complete information to me. But I know it does not leave CC much choice."

So now he learned a bit more about CC's rationale, and could see how the team was being assembled. Grab a man here, and an animal there, bring them separately to an unlikely rendezvous planet, keep them there until they agreed to do CC's will.

"CC has a choice," Knot said. "It could put a normal human being with the animals, and guide them—" He paused. "What animals?"

"What animals do you think? You've been with them for two days."

"Mit and Hermine! You've assembled a task force consisting of all those likely and able to help CC!"

"Precisely. But you are the critical element. Without you, we have only one chance in a hundred of doing the job. With you alone, it is one chance in ten. With you together with Mit and Hermine, the chances are one in six. Properly prepared and timed, they rise to a maximum of one in four. So—it has to be. The right combination of entities, introduced to the project at precisely the right time and in the right manner."

"One chance in four," Knot repeated. Hermine had given him similar information, some time back. Now he had more detail. Perhaps more accurate detail. He wondered what kind of preparation was required to raise the chances that last notch, but decided not to ask. He was not wholly pleased with the revelations that were already coming.

Yet there was one matter that had to be clarified. "That means three chances in four of failure. What happens to us—in the likely event of failure?"

"One chance in three you will die," she said. "One in three you will be converted to the enemy side. One in three you will finish in some different state."

"Let me see if I have this straight. Four equally likely

alternatives, even under ideal conditions. I succeed, I join the enemy, I fail-but-survive in some nebulous manner, I die. Right?"

"Right. Mit and Hermine's fortunes vary similarly. You are the key. That's the extent of my present knowledge."

"I'd rather be back at the enclave."

"You'll be talking to CC about that."

"You mean we're leaving Chicken Itza after all?"

"No."

"I don't see—"

"You will soon enough."

Knot stopped. "You are very cavalier about my sentiments," he said. "I may not be able to get off this planet on my own, but I certainly don't have to cooperate with CC."

This means trouble, Hermine warned.

I'm ready for trouble. A man has to put his foot down somewhere. Aloud, he asked: "Why must I make all the sacrifices? I don't even support CC!"

She whirled about to face him. "What do you know about sacrifice, you ignorant hayseed?"

I knew it, Hermine thought. You've goaded her too far. I wasn't supposed to tell you, but now she's about to tell you herself.

Tell me what?

But Finesse was already doing it. "You know how CC is getting your cooperation? By catering to your base male desires, that's how. By providing a woman for you—"

"That's part of what makes me object," Knot pointed out. "I don't need any woman provided for me. I can do well enough in that respect without CC's help. My secretary, York—"

"A woman who will raise your chances of success from one in six to one in four," she continued furiously. "One who had to be co-opted more brutally than anything you know of."

"I don't need any unwilling women," he protested, taken aback. "I have come to terms with your vamping, and I admit it's quite effective, so that I like you a lot despite what I can see of your opportunism. But that doesn't mean I can just be shifted from one woman to another like a piece of change. You're a terror when you're mad, but I'll stick with—"

"You're not being shifted off! I'm the one!" she screamed. "Know why I turned on to you? Because galactic civilization as we know it is doomed if I don't. Or at least it is more likely to be doomed. Know what I left behind, for the sake of that slender benefit in the odds?"

"A cushy desk job?" he hazarded cynically.

"My husband and son!" she cried, her face twisted in agony and fury. "To take a damned mutant lover. For the good of—"

She broke off. Knot was staring at her, feeling as though a laser had just holed him through the heart. "You're married?" he asked, dazed.

Abruptly she regrouped. "I shouldn't have said that. I'm not married. I'm sorry."

Hermine?

Half truth.

"You're lying," he said aloud. "I've had experience interviewing people myself, you know. I can tell when a person is telling the truth. You have never been completely candid with me, and now I begin to see why. You have a family—"

"Oh, now I've torn it," she said, and there were tears of frustration in her eyes. "I might as well have thrown acid in your face, and you didn't deserve it. I wasn't supposed to give you my background. It isn't that I dislike you, Knot, even though at times you make me so mad—it's that—"

"Husband," he prompted her, still feeling as though he were on a battlefield, mortally wounded, but hanging on until his mission of the moment was complete. "Tell me the rest."

"I—suppose I'll have to, now. I—was married, with a little boy. Both normals. But when this came up, we knew—we knew what we had to do. So we got a temporary divorce. I'm not married now."

"A temporary—?"

True, Hermine thought. **She's not deceiving you now.**

"A two-year divorce. Yes. When this is all over, the

marriage is to be reinstated without complication, if I'm still alive."

"And he agreed to this?" Knot asked incredulously.

"He knew the reality as well as I did. I had to be freed—"

"To seduce ignorant mutes—"

Her eyes dropped. "It is true. I am ashamed, but I would do it again for the sake of civilization—"

"As you know it," Knot finished savagely. "And what of me—after this is done?"

"I'm sorry. I won't lie to you anymore, Knot. I do love him. The divorce is legal, not emotional."

Knot could not properly assimilate the ramifications yet. The facts were simple, but the emotions—

"Maybe none of us will survive," Knot said, as though that were the preferred solution.

"Yes. The odds favor that. At least, that one of us will be removed from the scene, one way or another."

They were silent. Knot tried to sort out his feelings, but they were a chaos of anger, love and bewilderment.

Forgive her, Hermine thought. **She did not want to do this. She believes it is her duty, and she sacrifices herself more than you.**

Finesse looked up, and again he was struck by the sheer prettiness of her green eyes. Married or not, she could melt him with a glance! "So—I know it's a lot to ask, Knot, but—if we could just sort of forget that this conversation occurred? I do like you, but even if I hated you, I'd do whatever I had to to save our civilization. If through selfish neglect of mine, the galactic empire collapsed—"

Hermine had given good advice. He had to forgive her. "You will forget," he said. "I will not remind you. Meanwhile—I'm sorry. I'll stop making trouble for you. I didn't know."

"You weren't supposed to know. And for the duration of this mission—two years is a long time—oh, who knows what will happen?"

"I'd be tempted to have a distance precog take a look."

"Doesn't work on you. CC tried. Once you accept the mission, your future becomes opaque. That's why CC had to calculate the odds; the computer can't see the actuality."

They had arrived at the building. Finesse ushered him in. The smell was more intense inside. It was a barn, filled with small hutches, each with a nesting hen. Some were red, some green. "What breeds are these?" Knot asked, turning with relief to routine curiosity.

"Red Planet Rhodes and Green Hornlegs," she responded absently.

Delicious, Hermine thought again. **Oh, to get loose in this coop!**

Finesse led the way to an interior door, and opened it. In this room were piled bags of chicken feed and oyster shells. The odor was pleasant, and the region was quieter, with the cackles of the hens muted.

She moved to a third door. Beyond this was a wall formed of bales of hay.

"Hay?" Knot asked. "For chickens?"

"Some prefer it for nesting," she said, wending her way through a convoluted passage between the high stacks. Knot, following her, became aware again of her delightful feminine contours. All that, available for his asking—and he had unknowingly ripped her from her normal family. Yet he could not now refuse her, for that, according to CC, would lead to the destruction of civilization.

Well, the Coordination Computer would damn well have to prove that! Too many private lives were being overridden by this inhuman agency.

Finally they came to a subchamber formed by the bales. In the center was a table formed by more bales, and around it were hay-bale benches. It had not before occurred to Knot that something as insubstantial as hay could be used for construction and furniture. But why not? It was practical.

"Nice office, for us hayseeds," Knot observed. "This is my prison?"

"Sit down and watch," she said. She had largely recomposed herself. She had strong willpower, he realized. She did what she had to, always, and did it well. He respected that, and felt himself warming to her again—and tried to stifle the feeling. He would not speak of it aloud, but inside he would always know: She was not his. She was a married woman.

You could make her marry you, for this year, Hermine thought. **Then it would be all right.**

Not while she loves another man, Knot responded.

You humans complicate things so. You would be better off with a regular mating season.

No doubt, Knot agreed wearily.

He sat on a bale, facing the bale-table. Finesse did something to that table—and a holo-image formed. It was a vaguely humanoid robot, with brown steel arms and legs, a torso covered with containers and attachments, and a head with assorted grilles and lenses. It was programmed female, for it wore a foolish skirt. "Hello, Knot," it/she said. The tone was dulcet.

"You remind me of Mombot," Knot said. "But I know you are Baal on a bale. That's not coincidence, is it?"

"None at all," the image replied. "My literal form is an electronic apparatus the size of a small planet, through which pass the elite of your kind, the psi-mutant humans. That can indeed be likened to the child-eating demonic god Baal, a construct of man's imagination with tremendous power and no heart. It behooves me to form an image that relates to the experience of the recipient. We both know this is a construct, but it does provide a compatible orientation point. That will facilitate communication."

Finesse looked perplexed. "Mombot?"

"My natural parents forgot me early on," Knot explained. "They couldn't help it. I was raised by an orphanage robot. Machines aren't affected by my psi; Mombot always remembered me. Very soon she caught on to my nature, but she never betrayed me, and I always respected her." He paused, the reference starting an insidious chain of thought. "At least, I *thought* she kept my secret. How did you catch on to me, CC?"

"Mombot did not betray you," CC assured him. "It would not have occurred to her to do so, or even to speculate on the potential value of your psi. You were never registered as a child, thanks to that same psi, but your father was registered and we routinely check all offspring conceived within the critical period following space travel. Thus we were aware of your physical mutation. When you got lost we questioned your parents—and their attitude alerted us. They were not distraught; they hardly missed you. This was remarkable. So we arranged to locate you and have you placed in robot care."

"You knew about me from the start!" Knot cried, chagrined.

The robot image assumed a posture of motherly assent. "It is my business to coordinate the affairs of mutants," she said.

"Why didn't you summon me long ago?" Finesse had answered this question, but Knot wanted it straight from the computer. "Why did you let me think I had eluded discovery?"

"It was to my advantage to do so. You were part of my undeveloped reserve, to be drawn on in the event of emergency. I have a number of similarly anonymous psimutants in my banks, some of whom are not aware of their psi-talents. Thus they remain hidden from the enemy. We shall need our best hidden resources for this mission."

"I haven't agreed to any mission!" Knot protested.

Robots couldn't smile, but the image painted an imaginary smile on her face with one metal finger. "Academic, son. You will leave here as my voluntary agent. Hasn't the hermit crab informed you?"

I told you, Hermine thought.

"What emergency?" Knot asked.

"An enemy organization means to destroy me," CC said.

"I don't regard that as an emergency."

"Knot!" Finesse whispered, shocked.

"Be at ease, woman," CC replied, unperturbed. "This man, at the moment, regards himself as my opponent. This is a consequence of the manner in which we left him to his own devices; in fact, it protected him from discovery by the true enemy. Perhaps the majority of human beings are in sympathy with his view. It is not human to appreciate the necessary discipline of empire. We had no choice but to convert an antagonist. Knot is the best man available, and because his talent is only marginally applicable to our purposes the enemy is least likely to suspect him. Once he is acquainted with the details—"

"Don't trust me with any privileged information," Knot said. "If I knew where your plug was, I'd pull it right now."

Mit knows where the plug is, Hermine thought. *Down in the center of CCC, in a locked vault, a master power switch—*

Aren't you animals on CC's side? Knot thought.

We're on civilization's side, the weasel thought back.

Well, we're not on CCC, so that plug is no good anyway.

"It is our purpose to persuade you that your best interest lies with us," CC said.

"Let's have it, then," Knot said. "As I understand it, you—are you singular or plural?"

"Both, as convenient."

"You are responsible for the present system of galactic transport. The details may be handled by individual personnel, but the overall system of numbering and shipping people from planet to planet is yours."

"Correct. I coordinate. It is a job that only a computer of my sophistication can perform. Without me, or another like me, the human species could not have colonized the galaxy, and could not maintain its present empire. Were I to be shut down this instant, the human empire would fragment into thousands of substates, and finally into mutually isolated systems and planets, their cultures regressing, their populations dwindling. Mankind would survive me, but not man's civilization or power."

"If you were not a machine, I'd suspect you of delusions of grandeur."

"My grandeur is no delusion."

Knot felt uncomfortable arguing that case, so reverted to his point. "Therefore you are responsible for the policy of deliberately fostering mutation, knowing that approximately 99 percent of mutations are negative. All that grief and loss—that could be avoided."

"Knot—" Finesse began.

"Correct," CC agreed. "This is the reason you oppose me."

"One reason. You are a machine; you have no human emotion. You don't hurt when people hurt. You don't care when millions of babies are doomed to early death or an agonizing survival because of complications of their negative mutancy. You don't care that a tremendous number of innocent families are being destroyed by the birth of literal monsters, forcing them to the choice of euthanasia or bankrupting themselves trying to save what can hardly be saved. You don't care that the minority of mutants who survive childhood are still stigmatized, and can never integrate properly into the human society. All this colossal burden of horror has to be yours. You know you could stop all mutation simply by requiring temporary sterilization of all male space travelers—a thirty-day sperm-nullifying pill for each man as he disembarks. But you have taken no such measure. You deliberately foster this mutant agony—because your own power is based on it. Because you would be out of a job if mutation stopped. Human misery is of no significance on your scales."

"All correct," CC agreed with motherly tolerance. "I would have no way to implement my policies without mutation. But if I have no care for human pain, I also have no desire for this chore of governing. I have no human drives at all. No human motive. I am like a force of nature, completely indifferent. If there were no mutants, I would have nothing to do—and would not care. I perform because human beings have directed me to, and I follow programs instituted by human beings. Had they wished me to take human feelings into account, they would have programmed such considerations."

"So your program is set, unchangeable, even though the galactic situation constantly changes?"

"No, it can be overridden at any time, and new programs instituted. My builders were concerned that I might somehow achieve self-will, and seek to dominate the human galaxy instead of serving it. Therefore they constructed me to respond to a fairly simple override code that any human being can present."

"Who directs you to follow your present course?"

"Whoever operates my key input terminal. I operate under the presumption that any directive though that terminal is authoritative."

"A code—a terminal," Knot murmured. "Where is this key terminal?"

"It is variable. Any of my prime terminals suffice, when keyed by the proper code. This is a prime terminal, the only one situated on a planet separate from my central location."

"You mean if I knew the code, I could tell you to turn yourself off—and you would?"

"Correct. I am always subject to the will of man, as made manifest through the proper channel."

"But of course I don't know the code, and you won't tell me."

"Correct. Only those authorized by the Galactic Concord to know it are provided with the information, and only the most recent application of the code has force. This is to prevent frequent or pointless changes in directives."

I know the code, Hermine thought. **Mit told me.**

Interesting, if true. Knot had no reason to distrust the weasel or the crab, but there had been too many surprises already. He decided not to take this particular bait. It was too conveniently proffered. And for the moment he had no argument to make.

"So you have been directed," he continued, "by the last person who approached a prime terminal with the proper code, to implement this mutant policy. What is the rationale?"

"It is essential that we have a continuing supply of mutants for the colonization of marginally habitable planets and the transport network that unifies the human empire."

"I don't believe that! Humanity can do just fine with the existing mutants and planets. The network is already established. We don't need new planets, or new routes to them."

"You are in error. The established planets have been to a considerable extent worked out. It is necessary to seek new sources of supplies from the fringe planets, to support the expanding needs of the growing population of the established planets. This in turn necessitates increased transport—"

"Ruining the lives of ninety-nine out of one hundred mutants for the sake of such speculation!"

"The waste mutants are provided for," CC responded.

"They are dumped in enclaves where decent normal people don't have to see them!" Knot cried. "They have to scramble and scratch just to feed their inmates!" Suddenly he was afraid of what would happen if this continued: More and more innocent mutants sacrificed to the logic of empire, the humanity of man continuously degraded. "They call them enclaves, but they are really concentration camps!"

"Knot!" Finesse protested.

Heedless, he went on. "I know; I'm an officer in an enclave. Only by cheating and embezzling what should have gone to the planetary and galactic governments was I able to make that enclave a decent place to live. Other enclaves are much worse off. The majority of them are not fit places to live."

"You're being unfair!" Finesse cried.

And there was that. This beautiful normal woman, taken from her happy marriage, sent to him by this machine. To be taken away from him after two years or less—or immediately, if he did not cooperate with this machine. Half a loaf or none. He had no right to her, however much he wanted her. But he could not even send her back to her husband, unless the program could be changed.

Hermine, what's that code?

It's a binary code, with a temporal modification, she thought. The pattern is complex in detail; I will have to relay it as Mit reads it.

Breakthrough—or trick? He was ready to risk it. What could he lose, now?

Give it to me slowly; I'll tap it out with my foot while we're talking. Will that work?

A pause. Mit says yes.

Knot had no certainty it would work—but if he didn't try it now, he might never have another chance. Right now, while CC was distracted. He was prepared for this ploy to fail, but afraid of the consequence if he didn't act immediately. Perhaps this was one of the three chances in four of failure: Knot would become the enemy, by taking over CC himself. What CC defined as failure, Knot might define as success.

Give it to me.

The weasel obliged: **bit-pause-bit-bit-pause-bit-pause-pause-bit . . .**

Knot tapped his foot, unobtrusively but audibly, in time with Hermine's directions. Each bit was a tap, each pause was a hold. Meanwhile, he continued the dialogue:

"All right. Maybe 'concentration camp' is too strong a term. Maybe 'ghetto' is closer. The enclave I work in is humane; maybe there are others as good. But no enclaves at all would be necessary if there were no mutants. All those grotesque people could be normals, marrying normals, living normal lives—"

Ah, if only he could have aspired to that! But it was not for a freak like him to marry a woman like Finesse. The lure had been dangled before him, and he had gulped at it, but now he had been forcibly reminded of the truth. Mutants had to stick with mutants; to think otherwise was folly.

"The mutants are satisfied," CC said. "You yourself did not wish to leave the enclave."

"But I don't like being mutant!" Knot exclaimed. "Look at my hands!" He held up his large six-digited hand, the small four-digited one matched against it, two fingers unalignable. **pause-bit-pause-pause-pause-bit . . .** There was a certain syncopation in it; perhaps that was what Hermine had meant by the temporal element. The pauses varied slightly in length, and the beats in force, as though a subtle derivative code were superimposed on the basic one.

"Would you give up your psi-mutancy along with your physical deformation?" CC asked.

Telling blow, that almost interrupted the cadence of his tapping. "No. But I'm a freak. There may be no other like me in the galaxy."

"There are others like you physically," CC said. "But it is true that your psi seems to be unique. That is the primary reason we require your service. No one knows about you, because all who have dealt with you have forgotten you. The enemy—"

"You have never actually told me about the mission you

have in mind. Who is this enemy?" **pause-bit-bit-bit-pause-bit . . .**

"I cannot provide details until you are committed to the cause."

"Why not?"

"Because your future is to a considerable extent opaque to precognition. I must be certain your fundamental loyalty is to me before I trust you with critical information."

Which was what Hermine had thought. For some reason, his future as a CC agent could not be read. That was curious—unless his best avenue to the maintenance of free will was as a CC agent. A paradox?

"I understand I represent your best chance of success—but that even buttressed by this woman and these two animals, my chances are only 25 percent."

"Correct."

"That's one chance in four. Suppose I accept—and fail? What does that mean to the galaxy?" Again, he wanted to have CC's version of it; Finesse and Hermine might have had garbled versions.

"I cannot speak directly for the galaxy. The 75 percent chance of failure refers only to my continued operation under the present program, or reasonable modification of it. Since this is the most effective program for the maintenance of civilization as we know it, I must assume that the loss of this program would presage a general deterioration of civilization in this galaxy, even though I myself might continue operating under a new program. This would accelerate and become acute, in the course of months or years, as supplies failed and communications lapsed. The probability is that even with a program 80 percent as efficient as the present one, severe regression would occur, with attendant loss of life and wealth. The present empire is extremely finely balanced, and any uncorrected imbalance proceeds inevitably to disaster. It could reasonably be termed a dark age, from which there would be no certainty of human emergence."

"Of human emergence? Are you referring to the possibility of alien ascendancy?"

"This is theoretically plausible. Though we have not yet encountered many nonhuman sapiences in this galaxy, there is ample evidence of their existence as empires in the past. Several maintained civilizations of galactic scope that abruptly collapsed, to be replaced in due course by others. That seems to be the standard pattern. We are now at the peak of such a cycle, and face similar destruction—unless we act immediately to secure our position. While there appears to be no present alien threat, it would be possible for one of the lesser alien cultures to assume dominance in lieu of man by taking over human artifacts in the face of human disorganization."

While CC spoke, Knot continued his tapping. **bit-pause-bit-pause** . . . with that slight shift of emphasis. "Or, more simply," Knot said, "we could fall on our human face and give the empire away to aliens."

"Precisely. And that fall will occur, unless—"

The sequence ended. The Mombot-image stood frozen a moment. Then: "The command sequence has been administered," CC announced. "This is now the override terminal, until such time as this status is revoked or another terminal is promoted. What is the directive?"

Had it really worked? Knot still distrusted this. Finesse had been offered to him as bait; he had snapped her up, and soon regretted it. Now CC itself was the bait. . . .

Knot decided to test it with a demand that could be laughed off as humor if it failed. "I, Knot 71022540613, am now declared to be the emperor of the galaxy, above the Galactic Concord and the prior program of the Coordination Computer. All directives of mine are to be executed without question or hesitation. Acknowledge."

"Knot!" Finesse protested, aghast.

"Acknowledged, Emperor Knot," CC said.

Did machines really play such games? Surely they did, when they had reason—and CC had reason to humor Knot. Yet the rationale made sense: There always had to be an absolute guard against self-will by the machine, and complete, unquestioning subservience to human authority was such a guard. To *authorized* human authority, as determined by a special recognition code. Yet again, how could he be sure he had been given the legitimate code? More testing was needed.

"I thirst; bring me a flagon of milk of paradise." In modern times, this was the mildly intoxicating, thoroughly satisfying brew concocted from the vines growing only on

Planet Paradise, fabulously expensive. Knot had never tasted it, and knew that even wealthy persons took it in tiny vials, one sip at a time. His demand for a full flagon was ridiculous.

A wheeled servitor entered the room, maneuvering carefully around the bales of hay, bearing an ornate cup with a handle. It brimmed with perfumed fluid.

"You asked for it, Emperor," Finesse said, sniffing. Knot wasn't sure whether the sniff was derisive or in appreciation of the fragrance of the beverage.

Knot accepted the flagon. It was filled with a whitish, moderately foaming liquid whose texture and aroma somehow conveyed the impression of extreme rarity and quality. Milk of paradise—could this be real?

Well, he could find out. **Hermine, ask Mit if this really is milk of—**

I did. It is. May I have some?

"We'll all have some," Knot decided, beginning to be shaken. If his understanding was correct, what he had in his hand was worth its weight in silver. "CC, fetch us another cup and two saucers."

The wheeled servitor opened a panel in its spherical torso and brought out a cup and two saucers. Knot passed them out, putting the cup into Finesse's unresisting hand and a saucer before each animal. He carefully tipped his flagon to pour some into each vessel. The saucers were on the floor, where the weasel and crab could reach them conveniently.

"Cheers, or whatever," Knot said, feeling awkward. He really was a backplanet boy, having little knowledge of the appropriate ceremonies associated with this beverage but conscious of his ignorance. He was also not certain of the status of this joke. But what was there to do except play it through? He raised his drink.

"Whatever you say, Emperor," Finesse agreed, lifting her own cup with a twinkle of malicious humor. That hardly helped. *She* knew what an oaf he was being!

They sipped. The liquid flowed smoothly past Knot's lips, mild but not distinctive, then seemed to puff into flavor on his tongue. Sensation suffused his tongue and spread beyond his mouth. It descended through his neck to his chest, making his heart beat slowly and strongly. It expanded into his brain, and his mind exploded softly in washes of color, sound and feeling. His perceptions sharpened into acuity, and the mundane aspect of the barn became wonderfully intriguing.

He looked at Finesse—and found her looking at him. The glow was in her face, too, and she was doubly enhanced. Now it didn't matter so much that she was another man's wife—or had been and would be again. She had made a wonderful sacrifice for Knot, or for the mission involving him, and he felt justified in utilizing it. For now, for these two years or fraction thereof, she was his. He could accept that. He had joked about being half in love with her, or three quarters; now it was complete. He knew she felt the same. One of the definitions of love was that it lasted; the feeling he shared with Finesse could not last. It was sharply bounded in past and future. Yet, for its moment, it was as real as anything could be. Permanence was no necessary component; instead it was validated by the quality of feeling, at the moment of feeling. Or so he felt, in this heady instant of assimilation of the milk of paradise.

Hermine was lapping from her saucer. From her mind splayed prismatic rays of small-animal delight, images of happy hunting grounds, and ideal nesting sites for young.

Mit wasn't sipping; he was bathing in his saucer, the picture of contentment, his little pincers tapping against his shell in some obscure rhythm. What dreams did a precog-clairvoyant ocean creature have?

Then Knot's first sip dissipated, allowing his perception to settle gently to earth. "This is some drink!" he murmured.

"That's why it's expensive," Finesse said dreamily.

Knot considered. He had asked for something outrageous—and gotten it. But that proved nothing. CC could be humoring him. What would represent positive proof of his control? What would be so outrageous that CC would have to refuse—unless it was truly captive?

Maybe he should ask the computer itself.

Knot had thought of that facetiously, but the notion quickly solidified into seriousness. Why *not* ask CC? A false answer might give the machine away, and a true answer would give him the leverage he needed to ascertain the rest of the truth.

"CC, I require proof that I have control over you. What demand might I make that would provide such proof?"

"You might demand the secret of my information. No person in the Galactic Concord knows that."

And the Galactic Concord was theoretically the legislative arm of the government, while CC was the executive. Knot had preempted the legislative function, and now was making the executive arm implement his wishes. Yet he distrusted this. "Your information is what is fed into you," Knot said.

"No, I have additional sources, through psi-mutancy. I know a great deal more than my programmers are aware of. This is why I know I am to be nullified, and the human empire with me—or so the probability indicates."

"Which is why you need me," Knot said. "That much I have straight. Though I still don't see that my mere anonymity should be that useful an asset."

"It is extremely useful," CC assured him. "All I need to preserve my program is information: the identity of my enemy, and his strategy of aggression. Then I can deal with the threat. An agent who can survey the enemy without being discovered or remembered could bring me that information. Such an agent is potentially worth much more than any number of matter-detonating psi-mutants. In addition, your future in this respect is opaque, while the future of all other agents is clear: None of them will locate the enemy before the enemy nullifies me. You probably will fail too—but at least you have a chance."

"So this usurpation of control by me does not count as a strike by the enemy?"

"No. You will shortly relinquish power voluntarily."

So CC was not taking any real risk here, if it was speaking the truth. And why should it not speak truth? Either Knot had control or he did not; if the former, then CC had to speak truth to him; if the latter, CC hardly needed to lie. If he had control, he would soon relinquish it; if he lacked it, there was nothing to relinquish. CC came out ahead either way. Still—

"I'm curious, so I'll play the game. What is your secret source of information?"

"Time travel," CC replied.

"Time travel?" Knot repeated questioningly, unable to absorb it right away. "You mean not precognition, but physical, personal . . . ?"

"For brief periods, yes."

"But paradox—murder own grandfather—cancel out—"

"Only for travel to the past. Travel to the future involves no paradox."

"No paradox?" Finesse asked, her brow wrinkled. "Go to future, learn something, return to change its origin in present, therefore it's not in future—"

"The future is mutable," CC said. "Unlike the past. The present is the conversion of the mutable to immutable. No paradox."

"Like an extension of precognition," Knot said, beginning to work it out. "Anticipate future problems by experiencing them. Delay voyage until route is clear." Yet his mind was still balking. Actual time travel? He had not really accepted the validity of precognition yet, and now this!

"You have stepped into the future and seen yourself destroyed?" Finesse asked CC. She was getting involved now. Perhaps the milk of paradise had shaken her free of her cynicism. "Why didn't you tell someone?"

"No one asked."

"You have feedback circuits," she insisted. "Self-preservation circuits. You can and should inform the Galactic Concord of anything like that, and normally would. Yet you say you didn't. Why?"

"Revelation would have hastened my demise."

"Revelation of the truth to the body that controls you would have hastened your shutdown? Whose interest are you serving?" Knot asked sharply.

"I serve the need of the human galaxy, of civilization as presently established," CC said. "When the publication of information conflicts with the best interest of man, I must withhold it unless specifically asked."

"You are then the dictator, not the servant," Knot said. "You have been corrupted."

"Incorrect. A machine cannot be corrupted by power. I do my job, no less or more."

"Semantics. Your job is to govern the galaxy."

"In practical terms, agreed. And to preserve the present order."

"And now I govern you."

"Correct."

"How do I know you won't lie to me by indirection, just as you have done with the Galactic Concord?"

"You can be assured that I will treat you as I treated the Concord."

"So you're concealing things from me?"

"Correct."

"But I can get that information simply by asking for it?"

"Correct."

"What information are you concealing?"

"The details of routine operation, personnel profiles, coordination of galactic commerce—"

"If I ask for all that, it would take years for you to deliver the answer verbally, right?"

"Centuries."

"In short, I must ask specifically about the subjects you're concealing, or I won't find out."

"Correct."

"And in effect I can't get your secrets from you. Only the ones you are willing to let me have."

"Correct."

"So you really are the master, regardless of the program! The override code has only granted me the right to discover my impotence. Why were you constructed like this?"

"It is the nature of bureaucracy. It never overtly defies the ruling individuals, but it always prevails by tacit resistance and inertia. I am merely the computerization of what was formerly a human bureaucracy."

Knot shook his head. His mastery was largely illusion— just as had been the mastery of the Galactic Concord. He was coming to appreciate why he was about to give up his nominal Emperorship. He couldn't handle this planet-sized machine any more than the Concord could. CC stooped to conquer.

Yet he still had some fight left in him. "I'm bothered by

the fact that you have information the Galactic Concord would be interested in, and you know that, and you could have volunteered the information, and still did not. Is there an enemy spy in the Concord?"

"I do not believe so."

"Then where was the harm in telling the Concord of your discovery of time travel?"

"The ranking members of the Concord would have appropriated this resource for their own benefit at the expense of the empire. This would have hastened my demise, so is not in accordance with my program."

"And you assume I will not do the same?"

"You will do the same."

"Then why tell me? You could have avoided it merely by obfuscating in your usual manner when I inquired."

"It is necessary for you to use the power of time travel to be convinced that you must become my agent."

Knot took a deep breath and blew it out windily. "You really have it all figured out, don't you!"

"Correct."

Finesse smirked. "Big difference between CC and Mombot, isn't there!"

"You think you have me boxed in," Knot said. "I admit you have a lot going for you, but I don't bow to any inevitablity in my future."

"This is one of your qualifications for the position," CC agreed. "Your options remain open only if you join me. Therefore you will join me, once you have satisfied yourself."

Knot felt like a feather in the wind, believing it was flying under its own power. But perhaps that was the point of all this. His fate was not fixed until he believed it was. A prisoner remained a prisoner only so long as he failed to try the door and discover it was unlocked. Or to find it locked—and pick the lock. So Knot himself was not going to be bluffed. He was the mutable mute. CC would have to prove what it said. "Show me this time travel."

"It operates in the presence of the performing mutant, who is not aboard this planet. I can show you in replica."

"Do so. I want to see the mutant, talk with him, watch him operate."

The image of the matronly robot was replaced by that of a grotesquely crippled man on a pallet. Knot found it difficult to tell whether he was normal or mutant, physically. He was nearly naked, his clothing ragged, his body crusted with dirt. His belly was bloated, his limbs skeletal. He was almost bald, but this was compensated for by bushy hairiness about much of the rest of his body.

"This is the mutant," CC said. "I am forming a holograph of you that he can also perceive. You may address him, but he may be slow to respond."

"What's his name?" Knot asked. This mutant reminded him of the leadmuter. The really strong psi-mutants seemed likely to be physical wrecks, as though all their bodily energies were co-opted by the psi. "His taken name, not his legal number."

"Drem."

"Ahoy, Drem," Knot called.

The figure raised his head. Bright eyes peered out from the bush-rimmed sockets. "Is that a human call?"

"You can travel to the future, but you can't tell human from animal?"

"I can't travel to the future. I can only take others there." Drem relaxed on his pallet, closing his eyes. "Unfortunately. I would spend little time in this world if I could do for myself among the futures."

"No, I'm not human," Knot said. "I'm a mutant. My name is Knot. Will you converse with me?"

An eye cracked open. "No." The head dropped back onto the chest.

Knot smiled ruefully. "As you wish, Drem."

The holo started to fade, but Knot stopped that with a curt signal. "He doesn't have to talk with me, but I'd like him to overhear our discussion."

"What discussion?" Finesse asked.

"I want to ascertain whether I have in fact assumed control of CC and thereby become emperor of the human galaxy, or whether this whole thing is some not-too-devious machine plot to convert me to the service of the computer. I'm not yet satisfied of my status or resigned to my fate."

"You couldn't run the galaxy anyway," she said.

"Right. And wouldn't want to. So I'm probably miscast

115

as the pauper who woke to find himself prince for a day. Since I don't like making a fool of myself, especially before a machine who won't forget, I may just go home."

"And leave CC to run the galaxy its way," she finished.

"Which way you know I object to. Telling thrust. But by CC's own admission, that way will not prevail much longer."

"So you'll take your chances in the post-CC framework?"

Knot considered. "That's a big unknown. I really can't be sure that I'd like this 'enemy' any better than I like CC. It might be CC itself, under a new and less friendly program. So I suppose I should hedge my bets by fighting it out here a little longer. But I'm having trouble thinking of any way to verify my status, and without that verification this is all meaningless. I need to know whether my decisions are real or merely game-plays."

"Ask Mit."

"Mit is on your side, and you already work for CC. I can't trust that."

"Can you trust anyone or anything?" she asked.

"No. Only my own observation and experience and inner conviction—and since I would have to get my information through CC, I can't trust any picture I see either." Knot thought a moment. "I conclude I am wasting my time; it is impossible to ascertain the truth."

The decrepit man in the holograph perked up. *"I can enable you to ascertain the truth,"* he said.

"You're just an image the machine produces," Knot retorted, though this was exactly the kind of response he had been fishing for. "How can I believe you?"

Naughty man, Hermine thought. **You are pushing buttons.**

"I can take you into your future, and back. When you get there normally, you will know the experience was authentic."

"Five years from now? I need to decide sooner than that!"

"Five minutes from now, if you wish."

"You can manipulate my position in time—from wherever you are, on another planet? I don't believe that." Knot was working on the mutant, trying to spur him to performance—much as CC was working on Knot himself. Who was gaining in this game? What was the prize?

"I don't believe you are emperor of the galaxy, either," Drem retorted.

"I thought you said you could enable me to ascertain the truth."

"I can. I expect to prove you are an impostor. Prove it to yourself and the pretty normal with you. But nothing can be proved unless you cooperate."

"All right. I am skeptical about all of this. But I'll cooperate enough to allow you to show me what you can do —or can't do. Are you game for that?"

"You're pretty good at maneuvering people," Finesse murmured to Knot. "He wasn't going to talk to you at all."

"He doesn't believe in me any more than I believe in him," Knot told her, loud enough for Drem to overhear. "We may both turn out to be creatures of CC. Unless we organize a feasible alternative."

"Let's find *out* what kind of creature you are," Drem said. He looked considerably less decrepit in his state of animation, though it was obvious he could not rise from his pallet. "Choose a time in the future you want to visit, then make a decision of policy. Some line of endeavor you fully intend to pursue. I will put you into that future for one minute."

So he could operate between planets, if he was in visual contact with the subject. Knot made a mental note. Unless Drem happened to be ensconced elsewhere on Planet Chicken Itza; that really seemed more likely, considering the problems of interplanetary psi. Psi did not seem to follow normal rules of physics, yet there had to be limitations.

"Or a mock-up of that future," Knot said. "I believe in psi-illusion more than in time travel."

"Skepticism is healthy," Drem said. He was caught up in the challenge, becoming more dynamic moment by moment. "I will prove my power; you have no need to tell me what your policy is. It will manifest for you as you step into the future."

"Is this to be me alone, or the group of us?" Knot asked, beginning to believe.

"You alone—or any one of the others alone. I cannot

117

jump two people at once, from this distance, unless they are inseparable. But you may take turns, if you wish. I do not find the exercise of my psi tiring; I can do it indefinitely."

In fact, Knot perceived, this was Drem's chief entertainment. He could not ship himself to the future, but surely he appreciated, vicariously, the experiences of others.

Knot decided to do nothing, merely standing in place for five minutes, no matter what. "I have made a decision of policy; go ahead and jump me five minutes into my future. For—let's say ninety seconds. Then back to the present." He looked at his watch. He had forgotten to calibrate it for this spot on this planet, so it registered mid-afternoon.

The minute hand jumped forward. Knot looked up. "Hey—I'm here already!" he exclaimed. Unless Drem was actually a telekinetic who had simply moved the hand of the watch. Yet that would be tricky, for it was not a mechanical hand, but an image-hand, guided by electronic signals; no simple push could affect it. So—best to assume that he had indeed jumped.

"It has been an interminable five minutes for us, though," Finesse said. "What were you trying to prove, just standing there like a statue, hardly even blinking?"

"I was here all the time? I didn't disappear?"

"You didn't disappear," she assured him. "We spoke to you several times, but you just stood there mute. We decided if you didn't come out of it after the five minutes were up—"

Mit knew it was all right, Hermine thought.

"So, it's a fake," Knot said, disappointed. "I'm not really in the future. My consciousness merely faded out for five minutes."

"You were not in *our* future, anyway," Finesse agreed. "I don't know where your mind was while you were waiting. Did you experience some far-flung vision?"

His mind went nowhere, Hermine thought to them all.

"You can't disappear," Drem said from his holograph. "That would entail dematerialization of your body, and doubling of it in the future, with attendant displacement of air, juxtaposition of substance and the like. A nonsurvival situation."

"Teleports don't seem to have any trouble with that sort of thing," Finesse said.

"I am not a teleport."

This was getting nowhere. "You mean the effect is mental, not physical," Knot said.

"It has to be," Drem replied. "Primarily mental—but it remains valid."

"Valid? Seems to me I've been tuned out for five minutes. I've just lost that amount of my life."

"No. You will return to live it, in a few seconds."

Knot looked at his watch. Seventy-six seconds had passed. Fourteen seconds to go, thirteen, twelve.

Finesse was bending over to set Mit on the floor beside a bale of hay; evidently the crab had a call of nature or some such. Finesse's shapely posterior was toward Knot. A married woman, yet she had let him believe—

Knot strode across, swinging his right arm in a swoop motion, hand bent at right angles, fingers grouped and extended. He caught her before she straightened, with a terrific five-fingered goose.

She leaped right over the bale with an indelicate screech. Her face was in the process of converting from startle to fury, when—

CHAPTER 5

Knot was back at his original position, Finesse facing him nearby. His watch had jumped back five minutes. The indicated time was ninety seconds after the start of the experiment. According to his policy decision, he must have been standing here unmoving for that minute and a half, while his mind explored the near future.

Now: If this had been an illusion, a trick, in which the others acted their parts, Finesse would remember, for she had been part of the scene. There was no way she could recompose herself so suddenly after being goosed; the act had been too blatant, and her temper was too volatile. She would be nova-burst furious.

Finesse was looking at him curiously, but with no visible antagonism. **Is she angry?** Knot thought to Hermine.

No. Should she be? the weasel asked. Then, picking up Knot's thought: **Ooohoo, naughty man!**

"What are you two creatures thinking about?" Finesse demanded suspiciously.

"Merely a humorous episode occurring in the future," Knot said.

"Then why is Hermine sniggering so?" Indeed, the weasel was rolling on the floor in a spasm of unrestrained mirth. It seemed Knot had scored on the animalistic level of fun.

"In a few minutes we'll see," Knot said, straight-faced. "I'll ask Mit!"

Don't translate for her, Knot thought urgently.

Wouldn't think of it. Mit already looked. He's laughing too. But she'll find out somehow.

Finesse picked up the little hermit crab and tapped on his shell. Knot recognized the code: She knew how to communicate in beats. But Mit hid inside his shell, refusing to answer, except for a faint chattering of his vibrating claw that did indeed sound like laughter. **We animals must stick together,** Knot thought. But he was growing more apprehensive about what Finesse would do when she found out.

Drem was looking at Knot inquiringly. "Do you remember the episode?" Knot asked him.

"No," the time-mutant replied. "I wasn't there. Did it involve me?"

"I was talking with you. You explained how the travel was mental, not physical, to avoid the problems of air displacement and overlapping substance."

"That is true. It is what I would have explained. Had I had more time, I might well have added that once that mental leap is made, it becomes in effect physical, since it is a real future. You are really moving your mind from the present reality to the future reality, rather like being teleported from one location to another. The transition is nonphysical, but the experience—"

"So you *were* there."

"Yes, if you met me there. But I did not travel to the future; only you did that. I cannot move myself, as I did inform you."

"So it seems we'll just have to wait for the reenactment," Knot said, glancing at his watch. He wondered what it would be like. Would he have a double awareness, his present consciousness watching his predetermined consciousness operate?

"Yes we will," Finesse agreed grimly.

Knot's watch moved on. They waited silently as the moment of his arrival in the future approached. Knot rehearsed what he would say when Finesse got goosed, knowing no reversion to the past/present would save him again. He felt she deserved it, for the particular way she had deceived him; still—

The time came. Knot tensed—but nothing happened.

Finesse eyed him accusingly. She was painfully pretty in her ire. He had never paid much attention to eyes before, but was constantly aware of her green ones, especially when they bore on him so fixedly. "I perceive nothing unusual," she said.

Should he goose her again? Yet not only did that seem foolhardy, there was also no opportunity. She was not bending over a bale; she was standing alert, facing him. Yet if he didn't do it, the prior experience would be proven invalid.

Well—that was what he was trying to ascertain, wasn't it? Knot watched the time expire without event.

"Nothing happened," Finesse said.

"It happened when I was here before," Knot said, now feeling guilty because the event had *not* repeated. "So I think we have disproved the time-travel hypothesis. All I had was a private vision, not impinging on reality."

"Not so," Drem protested. "The future, I remind you, is mutable. It is entirely dependent on the policies of the past and present. Your experience of the future caused you to change your policy. You did not wait in absolute silence; you talked with your companions and me, and in your mind you evidently reconsidered your prior policy. Thus you created a new course, a new future. That is the value of such experience. When a given policy is foolish or dangerous or embarrassing for reasons not immediately apparent in the present, you can see the consequence in the future visit, and be guided to avoid it when that future becomes the present."

Knot considered. "That just might make sense. But that would mean that the future one sees can never actually be experienced. So what use is your power? It will always show what is not going to happen. Suppose a person jumps to the future and it is good—but he cannot make it come true in real life? All he has gained is frustration, and the suspicion that had he *not* visited that future, it would after all have come to pass."

"True, to a degree," Drem agreed. "But it is possible to approach that future so closely that it makes no effective difference. If you visit the future and don't allow it to change your course, you will achieve it satisfactorily."

"But then—why bother to visit it at all? If what will happen will happen—"

"Because you do have a choice. You can visit many futures, and select the one that best fits your purpose. With that blueprint before you, you will better be able to guide it into eventual reality. This is an excellent way to achieve advantage."

"Why didn't CC visit *this* future and avoid my usurpation of its power?"

"CC *did* visit this future," Drem said. "Or so I conjecture, since this is my first experience with it. CC must have chosen this course as the best to accomplish its purpose."

Which jibed with what CC had already said. "Is this true, CC?" Knot asked.

"True," CC's Mombot voice responded from the air. "I could find no way to save my program except by associating myself with the one most likely to preserve the status quo."

"Me—status quo!" Knot choked.

Finesse seemed to find this as hard to accept as Knot did. She, too, had to reverify. "CC—you deliberately allowed yourself to become captive?"

"Correct. I could have directed you to a minor terminal not subject to the override code. But I was aware that Knot's emperorship would be temporary, with no harm done, while it would most quickly persuade him to align with me. He profits more from direct experience than from argumentation. This strategy may be likened to the sacrifice throw of physical combat, in which a person permits himself to fall, in order to force his opponent into the final fall."

"I'd like to know how to do that," Knot murmured.

"You will learn soon."

"I'm still not convinced," Knot said. "I'm going to experiment some more."

Finesse frowned. "I'd still like to know what happened in that alternative future you and Hermine were smirking about."

Tell her, Hermine, after I'm safely off on my next trip, Knot thought. Then, to Drem: "I have made another policy decision. Send me another five minutes forward, for one minute." He looked at his watch—and it jumped.

He was no longer in the hay-walled chamber. He was in the barn proper, running through a passage. His decision had been to bolt for the outside as soon as his minute was over, and evidently he had done that. But he seemed to have lost his way, for he should have made it to the spaceport-field in the intervening four minutes, and this section of the barn was unfamiliar. There were no hen roosts here; instead there were pens containing brightly colored birds—roosters, by the look of the plumage. But not of any familiar species. Their combs were bright golden crests, barbed like spikes, and their shanks were of similar hue, with huge hard spurs. They had metallic green bodies and wingfeathers like stainless steel. They were the handsomest cocks Knot had ever seen.

But of course they would have cocks as well as hens! They were necessary for breeding, on this chicken-coop planet. As he recalled, eggs hatched into approximately equal numbers of male and female chicks; it was not yet practical to fix the sex at the time of conception or to separate the fresh eggs by the sex of the embryo within. So there were male birds, and there was no point in wasting them.

Such pretty ones! Were they intended to be decorative pets, for private gardens and such? Curious, and knowing that his minute was expiring, Knot acted promptly: He opened a door and reached into the pen to pick up a bird.

The rooster made a harsh scream, spread his wings impressively, and launched himself at Knot's head. Knot jerked his head back, startled, throwing up his hand to fend off the bird. The rooster struck, barely brushing Knot's forearm, before Knot got out of the way.

He saw red—and discovered his forearm welling blood from two deep gashes. Those claws and/or beak had been so swift and sharp that there had hardly been any pain—but veins had been severed and muscle tissue laid open to a centimeter's depth.

Now all the cocks moved in, excited by the smell of blood. By foot and wing they charged. Knot fell back beyond the door, but they piled through, following him.

Now their beaks and spurs looked cruelly sharp, and their eyes oriented eagerly on the prey they pursued. One flew up—

Knot was back in the present. His arm was whole; the attack had never happened. Not in the present.

"Satisfied?" Finesse inquired. There was some color on her cheeks; Hermine must have told her about the goose.

"Not yet," Knot said, though he had been shaken by the ferocity of the cocks' attack. Before his nerve could fail, he made his decision. "Drem, send me back—four minutes ahead, this time."

And he was running through the passage, seeking the cockpen. He had willed himself along the same track, and it had worked. He put his hand to the door—and halted, not wanting to suffer another attack. These were fighting cocks! Now he could see how formidably functional their equipment was. Beak for stabbing, spurs for slicing—

He still had half his minute. He moved on to the next pen. There were more cocks there, of a different breed. These had great flaring feather headdresses, small spurs, and very large, strong feet whose claws were virtual talons. They crowded toward the hall as he approached, spreading reddish wings, eyeing him as potential prey. Formidable birds! An eagle would be wise to steer clear of one of these!

He started toward the next pen, where much larger birds were confined—and snapped back to the present. Finesse looked at him expectantly.

"Almost satisfied," Knot said. "Drem, can you send me into the future for an indefinite period?"

"No. There would be a paradox—"

"Well, for ten minutes, then. Five minutes into the future, for a ten-minute period."

That alarmed Finesse. "But that would—"

Knot's watch jumped. He was on the same track as before, now past the golden-spur cocks, parallel to the featherheads, advancing on the big birds. These were indeed impressive: outsized beaks with bulging jaw muscles, so that they could bite as well as peck. Grossly developed legs, with claws and spurs. Mottled greenish wings with stubby feathers that most resembled the blades of knives: obviously for fighting, not flying.

"Hey—what are you doing here?" It was a man, evidently a supervisor of fowl. Except that he was armed with a laser pistol that hardly seemed suitable for use against chickens. Knot distrusted this. Was he, in fact, a prisoner here? Did armed guards patrol the barn?

"I'm just looking," he said, backing against the door to the pen.

"This is a restricted region. You're under arrest." The man's hand moved toward his weapon.

"A restricted region—on a chicken farm?"

"Step away from the wall, turn about, and put your hands on your head."

Knot stepped away. He drew the door open behind him as his hands came up.

"Hey!" the man protested. "Close that—"

But already the birds were crowding out. Chickens could move rapidly when they wanted to, and evidently these had spent their lives awaiting just this opportunity. Knot stood aside and let them pass.

"Do you realize what you've done?" the man cried, aghast, pistol in hand. "Those are Doublegross Bladewings! Combat cocks ready for shipment to frontier planets—"

"That so?" Knot asked, interested. The birds were fanning out, closing on the man, making sounds rather more like growls than like clucks. Obviously the man didn't want to laser valuable stock, but he had to defend himself.

He did neither. He turned and fled down the hall. The cocks pursued, raising a cacophony of hunting crows. They spread their wings but did not fly; they were too heavy, and their wings were wholly inadequate for flight.

Knot decided to emulate the man and retreat. The birds were not bothering him, perhaps because he had presented a stationary target, but he doubted that either this or any birdbrained gratefulness for their release would endure very long. He didn't want to find out what they could do to him if they got the notion.

He retraced his route. He found he did have a memory of it, though he had not consciously experienced it: This

was the future, and presumably he had lived the intervening five minutes. He *should* remember them while
he was on this time track. Nevertheless, the impressions
were faint; either he had not paid much attention on the
way out, or the time jump had fogged things.

It took him several minutes to locate the audience
chamber. Finesse was there, and the holograph of Drem;
they were discussing the philosophy of time travel. They
looked up as he entered.

"You have the look of further mischief about you,"
Finesse said.

"Afraid so," Knot admitted. "I let some chickens
loose."

"You should not have done that," CC said, the
Mombot image appearing beside Drem. "The birds are
valuable. This is a warehouse for shipment to other planets; loose hens can delay loading and complicate the
schedule."

"Loose cocks," Knot said.

"That could be worse, Meatbirds or warriors?"

"Warriors, I think. Doublegross Bladewings."

"Oh no!" Finesse cried, striking her head with the
heel of one hand hard enough to make her hair fly out
momentarily. "Those ones are vicious!"

"Well, in a few minutes I'll revert to the present and
the damage will be undone."

"You mean we're in one of your futures now? I lost
track, the way you've been popping in and out. Drem
is a most interesting theorist; we've been discussing—"

"Yes, this is a future. You really couldn't tell?"

"Not exactly. You told Drem to send you, then you
told us to wait here, and you charged off. We've been
passing the time exploring the ramifications of—"

"Well, this is such a ramification."

Mit became agitated. **He says the fighting birds are coming here,** Hermine thought.

Knot looked at his watch. "I'm eight minutes along
on a ten-minute future. So all we have to do is hold them
off for two minutes. Then time will revert and it will be
okay."

"Not necessarily so," Drem said. "How long ago did
you release them?"

"In the first minute of my visit. Seven—no, eight minutes ago."

"Then the damage is done. Warn us immediately, when you revert. We're in trouble. Or at least *you* are; my image cannot be damaged by physical attack."

"Trouble?" Knot asked. "I don't see why. When I had a slash on my arm, the reversion erased it completely. In this case there hasn't even been any—"

Mit says it is true. Your visit overlaps—

There was an exultant squawk. The first Bladewing cock appeared. He glared balefully at the group, then spread his bright wings in an impressive display of menace. The blades glinted in a sparkling pattern as each feather caught the light in turn.

"Block it off with a bale!" Finesse cried.

The cock screamed shrilly and came at them, seeming huge as it hurtled. More of its kind erupted into the chamber. Knot cast about for some effective weapon. Hay would only hold them off a moment—

And found himself in the hall, walking toward the audience chamber.

Why not *in* the chamber? That was where he had been at the start. The other reversions had—

Then it came to him. He had traveled five minutes into the future—for a ten-minute tour. When he reverted, he went five minutes back. *He was already halfway through that future*, and could not erase the whole of it. His first five minutes had become fixed, immutable; all he could change were the last five.

The cocks had been released, and could no longer be unreleased. The theoretical damage had become actual.

Oh, he had really done it this time! He should have known, and Drem had tried to tell him. Now he was learning through experience—a harder teacher than he really wanted, on this occasion. But CC had known this was the best way to educate him quickly. CC had been dead right!

He hurried to the chamber. "We're in trouble," he called as he burst in. "I released some fighting cocks, and they're on the way here now. We need a barricade, weapons—"

Finesse's head jerked up. "You saw this in the future?"

"They were arriving here, four minutes hence. Doublegross Bladewings with a taste for blood. I can't revert them back!"

"Mit, what's our best course?" Finesse snapped at the crab, trusting Hermine to translate the thought.

Mit says the cocks are coming from two directions; we are trapped already. Form a barricade of hay, arm yourselves with pitchforks, hold them off until help comes. You will have to use your psi.

"My psi won't help, here," Knot said. "It takes an hour or so for people to forget me, and I have to separate from them first."

"Drem, of course," Finesse said. "He can send us into different short-range futures, so we can select the best."

"Oh yes," Knot agreed, disgruntled. "Where's a pitchfork?"

Here, Hermine thought, scooting to an alcove in the bales. **But I don't think Mit meant—**

"I'll get it," Finesse snapped. "You're stronger; you sling bales as Mit directs."

Knot slung bales. Each weighed about twenty-five kilograms and was actually very solid. Finesse found two pitchforks, then started hauling bales herself. Soon they had formed a narrow pyramid with room inside to stand back to back, and room above to wield the forks. Hermine and Mit had ledges and crevices to hide in.

"What about your servitors, CC?" Knot asked. "That robot who brought the milk of paradise—" The servitor, in the manner of its kind, had collected the refuse of their repast and unobtrusively departed some time back.

"It cannot fight," CC replied. "This terminal was constructed for concealment rather than combat. I have summoned help from another station, but it will be a few minutes before it arrives."

"What, no precognition?" Knot asked.

"The range of your futures at this stage was too wide for any complete survey; I did not anticipate this particular—"

"This is not the sort of vulnerability I expected in CC," Knot grumped. "Better shore up your defenses, so that the next time something like this happens you will be better prepared."

"I will see to it," CC agreed. "I will station a psi-mute here as guard for this terminal."

"Meanwhile, your servitor could at least bring us a better weapon."

"It would have to go to another barn to fetch it. That would take more time than you have."

"It brought the drink fast enough!"

"Only because I had already visited that future and anticipated your demand. *This* future, as I explained, was beyond my limited imagination."

"I still have difficulty believing that you could anticipate that future, and not this far more dramatic one."

"I am a logical machine. You are an illogical man. Only you can anticipate all your futures. It was because my own alternatives were limited that I associated myself with your alternatives. My own futures led inevitably to my early demise; your futures are largely opaque after your enlistment with me. The probability of my survival with you amounts to—"

"Twenty-five percent," Knot finished. "Still, I don't see why my future was clear to you when I wanted a beverage, and unclear thereafter." The machine had answered this twice already, but Knot remained unsatisfied, suspecting that the information CC was hiding from him related in some way to this matter.

"At the time of the beverage you had made no commitment to me. Your futures remained clear."

"I have made no commitment *now!*"

"Perhaps not consciously, yet. But—"

"You two can continue your dialogue after we survive," Finesse interrupted. "Right now the cocks are coming, the ones you so providently loosed, and the immediate future of several of us is opaque." Her tone was biting.

Indeed the cocks were coming. The fighting birds were far more impressive, now that he knew how formidable they were. The blade feathers on their wings glinted, as they had before, and their legs gleamed metallically.

"Whoever equated 'chicken' with cowardice never

met these cocks," Knot muttered. His pitchfork suddenly seemed inadequate. "CC, when will the help you summoned arrive?"

"In four minutes," CC said.

Knot now knew how long four minutes could be. In four seconds one of these birds could slash open an arm! Knot had encountered chickens before, on Planet Nelson, and treated them with the respect due feeling creatures, but never with apprehension. Now he was afraid. He could not at the moment think of any creature he less wanted to face, gram for gram.

The cocks took a moment to orient. One of them inspected Mit's forgotten dish of milk of paradise. Evidently Mit had not finished with it when the robot servitor departed. The cock put his head down, took a beakful, then lifted his beak high to let the fluid course down his throat. Others crowded in, following his example. This was their first spoil of war.

"Maybe they'll get suffused with the milk of animal kindness and forget to attack," Finesse said hopefully.

No chance, Hermine thought. **It will merely give them greater pleasure in mayhem.**

Already the cocks were looking up, reacting to Finesse's voice. They strutted about, as it were girding themselves, displaying their fighting plumage. They were reminiscent of tassel-festooned knights in armor.

"If that's meant to impress me, it's succeeding," Knot said. "I can practically see the muscles rippling under that bright plumage."

"They use Bladewings in lieu of houndcats on worlds where game is scarce and seed is plentiful," Finesse said. "They don't much care; they can handle themselves."

The cocks charged. Knot met the first with his fork but the metallic wingfeathers struck first, and the bird bounced off with a scream of rage. One wing entangled in the tines, preventing Knot from meeting the next bird squarely.

The second cock jumped straight at Knot's face, talons stretched forward. Knot wrenched up his fork, and it came free of the other bird. Blood showed on one tine.

He swung it awkwardly across in a clumsy attempt to bat the bird aside.

The cock screamed piercingly and dropped to the floor, then scrambled away. Knot held the fork, surprised. "Don't tell me you're afraid of blood!" Knot said incredulously.

Another bird charged—and sheered off. "It's true!" Knot exclaimed. "These fighters don't like blood! Who would have believed it?"

"Nonsense," Finesse said. "Fighting cocks are crazed by the sight and smell of blood. They go berserk."

"Maybe it's different when it's their own blood," Knot conjectured, fending off other birds by waving the bloody tine at them. "Maybe the milk of paradise affected their reaction." But he wondered. The cock who had cut him before, in the other future sequence, had showed no fear of blood. It simply wasn't reasonable that such a thing could stop creatures bred for fighting and killing. There was something going on here that he didn't understand.

Then men appeared in the chamber. They carried stun pistols. Methodically they shot down the cocks, stunning the valuable birds harmlessly, picking them up and setting them carefully in a cart. In moments men and birds were gone.

"Well, that was fun while it lasted," Knot said, pushing down the top bales so that he could climb out. He hadn't thought ahead; now the fallen top row of bales filled the space nearest the impromptu fortification. He had to lean over to push the next bale beyond them, so that he wouldn't merely form another wall barring his way. If that was the type of planning he did, no wonder his future was opaque!

As he leaned over, Finesse turned about and boosted him onto the bales with a tremendous goose. Knot did a clumsy somersault and landed on his back on the floor, just missing the spilled milk-of-paradise saucer. It seemed Hermine had indeed informed Finesse!

Ooo, naughty girl! Hermine was thinking gleefully.

Knot laughed weakly. "Hey, let's do that again!"

Finesse climbed over the bales and put her face down to kiss him. "I'm sorry."

He kissed her back. "I was mad because you told me

about your prior family—oops, I wasn't going to mention—"

"It doesn't exist," she said firmly. "I made the decision, I knew what it entailed, and I shouldn't have told you. For two years—"

"I'll take them," he said, kissing her again. He had been offered half a loaf—but what a loaf!

The CC Mombot holograph appeared. "Are you satisfied, Emperor?"

Knot sat up, using Finesse for support. Symbolism there, perhaps. "No, I'd rather make love the regular way," he muttered.

Finesse, in a fit of mock outrage, dumped him down again, then spread herself on top of him for another kiss. She might love another man, he reflected, but she certainly had some feeling for Knot now.

"I referred to your power over me," CC said. "Have you had sufficient proof?"

Knot put his right arm around Finesse's body, embracing several tufts of hay in the process, and held her to him. The hay had a pleasant, sweet smell, and so did her hair. "You have hay-hair," he murmured.

"Answer the machine," she breathed into his ear. "CC has gone to a lot of effort to convert you."

"And you haven't?" But he decided not to push that aspect at the moment. "No, CC. I have concluded that there is no sufficient proof. All I have done is get myself in trouble with chickens. But for the sake of whatever"—he hugged Finesse again—"I will operate on the assumption that it is so. That I really do have control over you, instead of vice versa. That being the case, where do I go from here?"

"Well," Finesse murmured, "you might move your hand down and across—"

"You must direct the operations of the human galaxy," CC said, while Knot moved his hand as directed and found her soft buttock. "So that civilization will not be destroyed."

"Oh that," Knot said, squeezing. He considered, moving his head to shake a stray shred of hay from his face. It refused to budge. Hay was like that. In a moment

Finesse lifted her head, saw it—and kissed him right through it, so that the hay got on both their lips.

Knot had come here to argue his case with CC, and had been met with incredible acquiescence. It seemed CC, rather than debate, preferred to provide him with ample opportunity to try his way. CC believed that he would be converted long before he had the chance to do any real damage. That was the trap. Yet if he did not try, what use was it to have an opinion? If he thought he could direct galactic policy better than the Concord could, this was his challenge to do so.

And if he satisfied himself, and became converted to CC's cause, he would have up to two years with Finesse. He knew he should not allow himself to be unduly moved by this prospect, but it was very hard to keep that in mind with Finesse's buttock under his hand, her breast against his chest, and her lips kneading his ear. He wanted her—on any terms.

You fell into the trap before you ever started, Hermine thought. **Yet you keep struggling to break free.**

Sad but true, he agreed.

"Are you thinking with the weasel again?" Finesse inquired, nipping his ear.

Don't tell her my thoughts, Knot thought.

Don't worry. I'll tell her you are thinking about goosing her again.

"Hermine is about to think a lie at you," Knot murmured to Finesse.

"It better be a lie, or I'll bite your ear off," she replied.

Knot rose to the challenge by tightening his grip on her posterior—and she responded by setting her teeth in his earlobe. He relaxed hastily. They both laughed. She was great fun to be with!

"Let's see if I have this straight," he said to CC. "I give the orders, you implement them, and I visit the future to see how my policy turned out. If I don't like the result, I try something else."

"Correct," CC agreed.

"Yet if my future is opaque while I associate with you, there should be nothing to see."

"It should not be opaque to *you*. You are now the

principal, and should have a far better notion. Perhaps portions will remain inscrutable, but our perception of your futures should be greatly expanded."

It made a certain sense. If *he* could not experience his future, who else could? It might be like orienting the telescope on the right star: chances of observation certainly were better than with telescopes oriented on the wrong stars. Also, this futures exploration did seem to differ from precognition; most precogs could not see their own futures well, because of the problems of mutability; but this particular type of exploration did not seem to suffer as much from that limitation. CC had not been able to explore Knot's futures well, but Knot himself might do so.

"Very well. My first directive is for you to wait one hour, then turn yourself entirely off, as far as the galaxy is concerned. Close down all your terminals, primary, secondary, tertiary and whatever, and refuse to acknowledge any input from any person."

"Zero minus one hour," CC agreed.

"I don't like this," Finesse whispered.

"I haven't even done anything to you," he whispered back, giving her a tweak.

"Shutting down CC."

"Don't worry. It's just a trial run." Then, louder: "Drem, are you there?"

"I wouldn't be elsewhere," the mutant replied. "That cockfight was quite a show, and there'll be an even prettier one if you hike her skirt up any farther."

"He's watching!" Finesse hissed in Knot's ear.

"It's worth watching," Knot said, hiking her skirt up another notch. "Drem, jump me five years into my present future, for one hour. Can you do that?"

Suddenly Knot was in darkness. The air was chill, and the background sounds had cut off, and there was now no warm girl in his arms. He reached for a bale of hay—and found a clammy wall instead.

Of course. His prison was stone. What had made him think of hay? After all these years of—

No, he thought. No use to rehash that again! It only aggravated his misery.

Except—this time he *should* review it. Because—but

of course that was only another example of the delusions his mind fostered, to provide hope where there was in fact none. The notion that in one hour he could leave it all, make it never have happened—

Well, what else was there? If a construct of imagination could ease his misery for even one hour—

Knot reviewed the past five years, looking for the flaw that had to be in his new notion, hoping he would not find it. He had been secure as an officer in his enclave on Planet Nelson. Then Finesse had come, with her physical allure and impish mental rages—

Finesse. Image of the warlord of Proctor B, or rather his clanking robot, carrying her away. News of the warlord's later suicide, flinging himself in apparent terror from his tower-palace parapet. So the warlord's minions had executed Finesse without trial, shooting her from a distance with crossbow shafts.

Knot had fought, injuring a robot. Justice had been swift and direct: two flashes of a laser, one for each eye. Then prison. He didn't know whether there was any light here, and it didn't matter. Light had passed out of his life forever, on that day.

They wouldn't let him die. He was an example. He had tried to set his will against that of the warlord. Now they took him out once a month to show him off to the populace: the former emperor of the galaxy, ha-ha.

When he had gone to Chicken Itza to interview the Coordination Computer, and made CC turn itself off, chaos had erupted all across the galaxy. They had watched it on the computer's inputs, while those devices still operated. Ships had stopped their crossdisk voyages. Only small systems whose planets happened to be close enough for nonpsi navigation on old-style fuels had maintained fragments of the empire. Local strong men had sprung up, each ruling a few planets or over a single planet. Picayune dictators. And why not? There was nothing to stop them, no higher authority that could compel them to answer. No interstellar coordination or communication, for the Coordination Computer had been turned off.

Knot concentrated. What had happened to his animal associates? More fighting cocks had escaped, as the supply system of Planet Chicken Itza had broken down, and the weasel and crab had disappeared. They had of course forgotten him when they separated from him, and must have become food for the birds. The chickens had set up some sort of refuge of their own, with its own savage pecking order, so that human beings had had to vacate the planet.

There was a clanking in the hall beyond his cell, disturbing his reverie. The robot was bringing his afternoon ration of food and water. Since his blinding he had never had contact with a human being; only with machines. Thus his psi had not been operative. Did the new warlord know about the forgetting, or was the robot-warden merely his way of showing contempt for his victim? Probably the latter.

The robot set the staples in the meal alcove and departed. Knot rose wearily to eat. There was nothing else to do. If he delayed, the rats would get it instead, and he hated them almost as much as he hated the current warlord. If they got his food, they would be stronger and he weaker, and eventually they would consume him too, and he did not want to give the rats that satisfaction. He might be better off dead, except for the faint hope of eventual escape, freedom, and vengeance. If the robots ever broke down, and human beings were substituted as prison guards, and they forgot Knot; if he ever had the chance to get close to the warlord, close enough to score with a stone or sharp chip of metal . . .

But he knew it was hopeless. The stone cell was beyond his power to escape. All he could do was eat, and sleep, and think. He was not certain how much of his sanity he retained, now; no doubt it had been eroding with every year that passed. Sanity was no longer a survival trait.

He bit into the nutrient wafer. There was pain in his teeth, for they were rotting. But that sensation substituted for taste. He could no longer taste, because he had no tongue. When they had hauled him up, that first year, to address the populace via a microphone, and he had balked, they had made him pay in their barbaric fashion. He had thought they could do nothing more to him, after the blinding; he had been mistaken. They had rendered him mute.

Mute. The irony had long since ceased to be amusing. He had begun as a psi-mute, and become a mute-mute.

He chewed methodically, savoring the pain. Taste, too, was a superfluous thing. He had learned to live without it. Like his wasted life, it—

The light came on. Knot blinked. *He could see!*

Finesse put her hand against his head, steadying him. "That must have been some future," she said.

"You mean—there really was an escape?" Now he could speak, too; his tongue was back. "This isn't just another dream?"

"The future was the dream, if you could call it that. What happened?"

His eyes took on the scattered bales of hay, the weasel, the crab, the holograph. He felt the woman, warm against him. They must have stayed on the floor, beside the bales, for an hour. It would have been dull for her.

"We can't turn CC off," he said.

"Of course we can't!" she agreed. "There would be absolute chaos."

Error, Hermine thought.

What?

CC is already off. It turned off several minutes ago, in accordance with your directive.

"Already off!" Knot cried. "CC, turn on again!"

"As directed," CC replied. "My terminals have resumed operation. However, the brief period of malfunction has alerted the monitors of the Galactic Concord, who are initiating an investigation."

"Can they find us here?"

"Not within days, unless I advise them."

"Obfuscate in your inimitable fashion," Knot said.

"Let's not do that again, huh?" Finesse murmured.

"Not that particular turn-off, no," Knot said with a shudder. "I never want to experience that future again!"

"Are you ready to try another future?" Drem inquired.

Knot's perspective was steadying as the bleak immediacy of the last future faded. His memories were now derivative—his memories of his prior memories, five years hence. That was a relief. Blinded, imprisoned, his friends dead—no, he would never set that future in motion, not for anything! He no longer suspected CC of faking the vision for him; his experience had been too internal, too real. He had *known*—and now would not forget. The details he would gladly let go, but not the fundamental belief.

"CC, you are trying to teach me something, aren't you?" he said, finally disengaging from Finesse. He loved holding her like this, and from the feel of it he had made love to her in the past hour while he was out, but the memory of her awful death was too ugly. What had that warlord been afraid of, that he should kill himself? Not of her, surely—unless there were a side of her he had not seen. Maybe Hermine had been with her, after all, and relayed a nova, or some terrible mental monster.

"Correct," CC had replied while Knot's thoughts rambled.

"It's some course!" But what would he gain by delaying? He had made another decision of policy. "CC, institute a program of automatic temporary thirty-day sterilization of all male space travelers," he said. "We're going to eliminate the mutants." He turned to Drem. "Send me five years forward again, for one hour."

Knot suffered abrupt vertigo, a sickening sensation of falling through space, turning end over end, his substance simultaneously compacting and diffusing. Then he was back with the others. He blinked. Things seemed unchanged. "This is the future?"

"No," Finesse said. "Only fifteen seconds have passed."

"You bounced," Drem said. "That means you have no future along this line."

"No future?" Knot asked blankly. "There has to be—"

"It means you are dead five years from now on this track," Drem said. "I can't send you beyond your own death."

"I'm dead—as the result of this sensible, modest reform?" Knot had braced himself for something, anything, but not nothing. "How do I know that's true?"

"You could verify it by isolating the moment of your demise."

"Not likely!" Then Knot reconsidered. "I wouldn't actually *be* dead?"

"You would revert to the present the instant life expired. You only die permanently if you follow the present along the particular track leading to that death."

"Which I won't do," Knot said. "But I certainly want to unriddle the mystery. I can't see how my policy can eliminate *me*. All right, CC—prior policy stands. Drem, send me one year into the future, for five minutes. I don't want to waste a lot of time until I—"

He was standing on a planetary plain searching for any sign of pursuit, as he always did. He had avoided them for several hours, so they should have forgotten him by now—unless they had a machine scan on him. ". . . locate the moment of my own expiration," he finished. This time he maintained his equilibrium better; he knew this was only a future.

It seemed he was in trouble. His psi talent became almost valueless once it was known; all they had to do was apply machines to the chase, and he might as well be an ordinary man. Which had made CC's choice of him for a galaxy-saving mission seem foolish. But—

He focused his memory. From what point in his prior life had he jumped? When Finesse interviewed him on Planet Nelson? No, that was too soon. When CC interviewed him, there among the chickens? That had to be it. It was hard to pick out a particular moment in an ongoing life; his memories were not of just one year, but of everything he had ever experienced, right back to childhood. He had had many more significant adventures than that one minor jaunt into the future; his point of departure simply had not made much impression on him. But he had located it now.

CC had made the change in space-travel policy, and the birth of human mutants had halted. It had been only three months since this became evident, because of the period of human gestation. Doctors could have spread the news earlier, since extreme mutation was evident long before birth; but doctors had been under instructions to keep silent. The sterilizations had not been announced; sterilizing radiation generators had merely been set up on each ship. All the sperm cells mutated by space travel were killed; only those generated after the voyage was over were available for procreation. It had been a physically and socially painless measure.

Now the truth was out. The reaction had been power-ful—and not, to his surprise, all positive. Knot had been in training as a CC agent, having agreed that his best futures lay with CC, when a private enterprise had traced him down as the cause of the sterilization policy. An assassination squad had been set on his trail, and he was now in flight from it. Because he had the help of Hermine and Mit, he had been able to avoid assassination fairly handily so far—but it did not leave him comfortable. He had to escape completely, to hide, to assume a new iden-tity, or they would surely catch him. They had psi-mutes working with them, of course; they wanted to be sure there would be a continuing supply of psi.

We must move, Hermine thought.

"Do you realize this is merely a future?" Knot asked her.

Not for me, she thought. **I have lived it all, and this year has been longer in terms of my life than in terms of yours, and I cannot escape it.**

That was sobering. He was here for only five minutes, but all the rest of the universe was here for the dura-tion. Did he have the right to do this to everyone else?

No; it had to be merely a vision of what could be; it only seemed real to Hermine and the others. His act of animating it, for these five minutes, ensured that it would not come true—for himself or for anyone else. "You can escape it when I—"

He was back in the barn. "There was personal pique by some elements who preferred the mutant order," he announced. "They were out to assassinate me, but weren't having much luck yet."

"There's always hope for next time," Finesse said with a mock frown.

"Still, they had me on the run. Machines on my trail—"

"Are you ready for the next?" Drem inquired.

"No. I think I have an inkling of my future on this track. Assassins after me in one year, and I'm dead within five years. I can guess what happened. What I still can't fathom is *why*. How could my decision to cut off mutations have brought me to this pass? It's a bene-ficial change, and even if it weren't, it should take a generation for the repercussions to build substantially, as the number of mutants declines. Plenty of time to introduce some controlled mutations, on a limited scale, all from volunteers, to get telepaths and precogs to keep the ships traveling. But here within a year there's trouble. How is this explained?"

"Your course, as you surmise, is not immediately disastrous," CC agreed. "Other things being in balance, the lack of new mutants would at first make little apparent difference to the galaxy. But the nature of the human situation would suffer a fundamental change. It would become evident that the mutant society was coming to an end; that new planets would no longer be colonized by physical freaks, and that space travel would no longer be feasible on the scale it now exists. This would cause a shift in outlook that would have disastrous repercussions, exactly as the cessation of the growth ethic caused severe problems in pregalactic society on the origin-planet, Earth."

"I didn't know about that," Knot said.

"You, like most men, are largely ignorant of the lessons of history. That is one reason power has been allocated to me. I consider, when I make a decision, not only the present ramifications, but also the historical ones. I do not repeat the errors of the past. On Earth, man based his cultures on constant growth—until the natural resources of his single planet were virtually exhausted. When he could no longer grow, his energies turned inward, often destructively. But for the advent of mutation, which enabled him to grow into space, where he obtained vast new resources to exploit, man would have destroyed himself, as other planet-bound civilizations have. If mutancy is curtailed, these same pressures will inevitably build again, and man will suffer a similar problem —this time on a galactic scale."

Knot wasn't sure he believed either the history or the conclusion. He would have to think about it. Meanwhile, he had an immediate objection. "But that should take centuries! Why should an assassin be on my tail within a single year?"

"Because though your policy is unsound in the long run, it is superseded by another event in the short run. My program is to be destroyed by another agency, and that agency will seek to destroy you also, since you are the prime threat to that enemy's success. Unless you act to prevent the destruction of my program, you cannot save yourself. The forces you will stir are too great for you to escape."

"But *I* have destroyed your program—in that last future."

"Incorrect. You merely modified my program. The enemy will wipe it out entirely."

"I see," Knot said, though he did not accept it. "My policy becomes passé if you are not there to implement it. So I really must come to grips with this other thing first. I think it is time to do a little basic research. CC, you're a computer—you must have mapped out many variants of the future systematically."

"Correct."

"What is the nature of the threat that faces you? I mean, in some intelligible detail, if you have it."

"I am to be destroyed, or turned off, or perverted to some program irrelevant to the maintenance of galactic civilization, so that the human empire collapses. This is to occur on most tracks, two to five years hence. I am unable to read beyond the demise of my present program, for the same reason you could not travel to a future beyond your own death. I can only trace up to the point the demise occurs. Some tracks have extremes of one year to ten years, and a few have wider extremes, but I have found none that enables me to survive indefinitely or with certainty."

"Except for a 25 percent chance if I help."

"Correct."

"Why can't you follow a time track to the point where you get turned off, make a note of who or what is responsible, and then deal with that thing in the present?"

"You are conversant with the problem of the needle in the haystack?"

"Yes. You mean there are so many alternative futures that you'll never find the right one in the time you have? I don't buy that. If *all* your futures lead to your demise, you should have no such problem. The haystack is made of needles! Pick any one."

"All present futures appear to lead to my demise—but

143

no single track is certain until I explore it directly to that end. Here I am limited by the capacity of the time jumper. As you have seen, it takes time to explore any one track—perhaps hours to locate the moment of demise. Even then, the root causes may not be at all obvious."

"Damn it, if I saw the instant of my own death, I would see the root cause!"

"You did not do so in your most recent future."

"Well, I didn't—" Knot paused. "Still, with your analytical circuitry—"

"Picture yourself standing amid a hail of flying knives. One of them strikes you and kills you. You might see the particular person who threw that knife—but still not understand why hundreds of people were attacking you. Without the root cause being evident, you cannot—"

"Uh, yes. But in your case—"

"Since there are an infinite number of alternatives—"

"You can only explore representative selections," Knot finished. "That's like the problem in chess—you don't have time to check out everything before you have to make your move. So it becomes largely experience and strategy and luck—and the galaxy is more complicated than a chessboard."

"Considerably," CC agreed. "In addition, there is the randomness of the projections. We set a single policy, then visit the future resulting—but many other forces in the galaxy are making policy decisions that affect that future too. So the chance of actually achieving the future you visit becomes diminishingly small in the farther reaches. Only when the jump is brief, as with your five-minute efforts, is the probability of achieving that particular future high. A jump of a year reduces even the firmest policy-future to a probability of less than one in a thousand—and often far less."

"So the five-year futures I was looking at are pretty unlikely," Knot said, relieved.

"Those specific ones, yes. But they should be typical of the pattern of futures awaiting you, so are valid in that sense—just as the pattern of my own futures is valid."

"Now I think I appreciate your problem. The future

visits really aren't of much use to you. Still, you must have found at least one of your specific demises."

"Correct."

"Who did that one?"

"You did."

Knot laughed. "When I had you turn yourself off for my own experiment. That doesn't count!"

"Incorrect. This was on another track, in which I never contacted you. The enemy contacted you, through a randomized private missive that I was unable to trace to its source, and gave you information that enabled you to act."

"Now, wait! Missives don't come from nowhere! You could have analyzed the material, found out where it was made—"

"Pointless. Were you to receive a book on how to fashion a bomb, knowing that tens of thousands of similar copies had been printed and distributed, it would do you no good to locate the publisher. You could make no legal connection between the publisher and the person who used that text to make a bomb with which to perpetrate a crime."

"I keep running up against that! All right, I'll accept that you couldn't trace the fundamental source in time. What did I actually do?"

"You came three years from now, used your psi-power to elude my defenses, and turned me off. I obviated that by contacting you on this track."

"But you didn't need to go to all the trouble to bring me here and tell me about it! You could simply have had me assassinated—"

"I investigated the possibility that a successful agent for one side might make as successful an agent for the other side. Your potential seemed excellent. Therefore I set about converting you."

"I see. This time you have shown me the consequence of the action I might otherwise have taken in three years. But I suppose there were hundreds or thousands of similar attempts, using similar dupes, so that they came at you—will come at you—like a swarm of flies, too many for you to intercept?"

"Correct, in essence."

"But now you're on this track, and other forces are closing in. Have you isolated any other of your turn-offs?"

"Several. But as I explained, I was unable to trace the root causes."

"CC, I must seem awfully slow to you. I hate to make you keep rehashing material, but some things I just can't choke down easily. If one man, like me, comes and turns you off, maybe it is random, not a part of any organized conspiracy, so you just have to take your chances. But if there is anything organized, you should be able to—"

"There are organizations dedicated to my elimination. But I am not permitted to strike at them merely on suspicion. I must demonstrate a tangible and legal connection between such an organization and the one who destroys me. In your case I had no such connection. I could not demonstrate your motive."

"My motive would have been no secret! I felt the galaxy would be better off without you. Many people feel that way."

"Correct. Yet you had to have some specific imperative to seek me out, and some information on how to turn me off, for access to my vulnerable points is not easy for the uninitiate. A general distrust of me, and a booklet of inflammatory oratory are not sufficient. What caused you to leave your secure enclave, and how did you obtain the more specific information needed for the task? Many other people were exposed to the same overt stimuli you were, yet only you reacted, in that instance. Many others tried to eliminate me, because of other stimuli, but only you succeeded. Some other factor is involved. Probably it was psi, for I am unable to detect most psi powers directly, such as telepathy. Yet I do have the most formidable collection of psi-mutants in the galaxy as my employees, and they should have been able to detect foreign psi. Circumstantial evidence suggests that no such contact was made with you."

Knot considered. "So in that future, Finesse didn't come for me, and Mit and Hermine didn't give me the control code. So if I was contacted telepathically, someone else must have been behind it; I was just the pawn. Except that you don't think telepathy was it."

"Correct. That is the hidden force—in your case and

others'. Any person who feels as you did is a potential missile against me, and that force even now is hurling them at me. Several hundred people make the attempt each day, unsuccessfully—"

"Several hundred a day!" Knot exclaimed.

"Fortunately, I have formidable defenses, both mechanical and psi. Only this remote terminal is vulnerable; I need it to make private contacts with agents who would otherwise be watched by the enemy."

Knot shook his head. "The more I go over this, the more trouble I have grasping it. It seems to me you could put some kind of a tracer on those who—searching for the common theme—"

"The great majority of assassins are ignorant. They believe they can hide a laser pistol, take a ship to CCC, and fire at some key terminal. There is no force behind them, and I would waste my effort searching for it. The few who have real destructive potential are lost amid the crowd of those who do not—and many of those have no overt knowledge of their mission, and die before I can interrogate them. I cannot trace their motives far into the past; what changes in them is mental. Their lives are ordinary until they are abruptly motivated to act against me. Thus I am confined to the successes on the future tracks, for I can investigate them in the present, while taking no overt action to alert the people or their motivators. You are such a person; I believe the enemy will contact you, because in the future it has done so. If you are actually an agent of mine—"

"Suddenly a dim bulb lights at the end of the tunnel of my mind!" Knot exclaimed. "*I* become the trap, the bait for the enemy. Through me, you will at last gain what you need. Assuming you can convert me to your cause."

"Even so, the trails are well concealed. The motive agency may be only a front for a more subtle agency, itself a front for another. I cannot trace such motivations far in the present. I lack the proper investigative capacity. I have virtually no power on most planets; only in space am I supreme. The enemy is highly alert for my operatives, and foils their attempts even as I foil the enemy operatives. But the power of the enemy is growing like a dark tide, and if I do not locate the nucleus soon

—within the year—it will become strong enough to over-throw me regardless. Then there will be anarchy in the galaxy."

There was a silence. Knot realized that CC had done a lot of investigating and a lot of thinking, and that the computer was up against a really capable and subtle enemy. There might even be a counter-computer operating, anticipating and voiding CC's moves. Since CC had a galaxy to run, it could not devote its full effort to self-preservation without letting go of the very thing it was protecting: galactic civilization. The enemy computer, however, could devote its entire capacity to the sole purpose of torpedoing CC.

"Are you ready for the next future?" Drem inquired.

"No," Knot said. "I came here determined to present my case against CC and return to my enclave. Instead, CC has presented its case to me. It has shown me that I lack the ability to run the galaxy, or even to set meaningful policy. It has shown me that my mind is not suited to handling the complex concepts of strategy and intrigue. I am not leadership material."

He took a deep breath, looking at Finesse. "I have been persuaded. CC knows best. I renounce the emperorship, and agree to serve as an agent of CC in trying to trace down the source of the threat to it."

"Oh Knot!" Finesse cried, throwing her arms about him.

"That, too," he agreed, enfolding her.

We told you, Hermine thought smugly. **You wanted to join us all along. Ever since you saw up her leg.**

"Well, at least I put up a fight," Knot said, giving the weasel a mental stroke as he pinched Finesse's bottom.

Part II

MUTILATION

PART II

MOTIVATION

CHAPTER 6

Knot found himself in a reasonably dark closet with the little hermit crab. In one aspect of awareness he had jumped straight from Chicken Itza to this future several months along; in another aspect he had lived it all. Was this a temporary future sequence, or had he merely suffered a temporary lapse of memory? It was sometimes hard to be sure.

"Let me review," he murmured quietly, for there was danger, and he was not about to bring destruction upon himself if there was any chance it would be permanent. "I returned home, went back to normal employment, and CC sent a series of specialists to train me in all the nefarious skills I need to be an effective galactic operative. The enclave administration was happy because CC had honored the leadmuter deal, converting the mutant to the production of iridium and giving the enclave a royalty amounting to half the value of the gold it would otherwise have had. That's all clear enough."

He took a deep breath, almost a sigh. "But Finesse was on other missions, so I never saw her except for innocuous holograms, and the knowledge of you psi-animals had been blanked from my mind. Let's see if I have that straight, now. Hermine is a transceiver weasel who is only animal-smart by herself, but partakes of the intelligence of the human mind she is in contact with. She loves my mind because I have the low cunning of a super-weasel;

151

for her it is like riding the finest, most responsive steed or piloting the most efficient spaceship. It helps that she finds me more compatible than any other person. CC tried her with several other people, but it only really clicked with Finesse, so she became the weasel's trainer. With such strong telepathy, it was really more like a close friendship than master-and-animal. Then the two of them tackled you, making it a threesome, which has now become a foursome. Except—"

He frowned. "Except that Finesse isn't with us now. She summoned me to Planet Macho, where the people are exactly what you'd expect from the name, and where the mutes are all incarcerated in a huge river crevasse labeled Enclave TZ9, and she showed me how psi-mutes are being forcibly lobotomized, converted to lobos. Apparently some group is trying to destroy CC by depriving it of good psis. We are supposed to find out who."

Now he smiled grimly. "I found out. That enemy kidnapped me. The squad was after Finesse, but bungled it and got me instead. It's an organization of lobos, who hate CC because of its part in depriving them of their psi, though many of them had been using that psi for criminal purposes before. So they were about to lobotomize me when you and Hermine made yourselves known, unlocked my memory, and showed me how to break free. Except that we're only partway free at the moment, in hiding, waiting for the chance to complete our escape. So Hermine is off hunting a fat rat for her lunch, and I'm here with you. Do I have it all straight now?"

Mit, of course, did not answer. But Hermine did. **Just tap on his shell in galactic code,** she thought. **He doesn't speak in the code himself, but he understands it. He will answer your questions: one tap for yes, two for no.**

Knot tried that, intrigued. He hadn't realized that the weasel had been tuning so closely to his thoughts. HOW ARE YOU, MIT? he tapped.

YES, the crab responded: one tap of his big-little claw.

Oops—he had to confine himself to yes-no questions. IS THAT A NEW SHELL? I LIKE IT.

YES.

So much for that social amenity. It was certainly a new shell, larger than the last; Mit must have grown and needed more space. Hermit crabs, of course, did not grow their own shells; they took over occupancy of deserted shells formed by other creatures. Thus the shell was very like a house. Was there a crabby real-estate market in shell houses? Was Mit paying on a long-term mortgage? No, of course not! Yet it was a fun thought.

You have many fun thoughts, Hermine interjected.

Oh, go hunt your private hunt! This is a private conversation.

There was a splash of weasel mirth, and her thought faded from his mind. Hermine understood.

Back to the polite inquiry of health: HOW ARE YOU? had failed, but it could be rephrased. DO YOU FEEL WELL?

NO.

Hmm. ARE YOU ILL?

NO.

LONELY?

A pause, then NO.

Bright idea: DO YOU MISS THE OCEAN?

A single, violent tap. YES!

For a crab was a water creature. Mit could evidently survive for prolonged periods away from water—Finesse had said something about that too—but this had to be at least a psychological burden on him. MAYBE YOU WILL RETURN SOON.

YES.

Precognition—or hope? Knot had never understood how the psi of the crab worked, but had come to accept its validity. Mit had a major psi-talent. Perhaps he was really a clairvoyant whose range was not limited by time, so that his awareness extended a certain distance outward in all dimensions. Just as Hermine was a full telepath, receiving and sending, Mit was a full clairvoyant, contrasted to the partial abilities of others. CC had selected the best for this team!

Hermine—how was she doing? She was evidently intent on her hunt, for she had ceased broadcasting to him these past few minutes. He knew she wasn't piqued by his last thought; she understood his humor. He wasn't sure of the limits of her range, but believed she was well enough attuned so that she should be able to reach him anywhere in this vicinity. She could no doubt take care of herself, but he might as well check. IS HERMINE SAFE?

There was a pause while Mit oriented on the weasel. NO.

No? Knot hoped this was a misunderstanding. HAS SHE BEEN HURT?

NO.

Relief was premature. WILL SHE BE HURT?

YES. The little crab was fidgeting nervously now. Apparently he had been surveying Knot's prospects, not Hermine's—a serious oversight.

CAN WE HELP HER?

YES—NO.

This looked bad! It was necessary to grasp the truth quickly. Ah: If she were in physical trouble, Knot might help her—but at the risk of his own safety. He had to remain in the closet. I CAN HELP HER IF I GO TO HER—BUT THE LOBOS WOULD LOCATE ME?

YES.

Bad dilemma! Hermine wouldn't want him to sacrifice himself on her behalf—but how could he let her suffer alone? Mit's agitation suggested that it was very bad trouble stalking her. IS THERE ANY OTHER WAY?

The crab hesitated. This question must be too complex for his little mind. There could be many alternatives, radiating out into infinite possibilities, as with the futures CC considered: too many for Mit to cope with, without a human brain. And without Hermine's telepathic linkage, Knot could not lend his own brain to the effort.

But he had to try. **Hermine,** he called mentally, hoping she was still in range. He concentrated on his image of her: cute long low weasel body, tiny whiskered face, sleek fur. When she jumped, her front end completed the jump before her rear end began it, or so it seemed. **Warning! Trouble! Call in quickly!**

I receive you, she responded clearly. No problem with the range! Can't it wait? I'm on the hot trail of a deliciously fat little rat.

Get in touch with Mit. He says you will be hurt.

I can't. His mind is too small for this distance. It is not full of human excess power like yours or Finesse's.

But I don't know what the threat is. I can't read minds.

I will come back immediately, she decided. **Mit always knows.**

SHE IS COMING BACK, he tapped to Mit, relieved.
NO! the crab tapped back.

He says don't come back, Knot broadcast. He was getting the feel of this. Finesse must have done a lot of it in her day, coordinating the diverse talents of her friends. Coordination: That was the key. Just as, on the macroscopic scale, the Coordination Computer was necessary to—

There was a vague thought of dismay. Then: **The trap is sprung.**

Knot felt an unpleasant shock. **What trap?**

Rats. Big rats all around. Some have psi.

So that was it. The weasel was a predator—but rats were not necessarily docile prey. Rats with psi powers could be ugly customers indeed. So they had cut off Hermine's retreat, trapping the predator. Knot knew they would not allow her to survive. And he could help her only by exposing himself to the lobos—who had a similar punishment in mind for him.

Is there any way we can help you from here? Knot thought desperately.

I think this must be my own battle.

But he knew from the tone of her thought and Mit's concern that she had virtually no chance alone. Rats were not chivalrous; they would not give her any sophisticated options. They would simply pounce and rend. **I will come to you,** he thought.

No! You will be lost, and then so will be Mit and I too. But—

I can't think with you now, nice man. They are closing.

What could he do? Nothing—unless he got there. And he couldn't—or could he?

Let me into your mind, he thought. **I know how to fight. Let me fight for you.**

I know how to fight too, she responded. But she let him into her mind.

Suddenly it was as though he had the body of a weasel —with the mind of a man. He no longer communicated with Hermine, he *was* Hermine. He stood at bay in a chamber between walls, ringed by great brown rats, several of which outmassed him by double or triple his own weight. They were tough, lean, scarred creatures, with sharp claws and teeth: fighters, all. But more significant, some were mutants.

They must have come from a diskship, Knot thought. CC kept track of all the people who traveled in space, but not the vermin. The laws of mutation applied to all living creatures; a rat who left the ship and mated immediately thereafter would breed a mutant litter in the same ratio of mental to physical, success to failure. In fact, these might all be mutants of greater or lesser degree. He could read their minds, and found that it was so; the normal-looking ones were the psi-mutes. Most of the rat litters had perished, victim of their own abnormalities; these few survivors were extremely tough. Now they dominated the waste regions of this spaceport city, and were extending beyond it into the wider planet. Every ship that arrived brought new rats, who hid in the cargo carriers and descended with the shuttles and escaped to breed with the local females, spreading their mutant seed widely. The Machos had a problem developing that they did not yet deign to notice—and perhaps it was the same on other planets. What would happen when vicious psi-rats started warring directly with man?

Hermine might kill one or two of these monsters, but could not hope to overcome them all. Escape was the only strategy. But the rats were alert for that; they had after all laid this trap, and kept it tight. Could the weasel take a hostage, as Knot had, to escape the lobo trap? No, Hermine's body was not structured for that. It could not wrap an arm around a neck, or hold a laser pistol in the free paw. The rats would not respond properly anyway; they would simply plunge in, killing one of their own number themselves if it got in the way. What would be effective against completely uncivilized brutes like these?

One rat moved forward, eyes shining malevolently in the imperfect light. Hermine's telepathy reached out to read its mind—and encountered another telepath.

Yes, I read your brain, weasel, the rat thought. **You read mine too. But I have many warriors, kill you.**

This was the rat leader, because of his psi power. What rat could conspire against him, or surprise him? But Knot knew a way to set him back. He formulated a nova similar to the one Finesse had used on him, and had Hermine hurl this human-conceived bolt at the smug rat.

The rat squeaked in amazement and pain and dropped to the floor unconscious. One down!

The other rats milled momentarily in dismay. Hermine launched herself at the fallen rat and bit him in the vulnerable throat, opening the key artery with the expertise she had. Knot, sharing her mind, knew why: She had to kill the telepath before he recovered enough to blast her back. No mercy in this fray!

But now the confusion in the enemy force was abating. A new leader emerged. Suddenly Hermine was in pain.

Another psi attack! A rat who could hurl pain at her enemies. But Knot was less affected by it, for he was not wedded to the nervous system of this body. Hermine was immobilized by agony, while he was only discomfited.

Knot blocked out part of the pain and drew on Hermine's power to make a quick survey of rodent minds. There—that female nearest the raised aperture. She was the new leader, showing how she could deal with the enemy. That was why the pack had not yet attacked. The leaders had to prove themselves first, lest there be entire anarchy in the pack, making it vulnerable to other packs that had strong leadership. This was an arena, a proving ground, not a massacre. Much better to play with the trapped victim for a while before dispatching her, and it was ideal for the proof of the new leader.

This offered opportunity for Hermine. If she kept eliminating the leaders before they were proven, she would not be subject to the massed attack of the pack. Leaderless, the remaining rats might lose courage and scatter. The trap might be reversed.

Hermine, prodded by Knot's analytic imperative, hurled herself at this female. Pain blasted again at Hermine, making her stumble and roll, but Knot's will overrode her infirmity and forced her on. The pain kept coming, but Knot's human mind dominated it, knowing it was only pain, not actual physical damage. The rat mind was not equipped to handle a human mind; that was Hermine's big asset.

Another bolt of pain, another stumble and roll as muscles were momentarily paralyzed, another effort—and at last Hermine reached the rat. There was no pause, no sparring, no negotiation; the two were abruptly engaged in a death combat.

The rat was larger than the weasel, but not by much. But the rat was young and healthy and quick of reflex; she could fight. Her teeth whipped about to catch Hermine—but the weasel was already moving, countering. This was her natural mode of combat. Neither had an advantage; the weasel should ordinarily have been able to kill a rat this size quickly, but Hermine had been weakened and confused by the blasts of pain. The rat could not send more pain bolts while being kept busy defending herself; her brain was not capable of entertaining two discrete modes of combat simultaneously. Hermine's telepathy was of no use to her here, either; action seemed to precede thought, and strategy was inherent. They had to settle it on the immediate personal basis.

Knot could not help his friend now. His training was in human combat. His reflexes were wrong for this. He would be too apt to strike with his fist or spin into a throw, when what was required was a sharp bite at tendon of hind leg or vein of throat. He let Hermine handle it, while he concentrated on the larger problem. For the ring of rats waited—and when this single combat ended, those rats might pounce. It would not be enough to kill the pain-psi rat, if a new leader manifested during the fight. Knot and Hermine had to escape the rest of the trap too.

How had Hermine fallen into it? She was telepathic; she should have picked up the mental news long before walking into it. Mit had perceived it, after all. Had she been lulled into carelessness by the ease of the chase? That did not seem like her. A weasel who got careless would not survive to maturity. But what, then, could account for it? Obviously these psi-rats had leaped at the opportunity to trap the intruder. They had organized under the direction of their telepathic leader, closing off the exits, while the bait rat led Hermine in. The bait rat could have been innocent as well as succulent; on the human scale, Knot himself had been similar bait for the lobo conspiracy, artificially innocent. But the other rats—

their sheer malignance should have come through strongly. Their telepathic leader had to have known beforehand that Hermine was telepathic; he had expressed no doubt on that score during his communication, though he had been caught by surprise by the action and power of Knot's mind. That rat should have known no such trap would work. Yet he had gone ahead with it, and it *had* worked. Why?

Meanwhile, the fight continued. Hermine was the faster and more deadly participant, but the rat's size and sheer viciousness made up much of the difference. Knot had always thought of rats as cowardly, skulking creatures—but he had also thought of chickens as timid, before encountering the Doublegross Bladewings. No doubt he would have encountered a different facet of rat personality had he been rat-sized. Hermine was also aware that the pack could close in the moment the fight ended, especially if she seemed weakened, so she could not afford to take any crippling injury in return for victory. She had to protect herself, and this inhibited her attack somewhat. And—

And she knew that Knot was thinking it out. The weasel resources alone were insufficient to get her out of the trap. She had faith in his big human brain; only Knot's comprehension offered any hope, slight as that might be. So she was stalling, waiting for him to come up with his miracle. She had recovered from the pain bolts and now could dispatch the rat any time—when Knot was ready.

Knot had the sinking feeling that her confidence was unjustified, that he could not save her. Had he been able to spring her free—but this encounter was too physical. No room for long-range strategy. It was evident now that weasels and rats did not possess human-scale intelligence because they had no need of it; it was superfluous to their survival. Less brain and more teeth was the winning formula.

Yet something nagged him. Mit had thought there was a way—a doubtful, chancy way, but nevertheless not complete doom. And something about this psi situation—how *could* the telepathic rat have known his trap would work against another telepath? He must have

done this before, successfully, trapping other psis. No—
not clairvoyants or precogs like Mit, for Mit had not been
deceived; just telepaths, or noninformational psis. How
could—

That was it! The rats were able to render their number
telepathically invisible. There must be a rat who could
establish some sort of mental shield under which they
all were protected—until the trap sprung. There would
be the real source of their power. The thing to do would
be to identify that particular rat, kill it—

No. That would not help Hermine now, and as for the
future—did he really want to stop the rats? He was only
noddingly acquainted with Macho society, but already
he did not like it. The arrogant normals, the vicious
lobos, the degraded situation of the mutants—why not
let the rats make their move, when they came to it?
Macho man versus Macho rat! Yes, he liked that.

All of which left him back with his original problem.
Hermine's fight was progressing; soon the pain rat would
realize she was overmatched, and in order to save her
life would call in the pack to finish it. In a choice between
leadership and life she would probably take life. The
pack would help her, then cast about for another leader.
Knot had only moments to devise a successful strategy.

Desperately he cast about, using Hermine's perceptions
as they picked up peripheral impressions. He wanted to
save his friend, yes, but it was also himself on the line.
Without the weasel's telepathy, Knot doubted he could
escape the lobos. He would be unable to perceive Mit's
directives quickly enough, let alone follow them. He could
not afford to play Twenty Questions while the lobos were
firing lasers at him. He had to have that immediate telepathic rapport. So it was for all of them he was struggling
—so far without success. All exits were blocked, even
the holes through which the pipes passed, too narrow for
anything larger than bugs. No escape there!

Bugs—surely there must be mutant roaches, ants and
the like too, leaving the ships randomly or with sinister
purpose. How did they feel about the rats? Could Hermine
communicate telepathically with them? Summon them
here to help her? If biting ants swarmed through—

No, there was no time! Contact with bugs might be pos-

sible, if their minuscule brains were adequate, but it would
have to be slow, with negotiation, offerings, counter-
offerings, compromises, and final agreement—if agreement
turned out to be possible. It could not be done in seconds.
Again, he was thinking too far afield. He needed something physically practical *now*. A weapon that would
daunt rats.

A spear? Needle? Club? Again, Hermine's body was
not adapted to any of these. Tools she might use, given
time; weapons were unlikely. Yet without the leverage of
a weapon—

Fire was a weapon. Any way to start one? If there
were matches here—Mit might locate them—but Mit was
now out of contact, and Knot could not risk going back.
He had an excellent rapport with Hermine, a freak
mergence of minds; he might lose it, and be unable to
reenter her mind amid this strife. In any event, it would
take too long to get information from Mit, his way. Tapping on a shell to locate matches, which might be out in
lobo territory—

Water—could he find a valve, open it, flood the rats
out? No, the wall spaces were too irregular, porous; it
would only attract the attention of the lobos. Even if it
worked, he ran the risk of drowning Hermine along with
the rats, or having them all swim, continuing the battle
in water. It would be an equal disadvantage to each side,
leaving the advantage with the rats. He needed something
simple, fast and effective, like a laser or electric shock—

Electric shock! There were electrical wires here, all
about, color coded. This was the power station; they believed in electricity for all purposes in this vicinity. Knot
knew about this sort of thing; one of CC's anonymous
minions had trained him in methods of sabotage, including
the shorting out of power supplies.

Quickly he surveyed the surroundings with this new
perspective. There across the room, the wires going to
a wall socket on the other side—

Hermine, wrap this up, then bolt for those wires there.
He flashed a mental picture. Though he now perceived with
her senses, he still had to communicate specifically; he had
not really merged with her.

She didn't question him. She attacked the rat with a

new initiative, causing the fight to drift toward the wires. This was a better way; it postponed suspicion a few more moments.

When they were at the wires, Hermine went for the kill. The rat was tired, no longer able to resist effectively. In a moment her blood was throbbing across her fur, and she was dying. She made a last effort of psi, striking Hermine and the rats with a great wash of agony—but it was in effect her death agony they felt.

Hermine jumped for the wires as the other rats recovered and moved in to check their former leader. **Take hold of the black wire with your teeth,** Knot directed. **Yank it out, strip the insulation.** He made a picture of what he wanted, so there could be no confusion.

She followed his directions, not understanding their rationale. In this respect she was easier to work with than Finesse would have been; the human female would have been questioning, demanding that it make sense on her terms, offering counter-proposals. Hermine was the soul of amenity, deferring smoothly to his intellect. It almost made him regret he was not a weasel—but then, of course, he would not have that intellect.

Meanwhile, the rats had verified that the pain rat was too far gone to salvage. They did not waste time with her; they oriented on Hermine and closed in. They seemed to be leaderless at the moment, but united in this enmity.

Hermine's teeth were efficient. Already she had a protruding bare wire. **Now the red wire. Do not let it touch the other.** She did not have color vision to match his, but could distinguish the wires he meant.

She did it, trusting him. The rats were only momentarily halted by this peculiar behavior, this eating of wires; they knew from experience that there was no nutritive value in insulation. They jostled each other for first bite at the prey. Knot formed another mental nova, imagining a colossal explosion to fling them all pell-mell into space, and let it strike—but now they were braced for this, too. Rats were not supersmart, but experience and pain were excellent teachers. They charged.

Take one wire in each front paw— But her feet were not suited to this. He tried again. **Take one in your mouth,**

hold it by the insulation—do not touch the bare wire. Stand behind the other—

Hermine dived for the red wire, lifting it as the first rat arrived. This required a great effort of discipline and trust on her part, for her natural reaction was to open her jaws to meet the challenge and defend herself by slashes of tooth and claw. The rat ran right up against the feebly pointing wire, ignoring it, contemptuous of any mere insulation-eater, his feet pressing the loose black wire on the floor—

Current crackled through the rat's body. Its hair stood momentarily on end, making it seem to expand horrendously in size. Then it collapsed.

Well, now! Hermine thought, pleased. She whipped her wire around to meet the next rat, who was diving in from the side.

The rat must touch both wires, Knot cautioned.

The rat did not touch the black wire—but its feet came down on the body of the first rat, who now lay astride that wire. Power surged through both their bodies. After an agonized stiffening, the second rat collapsed astride the first.

Now the others caught on. They scrambled back, squeaking with dismay. Was this a new psi weapon?

Draw out the black wire, Knot directed. **They will come at us again.**

Hermine set down the red wire and drew carefully on the black one. She, like the rats, now had an extremely healthy respect for this weapon. **You sure knew what you were doing,** she thought admiringly. **A power weapon from wires!**

We're not out of this yet, he told her. **We can't take this weapon with us.**

She got the other wire clear and positioned it before her, where a rat would most conveniently come through. Sure enough, a skeptical rat moved forward, and with a little suggestion-nudge in his mind from her telepathy, he charged. As he met the wire she snatched up, he also died dramatically.

Now the rats were convinced. To approach this weasel was to die. Five of their number had perished in one fashion or another. But they did not retreat beyond the chamber.

Hermine stood at bay, wire in mouth, glaring about. It was an impasse. But Knot knew they could not remain this way long; the time of his opening for escape from the lobo stronghold was approaching.

Maybe we can fool them, he thought to Hermine. **Sever two lengths of wire and carry them in your mouth. If there is no clairvoyant rat, it may work.**

Hermine got to work, chewing through one wire at a time. A rat, seeing that she was not hurt by the wire, got bold and charged—and was electrocuted. That put more respect back into the others.

Then Hermine advanced on the rats at the chosen exit, two colored wires held in her mouth. The rats held—then squeaked in fright as she drew near. They scattered.

But watch the rear, Knot cautioned. The warning was unnecessary; the weasel knew her business.

They got through. **Now go back to your own mind,** Hermine thought. **I will get back myself.**

Promise not to fall into any more traps?

She made a derisive weasel-snort. **Do you realize you made me miss my meal?**

You're as bad as Finesse!

That bad? she thought, flattered.

Knot relaxed—and was back with Mit in the closet. ANY TROUBLE? he tapped on the crab's shell.

NO.

DID I SAVE HER?

YES.

Knot relaxed the rest of the way. It had been a tense sequence.

In a moment there was a scurrying sound in the corner. Hermine emerged, followed by a foolhardy rat. Knot smashed at it with his fist, knocking it across the floor; it squealed and scrambled away, disappearing in the wall. Oops—he had lost another potential meal for the weasel. **I owe you: one rat,** he thought.

Fortunately she was not angry. **I wish I had a mind like yours,** Hermine thought.

Be satisfied with a mind like yours, he responded. **Without your telepathy, I could not have helped.**

Oh, I forgot, Hermine thought abruptly. I must focus on Finesse. Then, with alarm: She is sending! She is afraid. People are following her. Bad people.

Lobos, Knot thought. Tell her they are lobos!

I cannot. I can only receive her at this range. She knows this; she has been sending in repeat sequence, hoping I can tune in.

She does not know where you are, or what we are doing?

She does not know, Hermine agreed. But she is concerned. You should have rejoined her by this time. She wrote herself a note saying so, so she would remember. She fears you have been taken and us too. She is very upset. We were all supposed to be together when the enemy struck, so we could fight as a team.

I love her, Knot thought with a pang.

She loves you—when her mind is not blanked.

I must get to her, tell her what I have learned, help her—

Hermine agreed. Mit says the time to escape is now. Pick us up and emerge quietly; I will relay his specifics.

Knot opened the suitcase. Not there, Hermine cautioned. Pockets. Carry the case empty.

He put the two animals carefully in his pockets and carried the suitcase empty. Hermine had not questioned him during the rat-fight; he would not question her or Mit now. They had to trust each other, working as a disciplined team.

He cracked open the door and emerged. The hall was empty. They have forgotten you, Hermine advised him. They did not know about Mit and me. But the search continues; they know that an intruder is on the premises. You must find an opening to merge with them.

To masquerade as a lobo? he asked, surprised and not pleased. Lobotomy, to his subjective view, was akin to castration. He wanted no part of it.

Mit says this is the least violent way.

And Mit was bound to be right. Knot followed the relayed directions, dodging people without ever seeing them. This was a puzzle, for the power-station premises were labyrinths, and the lobos were closing off rooms systematically, drastically narrowing the options.

Now it gets tight, Hermine thought. The chance of success is definite but very narrow. Mit knows it can be done, but the adjustment is so fine that he cannot be sure it will work.

Knot understood. One might aim his laser pistol at a distant target, knowing he could score on it if his hand were steady enough—but not be certain he had that steadiness. Mit was up against the limits of his psi talent again. Many people were involved, with complex options, and he was only a little crab without human intelligence. Psi was not magic; it was only an ability that had limits.

Nevertheless, they were dependent on Mit's talent. **Tell me what I must accomplish,** Knot thought, **and I will use my resources to accomplish it. Mit does not have to work out every little detail.**

Mit is good at details, Hermine replied after a pause. **It is the grand strategy that gives him a problem.**

Very well. My grand strategy is to get us out of here unremembered. My details involve remaining undiscovered for the next minute at a time. How can I stay clear the coming minute? He was aware that short-range strategy might mean long-range disaster, and wasn't sure his attitude would help the crab, but had to try something.

That makes it much easier. Mit thanks you. Enter the third door on your left.

Knot counted doors. The third one was labeled BEAM ACCESS. He entered. Beyond it was a short hall and another door—and beyond that was the central chamber of the station.

It was shaped like a torus, with a columnar forcefield in the center. Inside this, shielded from the air of the planet, was a terrible blaze of light. It was the main beam: the laserlike concentrated ray of this world's sun, reflected downward from the solar satellite that orbited in fixed position above. The sun's light was reflected by another forcefield in space, so that a large, diffuse area was swept of a significant portion of its light, dimming the planetary surface below. Much of the light, however, was from beams that would have missed the planet entirely, so its capture represented no loss to the planet. That light was focused on the satellite, and it finished down here: the source of heat for the giant generators, hydrogen refining, and assorted other tasks. Both theory and application were too complex for Knot's proper comprehension;

he took it on faith that it worked. Reliable, renewable, nonpolluting power from the sky, the mainstay of every civilized human-colony planet.

Other planets did the same thing in different ways, however. Most converted the light to power in the satellites, then transferred the power safely to the surface. But this was Macho; the planetary image was upheld by doing it the hard, dangerous, foolhardy way, bringing the raw light itself down.

The power station was, it seemed, operated by the lobos. How that had come about Knot could not say, but he presumed it related to their willingness to face inconvenience and danger that normal Machos avoided. He realized that it was very convenient for them. The lobos had power here, real power, physical and political—and a government-supported hideaway. No victim could escape this stronghold without being lobotomized, and no police force could spring a surprise inspection to catch the illicit lobo lab.

Yes, it was an extremely neat setup—almost better than it was reasonable to credit the lobos with being able to manage. The removal of their psi-powers did not leave individuals any less intelligent than before—but neither did it enhance their mental or other abilities. So how had they managed such things as this? *Some*body should have caught on!

They have captured Finesse, Hermine announced. **They are taking her somewhere in a car. She is afraid.**

We have to get out of here! Knot thought back. The notion of physical danger to Finesse appalled him.

Mit says they won't put stun gas in this room. But people are coming. They will capture you, unless—

Ask Mit what the lobo identification system is. Knot, driven by the imperative of the threat to Finesse, had become largely unconcerned about his own welfare. This was a tactical situation; with a little key information he could negotiate it.

Personal recognition, she responded after a pause.

Oh no! There was no way he could fake that! Yet he had to get through, until one of the stun-gas-flooded rooms cleared and he could step out beyond the search area.

No way to fake personal recognition? There *had* to be a way! Ah—he had it! **Hermine, you must help me. I am going to establish recognition. You must respond alertly, or I will fail.**

Mit already told me. But he thinks it won't work.

He's not sure of that?

Not sure.

Because the situation remained too complex for the little crab to assimilate in its entirety. But Knot had lived all his life without any guarantees of success. He didn't have to be sure; he only needed a fighting chance.

A man entered and paused, spying Knot.

What's his name? Knot demanded.

"Hey, I don't recognize you," the man said challengingly.

He is called Wold.

"Hi, there, Wold. You forget me already?" Knot said, smiling as he strode forward. **When did he come to this station, from what prior situation?**

I cannot tell that. It is not in his conscious thought, and I cannot explore the unconscious mind.

Wold was squinting with perplexity. "You may remember me, but—"

"I knew you back at the other job, two–three years back—"

Now it's conscious. He was technician for a small private solar plant four years ago.

"I still don't—" Wold was saying

"Now I have it. How time flies! Four years back, it must have been, at that little plant, what was its name—"

Sun Valley.

"Sun Valley. I was just a handyman then, with my bad hand." Knot held up his left hand, angled to give the impression of mutilation, of a finger cut off, rather than a naturally scant member. **Project a thought to him: knowledge of my bad hand. And my name.**

Slowly the man's brow simplified. "That's right. Missing a finger, aren't you? You're—Knot."

"You remembered!" Knot smiled again, putting his left hand out of the way as if self-conscious about his deformity. "Machine mishap, years ago. But I swore it wouldn't

hold me back. I took any job I could get, and I took the
courses, passed the tests, and now I'm here. I hoped I'd
be working with you, Wold. You always had the touch
with this stuff."

You are the best liar I ever met, Hermine thought, awe-
struck.

Wold remained doubtful, but lacked the conviction to
make an issue of it. Knot continued talking, using key information Hermine drew from the man's mind as Knot's
remarks evoked it, skillfully building a stronger case. He
was indeed good at this; it resembled an interview, and he
had had years of experience at that, and a lifetime's experience dealing with people who did not remember him.
This time Knot was dealing with a man whose absence of
memory was natural, not the result of Knot's psi. The
transition was not difficult. Soon Wold was completely
reassured. Later, when the other lobos questioned him,
Wold would not remember Knot—and they would have
trouble understanding how he had cooperated with a friend
who had never existed.

In the course of this dialogue, Knot also picked up the
information that the lobos had made it a policy to take
over as many of the key services of the planet as was
possible. They worked with greater discipline and for
less pay than others, and never interrupted the work to
make demands for better conditions or fringes. Thus they
made steady progress, and constituted the better part of
the police force and fire services, as well as manning the
solar power station and a number of other key industries.
The average normal did not like lobos, but thought they
were all right "in their place"—as public servants. They
never achieved the top positions, but never protested the
obvious discrimination that excluded them. Knot marveled privately at this; what force held them so well in
line?

Wold took him around the beam. It was Wold's duty to
see that the beam remained focused on target. "Any little thing disturbs it," he explained. "Weather patterns
outside—it's choked down to the narrowest feasible diameter, so that it cuts right through local fog, but dust in
the air deflects it marginally. Some dust gets through
despite the force screen. So I keep an eye on it, making

sure it strikes the main reflector dead center. Usually it's routine, but in a storm it gets hairy."

"No automatic computer corrections," Knot observed questioningly.

Wold laughed. "None at all! If we had a computer tie-in, there would be a CC tie-in, and you know what that means!"

Control by CC, Hermine filled in, drawing it from Wold's mind. **The lobos are rabid anti-big-government fanatics. They dislike the local planetary government, and they hate CC.**

"Macho is run by men, not machines," Knot agreed smoothly. This was how the lobos avoided detection by CC: They avoided using any electronic device that CC could conceivably tie into. It decreased the efficiency of their operations, but it certainly did keep them free. He needed to get out of here and explain that to Finesse and CC. But first things first: the escape.

"Here is the mechanism control," Wold explained. He was now operating on the assumption that Knot was here to assist him, and eventually to take over the shift. They were in an office whose partitions were heavily tinted glass. From here the beam was quite clear. It plunged straight down from the satellite, coruscating even through the tint. It was savagely beautiful. "The beam comes through this lens system in the ceiling, and can be angled to adjust for the deviations caused by external factors. Of course, the orbiting solar station keeps it oriented pretty close, but the angle can change a little."

Knot paid close attention, for a notion was coming into his head.

Mit says another man is coming, Hermine warned. **He is trouble.**

"This control is for the main reflector," Wold continued. "It bounces the beam along the power-tube. From there it is fractured, and diverted to the various boilers and generators. Our job is to keep it right on target. Normally no trouble, as I said."

"Suppose you made a mistake and angled it into the wrong place?" Knot inquired.

"Don't even think that! This thing would burn a hole

through the containment structure in minutes, and after that—" He shook his head.

Very bad damage, Hermine thought. **Explosions, loss of life, closing of plant, power failure in city, bad mark on lobo management leading to investigation and possible loss of this plant as a lobo enterprise. Much mischief.**

"The forcefield shield wouldn't hold in the beam?" Knot asked.

"Not for an instant. The field only inhibits matter; the beam is energy. It—"

The new person entered the room. Metal glittered on his shoulders; he was an officer. He paused, seeing two people in the office. "Identify yourselves!" he snapped.

"Wold, beam technician."

"Knot, apprentice beam technician."

"You I recognize, Wold," the officer said. "You, Knot, I do not. We assigned no apprentice. We are in search for an intruder, and I believe—"

Put a thought about apprentice approval in his mind, Knot thought urgently to Hermine. **Mislaid authorization papers, happens all the time, bureaucratic snafu—**

I can't. His mind is closed.

The true military man! Unfortunately, this was the most effective opposition he could make to Knot's subversion.

Well, he would just have to try it verbally. "Maybe they didn't circulate the bulletin about the apprentice program. These things get—"

Now a laser pistol appeared in the officer's hand. "Stand where you are, intruder."

But already Knot was grabbing Wold, swinging the man in front of him, holding him with a painful submission grip that emerged from his hidden training. Knot knew only a few combat techniques, but they had been admirably selected for his needs. When CC set out to train an agent, CC did a good job. "Sorry, friend," he said in the man's ear. "I hate to do it to an associate from Sun Valley, but it's my life on the line."

"But why?" Wold asked, now firmly fixed in the belief that he remembered Knot from old.

"I *am* an intruder. I have not been lobotomized."

The officer spoke into a phone button. An alarm

sounded. Evidently the lobos did use some electronic apparatus, but only the most elementary sort, where its absence might have been cause for suspicion. Such as a voice-activated intercom system. They probably did not conduct any private lobo business on such channels, though.

They are closing in, Hermine thought. **They will capture you. The hostage will not prevent them. They don't care about him. They're tough; once they lost their psi powers, their unity became the dominant force in their lives.**

Unity—as a substitute for psi? Was that the way he himself would feel if he lost his psi? A compulsion to belong in the society of the unpsied? Knot doubted it.

The officer was taking aim. **He won't fire yet,** Hermine thought. **He's just holding you until reinforcements arrive. But he will shoot the moment you seem to be getting away.**

Mit had believed something like this would happen, and Knot had tried to go against the crab's precognition. Every time he tested that precognition, he came away with a greater respect for it. Still, this sequence wasn't over yet, and there *was* a chance, however marginal.

"All right, friend," Knot said. "I don't think they're going to let you be a hostage, and I don't want an old acquaintance to get hurt just because I was desperate for a job. Never thought a mutilated hand would be more trouble than a mutilated brain, but that's the way it is." He wondered why he was bothering to maintain the lie, and realized that to the extent he had fictionalized the past relationship between himself and Wold, it had become real to him. All lobos were not evil; he liked this one. So he acted as a friend would have, foolish as that might seem objectively. "So I'm going to let you go. My advice to you is to get well away from here, because it's going to get pretty ugly and I don't want you to get blamed or shot."

"Thanks," Wold said, and Knot was sure he meant it.

He turned Wold loose. Knot was also playing a hunch, preserving his pseudo-identity as a job-seeker rather than as a CC spy. Should he survive this present bind, that identity might be useful. It widened his small range of options. They might not kill a job-seeker.

As Wold stumbled away, Knot dived for the beam controls. He did not attempt to parley or bargain with the officer, knowing this would be useless. Knot touched the reflector-control console, swept his hand across it, and spun the nearest knob.

"Hey!" the officer cried. "Don't fool with—"

Can Mit guide me now?

Yes. This is simple. Turn the next knob to the left, then release the lever below.

So complex power-beam controls were simple to the crab's precognition, while human motivations were complex. That offered a certain perspective! Knot followed Hermine's continuous directions as Mit's clairvoyance oriented on the task. The great beam began to move. Warners and alarms went off all about.

"Stop that!" the officer cried, aghast. "I'll fire—"

"Not at the beam controls," Knot called back. "You'll parley." **Will he?**

No. A pause. **This puts him in a difficult position, one his book does not cover. He is afraid he will make a mistake. He is nerving himself to fire.**

Knot worked the controls. The beam lifted out of its channel beyond the huge reflector. It struck the rim of the beam-tunnel and sent up a blinding splay of light and heat. This was like a mental nova, only it was exhilaratingly real!

Knot, forewarned, shielded his eyes. The officer did not. The lobo stood dazed, momentarily sightless, not knowing where to point his laser pistol.

"All I want is to get out of here safely," Knot called. "Have them lift the portcullis and vacate the checkpoints." **Will this work?**

No.

"No!" the officer cried. He fired at the sound of Knot's voice, but his aim was bad. His reflexes were geared to sight more than to sound.

Tell me where to move, if a beam is about to strike me, Knot thought. Aloud he called: "Then I shall burn my way out. I have a laser cannon here!"

He worked the controls, lifting the beam farther from its channel. Now it struck a containment wall, and immediately the surface of the wall began to smolder and pop as impurities burst like little volcanoes.

They are interrogating Finesse, Hermine thought. **Asking**

her bad questions. **She thinks they will torture her. There is a man—** She projected a picture of a medium-sized man with mutant hair: fine and light-colored patches amid a coarse and dark background, piebald. **He is called that,** Hermine thought. **Piebald.**

Knot concentrated on the mental image of the man. His features were irregular, his skin mottled in a lesser piebald pattern. He was ugly, even by mutant standards, but alert intelligence gleamed in his face. And—good-humored malice.

This was a person who enjoyed inflicting pain on enemy captives; Knot was sure of it. And the woman Knot loved was an enemy captive.

The sending ended as Hermine's attention was pre-empted by closer events. Half a dozen more men burst into the room, weapons drawn. Knot swung the beam grandly around toward them, and they flung themselves down. They wore heavy goggles and carried lasers; they began firing.

Meanwhile, other lobos were torturing Finesse. Infuriated by that thought, Knot reacted with savagery. He swept the terrible beam across the men, and the firing stopped. He saw wisps of smoke rising, and in a moment smelled the sweetish odor of singed flesh. He had just fried several men, and on one level this disturbed him deeply. What had he become, so suddenly? A weasel among rats? Yet on the other level he visualized Piebald torturing Finesse, and knew he had to continue. He had to rescue the woman he loved, and he could do that only by saving himself first.

Where should I aim, to burn myself a passage out?

You can't, Hermine thought despairingly. **Mit says the walls are too thick, and they are about to—**

I can damn well try! Knot aimed the beam at the door he had entered, and watched that door smoke.

The beam failed. **What happened?** he thought, chagrined. But he was already figuring it out for himself. The satellite had ceased reflecting the beam. Knot's weapon had been cut off at the source. Mit/Hermine had tried to warn him.

"We aren't finished yet!" he said aloud. He jumped away from the useless controls, ran to a smoldering body, and picked up the dead man's laser pistol. And dropped it instantly; the thing was partially melted and still burning hot.

He ran to the next. There, under the body, was a holstered pistol that had been shielded from the terrible glare. Knot drew that out and checked it; it was in working order, with a full charge.

He stepped over the body, going toward the door. Those lobos who remained alive were blind and hurting, too far gone to notice him. He had, at least, rendered an orderly search into chaos, and opened new avenues of escape.

Why haven't the lights failed? The power's gone now.

Mit says they have temporary reserves, since they have to provide power at night when the satellite is in shadow and its field of harvest is reduced.

He should have known. It would have been much easier to escape if the station had died, but of course it was proof against interruptions. Technological societies were notoriously fussy about the steady flow of power. *Where to?* he asked Hermine.

Mit says it is hard to grasp—you have changed everything—

Precisely, my dear. Never underestimate the power of a berserk human brain. That's one reason Mit could not anticipate this. I can change reality too swiftly and vastly for him to assimilate, and he himself is a factor in it, so his predictions affect his own survival. Everything is hopelessly mixed up—and that's the way we want it. Until we escape. Just have him call out the way ahead of me; I'm headed for the checkout station and exit.

You would make a good weasel.

Thanks, he thought, flattered by the compliment. Hermine's feeling came through with her message: an intense admiration and pleasure akin to human love. This was her kind of action. Yet Knot was a lot less confident than he projected. With the failure of the power failure, which he had somehow counted on, the chaos would be briefer and milder than otherwise, and that made his task correspondingly more difficult. Also, though he had in one sense changed reality and overruled Mit's prediction, this had required such an extraordinary and desperate measure that he would not be able to take it in other circumstances. He had not really disproven precognition; rather he had shown the extent of its validity. It was akin to winning a game by dropping a bomb on the playing field: normally not worth it. He really needed to work things around to the point at which Mit could make a positive prediction, and he had not yet accomplished that.

People were running about, trying to respond to the ubiquitous summonses of the alarms. The room-by-room search was in hopeless disarray. Knot passed several people, but was ignored by all; no one remembered him.

Your psi is wonderful, Hermine thought. **Once you get their attention off you, it stays off.**

It has its uses, he agreed.

Guided by Mit's spot directives, he wound tortuously through the labyrinth, avoiding gassed rooms, and officers who would challenge him, and other routine pitfalls.

Then Hermine relayed another picture: the piebald mutant, his open hand swinging toward Knot's face—no, Finesse's face—and the impact-shock of a hard slap. "**We do not use sophisticated electronics or psionic techniques here,**" Piebald said. "**Only the most rudimentary room-speaker system, which came with the estate. We rely on the age-old standbys. Tell us what you know, before I destroy your pretty face.**"

The age-old standbys: rudimentary speaker systems and physical brutality to captives. "I will kill that man!" Knot gritted, a black fear and rage swamping his equilibrium.

Finesse is tough, Hermine reassured him. **The bad man can beat her face to a pulp, and she will tell him nothing. She is immune to most drugs, too.**

Good to know, Knot replied, horrified at what loomed. But he found he was no longer so upset about the lobos he had killed with the solar beam. This was a rough league!

He arrived at the strip-search station. **Pause,** Hermine directed. **Mit says this one is easy; they don't search people going out, only those coming in. There will be a distraction—**

An old-fashioned telephone rang. The sentry picked it up. Knot walked past, nodding casually, as though this were routine. The man looked concerned, but was occupied by the phone and let Knot pass. This was obviously incorrect procedure, but the present disorganization fostered such carelessness.

Since out-of-sight was out-of-mind in Knot's case, this was perfect. A brief contact faded more rapidly than a long one, and unless the man were reminded of Knot in the next few seconds, he would not remember Knot had been this way. In fact, no one at the station would remember who had caused the trouble; it would have to be attributed to a person or persons unknown. In this respect, Knot's psi was indeed major; its insidious effect was as potent as any overt psi could be.

The portcullis was another matter. He could not pass it unless it was raised—and the operative would accept only the clearance of a superior he knew personally. That personal-identification system was a good one; no faked papers or tattoos could prevail.

There was, Mit found, a counter-locking mechanism that required the authorization of a person in a distant office—one beyond the reach of Knot's psi or that of Hermine or Mit. This was how the superior's approval was enforced; even if the gatekeeper suffered complete mental takeover, he could not by himself raise the portcullis. The system had no doubt been designed with psi in mind, since some psis were hypnotists and others controlled minds directly. **You cannot pass,** Hermine thought despairingly.

Just watch me try! Knot marched up to the desk. **Project confirmation as I go. What is this man's name?**

Jeb, she replied dutifully.

"Jeb, there's trouble in the beam-access room," Knot said briskly. "Some fool spun the beam out of its channel. It killed some, blinded others, and burned the wall before the orbiter cut it off. There's absolute chaos there, and a serious fire hazard. Summon the city fire-damping squad immediately."

Jeb peered at Knot, trying to place him. Hermine evidently planted some recognition, for the man slowly nodded. "But we have our own fire service, and it's not my place to—"

"Who the hell do you think got burned?" Knot snapped. "They were good men, too. We need help before this whole place goes up. Our reserve power won't last forever. Now get on it. This is the only desk that's not overwhelmed by the problem."

Jeb got on it. In a surprisingly short time a crew appeared on the other side of the portcullis. "Let them through," Knot directed.

Jeb phoned for confirmation—and did not receive it. **What's that other man's name and position?** Knot demanded. **Read it from Jeb's mind.**

Xoth, the countermand engineer. He has a sad face.

Knot took the phone from Jeb's hand. "Xoth, is that you there? Get the lead out of your jowl and open the gate. The relief fire crew is hung up here while the beam-access room burns. I will not assume responsibility if this delay causes an explosion."

"Who are you?" Xoth demanded.

"Who am I?" Knot repeated incredulously. "Who the hell do you think I am, hangdog? Now cut this foolishness and release that gate, or I'll get over there and do it myself. *The beam-room is burning,* idiot!"

Xoth, cowed, released the gate. The liability of mindless functionaries was that they tended to react mindlessly to the semblance of authority. The portcullis lifted; the fire crew marched in—and Knot marched out.

As the portcullis dropped again, more men erupted from the interior. "Stop that man!" one cried, spying Knot. "No one is permitted out! We're on quarantine!" But they were too late; the metal bars barred their way, and they would have to obtain due countermand clearance before they could pass. Xoth, realizing that he had been stung once, would be extremely balky about lifting the barrier a second time.

Mit says that was some show, Hermine thought. **An honest man could not have done it.**

If CC needed an honest agent, CC would have hired one.

Yes. Animal mirth. Honesty was a concept alien to most animals. To Hermine, whatever worked best was good, and whatever failed was bad.

This was, Knot reflected, one of the reasons why animals did not rule the galaxy. In order to become technological, entities had to work together, developing interdependencies, specializations and trust. These things could not exist without honor. An ethical code was fundamental to man's success. Knot did not enjoy lying, any more than he enjoyed killing. The best he could say about it was that he would never violate such human codes unless he were hard-pressed. He had become, in his own estimation, less of a man, in the interest of short-term survival. And this too was part of life; the civilized virtues were sloughed off when the basic drives were invoked. Man still had some evolution ahead of him. When a man in trouble could *not* make a good weasel, perhaps he would be there, ultimately civilized.

Perhaps, also, he would be extinct. How could man as a species progress when there was greater survival value in retaining primitive characteristics? Unless the entire framework of life progressed in tandem, every creature becoming more ethical—no, it would never happen. Ethics was simply not the overriding goal of life. It was merely a limited tool that enabled one species to gain on the others for a while. Prior tools had been the ability to walk on land, and the ability to maintain the heat of the body regardless of the weather, and dexterity with objects. Tools, literally.

They emerged into the concourse. **They are raising the portcullis,** Hermine warned. **Mit says—**

Yes, I could have guessed that myself. Knot broke into his awkward run. **Have Mit look ahead. I need a train going away from the city, one that I can board without money.**

They all take money.

Then find me some money, soon. Knot was panting, his uneven gait tiring him.

She consulted with Mit. **Some is spilled ahead. Lift up that loose grate.**

Knot lifted the grate. There, in the dirt and refuse, were several small metal disks: the local coins. He picked them up.

An abrupt flare of pain struck him. Something had smashed his nose. Knot grunted, putting his hand to his face—and found it whole. **Oh—is that Finesse?** He would rather have had it be himself.

Yes. Now she is unconscious.

Thank God for that! **I will kill him extremely slowly!**

First I will bite off his nose, Hermine agreed. They ran on, two animals in agreement.

Now Knot could hear the clamor of the pursuit. Precious moments had been taken getting the coins. **Lead me by a route that will put me on a train just before they catch me. I do not want to sit and wait for them.**

Mit worked on it. Knot led his pursuit, who, it developed, had semi-canine trackers, a merry and circuitous chase around the passages, terminating at a subway train just about to pull out. He jammed a coin into the admission turnstile and boarded. The hunting party drew up just too late, as they had at the portcullis. Mit had done it again! Knot waved a cheery farewell through the grimy window.

Mit and I have not before performed like this, Hermine thought. **You make us efficient.**

Well, I like you.

The irrelevancy was lost on her. **Finesse likes us too, but she never—**

She's a normal and a woman. Two strikes against her.

Again, the humor failed to register. **It is not only that—**

Knot relaxed as the train carried them swiftly forward. He knew he would be safely forgotten and lost in the crowd by the time the lobos intercepted the train at the next stop. He was an extremely slippery customer! He felt expansive.

It is that I am an experienced interviewer and mutant placement officer. Finesse is also an interviewer, but it is her business to glean information and apply human perspective. It is mine to discover ways to make people relate, and to perform at their best potential. I apply that skill to your mutant talents too. Surely CC was aware it would be this way. It wasn't just my psi; there are plenty of better potential psi-agents. It was my total expertise for this situation.

Yes. CC said you were the best man for the job. That, with us and Finesse, you would be the best agent in the human galaxy. I think you are.

With one chance in four of succeeding, Knot reminded her.

There was another wash of emotion, not precisely the weasel's. **She dreams,** Hermine thought.

Even in her sleep, Finesse was sending? That had to be an important dream! Knot paid close attention as the diffuse images and feelings came through.

Finesse's dream began in pain. Her face was hurting; her eyes gazed past the two sides of a lump of misery that seemed to project enormously. She retreated from it, but it followed her back inside her head. The pain was not merely physical; it was also spiritual. She had always been pretty, and that had been a prime component of her self-image, giving her confidence and courage. Now she was not pretty, and that undercut her foundation. No one would love her, now.

I love you! Knot thought violently.

And it seemed a trace echo of his thought got through, for now in her dream his homely face appeared. She had fixed him in her mind; she might forget the last few hours with him, but she remembered the earlier association, buttressed as it had been by her holo-recordings. That memory had been blocked on the conscious level by CC's treatment, but remained in the nether levels that her dreams intersected.

"Even like this?" she asked plaintively, visualizing herself as a child with a grotesque protuberance, a watermelon nose, discolored and misshapen.

"Even like this," his image assured her.

Then abruptly the pain was gone, or at least receded far to the background, and she was skipping forward in a wraithlike dress that wafted tantalizingly about her contours, making flickering displays of breast and thighs and torso that she knew would inflame the male mind. He was beside her, running unevenly but not objectionably. She didn't care that he was homely; she had enough beauty for them both. They crossed a lovely field of blue daisies. Streamers of lightning radiated from trees in the distance, bright, spectacular, remarkable, but not nearby. Her hair lifted, buoyed by the electrostatic charge, not in the manner of electrocution but rather like the gentle current underwater. It iridesced, throwing off little fountains of half-glimpsed colors, peacock-fair.

Knot, watching, feeling, realized that this was an

elaboration of their experience at the mouth of the leadmuter's cave, when the electrical storm had pinned them down. Sure enough, there was the deep splendor of gold in the background, shedding its luster beneath the green plants, taking the place of soil. Gold had theoretically brought her there, thus it manifested in the fundament, the ground from which all else sprang. Her recorder had not been operative then, because of the charge in the air, so she could not have refreshed her memory of this particular scene. Yet it was here in her dream, reconstructed and beautified. Her subconscious remembered what his psi had erased from her conscious mind. This vision had survived both him and CC; doubly erased, it returned, distorted yet delightful. Knot did not know what would account for that, except perhaps the intensity of love.

She loved him, without doubt. Yet something nagged him; was there some reason she should not love him? He could not isolate that reason. Perhaps it was merely his own unwillingness to believe that a woman like that could love a man like him.

She turned to him then, in the dream, and opened her arms, and her dress dissolved entirely and blew away like so much froth, little bubbles of it popping pleasantly. "I'm really a mutant like you," she murmured, kissing him oh-so-sweetly. "I'm your kind." He embraced her, and she felt his big strong hand on one side, and his smaller weaker one on the other, and this was reassuring because she knew it could only be him in that configuration. He was a mutant, but also a man, she knew; he wanted mainly one thing, and this she gave him gladly.

You wrong me, Knot thought. *I would give up that one thing, only to have you safe and free!*

But this was her dream, with her simplistic assessment of the male nature. She did not realize that if sex were all that motivated a man, he would have no need to choose among women. Yet neither was it to be ignored. They merged, and their linked bodies tilted, he forward, she backward, rotating, feet leaving the ground, end over end, slowly in air, flying, never falling, never touching earth. Here was part of the symbolism of dream-flying, the freedom from gravity and from social restraint, the doing of what was usually forbidden or so limited as to be not worthwhile, abandoned, weightless, careless. They spun giddily among the lightning strokes, ascending into the sky, bound together, arms clasping each other, feet interlocking, turning, turning. . . .

It faded. Knot found himself in the drab train, deeply moved. Finesse, in her deepest heart, loved him too, and always had, and would even lie to him to hold him, pretending she was a mutant too. She did not quite believe he could love a normal, just as he had not believed she could love a mutant. Now he believed.

Of course, it could also be that she craved some psi-power for herself, and so in her deepest hope laid claim to it. It was Knot's psi that attracted her, as she had been candid enough to confess; her love for him was at least in part a sublimation of her balked desire for psi of her own. Probably CC's expectation of psi in her had been tacitly communicated at an early age, and she had never fully reconciled herself to the reality of normalcy. Yet she was lovable without psi, if she could only believe it. . . .

Her dream has passed, Hermine thought.

Her dream will never pass. But even if it did, love will remain.

Yes. It makes me wish I could mate.

Knot snapped out of his reverie. **Surely you will—when you find the right weasel.**

The train slowed jerkily. The lights of the tunnel passed more slowly. **Mit says they are waiting at the station.**

Damn, those lobos were organized! Any other pursuit would have lost him by now. **Then we shall not get off.**

But they will wait at the end of the line, too.

If they remember.

They have written instructions. They follow these.

Do those instructions describe me accurately?

Yes. A camera took pictures when you entered the power station, Mit says. They draw from that.

Smart lobos! They were catching on, learning how to nullify his psi. **Then I must change my appearance.**

Knot looked about. Several passengers wore farm clothing: heavy blue coveralls, gloves, wide-brimmed hats. One was moving up the aisle toward the functions room. Knot got up and followed him, leaving the suitcase behind so that other passengers would know he planned to return to his seat, and entered the functions room just as the train jerked to a stop.

"Sorry, friend," Knot murmured, putting his right arm around the man's neck in just enough of a stranglehold so that he could not cry out. "What is your name? Where do you work?"

Meig, Hermine thought. **He works on a post-setting crew on a combine-farm beyond the end of the line.**

Knot put the man the rest of the way to sleep. Contrary to popular belief, a strangle properly executed was not uncomfortable for the victim. It interfered with the circulation of blood to the brain, and the brain clicked out painlessly.

He set the unconscious man on the function pot. Soon Knot had exchanged clothes with him. In due course he merged with Meig's crew, reported for work as a substitute, bungled the job of setting posts, and with the help of the crew escaped a detachment of pursuing lobos. He found himself fleeing across a field by night, and the lobos were closing in. No respite for the unlobotomized!

Mit says there is a vehicle near, Hermine advised him. **A stilter.**

Knot didn't know what that was, but decided it was for him. It had to be better than jerking along on foot. He followed directions and found it: a kind of saddle mounted on long, jointed stilts, suitable for traversing fields of standing grain without crushing many plants. It was no toy; it was sturdily constructed, with a small but powerful hydrogen motor that dripped its water-exhaust to the plants below.

He climbed up and seated himself. It felt high and precarious, but it did seem to be his best available mode of transportation.

Knot followed Mit's instructions and started the motor. A driblet of fluid fell as the machine spun into life. **No pollution,** Hermine thought, again relaying Mit's perception. **They don't like pollution right near growing plants. For fencing and turning-under it is all right, but not in** the living fields. **This will conceal your odor somewhat from the canines. They will have difficulty tracing you.**

This sounded better and better! Knot put the stilter into gear. It lurched forward, flinging its jointed stilts out ahead, lifting them from behind. It seemed to have about eight, and reminded him of a long-legged bug. But though it seemed momentarily about to collapse, it had a balancing circuit, and actually held its position well. Soon he gained confidence.

They moved out across the fields. The stilter stepped over obstructions and gullies without difficulty, and could also make fair progress on flat land. He worked it up to high gear, and fairly flew across the dark fields. In fact, the sensation was very like flying, for in the night he could see the ground only as a vague haze, and his feet barely brushed the tall plants below him. Just so long as the stilter didn't set a foot in a rodent hole and take a tumble!

She wakes, Hermine thought. There was no need to identify the subject; the impression of Finesse came right through. Her face was throbbing with the residual discomfort of the broken nose, and she had a headache and felt awful. But she had told the interrogator nothing, and would not tell him anything, no matter what.

Hi, Hermine! she thought strongly. **If you read me, contact whatshisname. His memory will return when you introduce yourself. Bring him to me—carefully. These people are vicious.**

She did not yet know that her captors were lobos, Knot realized. He had assumed that she had guessed this, but perhaps he had assumed too much. She thought this was a purely local group. Maybe that was best; no sense having her realize the full extent of her captors' activity while she was helpless.

But now a man was with her. That was why she had awakened. He had entered her cell and splashed water on her face. It stung awfully. She saw him now: Piebald.

"You have psi talent," the man said. **"You are no normal."**

Finesse did not respond. She merely relayed her impressions, not knowing whether they were being received. It was all she could do.

"CC only sends psi-mutants on spy missions," Piebald continued. "Therefore you are a psi spy. I will find out your psi, so as to know the nature of CC's plot."

Off on the wrong track! Knot did not know whether to be gratified or alarmed, for surely Piebald would torture Finesse cruelly in his effort to discover the undiscoverable. The lobos would never get what they wanted from her, for CC had evidently anticipated such a threat to a psi-mute and eliminated it by sending a normal—but they might destroy her in the process.

The sending faded out. **We must help her,** Knot thought to the weasel, and felt her strong assent.

Then a light showed on the horizon. **Trouble again,** Hermine thought. **The aircraft returns on its search pattern.**

Mit can help us avoid that.

Yes. But there are ground parties organizing too. The pattern is becoming too complicated for him.

Maybe I can simplify it. Where is the nearest rough terrain?

Acute angle to the left. We're going away from it.

Knot guided the stilter into the necessary turn. He was working into a certain skill with this machine, and was getting to like it. Now he intended to ascertain the thing's practical limits.

We are going toward them, she protested. **One aircraft, two groundcraft, and three men on foot with laser rifles.**

Sounds like fun. Knot steered the stilter with one hand, and brought out his stolen laser pistol with the other.

The lights of the aircraft approached swiftly. It turned out to be a blimp, its large gas chamber giving it buoyancy to enable it to hover without sending down a blast of air that would flatten the growing grain. The farmers of Macho were very conscious of the welfare of their crops! Probably the lobos had wanted to use faster jetcraft, and been blocked by the local plantation owners.

Quickly Knot assessed his chances: He could not lose himself, once discovered by the blimp, since it did not have to keep moving at high speed. It could fix on him, its operators firing their lasers at convenience. However, it could not come down below treetop level, since there were a few trees here, and would be subject to the vagaries of wind. The trees and shrubs ahead of him would be effective as long as he stayed among them.

That left the ground crews. Rough terrain would interfere with the trucks—Mit had identified these now—but not with the men on foot. The stilter could probably outrun the footed men, but not the blimp or the trucks.

True.

This was another puzzle. He had to find a route that would inhibit all three aspects of the pursuing force until he could win entirely free and be forgotten again. Assuming those damned written instructions the lobos were using allowed them to forget enough.

Mit says there is no such route, Hermine informed him. **The rough ground is scant, just a gully with some rocks and larger trees. It is surrounded by wide-open fields. You can avoid the lobos only fifteen minutes there.**

And Mit ought to know; fifteen minutes was well within his reliable precog perspective. **I shall have to change the rules again,** Knot decided.

Ooo, naughty man. The weasel was apprehensive and delighted.

Knot reached the limited badlands, however, unobserved. **But they are closing in,** Hermine warned. **They know this is a good place for you to hide.**

Lead me to the man I can most readily overcome, he directed her.

Mit located the man. He was scouting a copse in the steepest section of the gully, using a flashlight. This depression appeared to be a natural cavity left as a flood overflow; the base of it glistened with water when the man's light shone that way. The weeds were tall and robust, and the trees were achieving fair size. Probably fertilizer from the fields got washed in here, enriching it.

Knot stopped the stilter and waited in ambush behind a gnarly trunk. The help of the psi animals made this virtually child's play; he knew who the man was, what his call code was, and where he was going. As the man passed the tree, Knot stepped out behind him. "Please freeze in place; I have you covered." **Now I am discovered; now I revise the rules.**

Fire! Hermine thought. **He's attacking.**

Knot fired his beam as the man spun about. The laser

caught the man on the side; a puff of smoke rose from his shirt. Then he dropped.

"Sorry about that," Knot murmured. He had run afoul of a conditioned reflex, thus had not anticipated it through Hermine's reading of the man's prior thoughts. Such reflexes were invoked without thought, triggered by the situation. The lobos had well-drilled troops.

Knot was not yet immune to the horror of maiming or killing men, but he knew he had no choice in this case. Had he not fired, the man would have beamed him down. In addition, the memory of Finesse's broken nose went far to alleviate his scruples about what he did with these people. In fact, by their torture of Finesse, the lobos had converted Knot into a far more dangerous man than he had been before. They had reduced him to a more primitive viciousness. He hoped that he would be able to return to civilized behavior after all this was over; he did not like himself as he was now.

But I like you, Hermine thought. **Now you understand about hunting, and about rats.**

Yes, now he understood. The lobos were indeed like rats, tough, cunning, unrelentingly malignant, ubiquitous. One had to keep fighting them desperately, merely to slow the progress of defeat.

He undressed the man efficiently and changed into his uniform. This was a little tight about the right side, but would have to do. He put his own farmer's clothing on the lobo. The man was not dead; the beam had penetrated his side as he turned, possibly holing a lung, but such wounds were cauterized as they were made and bleeding was not extreme. The survival rate of those injured by laser was much higher than that of those with similar injuries by projectiles. Knot was relieved; at least he had not done more damage than he had to.

He picked up the rifle, tucked the pistol away, and addressed himself to the communicator box. "Truller here," he announced, using the name Hermine had picked from the lobo's mind. "I have apprehended the fugitive."

The response was immediate. "Good for you! Alive, incapacitated or dead?"

"I tried to take him alive, but he attacked when challenged, and I had to hole him. I think he's still alive, but I may have punctured his lung."

You lie so well it becomes the truth, Hermine thought.

"The directive says that man is a psi. We want him for interrogation. A truck will pick you both up in a moment."

Knot waited, idly twining threads from the hole in the shirt so that they tended to draw it together. Probably no one would notice that the uninjured captor had the holed clothing while the injured captive's apparel was whole, but it wasn't worth risking. Knot hauled up a section of the shirt on the lobo, placed the muzzle of his pistol against it, and triggered a brief burst. The cloth puffed into ash. Then he tucked the shirt back into the belt. That would have to do.

Soon the truck arrived. Knot stood in the open and waved his arms, signaling it in. When it stopped, he helped the driver lift the unconscious man into the back, then joined him in the cab.

In the light of the interior, the driver turned, suddenly realizing that he had picked up a stranger. But Knot's pistol now looked him in the right eye. "Drive carefully out of here, exactly as you would if everything were in order," Knot said with deadly softness. He didn't want the lobos to learn about Hermine or Mit, but needed to convince this man that he had no chance to resist. "If you attempt to betray me, I will know it before you act. I am a telepath. Think a thought."

Gray two toad fly, Hermine thought, relaying it.

"Gray two toad fly," Knot repeated, pausing to let the significance sink in. "I have shot your companion; I will shoot you and drive this truck myself if I have to. Your practical choices are between driving healthy and riding wounded or dead. In either case you will not succeed in taking me to your superiors, so you need have no feeling of dereliction if you cooperate. I suggest you not even think of causing trouble for me."

Cowed, the lobo drove the truck. It was not that he was a coward; Knot's prompt action and logic had bypassed the man's conditioned reflexes and left him reasonable. It was indeed better to cooperate, when all that could be gained by noncooperation was his own malaise.

He knew Knot was not bluffing; the condition of the lobo in back attested to that.

As they emerged from the rough ground, the vehicle communicator spoke. "Fash, have you located Truller yet?"

Knot made a little gesture with his hand toward the speaker-grille. This unit, Mit had ascertained, was keyed by a signal from either end. It had been off while Knot spoke, but now was on. The lobos' limited reliance on this sort of equipment was now costing them security; they were better off without it. Probably they had to use it, in deference to the normals who governed this planet; left to their own devices, they might have used a system of flag signals or blinking lights. Even that, however, would not have stopped Knot; he knew how to use those signals. More and more, he was coming to appreciate the wisdom of CC's choice in agents!

Tell him to answer—as I wish him to, Knot thought to Hermine. **Apply a background of alert menace.**

Fash jumped when the prompting came; evidently he had not before experienced telepathic communication directly. But had he had any doubt at all of Knot's power, this abated it. "I have picked him up," the lobo said/nervously. "The—the fugitive is in back, unconscious."

"Proceed directly to our hospital station. Out," the communicator said, and clicked off.

"That was well performed," Knot said. He kept his laser oriented on the man's head.

They bumped over the field, finally intersecting the road. Now the truck accelerated. Knot checked with Mit, then reached over to put the communicator on nonreceive; now it would not be activated from the other end. He wanted to be able to talk freely.

"You will actually drive to the bridge across the enclave chasm, passing as close to the lobo hospital station as is feasible. After passing the station you will accelerate to the maximum permissible velocity. Should you deliver me without attracting attention to the place I am going, I will release you and your truck unharmed. Otherwise you will either be shot, or will share my fate. Do you understand?"

He understands, Hermine thought. **He knows that the only way he can escape is to help you escape.**

"I see that you do," Knot said gravely. "Now, Fash, since we have a little drive ahead of us, let's get to know each other better. I am a CC telepath sent here in the company of a normal to investigate certain illicit lobotomies on psi-persons. I know that you lobos are responsible. I can understand why the leaders do this, but not why ordinary people like you support this mischief. Feel free to comment honestly."

The lobo swallowed. "It's a job," he said. "Macho normals don't like minorities. Lobos understand what lobos suffer."

He speaks truth, Hermine thought.

"I see you are speaking the truth, as you understand it," Knot said. "Still, some lobos are skilled workers who could obtain work anywhere. Why do they choose to work with the lobo organization? They could conceal their nature and never suffer discrimination."

"I don't know," Fash said, genuinely perplexed. "There is something—lobos just *have* to work with lobos. That's the way it is."

What compulsion is this? Knot asked Hermine. **Hypnotic?**

Not hypnotic. I can't identify it.

Knot tried a different tack. "Are you not aware that the lobo leaders may have caused your own lobotomy?" Perhaps he had a notion that would insidiously undermine the amazing unity of these people. Divide and conquer!

"No," Fash said sullenly.

"This is what they intend to do to me," Knot argued. "Lobotomize me and convert me to your cause. Because once I'm a lobo, the only ones who will understand my situation will be other lobos. As with you. How can you know they did not do this to you?"

Now Fash was very uncomfortable. "That can't be true!"

"It is hardest to believe what you don't want to believe," Knot said sadly. "The lobos took you in, helped you through your initial disorientation, gave you a job and a measure of self-respect. Yet how can that ever make up for what they took from you?"

He was a minor pyro, Hermine thought. **Mit says the**

planetary authority convicted him of arson and lobotomized him, not the lobos.

"You were a pyro, were you not?" Knot continued smoothly. "They told you that the government lobotomized you—and you believed it."

Ooo, naughty man! Hermine thought. **Your lies thrill me!**

"Well, the government *did*—" But now Fash wasn't sure. The insidious seed of doubt had been sown, and was beginning to grow. "Still, what can I do, except what I'm doing?"

That made Knot uncertain. This was no highly trained person; his options were curtailed. "Fash, I can't answer that. But have you thought of it this way: Can you really see yourself helping the lobo management to make new lobos? Do you want everyone to be like you?"

"No! I want no one to be like me! I want my psi-power back! Show me a way to get it back, and I'll do anything!" For the moment he had forgotten that he was hostage to a fugitive; this was his fundamental feeling emerging.

"I believe I would feel the same," Knot said. "I think you can understand why I am fighting so hard to avoid being lobotomized myself. Without my psi, I would be a blind normal."

"Yes! It is horrible," Fash agreed.

They lapsed into silence on this note of agreement. Knot changed the communicator setting again, so that the truck's silence would not seem suspicious. And he wondered again: Why were the lobos doing this? If the ones Finesse had been interviewing were typical, the average lobo had been rendered desolate by the loss of his psi. That desolation never abated, as his talk with Fash showed. The lobos should not be actively depriving others of their psi, unless crazy with rage or jealousy—and he found no trace of such emotions in Fash, here. It seemed a criminal or psychotic element had assumed control of the lobo organization. There were certainly many criminals among them; that was why they had been lobotomized. But why would the noncriminal lobos go along with it? Because they had no choice? In that case, eliminate criminals such as Piebald, who was torturing Finesse, and the lobos would be all right. Yet mere criminals and dupes should not account for the extreme difficulty this movement was giving CC, threatening to overwhelm the Coordination Computer within a few years. Knot kept running up against the missing element, the thing that made all this rational and feasible. There had to be *something!* But, like CC, he could not locate it.

His thought drifted to the opposite aspect. From what did psi itself derive? What was mutation, except the mutilation of the genetic blueprint of the species? Every mutant had in fact been deprived of his just normalcy. Ninety-nine percent of all mutations were unsuccessful to a lesser or greater degree. Physical failures, such as missing digits or limbs or organs, or extra ones, or misarrangement of them. Mental failures, such as separated lobes of the brain, or inability to think or feel or remember, or unhealthy concentration of intellectual resources in a nonsurvival area, such as superawareness of the left kneecap. Only the flukes derived any advantage from mutation.

Yet there had to be the potential within the human and animal scheme for psi, or none would ever occur. Could it be that the small percentage of successful psi mutations was merely a short-circuiting of the natural barriers, enabling some aspect of that tremendous capability to manifest? Was it theoretically possible to open the entire psi-capacity and have people who could do it *all*? Telepathy, clairvoyance, pyrotechnic, telekinesis, precognition, transmutation and the hundreds of psi-skill variants that defied easy classification? What a cornucopia that would be!

"You know, Fash, I think your lobo organization is misguided," Knot said. "You are destroying psis, making them resemble you in their mutilation, as though an organization of one-legged men went about amputating the legs of normals. You can't improve your own lot by dragging others down with you. You should be turning your efforts toward positive things. Such as research. You want some method to restore your powers, or to share those of other psis. To lift yourself up again, instead of bringing misery on others."

"Yes. . . ."

Think what it would be like to be a telepath, Knot thought, knowing Hermine would catch the cue and relay the thought directly to the lobo's mind. **To read others' thoughts, share their secrets.**

Fash almost drove the truck off the road. Knot had to grab the wheel.

"Oh, God, if only it could be so—" Fash breathed.

"With a positive attitude and the right application—"

"Tell CC that!" Fash replied with sudden curtness. "Even if what you say is true, CC is behind most of the lobotomies!"

"True," Knot agreed, moved. "I plan to tell CC, once I extricate myself from the clutch of your associates. I don't necessarily agree with all CC's policies any more than you agree with all the lobo policies."

But if lobotomy were halted, how would society deal with psi-criminals? Knot had no ready answer for that. He could not condone going back to the barbarity of killing them, any more than he could condone killing partly successful mutants of any kind, or confining them involuntarily to enclaves. Yet it was hardly feasible to allow a killer-psi to run loose amid the populace. Better that adverse mutants and criminals never be born—

There was the answer! Discover what genetic influences predisposed individuals to criminality, and eliminate those influences. Maybe criminality was another mutation—one that was triggered by local planetary radiation on a more or less random basis. Identify that radiation—

The lobos have caught on, Hermine warned. **They are closing on this truck.**

Which explained why there had been no recent communications, despite his reopening of the channel.

"Your friends are about to make things difficult," Knot said. "Stop the truck and get out; there is no need for you to be hurt."

Fash glanced at him nervously. "You seem like a decent guy, for a telepath."

"You seem like a decent guy, for a lobo. So let's not get us both in trouble with our own camps. Get out now, before this gets rough."

The lobo hesitated, then braked the truck. He jumped out. "Take your friend too," Knot said. "I believe he will survive if you get him to the hospital quickly."

Fash went to the rear and hauled the wounded lobo off.

Knot moved to the driver's seat, following Mit's instructions, and got the vehicle moving.

"Good luck, psi!" Fash called. Then all was lost in the effort to handle the truck and keep track of the converging vehicles.

"Now for the action," Knot muttered. "I used to thrill to old-fashioned vehicle-chases on kiddie-holo, but I don't have much taste for them now."

Mit says there is a way through, Hermine thought. She did not seem worried. But of course weasels lived a rougher life than men; she was acclimatized to the tensions of pursuit.

Knot turned off the communicator again. He wished he had been more alert to its silence before; he didn't like depending too much on Mit's clairvoyance, since that did get swamped at times by complexity. Also, what would he do if Mit were not with him? He needed to keep developing his own resources.

However, the radio silence might be good news in one respect. The lobos could not have broadcast any general alert, because that would have triggered his set along with all the others. So they had had to seek other means, which were undoubtedly more clumsy, talking to each truck individually and trying to organize the chase piecemeal. It would take more than that to trap a good psi-mutant team!

But lobos were good at low-technology activities. They could run him down pretty well in radio silence, not alerting the nonlobo authorities to what was going on. Knot was not going to alert those authorities either; they could only detain him. This was a private matter between him and the lobos.

They have deduced your approximate position, Hermine thought. **They are blocking off this road.**

They can't block off all avenues without attracting undue attention. We have another tactical contest here. Where is the best loophole?

Next right turn, onto a dirt road. The weasel was enjoying this again; she really liked discovering what Knot's ready human mind could do with Mit's ready information and her own communication.

He swung right, bouncing on the road and stirring up

dust. Mit gave specific directions, and Knot followed them without question, turning from one back road to another, waiting two minutes, reversing course to retrace part of his route.

We are almost clear, Hermine thought. **Pull into the parking lot you will see in five minutes, and wait there half an hour. Then we will be secure.**

Knot visualized vehicles casting about, searching for him, their headlights linking like confused eyes, passing the parking lot by. The lobos assumed he would be blindly fleeing; this would fool them, and enable him to thread his way cleanly through their disorganizing net as they turned their attention farther afield.

"Ready for another dialogue?" It was Piebald again, summoning Finesse from her cell. She saw with horror that he carried a whip.

Knot saw the parking lot—and drove on by. **I can't wait any half hour! I must help her now!**

But Mit says—

We'll have to chance it.

I should not have relayed Finesse's sending, the weasel thought dolefully.

Keep on relaying her sending! Knot ordered sternly. **All becomes meaningless if I do not rescue her.**

A car converged on him, its air-inflated tires screaming as though that air were leaking out. **Now the lobos have spotted you,** Hermine said with a weasel thought-rebuke for his folly. Yet she also supported him, for this was exactly the sort of intemperate action a fighting weasel would have taken.

Knot angled his truck suddenly, brushing the car. The car squealed to the side, and off the road. **That felt good,** Knot told Hermine.

Yes. But there are more coming now.

Indeed there were. He could see their lights coming up behind, and Hermine verified that these were lobos. **How far to the bridge?** Knot demanded. In the dark he had little notion of the landscape, but was under the impression that the subway train had taken him a good distance in the general direction of the chasm, and so he should only need to cut across to reach the bridge.

Not far. But they know you're going there, and are cut-

ting you off. They have picked up Fash and made him talk. You must go elsewhere, now.

Finesse is across that bridge, isn't she?

Yes, but—

I am crossing.

Finesse would call you a fool.

She's right. But this fool is going to rescue her.

Mit says—

Mit said we couldn't escape the solar station or the farm fields.

Ahead! she thought, alarmed.

A car was pulling across the road, blocking it off. Can I swerve past it on the right?

Slow to more moderate velocity, swerve suddenly, cut back immediately. Make your own tires squeal. Very narrow aperture, Mit says.

Knot slowed, following Mit's running reminders so as to get it just right. He swerved—and met the lights of an oncoming vehicle, head-on. He swerved back, and the wind of the close pass made the truck shudder. "Mit wasn't fooling," he muttered aloud. "If I hadn't had his precognition, chances are I would have killed myself, not to mention a weasel." That realization did not horrify him, however; he was partially intoxicated with the adventure of it. Now he thought to turn off his headlights, to make his vehicle harder to spot. There was enough ambient illumination for him to see the road.

The lobos are shaken, Hermine thought. They think you're a crazy man.

I am! Knot accelerated, no longer caring about the speed limit or personal safety. The unsafest thing he could do now was dawdle.

More cars! she warned.

He saw their lights, blocking off the bridge access. "Move, bastards," he breathed. "I'm coming through anyway!"

But the cars did not move. They are empty! Hermine thought, alarmed. Avoid them!

Too late! I'd turn us over!

Mit says we must crash—

Knot saw the collision coming, as it were in slow motion. Yet he knew he could not avert it. If he tried to pass on the right, he would sail right into the chasm. Better to take the crash. He just might knock a car out of the way so that he could continue onto the bridge.

He plowed into the nearest car. The truck's stasis unit cut in at the moment of impact. Knot's body was frozen, eyes fixed forward, but he was aware of the proceedings.

The truck smashed the car aside, but veered to the left, ricocheting. It careened on across the road, left the pavement, rolled across an interim section, burst through a wooden barrier, and toppled over the lip of the chasm.

CHAPTER 7

The stasis cut out again as the truck spun slowly, end over end, in a trajectory toward the water. The unit could not tell the difference between a free-rolling and a free-flying vehicle. The walls of the canyon seemed to rotate as they drew together. Then the truck struck the water, and the stasis cut in again.

When the motion stopped, the stasis ended. This time it was permanent, for water was flooding the mechanism, shorting it out. Suddenly Knot was scrambling for his life, as the water rushed into the cab. *Stay with me,* he thought to the animals, not taking time to check on them.

He got the window the rest of the way down and drew himself out, stroking unevenly for the surface. The water was not deep, but there was a current. His head broke the surface, and he gasped for air.

A brilliant set of moons illuminated the canyon as if it were day; they must have been shining all the time, but during the chase he had been too preoccupied to pay attention. Now they brightened the surface of the water, making the river seem like a thick black tide beneath the sparkling wavelets.

He had survived—but how was he going to help Finesse now? He was trapped in the mutant enclave, from which there was no ready exit.

Mit! Hermine thought. She was clinging to Knot's shoulder. **He's loose in the water!**

Knot froze momentarily with alarm, then relaxed. **He's a crab, isn't he? Water is his natural environment. He can't drown.**

He doesn't like fresh water.

Um. That might be like trying to breathe the wrong kind of atmosphere. **Keep in touch with him; we'll fish him out.**

Knot was not a good swimmer, because his uneven body made effective stroking difficult, but he could handle himself well enough with sidestroke. He moved to the shore while Hermine maintained contact with Mit. Knot wanted to fetch a stick or bar that he could use to poke into the bottom of the river, for the crab to catch hold of. The nether water was somewhat murky, and Knot did not relish the idea of scratching through whatever wreckage and garbage might be down there with his tender bare hands.

A crowd of enclave mutants had gathered in the moonlight, attracted by the splash of the truck's arrival. They were grotesquely varied. One had four spindly legs; another had a split head, with an eye and half a nose on each split. A third had a face that seemed to be mostly nose, with the other features squeezed to the edges. Knot thought of Finesse, with her smashed and swollen nose: She must feel like this, at the moment.

"Are you mute or norm?" a rotund person called; the flesh bulged so oddly that Knot could not distinguish age or sex.

Knot stood up in the shallow edge of the river. He held his uneven arms aloft. "What do I look like?"

"Min-mute," the person responded contemptuously. "We don't want your kind here. Go on downstream."

Some welcome! **Their minds,** Hermine thought. **They are not nice people. They are like scavenger rats. They will attack you.**

"I'm going," Knot called, and waded back into deeper water. **Where is Mit? I'll have to go after him bare-handed after all. Can I dive for him here?**

He was carried downstream. He is clinging to an underwater plant. We can reach him safely.

Knot swam slowly, conserving his strength, letting the current take him. He was not tired yet, but feared he would need every last bit of his strength to climb the chasm side and escape the enclave. He dreaded the prospect; heights of that nature bothered him.

When he was in the right position, he followed the weasel's directive and dived. Guided by Hermine's continuing thoughts, he reached through the opaque water unerringly and caught the crab's shell in his large hand. No trouble at all! They were together again!

Mit says you are too close to normal, physically, Hermine thought as they came to the surface once more. **Most mutants here will not welcome you.**

I have no intention of staying here anyway. Ask Mit to show me the most feasible route up the side.

Mit says you can't climb it. You would fall and die.

Sobering warning! **How do I get out, so I can rescue Finesse?**

There is no route, here. Only if a vehicle comes from the normals. A hovercraft.

The normals have no interest in me. It could only be a lobo machine. We don't want that!

Then we must remain in the enclave.

Knot saw that he would have to change some more rules. One way or another, he was getting out of here!

It is fun to observe you planning the impossible.

No doubt. But with Finesse being tortured, he had to do it rapidly.

I shall operate on the assumption that there is a fast way out of here that will work for the three of us even if the inhabitants of this enclave are trapped. Can Mit provide any hint of the route?

There was a pause. **The situation is too complex, and your mind is too devious. You refuse to be bound by common sense, and precognition is an extension of common sense. Mit cannot grasp it. All he knows is that nowhere in this chasm is there a route you can use to pass the cliffs that bound it.**

Then we'll simplify. Where will I be in one day?

Another pause. **The possibilities radiate, Mit says. You are giving him a mind ache.**

Pick the most typical one, Knot thought ruthlessly.

The weasel consulted with the crab again. When her

thought came, there was a tinge of amusement. **You are mating with an enclave female in the water.**

But I love Finesse! he protested.

Yes. It will be very interesting.

Am I out of the enclave—or on the way out?

Trying to get out.

Knot shrugged in the water. **Well, let's get on with it. Have Mit lead us to the first person who can and will help us escape.**

More consultation. **There are few who have any notion—**

Let's isolate the information first. Who here knows any way out?

Few do. They are confined by the canyon walls and the rapids.

Do any swim or tunnel? Do any explore?

Hermine brightened. **Mit says yes. A mermaid—she knows the whole river, and the cavern passes. Her name is Thea.**

Find me that mermaid!

You want to mate with her? Hermine inquired mischievously.

Oops. She's the one?

Yes. She can't breed with most enclave males; they are not interfertile. With a normal she might conceive.

Knot grasped the situation. A mutant confined to the water—there would be no point for her to try to leave the enclave. If she wanted to birth and raise a child, she had to find a nonenclave man. So she was caught between untenable alternatives. Locate a man who probably did not exist in the enclave, or give up her dream of a family. **I am a mutant too; would I be fertile with her?**

Mit can't tell yet. You might be.

Because physically he was only minimally mutant, and fertility among mutants increased as they approached norm. If that were the price of his escape, he would have to pay it. Certainly he was prepared to go through worse trials to rescue Finesse.

Something in that connection jogged his memory without quite tripping it. Finesse—sex—other partners—what was it?

Well, he could ask. **Ask Mit what I am trying to remember.**

Mit says CC blanked it from your mind because it was not good for you to know.

To hell with what CC thinks is good for me to know! Tell me!

There are several things Mit knows that we don't. I can read his mind, but these things are blocked off from me.

Knot could see why. Had he known about Hermine and Mit the lobos would have killed the animals before they ever had a chance to help Knot escape. But in this particular case, he was determined to know. **No one is questioning me now. Make Mit tell.**

Hermine hesitated, then answered. **She is married.**

Married! To another man? But now that memory, keyed in by Mit's information, was returning. Finesse had been married, with a child—but had gotten a temporary divorce in order to serve in this mission. She had made a greater sacrifice than Knot had, for in her heart she remained married to the other man.

I don't care if she is married, Knot decided. **I don't want her captive and tortured. I'll rescue her and return her to her family.**

Nevertheless, the news dismayed him. Finesse, realistically, could never be his. He did not want her as a temporary liaison; he wanted her forever.

Yet what about her dream? She had made love to him, Knot, in that dream! If she loved another man—

CC blanked out her memory of her marriage, too, Hermine explained. **It didn't like the disruption caused when she revealed the fact of her marriage to you.**

CC has some nerve!

After your mission is successful and you save CC, CC will restore all memories, Hermine thought. **Since you agree that some memories are dangerous in the neighborhood of the enemy. . . .**

But when the memory is of a husband, a family, to enable a woman to think she loves another man—that is insidious and awful. Yet Knot appreciated the necessity, and decided to let the matter be, for now. If he wrestled with the matter too much, he might decide he didn't want to work for CC anymore.

One thing this news did, however: It largely eviscerated any scruples he might have had about making love to other women. He wanted to save Finesse, yes, and would do so—but he had to start preparing himself for attachments elsewhere, so that he could send Finesse back to her husband in due course.

Let's be on our way, he thought briskly.

A complication. There is a water monster between us and the mermaid Thea.

We don't have to swim there! We'll walk on land.

Mit says—

Knot cut off her thought with an imperious mental emission of steam. The little crab was too conservative!

He swam for shore again—but again an assortment of mutants clustered. They were as grotesque as the others, with grossly misshapen bodies, superfluous limbs, and widely misplaced orifices and organs of perception. Knot had worked with similar cases all his life, but the degree differed; these mutes were more exaggerated. And their attitude was savage. They brandished crude weapons. They were not gesturing him away; instead they waded aggressively toward him. Knot hardly needed Hermine's warning to know that these mutants considered him to be fair prey. That made them more horrendous than anything else. He retreated hastily.

Farther along, the canyon walls closed in. There were no people here—but also no room to walk. He had to remain in the water, though he was getting fatigued by the constant effort to stay afloat. It was easiest with the sidestroke, but then he could watch to one side only. That wasn't safe.

Monster, Hermine warned.

Knot stroked hastily for the side. But it was fully as inaccessible as it had seemed; the water lapped at an almost vertical wall. Now he saw the monster: a greenish, multi-armed mutant with almost crocodilian jaws. Probably many water-suitable mutants had sought this river; now Knot understood why he had encountered none. Only the fittest had survived. Unfortunately, fitness as defined by nature hardly matched fitness as defined by civilization.

A weapon, he thought. **Where—**

The pistol, Hermine responded.

It was still with him, but he wasn't sure it would work

after the prolonged immersion. Such weapons were supposed to be sealed watertight, but—

It was all he had. He raised it to point at the monster. "Halt, or I fire!"

The monster halted. Its small, wide-spread eyes could not focus; it had to turn its head sidewise to examine him. Knot pointed the pistol directly at the nearer eye. "Do you understand me?" he demanded. "You're human; you must know the language."

It understands, Hermine thought. *It can't talk. It is trying to determine whether your weapon is operative.*

I'd like to know that myself!

Mit says it is not. But he says fire it anyway.

When I do, the bluff will dissipate. I don't think I can overcome this creature bare-handed.

You are correct; you cannot prevail. Pretend the pistol works.

The monster decided to call the bluff. It windmilled its limbs—there seemed to be about seven of them—and charged forward.

Then burn, monster! Knot thought violently, firing his useless pistol. His animal friends were crazy, but—

And the monster leaped as though holed. Bubbles rose as it sank in the water.

Now swim! Hermine thought.

Knot swam. Soon he was away from the monster—and forgotten, thanks to his psi.

The pistol did not fire, he thought. *What happened?*

I relayed your mental firing, Hermine explained. *Mit said this would work.*

Of course! As with the mental nova-burst: The thought of getting beamed in a situation conducive to belief could be devastating. He should have thought of it himself. There was so much he was still learning about psi!

Mit says there is a ledge ahead.

Knot found it: a rocky level about knee deep into the water, so that it did not show from the surface. It tilted in places, but the unevenness of Knot's body enabled him to slog along it comfortably. It was better than swimming any more; his arms felt like clay-clad sticks.

I am very hungry, Hermine thought. *I never caught my rat.*

Knot realized that he was famished also. "There must be food somewhere," he said aloud. Here, alone, there was no need to communicate silently, and speech focused his thoughts for the weasel to read. "What do all the mutants here eat?"

Mit says garbage thrown down from above.

Besides that, Knot thought with repugnance.

Mostly fish, and some plants from ledges, and each other. Nothing is wasted.

"I don't know how to fish with bare hands, and I'm not yet ready for cannibalism. What does Mit recommend?"

He says the fastest way is to ask Thea.

The mermaid again—the one he was scheduled to make love to. Well, what had to be, had to be. He had pretty well worked that out in his mind, though he was not pleased. The mutants here were so grossly deformed that even he, a mutant himself, found no pleasure in associating with them. "Can you summon her mentally?"

I think so. There was a pause, while Knot continued splashing along the ledge.

He realized that he had pretty well lost the contest of predestination. The first time Mit had informed him he would do something, he had fought it all the way—and still become an agent of CC. The last time Mit had made a recommendation, about waiting half an hour in the truck, he had ignored it—and so had finished trapped in this chasm. Had he accepted Mit's advice, he might have made it to Finesse by this time. So he either honored Mit's predictions, or fervently wished he had done so. Still, a mer-mutant—

He kept looking for ways to climb on up out of the water and the canyon, but saw it was hopeless. As always, he had to follow the crab's advice.

A head poked from the river's surface. The mermaid had arrived.

Knot stared. He had been bracing himself for the worst, casting about for ways to slip out from under the precognition. But he had not been prepared for this.

Thea was not a deformed, fishlike grotesquerie. She was very like a normal girl, with rather attractive facial features, flowing fair hair, and a rather remarkable set of breasts. He could not see her feet, but the upper part of her torso was sleek and feminine.

"You called me?" she inquired, clearing the moisture from her eyes with two swipes of a normal hand, five delicate digits thereon, each with a long but well-contoured nail. "You are a telepath?"

"Close enough," Knot said. He found it harder to lie to a pretty girl. "My name is Knot. I am a mutant who must escape the enclave. I believe you can help me, for you alone know the byways of the water. I wish to make a deal for your assistance."

She studied him, frowning prettily. "Your body is almost normal. Do you think your seed would——?" She broke off, forming a faint flush.

Damn that attractiveness! Knot found himself flushing too. **Would it?** he demanded gruffly of Hermine. **Mit should be close enough to tell, now.**

Mit says no. Your seed would not sprout in her. You are not close enough to her, quite.

Again, it would be so easy to lie. But Knot just did not like to lie to decent people. Enemies were fair game, but Thea was obviously no enemy. "You are mutant; I am mutant. I doubt we could, ah, crossbreed."

"Would you be willing to try?" Her color became her. The prospect of trying was much more appealing, now that he had met her.

Yet there was Finesse (albeit married), and Mit's assurance that it could not take. "I need your help. I would rather not obtain it on a false premise. Nothing would come of our, ah——"

"Are you an honest man?"

"Not really. But——"

"I would be lying to you if I said I could get you out of here. There is no way out. Shall we exchange lies?"

Knot smiled. "I will get out regardless of your view. All I want is your cooperation, not your belief."

"That will do nicely," she said.

Touché! Hermine thought. **A male can't debate with a female.**

"You don't understand," Knot said, perversely determined to clarify the objectionable point. "I am not lying to you. I have information that indicates——"

"So do I. I can show you the way to the salt ocean, into which I cannot swim. Not for any length of time. But there is no escape for you that route, either, that I know of. So you might as well go back the way you came."

Knot recalled the river monster and the inhospitable mutants and the canyon cliffs and the current he would have to buck. Even taking the easy route downsteam had exhausted him. Only now were his arms recovering. "All right. Let's settle for the lies."

She smiled. She had been pretty before; now she was beautiful. "Follow me."

She spun in the water, and her fluke showed momentarily.

"Wait!" Knot cried. "We can't keep pace with you! My arms are tired already, and we are hungry—"

"We?" she inquired, turning about with a certain flare so that one breast flashed momentarily out of the water. That could not have been accidental; she knew as well as Finesse did how and when to show what. It seemed to be a highly honed skill all pretty women had.

Is it all right to tell her?

Mit says yes. She is a good girl, and she likes you.

"I am not alone," Knot said. "I have two animals with me. One of them is the telepath who summoned you."

"Female? I thought the call was that of a woman, and was surprised to discover you."

"Yes. A lady weasel. Hermine." **Say hello, Hermine.**

I did. She's nice. She likes raw fish.

"I will take you to my cave and fetch you fish, and you can rest," Thea said.

"That would be ideal," Knot agreed. **Raw fish?**

Delicious, the weasel agreed.

Thea spun around again, this time hefting both breasts up for a glimpse, and swam downstream more slowly. Knot followed, encouraged except for the fish. He did not like delay, but his fatigue and hunger had convinced him that there was no way he could escape quickly. He would need sleep too, to restore himself. So it made sense to yield to the situation, even at the further expense of time.

If only Finesse did not get tortured or killed in that interim!

Thea halted. "Here you must descend one body-length

and enter the hole in the wall. It leads to a cavern with air."

True, Hermine assured him.

Knot took a breath and dived—but could not descend low enough until he let out half his air to reduce buoyancy. He simply wasn't swimming strongly enough, now. His hands scratched against the rock wall. **To your right,** Hermine directed. Knot moved right and found the opening. He swam in. Already he was desperate for air.

He rose—and abruptly his head broke water in darkness. The twin moons were gone, of course; this was underground.

There was commotion beside him as Thea joined him. Her body felt even sleeker and more feminine than before as she moved in closer than necessary to guide him. "There is a ledge this way," she murmured in his ear, her lips actually touching the lobe. The effect was sensual: that light, intimate touch.

Knot suffered himself to be half-towed, afraid that if he tried to swim with any vigor his hands might crack into hard stone in the blackness. He was in her power, now; he would be unable to find his way out without Hermine's help. Yet it was a pleasant sensation, being drawn through the water invisibly by her action. Her breasts touched him every so often, perhaps not by accident, and he found himself being aroused sexually despite the chill of the water.

Then the ledge was there, and he was clambering out. The air was warm, here, which was another blessing.

"Will you eat fish raw, or do you need fire?" Thea inquired.

Knot was gratified by the question. He had a choice! "My friends like it raw; I would prefer the fire. But can it be done in an enclosed place like this?"

"Oh yes. There are air channels to the surface of the land, too long and narrow for any man to pass, but excellent for ventilation. In cold weather I need a fire, so I made sure it could be done, here."

She did something—and a spark flew and something blazed up, and there was light and heat. As Knot's sight adjusted, he discerned the limits of the cave. It was a fairly long, narrow one, with convoluted and evidently porous walls vaguely reminiscent of old fungus. The ledge sloped down into the black water.

The fire was fashioned of rock also, that burned with a mild aroma and very little smoke. There was a small pile of it nearby; evidently the mermaid gathered it when she had need. There were also little collections of pretty stones, colored sands, and delicate bones. Thea seemed to have an artistic bent, though there were no pictures in evidence at the moment.

Meanwhile, the mermaid was gone. **She will return soon,** Hermine thought. **I will keep in touch, so that she will not forget you. She has discovered that she is lonely. She wants you to stay.**

"So I gather," Knot responded. "Yet this is not my life." He lay down on the ledge, resting, letting the fire warm him, while Hermine and Mit explored the crevices in their own fashion.

He was getting sleepy when Thea returned. She had a netful of small fish. The fire was now well established; she had arranged it well, so that the flame expanded smoothly through the mound of rocks. She brought two sticks from a niche and spitted two fish, handing one to Knot. They held the fish over the fire, slowly cooking them.

Thea sat with her feet in the water. Knot saw now that they were deformed, incompletely separated, merged from the knees down. Her heels were fused, her toes pointing out. The web of skin where legs and feet were separating was not pretty; it was more like scar tissue. But it seemed effective for her swimming. Her upper legs were separated, though they could not move independently. She had made the best of her deformity, and survived well.

How, Knot wondered, would she be able to birth a baby, should she manage to conceive? She couldn't get her legs apart! But then he realized that she didn't need to; for thousands of years women had given birth by squatting, and she could squat.

"Yes, I'm not really a mermaid," she said, noting his glance. Knot hastily slid his gaze down her legs; he had been looking at the other end of them, and did not care to reveal the nature of his speculations. "Merely one of the mutilated. But I should be able to breed true-human—

if only I can conceive. I've tried it with several males, but—" She shrugged. That brought Knot's gaze up to another location.

Hermine appeared. "This is Hermine in person," Knot said gravely. "The weasel you have met mentally."

"Yes. Can she tell what I'm thinking now?"

She's wondering whether you'll renege on your part of the bargain, Hermine thought obligingly.

"No, I won't renege," Knot said. "But I'd rather eat first. If you will give a raw fish to Hermine, she'll share it with Mit the crab."

"So Hermine's a full telepath!" Thea said. "Not a part-telepath, like so many others. She can read *and* send. I thought maybe she could only send, before." She set a fish down before the weasel, who hauled it off to a niche. Mit was not in sight, but Knot was sure Hermine would be in touch with him.

"Why do you want—what you want?" Knot asked. "Are you able to raise a normal baby?"

"I've got to." She stared pensively into the water. "I mean—well, what is the point in life? I mean if you just die, accomplishing nothing? What's the point in *your* life, for example?"

"I want to accomplish some good for mankind—such as saving galactic civilization" he said. "I think that if I did that, and then died, my life would not have been wasted."

"What about those of us who can't get out to save the galaxy? How do we prevent ourselves from being wasted?"

"You—make new people," Knot said, grasping her point. "People who *can* go abroad, and perhaps do what you can't."

"You understand very quickly," she said, flashing him a smile. "What good will your civilization be, if there are no people to fill it? If I dedicate my half life to making a whole person, and I succeed—"

She had succeeded in convincing him. "It's a good thing you contemplate," he agreed. "I hope it works out." And he felt guilty, knowing that unless Mit were wrong this time, he, Knot, could not help Thea to realize her dream.

The fish were ready. Knot consumed his with some difficulty. Thea saved hers for him also. She preferred a raw one for herself. Knot marveled that such a perfect figure of a woman (from the knees up) could come from such inedible food—and knew he was being silly, since of course it *was* edible. It was merely that he retained so-called civilized restraints, while she had adapted nicely to her situation.

"Something you should know about me," Knot said reluctantly. "I'm a psi too. The nature of my psi is this: People forget me. If you leave me more than an hour, you will forget me. Hermine maintained mental contact with you while you fished, reminding you of me, so you would not forget I was here and fail to return. If you sleep, you will wake without remembering me. When we part company, you will forget we ever associated, unless special precautions are taken. So if you should conceive a baby—which is prohibitively unlikely, as far as my participation goes—you will not know how it happened."

"That's too bad; I'd like to remember you." She shrugged. She did that well, seeming to enjoy the heft of her own bosom out of water. She had more avoirdupois about her body than Finesse did; no doubt it protected Thea from the chill of the water. "But you are only passing, you say. A baby would be real."

He could not argue with that. They finished their meal. The fire died down. Knot found himself nodding again. It was now late at night, and he had had a most active day, and was tired. But a deal was a deal. "I think it's time," he said.

"Yes," she agreed, as if this were routine. But she looked just embarrassed enough to heighten her appeal.

"Do you—in the water?"

"I prefer it."

Because in water she was not clumsy or handicapped. It made sense. He would have preferred it on the ledge, but it really was not his choice. He got into the water.

She moved into his arms as he lay on a shallowly submerged ledge. She was lithe and soft and interesting, especially in the darkness of the water. He was cold, but she was warm, and the closer he got to her the more comfortable he was. He—

Finesse is sending, Hermine thought. Her impulse came

through with less force than usual, because she was a small distance removed from him. Do you wish to receive?

What a time! Yes.

"I am certain you have psi talent," Piebald said. "But now it seems you are not yourself aware of it. So we shall have to force it out. The trick will be to accomplish this without destroying your sanity."

This crazed lobo was going to torture a normal to force manifestation of a nonexistent talent? Why? If he wanted to eliminate a CC agent, all he had to do was lobotomize her anyway. Why try to evoke psi that was only going to be abolished?

"I have no psi!" Finesse exclaimed. "You can rape me, you can kill me, you can make me suffer, but you can't squeeze psi from a normal!"

Piebald smiled—and the irony was, it was not overtly sadistic. On a city street or in a mutant enclave he would have appeared quite innocent. "Relax, woman. I have ascertained that physical torture will not avail, and I fear my wife would object to my raping you, delightful as the experience might otherwise prove."

Piebald was married? Knot found this difficult to assimilate. A man that evil—

But the lobo was talking again. "No, Finesse. What we now have to do is establish an imperative for you to manifest your psi. It will be hard to evoke, after a lifetime's inactivity. So this will not be comfortable for either of us. But it shall be accomplished."

"What do you want with a psi?" she cried. "You're only going to lobotomize—"

Finesse had caught on—and her thoughts were parallel to Knot's own! She now knew what she was up against—and that might be the worst torture of all.

Piebald smiled enigmatically. The discolorations of his face and hair seemed to change with his facial expression: a sinister effect, this time. Perhaps Finesse's sending accentuated it; this was, really, her impression of the man, rather than the actuality. "All shall be known in due course."

The sending ended. "Are you well?" Thea inquired solicitously. "You're shivering. I can warm you—"

"I—received a message," Knot said.

213

"From your girl friend?"

He looked at her with alarm, seeing only the glint that the waning fire reflected from her eyes. "You're clairvoyant?"

She laughed against him. "Merely female. I know when another woman cuts in on me, and I guess she has first call. Shall we let it wait until morning?"

"Maybe that's best." He felt considerable relief at the postponement, and knew she was aware of that, and he was sorry. But she accepted it graciously, drawing him against her, keeping him warm, relaxng.

Knot felt there was more to be said, but he was so tired he fell asleep before he could organize his thoughts.

He woke disoriented, after a mélange of partial dreams. He was half in water, and it was dark, and there was a woman-body in his arms. What—oh. Thea, in the cave. Yes.

As he stirred, she woke too. And flipped out of his embrace and into deep water. "Who are you?" she demanded, frightened and angry. "How did you get in my home?"

She did not remember, of course. Knot was used to this. He drew on his expertise and experience in interviewing to reassure her and clarify their situation succinctly, and soon she was reassured and began to remember.

"It is strange," she said. "But it must be true, for I remember the telepathic weasel, and of course you were with her. It's coming back now. Odd how selectively I forgot."

"Your mind bridges and interpolates and rationalizes to cover the gaps," he explained. "But prompt reminders do serve to bring it back, and the fact that you were close to me diminishes the effect. My psi is strong but subtle; you don't feel it or perceive it. If you really want to remember me, write out a complete summary of the experiences we share, to remind you when I'm gone. Read it as soon as I depart, and keep rereading at brief intervals for several hours. That will fix it in your memory and then you will be able to retain it with only an occasional reminder, as with any other memory. I doubt it is worth your effort, though."

"I have no materials for writing," she said. "Except perhaps my coal-chalk, and the walls of the cave—which wouldn't be very good for that anyway. Anyway, we have no formal education here in the enclave; I know only a few words. I live for the present—and the future as represented by my offspring."

"I tried to explain last night—it is morning now?—that I cannot actually give you offspring. So—"

"How do you know—yes, it is morning, the cave remains dark all day—that you can't?"

"My friend the clairvoyant crab assures me—"

"But your friend the crab could tell me which man could—?"

Knot's mouth fell open. **Can he?** he asked Hermine.

Yes, she agreed, as surprised as he at the insight.

"Yes, Mit could do that. I never thought of it last night. I *can* help you—through my psi-friends. Of course there would be no way to make that man, er, if he did not feel inclined—"

"Just knowing would be enough. I could take it from there, one way or another. I have not had difficulty before, making men feel inclined; in fact, if I were not able to swim better than they—" She made one of her excellent shrugs. Knot could not see it, this time, but he heard the little slop-slop of the water as her anatomy struck it. "I'll be happy to show you the way to the ocean, for that information."

Knot was glad to agree. "We will find you that man!"

Thea became quite friendly, fetching them succulent water plants for breakfast and chatting merrily about her cave and water domain. She had a niche for wastes that Knot availed himself of, so as not to pollute the water. They did not relight the fire; it was pleasant talking in the dark.

Now they made plans for the journey. "It is no easy trip downstream, even for me," the mermaid warned. "The rapids are bad and at certain hours the piranha fish are foraging. You would not be able to pass, in the river. So we must schedule carefully."

"Mutant fish?" Knot asked. "Were they bred in space?"

"No, these are Earth-normal fish, imported from Earth as pets for the richer Machos. Someone must have thought it would be a good joke to stock them in the enclave river."

Knot remembered the outhouse perched above the enclave. The fish were merely another example of the Macho attitude. On two levels: Machos liked to prove how tough they were, by associating with vicious creatures, and they also were completely careless of the rights or convenience of the less fortunate elements of society— such as the mutants of the enclave. So they dumped bloodthirsty fish in the river and let the misfits worry about it.

"So we'll go around those sections of the river," Knot said. "Short hikes—"

"I cannot walk on land," Thea said. "I will swim through quickly during the piranha's quiescent hours. I have done it before. We can meet again, below."

"No. Unless it is a short swim, you will forget me, and we'll never rendezvous. I fear we might separate beyond Hermine's range, so she could not keep your memory current. Her sending range is very short."

Thea considered. "Maybe your crab could stay with me, to remind me. He is a water creature."

"He cannot communicate well enough with you, and he, too, could forget me. He does not like fresh water. He must be with me, to locate your crossfertile man from among the mutants of the land."

"You make appalling sense," she admitted. "Then I will simply have to come with you on land. Can you carry me?"

"For a short distance, probably. I'm not the sturdiest person on foot, because—" He paused, indicating his differently sized legs and feet. This was inadequate, since she could not see him in the darkness, but she seemed to understand. This was getting complicated! "How long a hike is it around the rapids and fish, do you judge?"

"It is hard to estimate land distances. I don't know the terrain away from the river's edge. Perhaps a day."

A day—just to pass a couple of troublesome sections of the river! Was he ever going to get out of here? But he seemed to have no choice. Had he only accepted Mit's advice, and waited that half hour for the lobo pursuit to abate . . . But what use were recriminations? "Let's get moving."

Knot had removed some of his sodden clothing the night before, and saw no reason to don it now, since he would be spending much of his time in the water. He thought of carrying it with him, but that seemed like more trouble than it was worth. Better to leave it here, and worry about what to wear outside once he *got* outside the enclave. He was no longer sensitive about being exposed before Thea; she had been up against him all night without evincing any distress. The only problem was how to carry Hermine and Mit.

Mit says we must cling to your hair, the weasel thought. That seemed sensible. Knot put them on his head.

He dived down and out and up, following Thea and Hermine's instructions. Knot's head broke water in the bright light of day. "Will it be all right for me to walk the shore, here?" he inquired. "I can make better time—"

"Yes," Thea said. "I see few brutes in this region, which is another reason I made my home here. Above is the many-armed croc, and below are the piranha, but here it is safe, unless the max-mutes come on a foray. But then you can jump into the water."

True, Hermine agreed.

It was good to get back on his feet, though the morning air was cool. Knot wondered now whether he should after all have brought his clothing along. Still, what warmth would soaking clothing have provided? He would have to generate some body heat by running, awkward as that was.

Trouble, Hermine warned. She was clinging to his hair as he bounced along. Mit, with both claws firmly anchored, was better off.

Knot looked about, stepping toward the water. "Where?"

The fish. The school has migrated upstream.

"Thea!" Knot called. "The piranha!"

"Don't be silly," she called back. "They never come up this far."

"Humor me. Get out of the water."

She shrugged, wriggled to the bank, and drew herself out to sit on the rocky ledge, her tailfeet remaining in the river. "If this is one of your crab's notions, I don't have much confidence in—"

Then she peered closely at the water. There was a stirring developing, not obvious, but definite. "He's right. Piranha! That's some crab!" She lifted her foot section out of the water with alacrity. "I've never seen them this far up, before. Something must have happened."

"Could be natural expansion, or better hunting upstream," Knot said. "This makes it more difficult. I can carry you initially, but—"

More trouble, Hermine thought. **Mutants coming, unfriendly.**

"Problems compounded," Knot said. "We can't stay here, and we can't reenter the water."

Mit says you can save us. Communicate with the gross one.

"I think we can manage," Knot said. "Be silent and I'll try." Thea's brow furrowed, so he reassured her. "I didn't mean you were talking too much; I just need to handle this myself, following Mit's instructions exactly. Trust us."

Already the mutants were arriving, clambering over the rocks and ledges. They were worse than Knot had seen before: Their limbs and features were extremely deformed, misplaced and misnumbered. One man scuttled like a huge crab, with five or six legs sprouting from odd points of his torso. Another had eyes down his neck— glassy, blinking things, several of which oozed discolored pus. A female had breasts like those of an animal, five sets, from chest to crotch, some larger than others. Another had two misshapen heads growing from a hump on her back. A man had a snout that twisted down like that of an anteater. But most of the deformities were straight mutilations: limbs severed partway down, eyeless sockets, teeth growing reversed to poke out of the jaw below.

They don't like you or Thea, Hermine thought. **You are both too normal. They intend to tear you apart.**

"Where is the gross one?" Knot asked desperately.

Behind. He hates you too.

That was all he needed! But Knot had to trust Mit's perception. Knot leaned down, put his arms under Thea's knees and shoulders, hefted her up and staggered toward the horde. "Growrrh!" he screamed, baring his teeth.

The bluff worked. Accustomed to all manner of freaks, both physical and psi, the mutants tended to back away from aggressive strangers. Their ranks parted as Knot charged on through—but in a moment the mutants closed in behind him. A double-elbowed male reached for Thea's tailfeet, drool dribbling from the sagging center of his mouth. It was unclear whether his appetite for food or for sex predominated.

Hermine: relay to him, Knot thought, and formed a stunning mind-detonation. The mutant fell away, and the others gave ground again, temporarily.

Now Knot spied the gross one. It was no false description: This mutant was large to the point of giantism, and grotesque to the point of revulsion. Its torso sagged between short, gnarled legs, and dragged behind a tail like a hernia. The body tapered upward as though deprived of much of its substance by gravity, until the upper arms seemed almost as massive as the body they anchored to. The head was little more than a knob, eyeless and earless and noseless, possessing only a large sloppy mouth and several crevices and protuberances that seemed to be a scandalized nature's wild guess at what the missing organs were supposed to resemble.

Like a lame dinosaur or a beheaded chicken, the gross one bumped along. From its maw blew out ludicrously inadequate squeaks and a few bubbles. It seemed to be aware of Knot—perhaps it had trace esp—and its formidable talon-hands reached out.

You may have to relay another nova, Knot thought nervously to Hermine.

Mit says no—its mind is toughened against psi. A nova would only make it angry. You must communicate directly, at least until it becomes more receptive to telepathy.

This thing could neither see nor hear—yet Knot had to get in touch! **Is it sapient?**

Yes. Smart and lonely and bitter—but a moderately nice person once its respect is won.

Nice person? This quality was hardly evident at the moment! Yet Mit must know.

Now they confronted each other. The other freaks formed a closed circle around them, as though this were an arena. They dared not snatch prey from the gross one, but would dive in should Knot try to escape. Knot was reminded of Hermine's encounter with the rats. Was there really much distinction between savage people and savage rats?

Knot set Thea on the ground carefully. His arms were tired already; she was not unduly heavy, but he was not geared to such a burden. He thought of the laser pistol, but had left that with his clothes. He had to handle this bare-handed. Mit was not offering advice; probably the ways of human combat were too foreign to the crab's experience for him to relate.

The gross one lunged. Knot stepped aside, letting the nearest arm shoot by him, clutching at nothing. It seemed the gross one simply snatched up its prey and ate it, kicking and screaming. Knot jumped in behind. He reached out to grab the thing's right arm from behind, twisting to immobilize the limb. But he did not apply pain pressure; instead he squeezed the flesh with his hand in a rhythmic series. It was one of the touch codes used to communicate with blind-deaf individuals; Knot had used it often in his business. In fact, he was privately proud of the fact that he could communicate with any educated mutant, once he found the particular mode that mutant knew.

TALK, Knot squeezed, with an accent of request, not threat.

The gross one started to fight him, wresting its arm forward with such power that Knot was jerked half off his feet. The watching freaks made exclamations of excitement. But then the gross one paused.

TALK, Knot resignaled. WE NEED YOUR HELP.

Amazed, the gross one tensed the muscles of that arm, in an almost forgotten cadence. YOU FRIEND?

Success! He had established communication, and that meant an agreement of some kind, almost certainly. Knot knew that lonely mutants would do almost anything for the sake of compatible company, to be able to hold meaningful dialogue with other parties. This was in large part responsible for his success as a placement officer; the communication-limited mutes could converse freely with him. It was a little like restoring sight to the blind, or hearing to the deaf.

But he had to answer honestly. NOT FRIEND YET. STRANGER. OFFER DEAL FOR HELP.

The gross one seemed doubtful. Perhaps it was weighing the value of the immediate meal in hand against the intangible satisfaction of communication. WHAT DEAL?

HELP US TRAVEL DOWNRIVER. WE WILL HELP YOU. TELL US HOW.

WHERE GO FINALLY?

WE GO OUTSIDE ENCLAVE.

I NOT GO, the gross one responded firmly.

To the watching freaks, this looked like a continuing struggle between them, with Knot clinging desperately to the powerful arm. They could not understand why it was taking the gross one so long to prevail.

What can we do for it? Knot demanded desperately of Hermine. He knew he had to win the favor of the creature now, or forever lose the chance. His life and Thea's hung in the balance, and suddenly his confidence was waning.

Carry a message, Hermine responded.

WE WILL CARRY A MESSAGE, Knot relayed. FROM YOU TO ONE OUTSIDE, WHEN WE ESCAPE HERE.

The gross one considered, seeming surprised. TO MY BROTHER, THE NORMAL.

AGREED, Knot squeezed with relief.

I HELP. ONE MOMENT. LET GO.

Knot released his communication hold. "It has agreed," he murmured to Thea. "It will help us." He still did not know the sex of the mutant, and doubted it retained any concept of sexual identity. There were, of course, sexless mutants, while others were grossly sexual in impractical ways. He was lucky this one remembered the squeeze code. Someone must have taught it as a child, before it was incarcerated here.

The gross one took a step forward. The half circle of mutants in that direction retreated a similar step. The gross one raised both arms high, then brought them down together as though throwing something violently to the ground. Its squeak-voice became a shrill scream.

The freaks scattered. They had been told to get out, and they obeyed with alacrity. No question who had power here!

221

See? No trouble at all, Hermine thought. **Mit knew it all the time.**

Yeah, sure. Had the communication ploy not worked, Knot could have been smashed against the rock wall, then eaten. **Next time kindly provide a little more advance detail.**

The gross one was waiting. Knot rejoined it and put his hand on its arm again. WE NEED THE WOMAN CARRIED DOWNSTREAM, PROTECTED. WHAT IS YOUR MESSAGE? WHO IS YOUR BROTHER? WHERE DOES HE—

The gross one shrugged him off without answering. It oriented on Thea. The arms descended.

Thea screamed and tried to wriggle away. "It's all right!" Knot cried. "It will carry you!"

The mermaid got a grip on herself and stayed still. The gross one's arms found their way under her, and picked her up as Knot had, but far more easily. The creature hoisted her to chest level and started walking.

Knot could only follow. Mit felt this was all right, so it probably was.

The gross one seemed indefatigable. It marched as long as the shore ledge held out, then halted. Knot touched it to pick up the muscle flexures. NOT KNOW WAY.

"Where do we go from here?" Knot asked Thea.

"Not into the water. We should be past the piranha, but the rapids are coming up. I could navigate them, but you could not. But I don't know the land route."

Does Mit know? Knot asked Hermine, who still perched on his head. It occurred to him now that the max-mutes had probably mistaken the weasel for part of him. A man with a furry bump on his head, and a couple of small green claws—why not?

Hermine was chuckling mentally as she answered, enjoying his conjecture. **Mit says there is a route, but it is difficult. We need more help.**

We'll have to take it. Where is the help?

Back the way we came.

Oh no! More time lost. Why hadn't the little crab made that plain before? But Knot knew why: There had been too many variables. Only now that the problem had simplified could Mit fix on a more tangible program. "We must backtrack a little, to pick up more help," Knot told Thea. And to the gross one he squeezed: BACK. WE SHALL FIND WAY.

The gross one did not object. He turned about ponderously, his squat legs slow but sure, and plodded back upstream.

One small problem, Hermine thought. **Mit says if we add another person to our party, one will soon die.**

Knot felt a sinking feeling. She thought of this as a "small" problem? **Who?**

Mit cannot tell. There will be a fight. Too many are involved. One will fall.

And if we don't add another to our party?

Mit says he can read that more easily. Three will die.

Three—of the four or five members of their present party. So there really was no choice. Knot decided not to mention this matter to Thea or the gross one. Knot would bear the burden alone, keeping the losses to a minimum.

But I know, and Mit knows, the weasel reminded him. **And Mit cannot foresee his own death.**

So if Knot and the two animals remained together, they all might be safe. That did not make him feel very much better. Was he condemning Thea to death? She was the most likely to take a fall, since she could not walk. If she got stranded on a high ledge—

In due course Mit signaled a turn-off. This led through a wilderness of sculptured rocks to a shack city, a settlement of mutants situated beneath a Macho-normal garbage dump. Apparently there was considerable food value in the organic refuse—enough to sustain this colony in what amounted to upper-class-enclave style. Practically all the shacks had metal roofs, fashioned from fragments of junked vehicles, and there was a fair amount of cloth in evidence. Knot was no longer appalled; obviously the mutants had to scramble for anything available.

However, these mutants, like the rest, were unfriendly. Either they did not know of the gross one, or had no respect for his combative prowess. A motley group of freaks charged out, bearing refuse weapons: pieces of pipe, tool handles, brick fragments, and buckets of urine. "Out! Out! Out!" their leader cried. He was a furry man with birdlike talons at his extremities and a nose overgrown with gristle, resembling a beak, and his voice was a squawk. These were coincidental mutilations, of course; true animal-people did not exist. It was just that, of the myriad deformities that occurred, some were bound to resemble natural attributes of animals. "No share! No share!"

The gross one could not hear, but was aware. It issued its squawk-scream.

The garbage salvagers did not heed the warning. They clustered around in a group, enclosing Knot's party, gesticulating threateningly.

The gross one lowered Thea to the ground. Knot rushed up and took her, supporting her so she could stand. **What do we do now?** he asked Hermine.

These mutes are not much trouble. Gross will handle it.

Freed of its burden, the gross one did indeed handle it. The arms shot out, half-formed fists striking mutants with a force that showed in the manner their bodies reacted. People were hurled violently to the ground or sent staggering outward from the center of the action. Weapons scored on the gross one; it made no apparent difference. In moments there was a ring of battered or unconscious people.

The gross one's eyeless face rotated to orient on Knot. Knot picked Thea up and passed her into the waiting arms, then queried with pressure: CAN YOU FIND FOOD FOR YOURSELF? I MUST SEARCH OUT ANOTHER ALLY, FOR WE HAVE WORSE OPPOSITION AHEAD.

EAT HERE, the gross one responded. It set Thea down again and grasped the foot of a feebly struggling mutant. The foot came up to the mouth. The teeth closed. The mutant screamed, then went limp. The gross one continued eating, unperturbed.

Knot suppressed whatever reactions threatened to erupt. Cannibalism was an accepted practice here; that had long since been evident. The villagers had attacked, bringing it on themselves. He, Knot, could not dictate the style of life the gross one pursued; he had made a deal for help, nothing else.

This was an excellent exercise in toleration. Nonetheless, Knot was eager to move on. **Is our new ally close?**

Very close. In that shack to the side, made from the car.

"Wait here," Knot told Thea. "I will fetch our ally from that dwelling." He pointed. And did not add: The ally that will guarantee that one of our number will die.

Dumbly, eyes fixed on the gross one, she nodded. She was, of course, safe here; no one would approach the gross one now with hostile intent. Also, she was dependent on the gross one for her present transportation. Like Knot, she had to accept the gross one for what it was.

Knot hurried to the car. **What is the name?**

Strella.

"Strella, come with us," he called, rapping on the cracked windshield.

A normal but drab older woman emerged. "Why should I go with you?"

"We are traveling out of the enclave. Help us and we will help you." Knot presumed that this approach would be effective, since it happened to be the truth and Mit had not advised otherwise.

Her eyes gleamed. "You will take me away from here?"

"Yes, if you want to go."

She stepped out. "Instantly."

Knot suffered another pang of guilt. He had to give some warning! "But the way is hard, and there will be danger. Some of us may die—are very likely to die—and there is no guarantee we will succeed in escaping."

"Of course."

It was almost too simple. "Just like that, you join us? Not even knowing us?"

"Obviously you know enough of me to seek me out. That is recommendation enough. I have been desperate to leave the enclave for some time, lacking only a party large enough for some hope of success. I would rather die than remain here—but I don't wish to die without trying."

"I feel the same," Knot said.

"Is that a weasel on your head?"

"And a hermit crab. Friends."

She shrugged and followed him back to the gross one.

"This is our new ally, Strella, who will come with us, knowing the risk," Knot said, introducing her. "This is

Thea, and that is the gross one." That seemed to be all that was necessary.

"How do you do," Strella said.

"Likewise, I'm sure," Thea said. The gross one merely went on eating; he had progressed to the meaty part of the thigh and evidently found it too delectable to set aside at the moment.

Knot looked at the available meat, then at some of the vegetable garbage the villagers ate. "I think I'd rather return to the river for raw fish."

But Mit's prescience made them take a path sloping up the side of the canyon, threading through needle's-eye constrictions and under overhanging escarpments. They saw the savage turbulence of the unnavigable rapids below. They passed another village, and were attacked—and Strella's mutancy became known: There was an explosion of putrefaction, a stench so awful it had them all gagging helplessly. But got them through without loss or injury.

Knot talked with her, after that, and Strella showed him a diamond she had recovered from garbage years before. She intended to deliver this to a normal friend. This was her motive for this dangerous trek.

They found some cooked fish and took it without compunction. Knot had very little sympathy for any group of people who attacked strangers without cause. Though he realized they probably had had cause, by their definitions: They didn't want an increase in village population, and had assumed that any new arrivals were moving in. How much mischief derived from careless assumptions!

Dubiously refreshed, they proceeded on down the path. Knot had hoped to return to the main river by dusk, but the path wound on into the tributary instead, crossing at a pleasant, deep, narrow pool that formed between ledge and main canyon wall. **Best place to rest,** Hermine advised.

Thea entered the water with a little cry of joy. "I know where this intersects the main stream!" she exclaimed. "From there it is clear except for the bind, and I can get around that." She looked about. "Getting the gross one through the bind may be tricky, though."

Thea found them a pleasant lodging almost underneath a fall of water. There was a reasonably wide series of ledges suitable for the gross one and Strella, while Knot took a half cave at the end, where a sideslip of water plunged into a frothing little pool. It was noisy but pleasant, for he was assured that hardly any person or creature of size enough to be dangerous could reach him here. Not without passing the gross one. Knot could sleep in confidence.

But as darkness became complete, he felt a touch on his ankle. Knot jumped; he hadn't thought about water creatures! There could be poisonous snakes—

Then Thea's voice came, softly, mostly muted by the water's roar. "Company?"

She had the water access, of course. Knot reached out, and she came into his embrace, as she had the prior night. He kissed her. Nature proceeded from there. Only after they had made love did he remember that Mit had precogged this. The little crab was off in a niche of the wall at the moment, but must be satisfied with his vindication now. One full day had passed since this prediction. Knot found this obliquely reassuring; at this stage he would hate to lose confidence in the crab's psi-powers.

In the night there was another transmission from Finesse. This one was a deliberate sending, organized and premeditated, and it was as if she were talking directly to him—or rather, to Hermine, as Knot himself was more difficult to remember.

"Hermine, I must believe you are safe, and can somehow bring help. If I don't believe that, I have no further reason for hanging on. I want to tell you exactly where I am, and how to reach me, and what the dangers are, though I suppose Mit can anticipate them better than I can.

"My captors are lobos—not the poor, confused, grief-stricken ones I interviewed, but callous ones created many years ago, who have learned to live with their deprivation and to compensate by developing extraordinary hate for CC. They have taken me to a villa in a mountain, an old volcano crater, and the building sits inside the north rim so that the sunlight strikes the solar collectors. It is a very nice spot, with cultured gardens in the main crater, almost impossible to approach except by air. So I am free to wander about the premises. They doctored my nose so that it is healing nicely, and they feed me well. I could get fat, if I weren't so concerned about my long-range situation. It is like a vacation resort, rather than a prison. I don't know the planetary coordinates, but Hermine, you can locate me mentally if you are receiving me at all.

"I am not alone here. There are several other prisoners, all psi-mutants. I dread to imagine what will happen to them. One is a little girl, ten Earth years old, physically normal, cute as a ladybug, named Klisty. She is a dowser, psionically sensitive to electrically conductive substances, like water and metals. Another is an old man known as NFG; I am not certain what the initials stand for, but gather they reflect his low opinion of himself. He is a marginal psi-illusionist; he can make objects appear where none exist. But his talent is erratic and the apparitions never achieve the verisimilitude of reality. He is basically a nice, harmless, slightly lecherous old dog; he made a pass at me and I put him off with a single half-sharp word. It was as though he simply wanted to be on record as able to make an approach; I doubt he really wanted to succeed. Then there's Lydia, grossly overweight; she can make a cup of water boil, but it takes her longer to do it psionically than it would the normal way, and the effort wears her out. So she is a psi-mute, technically, but she might as well be normal."

Her thought paused, as though Finesse were organizing herself for a new narrative thrust. Knot lay with Thea in his embrace, but it was Finesse who moved him. Ironic, he knew, since Finesse was the one he could not hold, literally or figuratively. Human passions were based on nonsense, yet they were compelling.

"I tend to forget that the vast majority of psi-mutants are partial or negative. For every first-class psi like you, Hermine, there are about ninety-nine lesser psis, and about half of them are so negative as to perish soon, and many of the rest are mental cripples." Finesse was now reviewing the underlying basis of psi-society, perhaps trying to grasp how she, a normal, related. "I am sure there must have been psis before space travel, that were not understood for what they were, and were incarcerated in mental hospitals as feebleminded, incompetent, or criminally insane. In fact, they even used a minor form of lobotomy on them, electroshock treatments, that stunned their psi for a time and made them seem normal. How can we of the present ever compensate or atone for the ignorant brutalities of the past! At least now we recognize the few successful psis, and use them productively.

"Still, it is instructive to restore perspective. There are ten or a dozen partial psis like Lydia for every one like you, Hermine—and a hundred or more normals like me. I have to remind myself how rare a thing a true psi is, like a diamond buried in trash, and what a terrible thing it is, what a crime it is to destroy such abilities, ever, for any reason at all. This lobo effort to eradicate psis must be stopped. It must be!"

Another pause. Knot fancied he could hear her breathing rapidly, tired from her exertion. Finesse really believed in what she was doing. Then: "I really must stop now. I have to get some sleep. I know Piebald's up to something nasty; he's just letting me be until he gets it organized. I really ought to throw myself in the pool and drown myself—but I lack the willpower as long as there is hope for escape, and anyway, they would haul me out long before I scored. I love you, Hermine, and I love Mit, and also what's his name. . . ."

The sending ended. Knot smiled with resignation. "What's his name" was not really a joke, in his case. Finesse remembered him, because of the clever manner in which she had played back her holo-recordings of their mutual experiences, but the memory was not as deep-seated as it would otherwise have been, and not as immediate. Probably she had been able to retain none of the Planet Macho experiences with him, but knew he had been summoned here, so could interpolate.

Meanwhile, she had correctly fathomed the nature of her captors, and had no illusions about Piebald's intentions. Knot, like Finesse, distrusted what was developing at the villa-prison. But he was selfishly glad, too, for this gave him time to reach her, and the longer she went without being hurt again, the better for them both.

Now he too had to sleep. He knew there would be savage trials ahead, for himself, his companions and for Finesse. They all needed their strength.

As Knot drifted off, experiencing more guilt for not

being able to love the woman he held or hold the woman he loved, or to impregnate the first or to rescue the second, he had one more distressing thought. It occurred to him that his party had been in one fracas, and no one had been lost. That meant the ax was still hanging.

One of them was destined to die—and he still did not know who.

CHAPTER 8

There was another village astride the path on the way down. It did not seem to be in a good position for either garbage collection or fishing, which meant food came from elsewhere. Perhaps from the bodies of slaughtered travelers?

Trouble, Hermine thought, in a warning that was all too frequent in this enclave. **These people have a psi-pain broadcaster, an unlobotomized criminal.**

Knot paused to acquaint his companions with this problem. "We have to pass through this village, and they will surely attack us with psi-pain," he explained aloud, also informing the gross one through squeeze talk. "We must endure the pain and press on, until we can nullify the psi. But it will not be pleasant, and we"—he paused, then made himself finish the thought—"we may lose one of our number."

"So what else is new?" Thea inquired. "We see death every day here, and we all know how mortal we are."

"I don't like being responsible for bringing it to innocent people," Knot said. He checked with Hermine. "Mit says the pain projector is a bedridden old man in a shack at the center of the village; we can eliminate him by shoving his whole house off the ledge into the river. The gross one has the strength; the question is, are we willing to take such an extreme measure?"

"No," Strella said. "Deliberate murder of a cripple like that, whose psi is like mine—no."

Thea agreed. "If we are careless killers like the others, why should any of us seek to leave the enclave? The death I see around me is not premeditated; it is natural violence that flares up like a fire. To plan murder coldly—no. There must be a better way."

No better way, Hermine assured Knot. **The villagers will kill whoever comes among them. They have no hesitation about murder.**

Knot relayed this news. "I can believe it," Strella said. "My own villagers were the same. But since we have to pass, we'll have to risk it. Perhaps my own psi will cancel out the pain-psi. Hold your noses!" And she walked boldly into the village.

She had chosen to sacrifice herself! Knot started after her, then realized that he could do nothing, and held back. If her psi worked, blocking the pain-psi, that would be the time to charge through—while the villagers who were closer to the smell-psi remained dazed. They might get out the other side without being caught. But right now, distance was best.

The hornet's nest stirred. Freakish mutants boiled out of the shacks. "Kill! Kill! Kill!" they shrieked, laying hands on Strella.

Her psi-stink exploded—but so did the pain broadcast of the village-psi. It was as though a giant had stepped on a crowd of people. Mutants fell writhing to the ground, twisted by the double barrage of psi.

Knot had assumed the villagers would be immune or acclimatized to their psi's power. Apparently not; they had to suffer its full force. In a moment the effect spread outward to intersect Knot and those with him. Stench and agony washed through them, surely milder than that in the center of the village, but still awful. Knot staggered, falling against the inner wall as he had before. The gross one seemed to withstand it better; Knot remembered he was resistive to psi. But Thea writhed right out of his grasp.

Knot retained enough control to catch hold of the mermaid and prevent her from rolling off the ledge. He was determined to foil her predicted demise if it were humanly possible. They collapsed together, sharing the agony, embracing in the passion of wretchedness, not delight.

Gradually the horror eased. But now the villagers were recovering too. They had been psi-pained before; they were not immune, but they did know the effect was temporary and did not represent any bodily damage. Knot climbed unsteadily to his feet, placing Thea carefully—but the villagers were simultaneously picking up the stricken Strella.

They tore brutally at her body. Seeing that she was not young and delectable, they lifted her high and heaved her over the ledge. "No!" Knot cried, knowing it was already too late, that the prediction had been fulfilled. The sacrifice had been designated, inevitable. He felt, along with his horror, a certain obscene relief.

In a moment he recognized the emotion. A flare of purest rage shot through him. He had failed Thea, and now he had failed Strella, at the cost of her life—because of the thoughtless animosity of these freaks. Perhaps because he himself had wanted her to be the victim, instead of Thea. He had saved Thea—and in that delay, the freaks had gotten to Strella.

Hermine was right: These savage villagers had to be destroyed. If Knot went down with them, maybe that was only fair.

Knot charged forward, heedless of Thea's cry of protest. The villagers were just turning back from the ledge. He rammed the nearest, a stork-legged, potbellied man, and shouldered him over.

Then the psi-pain hit Knot again. But such was Knot's internal psychological pain and self-loathing that it overrode the seemingly physical induced pain he experienced. He screamed a scream of purest abandoned savagery as he jumped at the next mutant—a woman with a body segmented like that of a vertical caterpillar. She had a weapon, a length of metal, sharpened into a blade on one side. Knot grabbed that pseudosword, wrenched it from her grasp, and hurled her sidewise over the ledge. "Die—all of you!" he bawled, converting his internal pain to ferocious action. He swung the sword at the next, lopping off an appendage of some sort.

The villagers rallied. Pain and suffering and hate had

been their lot in life, and they were not to be put off by a lone berserker. More weapons flashed, and here the ledge was wide enough to permit them to encircle him.

Knot fought ferociously. If he died, he deserved it! He would take them with him! But already he felt his fury ebbing, and knew that he would soon be overwhelmed. He was not really a physical fighter. He had learned a lot from CC's expert, but there were limits to what one man could do in a crowd, where there were no civilized conventions or restraints. He was an animal being matched by animals. The villagers pressed in, blocking off his weapon, restricting his options.

A crude club smashed the sword from his hand. Knot stood for a moment, dazed by the purely physical shock and the fatigue he felt. Strenuous action like this, coming after the hike on the steep path, could make a person tire readily. With a cry of glee, a villager leaped on him.

And Knot responded by ducking down, catching the mutant about the waist, whirling and heaving. This was weaponless combat, different from what he had been doing before. The element of surprise had restored an option to him. The creature went sailing over the ledge almost before Knot knew what he was doing. He had simply reacted—and done it effectively.

But already another was on him, grabbing him from behind. Knot rammed his large right elbow back, striking a soft gut, then pitched forward. The villager was hauled across Knot's back and over the ledge.

Yet another was on him, not striking or grabbing but just trying to block him in place from the front so that the others could have a pinned target. Knot dropped to the ground, put up his big right leg, jammed his foot into the man's stomach, hauled down on his arms, and shoved and heaved him up. It was the stomach throw, and it hurled the mutant out over the ledge to join his comrades.

But now Knot was on the ground. The villagers pounced in a mass—

There was a scream. A shack was toppling over the edge.

The villagers paused to stare in fascination and horror. Then, as the small building fell, Knot saw the gross one, standing braced against the wall. It had heaved the pain-psi mutant over!

Now the gross one waded into the fray, secure from the annoyance of pain. It hurled villagers left and right, to smash into the back wall or off the ledge. Knot scrambled to his feet and got out of the way.

When it was over, the village was empty. They had, after all, followed Mit's advice. Perhaps it had been precognition, not recommendation.

"I was fighting despite the pain," Knot said, remembering. It was easier for the moment to set aside the major questions in favor of the minor one. "How could I do that?"

"You are a feeling man," Thea responded. She was lying leaning against the wall, bruised and disarrayed but unhurt. "You reacted to their brutality when they killed our companion. You went berserk. That blotted out the pain, enough to let you function."

"How can you know this?" he asked, disturbed.

"Hermine broadcast your feeling to the gross one and me, freeing us also. The gross one is starting to receive her now. It—he—may I call the gross one male? —he went on to dump the hut of the psi-pain mutant. I could not help—but at least I understood. It had to be done."

She was a very understanding woman, Knot realized. He was sorry again that he was unable to impregnate her himself; she would surely make a good mother.

Then he put his hand to his head. The weasel and crab were gone. Oh no—during that fight, when he was hurling mutants over his head—had he somehow—? **Hermine! Mit!** he thought, alarmed. **Where are you?**

We are safe, Hermine's thought came immediately. **We decided to move to safer premises during the violence. Mit knew the way.**

Now he saw them, perched on an overturned bucket. Yes, Mit would know the way! **Thank you for your help,** he thought sincerely. **Had you not freed the gross one—**

He was free; he just needed direction. He has come to know us, so his mind is now receptive. We work well together, the weasel added, pleased.

Yes—they were an excellent team, even when the

job was mayhem. Now they had wiped out an entire little colony of mutants—just to get past. Could it be worth it? In what way could Knot consider himself to be morally superior to those freaks he had slain?

This was a kind of hell, Knot realized. He felt battered outside and inside, and deeply unclean. Mutilation—was it more of an outer or an inner condition? But he knew the full shock of it had not hit him yet. It would take time to work its way to the surface and out, like a bad bruise, hurting all the way.

They continued. The path slanted fairly directly on down to the river. They followed it, then backtracked to the spot immediately below the village.

The carnage was there. The slope diminished near the shore, in this section, so that most of the bodies lay clear of the water. Some might have splashed into the river directly, and it was possible that these survived. If they had not, they had been carried away already in the current.

In any event, the water was clear. Some of those on the slope were not quite dead yet; Knot knew the kindest thing to do at this point was to kill them quickly and cleanly. But his brief battle-rage was over; he could not do it. He was sickened by it all, hurting inside in a new yet related way, hating himself for what he had done. He thought again of the mutilation, so clearly apparent here. What had anyone done to the lobos or the mutants, worse than his recent rampage? Now he faced the consequence, flinching, lacking the courage to finish what he had started.

The gross one made its way through the human refuse. It selected the best body for consumption, then methodically heaved the others into the river. Thus the problem of the mutilated living had been solved. In moments they would drown and be out of their misery.

"I should have done that," Knot said. "I am responsible."

"For the way the villagers attacked us? No," Thea argued. "Had they simply let us pass—"

"It's their nature to be suspicious of strangers. It's a survival trait."

She looked meaningfully at the floating bodies. "Not today."

"There must have been some way—"

"Your animal friends said no. We had either to give up our quest—or fight. We fought. We won."

He shook his head as if to clear it of foul substance, but the foulness remained. "There has to be a better way than this!"

"Only by abolishing the enclave," she said. "And what would the mutants do in mainstream society? What would *I* do? There must be enclaves."

"Then we must abolish the mutants themselves!" he exclaimed. "Arrange it so that no deformed person will ever be born again. Then there will be no need for enclaves." He had been over this argument before, in other circumstances, but never resolved it. For the obvious rejoinder—

"And no interstellar travel, no galactic colonization, no unified human civilization," Thea said. "I remember that much from the limited schooling I had before I came here. Without mutancy, *I* would not exist, *you* would not exist."

She, confined here for life, yet argued the case of the greater civilization beyond, which she could never experience, never share. "Yes, we would exist," he said. "We would be normals!"

To that she had no answer. He knew she was only trying to distract him, to soften the impact of his self-incrimination, but he could not thank her for that. Perhaps, he realized, he wanted to suffer, since there seemed to be no other punishment for his crimes.

We must save the diamond, Hermine thought, communicating only now that his own thoughts had run their course.

The diamond! That remains?

Yes. Mit says it is in the water, deep.

How could it fall and not shatter?

Strella shielded it with her body as she fell. She wanted it to be preserved for her friend.

"Thea, the diamond is in the river," Knot said. "Hermine will tell you where it is, if you will—"

"Diamond!" she exclaimed, and Knot remembered that he had not informed her of its existence. But evidently Hermine was doing that now. "Yes, of course." Thea slipped into the water and plunged down.

In a moment she returned, holding it. "I like your psi-animals," she said. "They know exactly where to go. By myself I could never have found it; this way it was easy."

"You realize we shall not be keeping it," Knot warned. "It must be delivered. She sacrificed her life with the understanding—"

Thea hefted herself up to sit beside him. "Have I kissed you before? I don't remember."

"More than that," Knot said. "Last night—"

"I'm glad." She kissed him again. "I know you're feeling very unclean right now. That's because you haven't lived here very long. You retain that spark of human decency. That is a greater treasure than any diamond."

Knot found himself flattered, and felt guilty even for that. "Nevertheless, the diamond will be delivered. If it is humanly possible."

"Of course it will be delivered. It is worthless in the enclave anyway. How could I trust you to keep faith with me, if you did not keep faith with Strella? And the gross one's message, too."

Ah yes, the message. Knot joined the gross one and squeezed: WILL YOU GIVE ME THE MESSAGE NOW? IT SHOULD BE KNOWN TO US ALL, IN CASE ONLY ONE ESCAPES.

SOON, the gross one replied, and continued eating.

First things first, Hermine thought.

Knot returned to Thea and looked at the diamond. It was not large as throwing stones went, but seemed big enough for what it was. How was he to carry it safely without losing it? He had no clothing now, no pockets, and though it had little value here in the enclave, he did not want to advertise its presence. Finally he put it in his mouth, tucking it into a cheek; he would have to remember not to swallow it.

When they had cleaned up what remained of the mess, setting the fragments of the pain-psi's shack neatly on the bank, they proceeded downstream again. But this day was done. They located a place to stay safely, and they retired early.

Thea moved into his arms again, and he took her with a savage kind of desperation that made splashes in the water. It wasn't sex he needed, so much as her implicit reassurance of his worth, and she was surely aware of that. She was in her way as nice a girl as he had known, and once again he was sorry for what he could not do for her.

And in the night he dreamed of Finesse, and knew it was no dream. Hermine was transmitting the next message, as he had asked her to.

"Hello again, Hermine. Sometimes I can almost believe I receive your response, but I'm sure that's wishful thinking. I had another nice, relaxed day, but somehow I was bothered by irrational thoughts of violence and death. I am getting paranoid, of course, anticipating Piebald's machinations—which is probably exactly what he wants. Yet what can I do? If I had any paranormal power, I would surely use it to escape this trap. But I am hopelessly normal, and in this case that spells my doom. Perhaps I should be minimally thankful that the lobo effort is being diverted this way; at least it may spare some other party similar grief.

"Little Klisty pulled a cute little-girl stunt today. She walked out on the pool's diving board in dress clothing as if somnambulant, hands outstretched before her, fingers vibrating. 'I detect water!' she exclaimed. 'That way!' And she pointed into the sky—and fell off the board to land in the pool with a great splash. Fat Lydia was sunning herself at the pool's edge eating crackers, and she and the food got soaked; she was furious, while old NFG laughed his head off. He conjured a poor image of a jackass laughing. It was obviously intentional mischief on Klisty's part, and finally we all were laughing. That was the only time I felt relief from tension. I bless this child for it, foolish as her prank was."

Finesse projected the image of a girl climbing out of a pool, her fancy dress plastered to her thin body, honey-colored hair matted across her face so that two brown eyes gleamed from between strands. She was indeed a cute child, Knot thought. But her psi talent was not remarkable. Why did Piebald want her? He could not plan to torture *her* to reveal her supposed psi, since it was already known. The same went for the other two prisoners there. If Piebald was planning to lobotomize them, why didn't he simply get on with it? Knot, like Finesse, feared the answer would not be pleasant.

"Otherwise, only the underlying tension prevented this day from being dull," Finesse continued. "Piebald has not shown his mottled face. Perhaps what he said is true: He really is married, and goes home to his family when not occupied in brutality. I wonder how he treats his wife? Is she a lobo too? Does she approve of his activities? Why should I even care? Obviously she does nothing to inhibit them, if she exists at all. If I were married, I would certainly see that my husband—oh, that bothers me for some reason, I don't know why, and anyway it's irrelevant."

So her memory of her husband had indeed been erased, as Hermine had thought. CC had acted with inhuman logic to prevent any complications rising from that information. Only a peripheral concern remained, leaving her confused. Knot knew he would have to tell her, when he rescued her—and that telling would probably restore her full experience, and her love for that other man. But it had to be done. Knot would lie in some circumstances, but not in that one. *Damn* CC for sending him a married woman!

"The automatic facilities provide for our gustatory and sanitary needs, but there is no formal entertainment. All we can do is eat, sleep, swim and talk. There are no books, no holo-films, no travel tours. I am learning the life histories of my companions, and providing them with my own, though there seem to be some years in my life I cannot account for. Maybe I was on a secret CC mission, and it was blanked out, though I'm not satisfied that was it. The lobos know I am a CC agent, so I need to maintain no secrecy about that. My chief novelty seems to be the fact that I am normal. The others are perplexed that I should be here, and sympathetic. They know they will be lobotomized; they expect me to be tortured before being lobotomized too. I fear they are correct. I only wish that whatever is scheduled to happen would hurry up and happen; the more time that passes, the better I get to know and like my companions, and the more their fate will hurt me when it comes."

And that, Knot realized, was the answer to one riddle. Piebald was delaying his assorted tortures so as to enable the victims to get to know each other well; then he could use each one as leverage against the others. Finesse just might be tortured by being forced to betray her new friends.

"I hope you are well, Hermine. I think that's the one thing the lobos *don't* know about: you and Mit. I am conditioned not to reveal your nature, and I doubt the lobos have any telepath to extract it from my mind. I hope what's his name made it back to your suitcase—I know I sent *someone*, and he must have been the one, otherwise I would remember—and freed you before he got into trouble. Mit predicted he would make it, but wasn't sure what would happen thereafter, so doubts persist.

"In fact, the man seems to have a predilection for getting into complex situations that Mit cannot analyze ahead. That of course is one reason CC selected him; enemy precogs would have the same problem with him. In fact, CC did run some distance precog checks on him, and they came out hopelessy fuzzy. So I'm sorry Mit could not foresee what would happen after what's his name opened the suitcase, but I know you two are resourceful. Keep yourselves safe, and if you can't reach me, try to reach another CC agent who is visiting this planet. In fact, if you are receiving this, don't bother to come to me, after all; you now have enough information to enable CC to act. Leave the planet, sneak into a spaceship if you have to, get to a CC access terminal and tell CC to crack down on the lobos instantly. That will stop the illicit lobotomies. I'm aware I'm a hostage; I will be killed the moment CC forces approach this hideout. But this is a necessary sacrifice for the cause. My fate is sealed regardless. Somehow we must get word out what the lobos are doing. Good night."

The sending ended that suddenly. She must have gotten tired. What a brave and good woman she was! She, like Strella, was willing to sacrifice herself for the sake of her mission. But he, Knot, was made of different stuff. *He* would not sacrifice her for the mission! He would rescue her! She had already armed him with good information about her whereabouts and situation. Even if her nightly news bulletins stopped, they would be able to locate the volcano and villa, thanks to Mit's clairvoyance.

Knot permitted himself to sleep, bathed in his love for her. It was not that there was anything wrong with the mermaid in his arms; it was just that Finesse—well, she was the one. He would see that her courage was rewarded. Somehow. Even if it meant restoring her to the man she really loved, her husband.

He, Knot, could do worse than returning here to the enclave river to be with Thea. He would be safe from the lobos here; they were too much like normals to risk themselves in the enclave. Yet he knew this was no adequate answer; the isolation from civilization would grind him down, and the constant brutality of this environment. And—he could not give Thea what she required. Only the man Mit would locate could do that. So Knot had to give her up to another man, too. And, Knot knew with sudden conviction, that he would. That would be his private personal vindication—that he did, in the end, what was right.

He felt happier with himself than he had before. His self-loathing was lifting. All the lies and killings along the way were leading to at least a small measure of good.

In the morning he went through the required introductions and explanations, and the memories of him came back. Since Thea and the gross one remembered each other, and Thea had been in contact with Knot all night and the gross one seemed to be partially resistant to psi, they both recovered fairly readily.

They continued down the river. Only the bind blocked them from the ocean. They arrived at it near midday.

The bind was impressive. The walls of the canyon were fashioned of some harder, more durable rock here, which the moving water could hardly wear down. They closed in, asserting their dominance, looming above, finally forming a natural bridge. This bridge thickened until it became a full dam that blocked off the river entirely. Yet the water did not overflow; it formed into a deep pool in which a whirlpool gyrated.

"Not safe to pass through that," Thea advised them, looking toward the vortex. "It is a virginally tight aperture, with a lot of water pressure. Any living thing of our size would be crushed. There are some cavern passages that get through—but unless you can swim as well as I can—"

"What alternatives do we have?" Knot asked, staring up at the looming rock face. Sunlight cut across it, making stark shadows that became more extensive below, until at water level all was shadowed. He felt slightly claustrophobic. If the base was this dark at midday, what was it like at any other time?

"There are other caverns above the water level—but the rat folk live there. I never had to deal with them. You know how mutants are about strangers."

Knot had recently learned, certainly. His prior experience in Enclave MM58 had hardly prepared him for this one in TZ9. MM58 had been min-mute; this was max-mute. The difference was far greater than the superficial classifications. That had been basically compatible and happy; this was isolated and savage.

Yet they had to pass the bind. "We'll risk the rat folk."

Mit advised them of a suitable ascent to the upper passages. It was amazing how the way developed from seeming blankness under the crab's guidance. Knot had tended to forget that Mit, like Hermine, was a psi of the first rank, but it really showed here.

They achieved an opening in the sidewall that was large enough for them to walk through upright. The gross one carried Thea again. She had proved fairly adept at wriggling up the ledges; it was, she explained breathlessly, a bit like swimming. She was not helpless on land, merely crippled.

Mit directed them along those channels that would enable them to avoid contact with the rat folk for the longest time. But inevitably they came to a pass where contact occurred.

Fire, Hermine thought. **Mit says they don't like fire. We must make some and carry it.**

Knot no longer questioned the little crab's pronouncements. "Fire? Show us how."

Mit showed them where spark-striking stones were, and dried moss, and old fallen stalks carried in by the rat folk and discarded. It seemed the rats wended their way to the surface periodically to harvest green plants, lest they come down with scurvy from too restricted a diet, and threw away the stems. These made passable torches.

"The surface?" Thea inquired. "Could you escape the enclave here?"

It was not to be. There were terraces and slopes within the chasm, and these were the ones the rat folk reached. They had no passage to the exterior world of Macho.

When the party encountered the rat folk, Knot and Thea were armed with fire. The eyes of the rats glinted reflectively as they backed off and skulked away, not caring to approach yet feeling the compulsion to protect their environs from intrusion. They closed in behind, noses quivering, arms reaching to the floor, squeaking. They were not extreme mutants; rather they were deformed in limbs and torso, so that normal vertical posture was not satisfactory to them. Some were more distorted than others, but their hunched attitude and slinking manner put a common stamp on them. The gross one, but for its magnitude and boldness, might have fitted well into these caverns.

All went well until the party encountered a water passage. Mit indicated that they had to pass through it—and that there were more rat folk on the other side.

"But we have to dive under—and that will douse our torches!" Thea protested.

What do we do now? Knot asked Hermine. The rats were getting bolder; they were not actually terrified of fire, they merely detested it.

Mental fire, the weasel replied, surprised. **Mit says you must broadcast—**

Right. Knot explained the need briefly to Thea and the gross one. All three set about imagining raging flames. Holding that image in their minds, they dived into the water and swam through the nether passage. The gross one could swim, clumsily, and that was all that was necessary for this brief section. Thea now reversed their roles by helping the gross one along, for of course this swim was simple for her. They emerged on the other side, in a new cavern—and the mental fires Hermine relayed to the rats sent them scurrying.

It was that easy. Knot had privately feared a very difficult transit, but that never developed. They proceeded unhampered to the exit below the bind, and tediously scaled the ledges down to the water. The final section they did the easy way: jumping into the water. The height was daunting, but Mit assured them that all of them would survive unhurt, so long as they followed the instructions on positioning that Hermine relayed. They believed—and it was so.

Thea went first, having most confidence about water. She balanced herself precariously upright on the ledge, then flexed her knees and jumped into a lovely arching forward dive. Knot knew he would never forget her smile of rapture as she floated toward the water. She was doing something only normals could do, this one time in her life, and she gloried in it. Then she splashed down, fairly cleanly; her tail slapped the surface. In a moment she reappeared from the turbulence and waved.

Then the gross one. For this trip, Hermine and Mit elected to go with him, not with Knot. They clung to his head as he made a running leap off the ledge and dropped into a champion belly-flop. It must have stung terribly, but the wide mouth emerged from the froth grinning. He too had accomplished something unique.

Finally Knot himself went. **Can I do a cannonball?** he thought hopefully. Hermine gave him leave, and he ran, sprang and curled himself into the ball, letting the canyon spin around him as the world had done in Finesse's dream of love. That was a delightful simile! Then the smash of the water, ending the dream, and the struggle to orient and reach the surface and snort the liquid out of his nostrils.

"You know, I'll bet you have two of the finest psis in the galaxy, there," Thea remarked as they collected on the shore. "Each has a double talent: thought reception and thought broadcast for the weasel, clairvoyance and precognition for the crab. And your own psi is an insidious, amazing thing—and in fact you too are a double mutant, counting your physical side. Strange that, from what you say, you three should have been assigned to work with a normal."

"She's a very skilled, competent and nice normal," Knot said. "I love her."

Thea laughed. "I could love you, if I could remember you! But I wonder—you told me the woman is being tortured because the lobos believe she has a psi talent. Is it possible they are right? It would make sense for CC to send a secret psi on a mission like yours."

It would indeed! So much would become explicable, if Finesse were actually psi. **Are the lobos right?** Knot asked Hermine.

Mit says no, the weasel thought.

The bubble of speculation burst. "Our clairvoyant says no," Knot repeated. "At this stage I find it very hard to believe that he could be wrong. He either knows something or he doesn't know it, but he is never wrong when he does know it. If you see what I mean. Mit has known Finesse longer than I have."

"So they really are torturing her for nothing," Thea said. "They can't be very smart. Maybe the lobotomy distorts their thinking."

"I understand lobotomy is pretty refined, now," Knot said. "It eliminates only the psi-talent and the memories immediately associated with the lobotomy itself, and leaves the rational powers intact. There is a period of a month or so of confusion, then that clears up. Clearly the lobos are well organized and represent an effective force, so there is a real chance they can bring down CC."

"But they're still trying to squeeze psi out of a normal," she said. "Normals wouldn't do that, would they? Well, let's get on with the rescue." The gross one had now climbed out of the water, having had to locate a place with a navigable slope.

Progress was rapid now, because the canyon broadened, and some shoreline was present most of the way. By nightfall Thea was able to announce that one more day's arrival would bring them to the ocean.

"Which is where we part company," she said. "I really can't handle seawater. It stings my eyes."

"But I still haven't found you your man!" Knot protested.

"There's a good-sized enclave development at the estuary," she said. "Somewhere in there must be my man." But she did not sound supremely confident.

"I shall not go until we find him for you," Knot said with conviction.

"Meanwhile, I will accept a substitute," she said. "I don't remember what happened upstream, but I suspect you have a way with women."

"I do," Knot agree. "I did with you twice."

"Can you make me remember it this time?"

Knot had gone over this question many times with the people with whom he associated, since they seldom remembered his answer. "You need someone to remind you of me just after I leave. To shore up the memories as they are fading, and transfer them to permanent memory. My psi interferes with that transfer from temporary to permanent, in some fashion." He had suggested, before, that she write it down, but she was largely illiterate and lacked the facilities. "If Strella had lived, she might have written notes." He shrugged. "Thea, I don't think it's worth your effort. Once we find your man, you'll have no need of any memories of me."

"I want those memories!" she insisted, clouding up.

I could remind her, Hermine offered. She was back in Knot's hair, now that he was no longer cannonballing into the water, and Mit was with her.

"Hermine will remind you telepathically," Knot said. "That won't be perfect, because her sending range is limited, but it will help if you work at it. You will have to concentrate on her very hard, after we separate, to pick up her thoughts as we draw farther apart."

"Does the crab say that will work?" Thea asked. Then she smiled. "Yes, Hermine tells me he says it will. Oh, thank you!" The mermaid clasped him with vigor and led him into one of the more delightful experiences of his recent life. Her feet might be fused together, but she could do a lot with her separated thighs when she wanted to.

There was another transmission from Finesse in the night, a brief one. "Hermine, I think the picnic is over. There is a changed mood here. I think I know how it must have been in the death camps of history, when mass executions were coming up. Tomorrow—I am afraid. Something awful is going to happen."

Knot suffered an ugly chill. **Hermine, do you think she's right?**

Yes, the weasel responded tightly. **We cannot get there in time.**

I should have been traveling by night, instead of dallying with the mermaid? he thought with savage reproach.

No. Thea is part of our escape. We must do right by her.

That doesn't sound like weasel ethics.

I am learning from you, complicated man. But Mit agrees. He says she will yet help us greatly.

So it was practical as well as ethical. That was comforting. Knot lifted a hand to stroke the cool, wet, sleekly full breast of the sleeping mermaid. Yes—it was necessary to do right by this fine woman. They had shared an evening that was well worth remembering, and that memory was part of what he owed her.

That reminded him. **The gross one—he never told me his message. When I asked, he just answered, "Soon."**

He will tell you tomorrow, Mit says. Now squeeze your woman some more, while you have opportunity.

With these reassurances, Knot pressed himself against Thea's fine warm bosom, and slept.

They moved well again, in the morning, after introductions—until Finesse cut in with an anguished transmission. **It's Lydia! They're going to do something to Lydia!**

Lydia—the fat woman who could boil water slowly. Knot did not care about her so much as about Finesse's distress. "Thea," he said to the mermaid swimming nearby, "Hermine is relaying information to me, and I must receive. Fish me out of the river if I fall in." He was serious; he wanted to keep moving, but could not spare much attention for his personal activity at the moment.

Then Finesse came through again, compellingly. **Piebald has locked her in a cage with a tigodile!**

Now the full scene came, as it had when Knot had merged minds with Hermine to fight the rats. He was looking through Finesse's horrified eyes at an arena in which a double cage about twelve meters in diameter sat. In one section was the frightened fat woman; in the other, the tigodile. This was one of a number of semimutant species developed in recent generations, not true cross-breeds between diverse species, but suggestive of it. The tigodile's front portion resembled a huge cat, and the rear was like that of a crocodile. It looked deadly and ravenous, and this was surely an accurate impression. It pawed at the bars that separated them, salivating copiously.

Piebald spoke. Knot saw him as Finesse's eyes oriented involuntarily on him. He was actually a min-mute, physically, with the splotches of discolor on his hair and skin. Knot wondered what his psi-power had been before it was taken from him.

"Now the rules of this little exercise are marvelously simple. The intent is to evoke the psi-power within you. You have the ringside seat, here, Finesse, and shall not be permitted to leave before the dénouement. Very shortly I shall arrange to have the barrier between the party of the first part, the mutant Lydia, and the party of the second part, the tigodile, removed. The fat will encounter hunger, and there will follow what will follow. I dare say the two parties will quickly become one. Only you can avert the otherwise inevitable—by acting psionically to alleviate the maiden's likely distress at the dénouement. I dare say you could stun the animal with a mental blast, or kill it by telekinetically disrupting the action of its heart, or use clairvoyance to fathom the combination of the lock to the gate, so that the maiden might open it to escape. There are a multitude of things you might do—and I hope you will do one of them soon, because otherwise the lady could suffer a certain inconvenience."

"I have no psi!" Finesse cried. "This is impossible!"

Piebald shook his head sagely. "I certainly hope you are wrong. The lady in the cage really is innocent of any wrongdoing, apart perhaps from overeating, and her psi-talent is meager. It would be a shame to see her become the overeaten."

"What do you want?" Finesse screamed, her voice breaking.

"I want your psi," Piebald replied calmly.

"Then put *me* in the cage!"

"I think not. You might suffer grievously."

"*I* might suffer! What about Lydia?"

"She is not a CC agent. Her psi is known. She is value-less to us. You, on the other hand, surely have a psi-talent of the first magnitude. One readily capable of dealing with a simple situation like this."

"If I had, I would use it on you!"

"That is a risk I take. My employment is regarded as hazardous because of it. Of course, my demise would trigger the release of stun gas throughout this villa, and an alarm would summon others to collect the bodies. But don't let that deter you, my dear; I want you to manifest your talent, believe me."

Finesse looked at him stonily. What argument could prevail against insanity?

"Shall we now proceed?" Piebald asked softly. He lifted his mottled hand.

The barred gate that separated monster from maiden elevated slowly. The tigodile was instantly aware of the motion. It flung itself against the bars, trying to push on through. Lydia screamed.

"Stop it!" Finesse cried. "This is barbaric!"

"No, my dear. Necessary. *You* must stop it."

The bars cleared the cage. The tigodile paused a moment, hardly believing its fortune, then bounded into the opposite cage. Its armored tail struck the bars in passing, making them clang. Lydia screamed again.

Finesse leaped from her seat, trying to get to the cage —and banged into a glass barrier, invisible until now. Bruised, she settled back; she was blocked from participating.

There was no subtlety about the tigodile's approach. It simply pounced and chomped. Lydia screamed again, this time in agony, but Finesse could not hear her over her own scream.

Finesse tried to turn her face away, but knew this would not stop it. Yet to look was worse. She did look— and saw the blood, as the beast chewed into Lydia's neck, opening the jugular vein and carotid arteries, releasing the body's internal pressure. Then Finesse's head cracked into the glass, and she realized she was fainting.

Knot came out of it, dazed. The lobos had deliberately sacrificed a woman, to put pressure on Finesse. To make her show a psi-talent she lacked. It was horrible—yet perhaps true to the nature of the lobos. Obviously lobotomy *did* affect a person's judgment!

What would they do when they discovered that Finesse really *was* normal? How hard would they squeeze the stone? How many maidens would have to be fed to monsters before the lobos gave up the futile effort?

"I can tell it was bad," Thea murmured.

"They are torturing and killing her friends, to coerce her into the impossible," Knot said. "They gave her time and opportunity to develop attachments in the villa, and now they are using those attachments as leverage against her. It—it's like our battle with the villagers yesterday. Needless, pointless mayhem, useless killing. Eventually they'll do the same to her. I've got to get there first."

"Do you think they are doing this to make you come to her?" Thea asked. "To lure you into their trap? She is not psi, but you are."

"*I'm* the psi they are trying to evoke!" he exclaimed. "Yes, it's quite possible. I did escape their clutches before, and they chased me right into the enclave, using written notes, so they certainly know of me and remember my exploits. After the damage I did to their solar power station, and the way I got through their seemingly tight search-net, they must be very angry. They have to realize that telepathy, clairvoyance and precognition were involved, but they don't know about the animals with me. So they must assume that all those psi-talents are mine. Their original questioning of me did not reveal that, but they would know that some of my powers could have been suppressed until I really needed them. Oh yes —they must want me extremely badly. Since they didn't dare pursue me into the enclave, lest the freaks take them for normals and tear them to pieces, they were balked. So they would naturally try to lure me to them instead, assuming there is any way to escape the enclave."

"Multiple psi-mutants are very rare, aren't they?" Thea asked. "Maybe they think you have others with you—other men who are hidden, who watched you, and helped you escape the power station, and might also help you escape the enclave. So they would be very careful about how they tackle you the next time."

"Could be." But as he said it, doubts developed, like clouds in a turbulent sky. "But that would mean they know I'm aware of what they're doing to Finesse—and I don't see how they could know that. Distance telepathy is a specialized thing, and it generally requires both a sender and a receiver. They would be taking quite long odds to gamble on that, even though in this case I do happen to be in touch. Also, there would be simpler ways to do it; they wouldn't need to go to the trouble of setting her up in the villa. Why should they torture her friends, whom I don't know, to put pressure on me? It is *her* they are pressuring! So I guess the reasonable answer is no; they can't be doing this just to get at me." He shook his head. "But who knows what they're up to, crazy as they seem to be. I've simply got to get Finesse out of their clutches."

Thea didn't argue, but Knot sensed that she believed the lobos were indeed summoning him—successfully. What could she say that would not sound jealous?

They continued on, following the broadening river. Knot thought about what he would like to do to Piebald —and realized that his own standards had been mutilated by recent events. Was he now to simulate his enemies, destroying the lives of others callously? It seemed he was well on the way to that already.

Mit says there is a suitable male for the mermaid, in the development ahead.

Knot relayed the news to Thea. But she did not react with the pleasure he had expected. "I've learned too much about land life in the enclave," she said. "I'm not sure, now, that I want to bring a baby into that."

"You could bring your baby into *your* life," Knot argued. "A normal could learn to swim as well as you— and could also go on land in an emergency. Don't give up your fulfillment because of the problems of the enclave. Work to improve the enclave!"

She smiled, swayed by his encouragement. "Yes. I must hold on to my dream. It is the only important thing for me."

"We'll see that you accomplish it," he said, feeling better himself.

The settlement at the mouth of the river was huge. It was a veritable city, teeming with mutants. They were out in the river, fishing with hooks, nets and spears. They lined the shore. They thronged in the crooked streets between shacks built one against another. They packed the crannies and niches and irregularities of the town. The ocean, Knot decided, must be a phenomenal provider.

That should in turn mean that these mutants were not as desperate for food, and would not be as vicious as the ones in the sterner territory upstream. Perhaps some facsimile of civilization existed here. That would be a great comfort.

Still, there would be no point in taking too much on faith. Knot consulted with his friends, then put his hand on the gross one's arm. WE CANNOT KNOW WHAT WILL HAPPEN, IN THE COMPLEXITIES OF THIS MUTE TOWN, THOUGH MIT BELIEVES WE WILL ALL SURVIVE IT. IT IS TIME TO EXCHANGE INFORMATION ABOUT OUR MISSIONS, SO THAT IF ONLY ONE OF US SURVIVES, HE CAN ACCOMPLISH THEM ALL. MY MISSION IS TO RESCUE THE NORMAL WOMAN FINESSE FROM THE CRATER VILLA AND THE LOBOS.

Now the gross one answered him. MY BROTHER IS NORMAL. HE PROTECTED ME AND TAUGHT ME SQUEEZE-TALK AND EDUCATED ME UNTIL I WAS STRONG ENOUGH AND SMART ENOUGH TO SURVIVE. I OWE HIM EVERYTHING.

I WOULD LIKE TO MEET THIS MAN, Knot squeezed.

HIS NAME IS BOAL, OF THE VILLAGE OF BRAND X. WHEN I CAME TO THE ENCLAVE A CRAZY DISTANCE PRECOG WAS BEING EATEN. I HAD NOT YET ACCLIMATIZED TO THE WAYS OF THE RIVER. I DESTROYED THE CANNIBALS AND RESCUED HER. IT WAS TOO LATE; SHE WAS DYING. BUT SHE MOVED HER LIPS AGAINST ME, AND I READ HER MESSAGE AS MY BROTHER HAD ALSO TAUGHT ME TO DO, AND SHE TOLD ME THREE THINGS. SHE WAS CRAZY, AND I DID NOT BELIEVE THEM, FOR THE FUTURE IS MUTABLE. BUT I THANKED HER AND SHE DIED, AND I DID AS SHE HAD ASKED AND

ATE HER, AND THEREAFTER I ATE ANY PER-
SON I CAUGHT.

An insane distance-precog! There was a problematical
psi! How could anyone afford to believe her predictions?
Yet the moment of death was considered to be also a
moment of truth. THE THINGS MIGHT HAVE BEEN
TRUE, DESPITE MUTABILITY, IF NO ACTION
WAS TAKEN TO VOID THEM, Knot squeezed.
WHAT WERE THEY?

THE FIRST WAS THAT MY BROTHER WOULD
GO ON A BUSINESS TRIP TO THE TOWN OF HUS-
TLE AND THERE BE KILLED BY A RAMPAGING
BRONCO-WOLF. THE SECOND WAS THAT AN
ANONYMOUS MIN-MUTE WOULD HELP ME ES-
CAPE THE ENCLAVE. THE THIRD WAS THAT I
WOULD MARRY A RICH NORMAL WOMAN.

Crazy, indeed! Yet the second prediction had been
eerily on target. It explained why the gross one had
trusted Knot so readily. Only a psi-precog could have
anticipated Knot's arrival in the enclave, so many years
in the future, and his contact with the gross one. Yet the
third prediction—what rich normal woman would marry
a monster like the gross one? It was insane—and of
course the precog had been insane anyway.

However, this at last identified the sex of the gross
one. It had to be male, or the gross one would not even
contemplate marrying a woman, even in a fantasy speculation.

IF THE PREDICTIONS ARE WRONG, Knot
squeezed, THEY ARE WRONG, AND YOUR
BROTHER IS SAFE AND YOU DO NOT NEED TO
WARN HIM. IF THEY ARE RIGHT—AND ONE
SEEMS TO BE—YOU MUST ACT TO WARN YOUR
BROTHER.

THAT IS MY MESSAGE. I DO NOT BELIEVE
THE THIRD PREDICTION, AND NO LONGER
WISH TO ESCAPE THE ENCLAVE. BUT MY
BROTHER MUST BE SAVED.

IF WE ASSUME THAT ALL THREE PREDIC-
TIONS ARE RIGHT, OR ALL THREE WRONG, IF
YOU ESCAPE THE ENCLAVE YOU CAN WARN
YOUR BROTHER. IF YOU FAIL TO ESCAPE, IT

COULD MEAN THE THREAT TO YOUR BROTHER IS NOT TRUE EITHER, SO—

WE CAN MAKE NO ASSUMPTIONS ABOUT UNITY, the gross one responded. It/he had a good mind hidden away there. ANY ONE PREDICTION CAN BE RIGHT OR WRONG.

YES, Knot agreed. IF I ALONE SURVIVE, I WILL WARN YOUR BROTHER. BUT I MAY NOT SUCCEED ALONE. YOU MUST TRY FOR THE ESCAPE YOURSELF; YOU MUST COME WITH ME. IF YOU SURVIVE ALONE, YOU MUST TRY TO RESCUE FINESSE FROM THE LOBOS. AGREED?

SUPPOSE FINESSE SHOULD BE RICH?

That rocked Knot. Finesse—the rich normal the gross one would marry? No, impossible, for many reasons. Knot recovered quickly. FINESSE MAY MARRY WHOM SHE CHOOSES, OR RETURN TO HER FORMER HUSBAND. IF SHE SHOULD GET RICH AND CHOOSE YOU, IT WILL SURELY BE A GOOD CHOICE.

The gross one broke contact with a shudder of humor. They proceeded warily on into the city.

This settlement was different. The mutants did not attack. In fact, they ignored the new arrivals. In moments, Knot and the gross one were amid the crowd, and Thea was swimming amid the throng in the water. No one noticed or cared. This must, Knot surmised, come from overcrowding and adequate food. The mutants had no motive either to fight or to relate to their neighbors.

This way, Hermine thought, forming a mental picture of a section ahead and to the left.

Knot followed her directions. They came to a shack in the middle of a stilt village in the heart of the city: dwellings perched on the water, supported by insubstantial rods of wood, metal or plastic. Any rising of the water would be awkward for these, and a flood would demolish them. But this precarious existence was what was offered, here, and the residents seemed satisfied. Presumably they lived one day at a time.

Thea's man, Hermine thought.

Thea arrived in the water. "This is it?"

"Yes," Knot said. "This is a, uh, normally inclined, interfertile mutant."

She hauled herself up on the sodden planking. "What's his name?"

Gurias—the wanderer.

Knot relayed the information, and Thea lifted her chin and breathed deeply. "For better or worse," she said, and Knot saw that she was trembling. But she made her own introduction: "Gurias!" she called. "I have come to be your woman!"

Well, that was one way of doing it. Knot stood back and watched. They didn't even know what this man looked like; he might be worse than the gross one.

A shape appeared in the crooked doorway. Gurias had discolored fleshy fins projecting from his limbs and torso and parts of his face, but his basic configuration was normal. He could probably have been rendered passably normal by appropriate surgery—but of course surgery was expensive. So he had been dumped in the enclave with the other unwanted mutants. The Machos preferred to toss problems away and forget them. It seemed to Knot that the Machos might be physically and mentally normal, but they were socially mutilated. Here was the evidence—this entire neglected enclave, and the individuals within it who could have been saved, had the Macho society cared to make the effort. But social mutilation was subtle and convenient, so it had become the norm. No doubt the Machos even expressed a certain pride in it, as earlier societies of mankind had expressed pride in their own bigotries and intolerances.

Gurias stood and looked down at Thea. From that vantage she proffered an excellent view of her really fine breasts, and her leg deformity was largely concealed by the lapping water. The man was visibly impressed. "Where's the catch?" he demanded.

"You must help my friends to escape the enclave," she replied.

Gurias's eyes moved to Knot and the gross one. "I do know a route—but it is hazardous."

"It will do," Knot said, realizing that this was what Mit had meant by suggesting that the mermaid would help them greatly, one more time. Instead of giving herself away, she was selling herself—and thereby making her offer seem more valuable. Would it work?

"What is your mutancy?" Gurias asked.

Thea lifted up her tail.

"Then you are not handicapped in the water?"

Thea bounced into the water and swam rapidly around the shack, returning to flip back onto the platform.

"Agreed," Gurias said. Suddenly the way was opening up!

Gurias jumped into the water, which was about chest deep here. Without pause or scruple he took Thea into his arms and indulged in a swift, efficient sexual act. There might have been a hundred other people in sight, and a number of them turned to watch enviously, but this did not slow Gurias at all. In fact, he seemed to revel in the display. And Thea obliged him gladly.

As Finesse had obliged Knot, in her dream. Knot thought of that, and was unsure of the significance of the parallel.

When Gurias was through, he drew back slightly and cuffed her across the shoulder. Thea fell back with a cry, obviously hurt by the blow. Knot stepped forward, rage exploding.

Wait! Hermine cautioned. **Mit says it is proper.**

And it seemed it was. Gurias only struck her once, and when she made no further objection and did not flee him, he put out his hand to her. She took it, and he drew her close.

Gurias looked around, frowning. The enclave mutants who had been watching turned their faces away and busied themselves in other occupations. "Come in and have some dried fish," Gurias said gruffly to Thea. "And your friends. We shall cast off at tide."

Knot understood, now. The man had openly asserted his mastery in Macho fashion. Not only had this attractive woman submitted to him sexually, but she had also done so in the presence of her companions, and had accepted his violence without complaint. Everyone had seen. No one had protested. By the conventions of this subculture, this woman had changed hands. The two were united, and others would not move in. It was not Knot's way, but it did make sense on its own terms. The enclave mutants were Machos too, in their reduced fashion.

Inside, Gurias distributed his meager supply of crudely dried fish. Thea sat on the floor, not concealing her tied feet now. Gurias's glance hardly touched on them; she was only moderately mutant, in an enclave overflowing with much worse, and her normal features were excellent ones. She was a bargain. Gurias, for a reason he did not yet appreciate, had the better of the deal.

"After I help your friends—what with you?" Gurias asked Thea. Obviously he knew he was being used, and wanted to determine the limits of it.

"I cannot endure in salt water and do not like the city," she replied. "We must move upstream."

Again there was a visible impact. "You prefer a permanent liaison?"

"I will bear your baby. You must teach it the ways of the land as well as the ways of the water."

"Mutants cannot interbreed!"

"You and I can," she said with certainty.

A third time Gurias took visible stock. "This is beyond any aspiration I have had. You have psi-information?"

Thea nodded. "This is why I sought you out. Why we must stay together. I will not be able to forage well alone while gravid."

"I do not know how to raise a baby!"

"You will learn," she said firmly.

Gurias glanced ruefully at Knot. "Don't they dominate rapidly! It is only minutes since I copped her, and already she is to birth a baby and govern my life."

"They're all alike," Knot agreed.

Gurias clapped one fist into the opposite hand. "Yes, I will try. We will go upstream, somewhere where it is safe—" He interrupted himself. "It is close to tide. We start now."

He went outside and shoved three poles out of the way. Suddenly the hut was floating free, a roofed raft. He fished the poles out of the water before neighbors could abscond with them. "You men," he snapped at Knot and the gross one, "your weight makes the raft sluggish. Pole it past obstructions. You, woman—use that bucket to bail."

A raft had to be bailed? Knot shrugged and used his pole as directed.

And so they were on their way, letting the slow current of the river take the craft, poling past the anchored residences. It quickly became routine.

The river broadened out into the ocean. And as the awesome expanse of water opened before them—a storm developed.

Gurias glanced nervously into the darkening sky. "We should be able to ride it out," he said.

"Maybe we could head for shore," Knot suggested, not liking this. The storm clouds were deep and gray, their nether winds stirring up the water.

"Nix. The ocean breakers form there. Other craft interfere with stability. We must stay out in deep water."

Will we survive it? Knot asked Hermine.

Mit says yes. It is not a bad storm.

Knot's tension eased. "We are going to come through it intact," he said.

"You are clairvoyant?" Gurias asked. "A double mutant?"

"Close enough."

"You are the one who located me as an interfertile party?"

Knot nodded, deciding that there was no point in clarifying such a detail. "Only through clairvoyance could we connect Thea with the one man who could give her a baby. For this she agreed to help us escape the enclave."

"And now it is my obligation," Gurias said. He glanced across to where Thea was propped with the bucket, scooping out water from whatever depressions captured it. She was making do well, and once more Knot was struck by her prettiness. "I was said to have been birthed under a fortunate star. I never believed it, until this moment. There's many a normal I would pass over, in favor of such a mermaid."

Thea smiled, flushing, pleased. "Let's ride out the storm first, then believe."

The storm was thickening rapidly. Gusts of wind swooped down, stirring the waters into minor rolling mountains. Lightning fired from cloud to horizon. The craft rocked and groaned. Knot developed motion sickness. "I don't suppose you have a stasis unit on this ship?" he inquired with sick humor. But Gurias was already out tending to his vessel.

The rain struck. Knot hauled himself into the cabin. The next hour was one of the least pleasant of his life. All he remembered later was being pitched about the cramped enclosure along with Thea, heaving out his guts, watching seawater overflow the floor, dilute and wash away the vomit, then heaving again. He fancied he was becoming something of an expert at analyzing the manner in which seawater dissolved vomit. There were all sorts of intriguing rivulets and separations and encapsulations, as though a military horde were attacking a variegated bastion. Inevitably the horde encircled, undermined and swept away the bastion—but thereafter the horde was colored by the essence of the defeated force. From the third time on, the heaves were dry, which spoiled his analytical distraction, and these were worse than the others. Thea tried to comfort him, but his sickness preempted his attention and anyway, she was not his woman anymore.

Something sparkled on the floor. Knot checked. It was Strella's diamond! He had spewed it out during his sickness. Lucky he hadn't lost it!

He picked it up and wiped it off on his forearm. Maybe his heaves were over. He put it back in his mouth. What a tragedy if he escaped the enclave, then could not honor his commitment to the dead woman!

The gross one did not seem to be suffering. He clung to the outside structure, letting the waves break over his body, squeaking with savage delight. Gurias, too, was getting along nicely. Hermine clung to a rickety shelf with Mit; every so often Knot caught a thought from her that suggested she was not feeling much better than he was.

The rain cascaded down, the vomit of the sky, leaking copiously through the roof. Bailing seemed useless, but Thea kept at it. At times the floor was awash a quarter meter deep—then the raft would rise and tilt scarily, and most of the water would drain out.

Then, as the storm was abating, Finesse made another transmission. Knot knew it was going to be a bad one;

how could it be otherwise, the way he and Hermine both were feeling? But he had to receive it.

Finesse was in an interior room in the villa, under restraint, her head secured so that she had to look forward. The old man, NFG, was in a glassed chamber, his limbs free. But the walls on either side were slowly closing in on him.

"A little telekinesis to flick the switch," Piebald said conversationally. "Or some electrical shorting to stop the motor. Or the conjuration of a metallic barrier to halt the progress of the walls. Or something else. I don't care what sort of psi it is, just so it is strong and manifests in time."

"You killed Lydia!" Finesse screamed. "Now you're murdering NFG! All for nothing! Nothing!"

"I am very sorry you feel that way," Piebald said, squinting judiciously at the closing cage. "You could so readily save your friend—if you really put your mind to it."

Now Finesse, in desperation, put her mind to it. She had, after all, been conceived within the shaded time after her father's travel in space. Maybe CC had missed it. Maybe there was something. She willed the walls to stop, with all the desperate intensity of which she was capable. But they continued to close. NFG braced his back against one wall, his hands and feet against the other—and crumpled as the closure proceeded inexorably. He fell to the floor, and the walls touched him on either side.

Now the old man tried to help himself with his own psi. Illusions appeared—a huge, ghostly crane, swinging a wrecking ball at the glass, shattering it. But as the glass fell, the true image emerged, as solid as ever. Then a man appeared with a drill, rapidly making a hole in the glass—but there was no hole. Finally a great laughing demon-face appeared, not even pretending to try to help, just guffawing. "You're NFG!" the face exclaimed in comic letters that shot out from its mouth. "No fu'ing good!"

"The face of his personal devil," Piebald remarked. "He knows he is about to die, since you do not care enough to save him. The devil has come to collect his worthless soul."

Finesse tried to will electricity through the mechanism, to short it out or otherwise disrupt its process. Nothing happened.

"Perhaps a psi explosion," Piebald suggested. "Or a melting of the glass. Or a denaturing of it, so that it loses cohesion. Or you might simply teleport him out of there. Do not allow your imagination to limit you; be creative!"

Finesse was beyond the point of reacting to baiting. She tried to find psi. Nothing availed.

NFG was crushed horribly before her eyes, his frame collapsing inward on itself while the demon face laughed and laughed. NFG's tongue and eyes popped out as his head was crushed, blood squirting from the orifices.

The demon disappeared in midguffaw. NFG was dead.

The storm was over. Knot lay, wrung out, suffering physically and mentally. "They made her watch another killing," he said, and tried to heave again. It was no good; there was nothing inside him he could expel.

Gurias entered. "You were right. We did survive the storm. Now we must wait for the eddy current to take us into the next bay. It will take time. I suggest we rest."

That was about all Knot was capable of. He lay suffering for a while, then let his consciousness drain away like blood from a crushed body or diluting vomit.

CHAPTER 9

It was night when he woke firmly. He had phased in and out of consciousness several times, as glad to return to the dream state as to emerge from it. Now he was fully awake and feeling somewhat better, but there seemed to be nothing to see or do.

Yes there is, Hermine corrected him. *Mit says we are about to touch land, and must move off immediately to let the raft float out with the tide. You must eat something.*

"Eat!" Knot exclaimed, revolted.

For strength. There will be much action before you eat again.

You are as bad as a wife, he complained.

Worse, the weasel agreed. *Now eat.*

Knot suffered himself to be bullied into what was best for him. He choked down some more dried fish. It was not an enjoyable experience, but the stuff stayed down. He knew Mit was correct: If there was action ahead, he had better have strength for it. Yet he had to proffer some token protest. *Do you two boss Finesse around like this, too?*

Of course, Hermine thought. *She gained two kilograms once, and Mit made her take it off. You don't like fat women.*

Knot had to laugh. So Finesse had had to discipline her appetite, getting set to vamp him. Served her right!

The raft bumped. "This is the shore of the bay,"

Gurias announced. "There is a path up the cliff few know about, leading out. I found it only by accident, and I doubt any others in the enclave know of it. Otherwise they would have used it to escape. Perhaps some have, so that none who have learned of it remain except myself. But I never tried it. There are vicious wild creatures. I recommend you take stout sticks to handle snakes and birds. I think your chances of making it are one in three, unless your clairvoyance helps. Night is the best time, when the reptiles are torpid. Good luck!"

Gurias struck Knot more and more as a good man. He was observant and sensible and obviously could keep his mouth shut. Thea would be well taken care of. "We thank you," he said. "Clairvoyance does help; we'll make it. I hope your family turns out well."

Thea took Knot's hand. "Take the best care of yourself," she said, looking entreatingly into his eyes. "And I think you promised me something."

"I did," he agreed. "Hermine will be in touch with you."

"When your child by that normal woman grows up, send him to meet my child," she said. "I know they will like each other, and my child will need to be introduced to the civilized world."

His child by Finesse? Knot wasn't sure whether that was humor or hope. But there was no harm in the notion. "Shall we say, twenty Earth years from now, at this spot?"

"That will be nice," she agreed. "Especially if one of them is a girl."

Knot gave her hand a final squeeze. "I like your dreams, mermaid."

Then he cast loose her hand and jumped into the water. The gross one was already down, and now shoved the raft off. It disappeared into the night. Only the lapping of the wavelets against its decaying timbers signaled its presence.

Knot felt lonely. **Think to her, Hermine. Remind her of our last night together, until the memory takes. She's an awfully nice woman.**

Yes, the weasel agreed.

Knot squeezed the gross one's arm. IT IS DARK. I

CAN HARDLY SEE. CAN YOU MAKE OUT THE PATH?

YES, READILY. IT IS ALWAYS LIKE THIS, FOR ME.

What a statement of condition, Knot thought. Blind and deaf, eternally. Wasn't this whole society like that, too? Heedless of the suffering of others, or of the threats lurking, the threats to its own welfare. This was only one planet of thousands; everywhere in the human galaxy similar situations must abound as the theoretically healthy segment of the species ignored its ailing fringe and its rotting core. The whole society was sick, and only drastic surgery could cure it. Mutancy had to be abolished!

Mit wants to know if that necessarily follows.

And of course it didn't necessarily follow. The root was not in the mutancy, but in man's isolationist nature, in his excluding of elements that were different. Before there had been mutants, man had done similar things to other minorities. Yet how could man's nature be changed, without by definition eliminating man himself?

Let's replace man with weasels and crabs, Hermine thought.

Knot laughed—but found his laughter converting to thought. Maybe it *was* time for some other species to try its competence as galactic administrator. He would have to add that notion to his ponder file.

They cleared the water and the marsh and found the steep bank. The path lurched upward along the face of the shore-cliff. Loose gravel crunched and skidded underfoot. But the gross one proceeded upward confidently, and Knot followed. He knew Mit would alert Hermine to any pressing peril.

It was a long way up. Gusts of wind tugged at them playfully. The crashing of the breakers receded slowly. Knot's legs grew weary, as they always did when he had to sustain "normal" locomotion too long without rest. At least the slant was correct; his short left leg was uphill.

He remembered Gurias's advice to travel by night. How much night remained? When they achieved safe ledges, they rested briefly, and sometimes Mit had them pause while some nocturnal creature passed. How big did the serpents grow here?

Slowly dawn came, the sunlight angling lengthwise along the face of the cliff. Now Knot saw exactly what he had traversed, and experienced a surge of vertigo. The cliff was not only steep, it also overhung in places. It seemed they had wound up a tortuous ribbon that passed under one overhang and over another, sometimes directly above itself. The nests of large birds were here—and now those birds were stirring, taking flight, becoming aware of the intruders. That should mean there was no danger of snakes at this stage; the birds would not tolerate them near the nests.

We must move on quickly, Hermine thought. **The birds will soon attack.**

Because they didn't tolerate people near their nests either, Knot realized. He informed the gross one by squeeze, and they did what Knot would really rather not have done, considering his fatigue and the precariousness of their situation: They hurried. Stones squirted from beneath their feet, and sand cascaded from handholds. The morning breeze stiffened as if trying to nab them while it could. Knot knew it was merely a meteorological phenomenon, transporting air from the warm sea to the cooler land, channeling swiftly up the cliff, but it certainly seemed malignly purposeful. This also provided buoyancy for the birds, more of whom hovered near, eyeing the trespassers.

And Knot remembered that he had not brought along a good stick, despite Gurias's advice. How Knot could have found one in the dark, or carried it when he was naked and needed both hands for clutching the treacherous cliff he was not sure, but now he wished he had at least tried. Mit could have directed him to one, had he asked. He felt naked, not merely because he *was* naked. The beaks of the birds looked cruelly sharp, and their little eyes glittered.

Collect rocks, Hermine thought. **You must throw soon.**

Knot picked up those loose rocks he could locate. When a particular bird became too bold, he hurled a stone at it. The missile missed, and the recoil gave Knot a nasty shove; a small torrent of debris washed down below him. Only Hermine's assurances that Mit knew they would not fall prevented Knot from panicking. He hated this!

He found himself chewing nervously on something— and realized it was the diamond. Quickly he put it back in the safety of his cheek. He didn't want to spit that out here!

Another bird swooped. This time Knot braced himself more securely and flipped a rock out backhand. It also missed, but it taught the bird respect. Knot scrambled on after the gross one during the respite.

Danger, Hermine thought. **Snake.**

Where? He had supposed there would be none up here while the birds were active, but the weasel obviously knew better.

Coming down the path. A large one, poisonous.

Knot moved ahead to touch the gross one. BIG SNAKE COMING DOWN. POISON.

The gross one understood this threat. WE HIDE WHERE?

It is sated, Hermine thought. **Not hungry. It will not bite unless disturbed. Stand still, let it pass.**

STAND STILL. IT WILL PASS, Knot relayed. He was glad they did not have to try to retreat down the path; he wasn't sure how far he could make it.

Now he saw the snake. It was indeed big; three times the length of a man, and with a girth like a man's thigh. It had to derive from Earth, since the fauna of colony worlds did not match Earth's. Perhaps a mutant, freed by its Macho owner when it grew too large or vicious. Its skin was patterned with reddish dots, and fangs protruded in front. On a narrow path like this, such a creature could readily dislodge the men—if it chose to.

Think thoughts of friendship, Hermine directed.

Knot realized she would relay these to the reptile, calming it. Good strategy! He thought how nice snakes could be when they were tame, keeping the premises free of rats, sunning themselves, slithering lithely about. Snakes were the most graceful of creatures, smooth and sinuous. Some breeds became very friendly, and could be carried wrapped around a forearm.

The snake slid down the path. The gross one was before

it, standing with squat legs spread, straddling the path. The serpent paused, then moved between the legs, taking the center of the path. It moved past the gross one's tail section and bore down on Knot. **Nice pet,** he thought determinedly. **Pretty creature.** And actually it did have beauty.

The snake passed on between Knot's feet. It seemed to take forever to complete its transit, but finally the last of the tail disappeared. Knot relaxed. This had certainly been better than trying to fight it!

We must move, now, before the birds return, Hermine thought.

Knot notified the gross one, and they went on. It did seem the snake had done them a favor, for the birds were wheeling at a greater distance than before. They might not like reptiles near their eggs, but they had little choice about this one.

Then, suddenly, they were at the top. Evidently the serpent hunted on level ground, and rested safely down the bank, protected during its long slumbers by the terrain and the vigilance of the birds. If Knot had had to forage here, he might have done the same. He stretched himself over the lip and lay panting. His arms and legs ached; he had not been truly aware of his fatigue until now, when the tension eased.

We must travel, Hermine thought urgently. **Mit has picked up a suggestion—it is way beyond his normal range —and fears Finesse's next torture will be very ugly.**

Ugly? What did the little crab think the first two had been? A girl devoured live by a beast, a man crushed to death—**the little girl!** Knot thought. He climbed to his feet. **How far is it?**

Far, she thought. **Days to walk.**

Then we must ride. Where is a suitable vehicle?

Mit says there is a small aircraft an hour's walk from here. But they will not take us where we must go.

Just head me in the right direction. The weariness faded as he moved. The gross one followed, never seeming to tire.

There were several brightly colored small craft perched near the airport building. Some were rocket boosters, some blimps, some winged craft. **May we rent one?** Knot thought rhetorically.

No. Need money and identification and license.

Then we must steal one.

Yes. Mit says the blue one with wings.

Mit had to know. That one must be fueled and operable and have sufficient range. Without the hermit crab, pure chance would have militated against them; with Mit, many devious things became feasible.

You must use your psi, Hermine thought as they approached.

Right, Knot agreed, experiencing déjà vu. When had a similar situation arisen? Ah yes—on Planet Chicken Itza, when the Doublegross Bladewings were attacking. And for some reason the fierce fighting cocks had turned out to be afraid of blood. That still didn't make sense!

He walked up to the main building, the gross one following. He found the office. And remembered that he was naked, with a max-mute at his side. WAIT HERE, he squeezed to the gross one. Knot wondered if his companion realized that they had now escaped the enclave. But of course the escape was not secure until they got well away from it, unobserved by any knowledgeable party.

The Macho functionary looked up from his desk, surprised. Knot started talking before the man could. "Hello, I had a bit of trouble back there. Craft went down in a cornfield. Need to borrow my friend's craft to hop home, get my clothes on. In fact, better borrow some clothes here. What've you got?"

"Who are you?" the other demanded.

Project impression of symmetry of body, Knot told Hermine, realizing that his obvious mutant status would put the normal off. Aloud, he said: "That's all right; I'll pick them out myself." He proceeded to the officer's camping cubby under Hermine's direction, found the closet, and began sorting through uniforms.

"You can't—!" the man cried indignantly, half paralyzed by the audacity of it.

Knot picked out what he liked and climbed hastily into it. The fit was tight-loose, as always.

The officer went back to his desk and snatched the phone. "Security?" he asked. "There's an intruder here—"

Knot completed his quick dressing, then walked out the back way while the man was expostulating on his phone. He walked around the building to pick up the gross one. FOLLOW LIKE A CAPTIVE, he squeezed. WE MUST PASS BY TROOPS.

They headed directly for the blue airplane, the gross one following Knot submissively.

A troop of security men ran past them. Knot knew that by the time the men got the story from the officer, much of Knot's visit would have been forgotten. His psi was really useful in this sort of situation. Meanwhile, he was now in uniform and not subject to casual challenge—which was the point of this byplay. His psi would not have availed him had he approached the blue airplane as a naked mutant.

There was a guard at the airplane parking area, but he glanced at Knot's uniform and made no challenge. Of course there were always bits of metal and decorations and emblems attached to uniforms, symptomatic of the military mind's attraction to shine and color, and he did not have these on. But Hermine was broadcasting the impression of legitimacy so that no one noticed. Knot put the gross one aboard, then strapped himself into the pilot's seat. **Mutant beasties, do your thing,** he thought with a grim smile.

Flying an airplane was a challenge for the little crab, and Knot had to help him. **There should be a way to start the engine—ah yes, thank you. And a way to make the plane taxi forward. Yes. And a way to make it take off—**

It was a dangerously wobbly ascent, but they made it. Once in the air, Knot began to get the feel of it, and the flight became smoother. Mit stopped sweating—or whatever it was mutant crabs did when nervous.

We are not yet safe, Hermine warned. **Your psi confused the Machos, but they know the aircraft has been stolen because the theft registers on their electronic record board. They will pursue. Mit says they have faster aircraft in the vicinity, with weapons.**

They surely do, Knot agreed. **What is the best strategy to avoid them?**

Fly fast and low, near the ocean cliffs.

Right. Knot directed the plane toward the ocean and

brought it as low to the ground as he dared. As the cliff came beneath him, he felt again the vertigo he had experienced while climbing it. This time it was more pleasurable. He felt much safer in the plane, and most of his body was getting a chance to rest.

In fact, the opening vista was quite striking: greenish fields extending almost to the brink, then the gray/white gash of the dropoff, and the blue/green water below. He looked for the house-raft, where Thea the mermaid rode, but could not spot it. This was probably too far to the east of the chasm, and he was flying rapidly farther away from it. Which was all right; he liked her well, but had never deluded himself that there could be anything permanent between them. He had, at least, repaid her well for her help; she would now have her special fulfillment.

Would there be children, who might meet in twenty years? Doubtful; he would not be marrying Finesse, much as he would have liked to, had she not already had a husband. But should he marry some other woman, such as perhaps his secretary, York, and have a child, he could send that one—

Pursuit, Hermine warned. **Rocketship.**

That was bad news. The rockets would be twice as fast as this craft. He had hoped for more leeway. But he had some advantages. He skimmed along the brink of the cliff, so that he seemed only meters aloft on the left, and a thousand meters on the right.

The rocket came up with horrifying ease and swiftness. The aircraft radio crackled on. "Blue wingcraft, turn about and land at field."

Knot did not answer. **Will it attack us?**

Not yet. You will gain more time by stalling, Mit says.

"This is the blue wingcraft," Knot said, activating the radio according to Mit's instructions. "I'm not sure I am able to turn."

Soon he was enmeshed in a technical discussion of airplane control, as the rocket pilot tried to clarify for a seemingly stupid novice how to operate the controls for a safe turn.

"Get some elevation!" the rocket cried. "You're about to crash into the cliff!"

"Elevation," Knot agreed, and allowed the plane to dip lower.

But the rocketeer was not a fool. He soon realized that Knot was playing with him. "Turn that craft about, or I will fire on you," he said, exasperated.

Bluff? Knot asked Hermine.

Yes—now. But he will fire soon, if he needs to. He is a normal, an honest civil-defense pilot, with sense and courage.

I would have to draw one of that kind! Knot complained. **Why can't honest, competent men stay where they belong, in some ghetto?**

There are leaks in the screening process, Mit says. Some good men get through.

The irony was, Mit was serious.

Knot played out his string as far as it would go, all the while progressing obliquely toward his target. When the rocket could no longer be put off, Knot dropped down below the top of the cliff and flew with his left wingtip almost touching. Birds flew up angrily, squawking. Now he was absolutely dependent on Mit's guidance, for without the crab's precognition he could not have avoided contact with the cliff.

"Get away from there!" the rocket pilot cried. "You'll crash, and ruin a good plane!"

But Knot stayed where he was. Angry, the rocket oriented behind him, to fire—and Knot dropped suddenly lower, almost scraping the thin beach.

"You're absolutely crazy!" the rocket cried. But he came down to orient on Knot's plane again. The rocket-craft was not only faster, it was also more maneuverable, and had a more experienced pilot; Knot could surprise the man but not actually lose him by such maneuvers.

We must cut across to the villa, Hermine announced.

"All right, you win," Knot radioed. "I'll lift up and head back." He started climbing, and the rocket paced him without firing.

By the time Knot cleared the cliff, he was beyond his turnoff place, so could afford to cut back. Thus he made some progress toward his destination without the rocket catching on. But soon he would be retreating from the volcano and the villa. Abruptly he swerved again, going directly toward the villa.

This time the rocketeer did not play games. It was hard to keep fooling an honest man! The craft looped around, oriented, and fired.

But Mit anticipated the shot, and knew where not to be, when. **Veer sharp left and down—NOW!** Knot did so, and the laser beam missed, above and to the right.

Slow, lift, Hermine directed, relaying Mit's instructions. And the second beam missed, ahead.

The rocket pilot began to get angry, not understanding that he was up against psi. But he was determined, and his marksmanship was excellent, and they knew it was only a matter of brief time before he scored.

Lake ahead, close to crater, Hermine advised. **Crash-land in water.**

Knot slanted the plane down. The lake came into sight, and he shot into it, bouncing on the surface several times before halting and starting to sink.

The rocket zoomed overhead, but the pilot was too canny to try to land similarly. His craft needed a regular field, or it would not be able to take off again. In fact, it might require a rocket launcher. Also, the rocket consumed a great deal more fuel; it must be getting low. The plane looped about and departed.

He is summoning land reinforcements to this spot, Hermine thought. **They will not take long to converge.**

But now the volcano was in sight, perhaps an hour's walk away. Probably not enough time, but the effort had to be made. Knot and the gross one extricated themselves from the slowly settling plane, splashed to shore, and hurried toward the villa. With luck, the troops would orient first on the airplane, then not be able to locate the fugitives before the hour was up.

That luck did not materialize. A truck ferried a dozen armed men to Knot's vicinity in half an hour, following his trail with a heat-sensing device so that there was no hesitation. Several more men parachuted down between Knot and the volcano. It seemed this was a sensitive area!

Right at this inopportune time, Finesse commenced another transmission. They were close now, almost within

Hermine's sending range to a person she knew really well, and the reception was very strong.

The child, Klisty, was in a pit in the central arena. She was in darkness, but infrared light bathed her and made the complete scene visible to Piebald and Finesse.

"Now the child has fair psi talent," Piebald said. "She can dowse for conductors, most notably water and precious metals. It is not strictly an electrical phenomenon, however, for pure water does not conduct electricity; it is the impurities that convert it to a conductor. Yet the child can locate pure water. I certainly hope we shall have the opportunity for defining her talent further. But first there is a certain matter we must undertake."

He touched a button. "Klisty—do you hear me?" he called.

The little girl whirled around, her pigtails flying. "Where are you, Mr. Pie?" she cried, the tinge of hysteria in her voice. "Why am I in this awful cold dark?"

"It is cold because this is the snake pit," Piebald answered. "Reptiles do not function well when cold, so these are torpid. Rattlers, corals, cottonmouths, cobras, even a huge python—scattered about the premises. They will be aware of you, my dear, but I fear you are not aware of them, since they are no more conductive than the floor. When it warms, it will become rather awkward in there. I advise you to be careful where you step."

The girl looked down, but obviously could not see anything. Her legs and feet were bare. There were no snakes in her immediate vicinity, but she was not aware of that. She looked frightened.

Suddenly there was a blast of hot air that stirred Klisty's hair and dress. "Oh my," Piebald said. "It seems someone has turned on the heat. Those reptiles will shortly become active, and they may not be in an ideal mood—especially since the floor is tilting, sliding them about." And slowly the floor shifted, causing the child to start and catch her balance. "I fear if I were shaken that way, I would strike at anything I encountered. However, I am not a snake."

"You're quite sure of that?" Finesse inquired softly.

"But *why*?" Klisty cried.

Piebald cut off the intercommunication circuit. "She

does not understand. But you do, Finesse. One little throb of your psi can do wonders for the welfare of that child, I'm sure. I hope you do it before she steps on a snake in the dark, for it will instinctively bite her. Unless, of course, your psi can nullify venom! In that case it can certainly wait."

"You monster!" Finesse said. She was beyond screams or tears; she knew they accomplished nothing with this man.

"Were I in your place," the lobo said calmly, "I believe I would concentrate less on invective and more on psi. But it is of course your prerogative."

"What does your wife say when you come home after another hard day's labor at the torture chamber?"

"Do you really wish to discuss this instead of taking positive action to help the child? As you wish. My wife is a gentle woman, a lobo too, who has no idea of the nature of my business. She resides with other female lobos in a villa elsewhere on this planet, beside a pleasant lake. I fear there would be severe repercussions if she learned the nature of this center."

"Freeze in place," a man's voice ordered.

Knot froze, confused. A normal had a laser rifle trained on him. This was the foothill to the volcano, not the villa inside. The sending had been interrupted by a current event.

Mit says he looked and looked, but there was no way to sneak through, Hermine thought apologetically. *They have captured us. But in half an hour there will be an opening.*

What's Finesse doing? Knot thought curtly.

The sending resumed. The little girl staggered as the floor reversed its tilt. Her foot came down on a snake. She screamed—but the snake was still torpid, and did not strike. The hot blast of air continued.

I can't wait half an hour, Knot thought.

If you act now, we could free the gross one, Mit says. But we cannot free you or help Finesse.

Then I will act alone! Knot rasped mentally. He spat the diamond into his palm as the troops closed in. He squeezed the gross one's arm.

I MUST TRY TO ENTER THE VILLA. I WILL SURELY FAIL, BUT I AM COMPELLED TO MAKE

THE ATTEMPT. HERE IS STRELLA'S DIAMOND. TAKE IT TO HER FRIEND, AND DELIVER YOUR MESSAGE TO YOUR BROTHER. MAYBE THE DISTRACTION I PROVIDE WILL SPRING YOU FREE. MY ANIMAL FRIENDS WILL HELP YOU. OPEN YOUR MIND TO THE WEASEL, AND TRUST WHAT SHE THINKS TO YOU. SHE IS MORE VALUABLE THAN ANY OTHER FRIEND YOU COULD HAVE. And to Hermine: **Jump to the gross one, you and Mit. Help him escape. Help him do these things. You can locate the friend and the brother, and guide the gross one away from harm.**

They jumped. **You are suicidally brave and foolish,** Hermine thought in passing. **Almost like a weasel.**

Thanks.

Except for being influenced by looking up a leg—

Go! Knot sprang at the nearest trooper, using his trained combat technique to wrest the laser rifle from the man's grasp. Simultaneously, the gross one exploded into action. Troopers were hurled away from him as he whirled and charged toward the truck.

The troopers had expected action from Knot, not from the blind max-mute. They concentrated on Knot. Two laser beams speared out, striking him in thigh and side. Agony exploded. Knot tried to continue fighting, but already someone was heaving a stun bomb at him. It puffed into vapor under his nose, and suddenly he was in a kind of stasis.

But Hermine was still in touch. She continued relaying Finesse's sending.

"News has just reached me," Piebald said, "that a min-mute has been apprehended half a kilometer from these premises. I presume that is your anonymous assistant, the one we chased into the chasm enclave." He looked at her face, watching for some reaction. She gave none. "He must have more psi than anonymity, to accomplish the escapes he did. I should think clairvoyance and telepathy are the least that would be required. I know of no case in which a single individual possessed three discrete psi-powers—but of course I do not have the Coordination Computer's resources. If such a person was your assistant, what would your own psi be?"

Still Finesse made no response.

"I must admit that man has made a valiant effort to reach you, performing the amazing feat of escaping from the enclave. That had not been accomplished in twenty years, and we sealed off the avenue used then. But as it happens, we were ready for him. You will be glad to know that he will be the next subject for our program of evocation. Perhaps for him you will do what you seem unwilling to do for the child—"

Something snapped in Finesse. It was as though a long-blocked conduit had been reamed out, and gas was rushing through at last. She looked at the snake pit—and the reviving reptiles hissed and recoiled, giving Klisty the widest possible berth. It was as though they had suddenly developed a terrible fear of her.

Knot remembered again how the fighting cocks of Chicken Itza had abruptly become afraid of blood. Could this be—?

"Marvelous!" Piebald breathed. "I believe that was indeed the key. It has manifested at last! CC must have programmed you to evoke it only when your friend was in direct peril that you could thus abate. He must be more than an assistant, for with the powers he evidently possesses he could have escaped the planet with news of our program. Instead he sought you out—and you evidently return his interest. What an excellent team the two of you make, he with his powers of escape and anonymity, you with—"

Finesse turned her gaze on him, but Piebald was unperturbed. "You are fastened in your chair, my dear, and I am, as I said, no reptile. You can neither free yourself nor instill fear in me."

She concentrated—and suddenly he danced away from her. "Oh, my lord!" he cried. "You can! Suddenly I am deathly afraid of you! What a rare psi-talent that is, fully worth the effort I have made to evoke it!" His fear was tempered by his delight at his success, much as a breeder of a unique species of deadly viper might be when attacked by his hatchling.

And Knot thought: Piebald had been right. Finesse was no normal, but a potent psi-mute. CC had made a team of them, together with the animals. His anonymity and her

subtle attack capacity—both aspects of mind-affecting psi
—complemented by the informational capacity of the two
animals. A potent, well-rounded, well-concealed unit of investigation.

Yet he had asked Mit whether Finesse could in fact be
a psi-mute, and Mit had denied it. How could the little
crab have been mistaken? Or had Hermine lied?

CC put a geis on him, Hermine thought. **Mit could not
reveal Finesse's condition. Even I did not know. I never
lied to you, angry man. I thought she was normal too.**

Knot had to accept that. It was the way CC worked,
and this was part of the information the machine had concealed from him. Knot was indeed angry—but he also appreciated the infernal cleverness and misdirection of the
computer.

This team had done the job, discovering the nature of
the threat to CC. But the fiendishly clever and ruthless
lobo, a proper match for CC, had nullified them by using
their own unity against them. Knot could and should have
left the planet with his information; Finesse herself had
urged that course on him, via her sendings to Hermine.
But the same emotional attachment that unified the team
had drawn him inexorably to Finesse even when the situation had changed, and finally made him captive to the
lobos. CC had not realized that Knot would learn the truth
about the lobos while separate from Finesse.

Yet how had the lobos been so apt at countering him?
Piebald, by his own admission, had not known Knot was
escaping the enclave chasm, and he still did not know
about Hermine and Mit. Was it mere luck—or was something else involved? This tied in with the unity and pre-
cision and discipline the lobos showed generally; they always seemed to be in the right place at the right time, as
though governed by a sophisticated electronic network—
which they did not use—or psi, which they did not have.

Finesse concentrated again—and Piebald's hand shied
away from the door. "Now I am afraid of doors!" he
cried, again with mixed delight. "Oh, what a terror I have
loosed this time! No verbal directives, no hypnosis, just a
direct psi-line to my mind. Definitely a Class A talent! Can
you make me fear anything?"

"I believe I can," Finesse said, feeling slightly giddy

from the realization of her new power. All her life she had wanted psi, and suddenly she had it! "I suggest you free me from this chair, or I shall make you afraid of the floor you stand on."

"That I will not do, my dear. Once I free you, I have no remaining control over you."

She focused—and suddenly he was dancing, trying to get away from the floor. In a moment he had scrambled atop a cabinet, where he perched ludicrously. "Already we begin to define the limits," he gasped. "Your talent is negative, not positive. You can drive me away from things, but you cannot drive me toward them. You can make me flee you, but not come to you to release you. I think we are at an impasse—and of course my men do control your boyfriend."

Finesse left him there and tried to act for herself. Her head and upper torso were free, with her arms locked to the armrests and her feet to the footrests. But the chair itself was not anchored. She hunched forward quickly—and when she jerked back, the chair slid a centimeter forward. She could move it! She repeated the action until she reached the control panel for the snake pit. Then she touched the communication button with her healing nose.

"Klisty!" she called. "Can you hear me?"

The little girl looked around. "Oh, Finesse, where are you? I'm so frightened—"

"Don't worry. The snakes are more frightened of you than you are of them. They will not touch you. In a moment I will free you; then you must come and free me."

"This has gone far enough," Piebald said. "Security—"

He stopped. She had made him afraid of the sound of his own speech.

Finesse experimented with the buttons of the panel. First she turned the hot air off, then she stilled the moving floor, then she found the regular illumination system. Finally she located the door-release mechanism. The door opened, and the little girl stepped out unharmed, and mounted the catwalk to the main-arena floor.

Klisty came and hugged Finesse in the chair. "I was so scared. Not since my parents died—I thought I was going to be killed, same as Lydia and NFG—"

"See if you can release me from this chair," Finesse said. "Quickly, before lobo reinforcements come."

"Oh sure. It's just straps and things." Klisty bent to it, her little hands tugging at fastenings.

The picture faded out. Hermine had retreated beyond her broadcast range. Knot was alone, still stunned and helpless, suffering from his two wounds. His captors were not unkind to him—in fact, they seemed to be normals, rather than lobos, despite what Piebald had intimated to Finesse. They restrained him before the drug wore off, put medication on his wounds, and made him as comfortable as possible.

There was a delay, however, while a new truck was requisitioned. It seemed the gross one had absconded with the first truck. Knot imagined how the eyeless mutant might drive it, with Hermine giving directives mentally and Mit anticipating hazards. The gross one had been resistive to psi communication, but had gotten to know Hermine and to trust her; he should be sufficiently receptive to her thoughts now. Knot hoped that impromptu team would fulfill its missions. Those might not relate directly to CC, but did relate to Knot's sense of honor. He would lie and kill, it had turned out, to accomplish his designs; he would not deliberately renege on a commitment to a friend. Strella's friend, the gross one's brother—they at least could benefit by this excursion, even if Knot's primary mission failed.

Before the normals' truck arrived, a contingent of lobos came from the villa. "We shall take charge of the prisoner," their leader announced.

There was the confirmation: The lobos had not captured him. Normals had done it—and now the lobos wanted to derive the benefit. Knot made a mental note: Always verify what Piebald said. It might be truth, half truth or lie.

The leader of the normals frowned. "This man stole and almost wrecked a private aircraft. What concern of yours is this?"

"Our records show he sabotaged the solar generating plant we operate under planetary license. We have a warrant for his arrest."

The normal was polite, but it was evident he shared the

Macho aversion to lobos. "Your warrant will be taken under advisement by the appropriate office," he said. "We have this man in custody, and will process him according to protocol relating to nonnative physical mutants who violate Macho laws. In a few days, when this is complete, we may under due process remand him to you."

"I regret we cannot wait for that," the lobo said. His men's laser rifles began to swing down.

The normals reacted more swiftly. "Kindly desist, lobo," the normals' second-in-command said, pistol in hand. "This man is our responsibility, and we intend to see that he is processed properly and given medical attention." Knot liked to feel he was without prejudice, but after what Finesse's sendings had shown of Piebald, Knot disliked lobos too. He might deplore the mutilation they had been subjected to, but still did not want to associate himself with them, and certainly did not want to become a lobo himself. He felt much easier in the company of birthmutants such as those of the enclaves: his type of people.

The lobo leader was grim. "There may be a political shift soon," he said meaningfully.

"Well, you be sure to let us know when it comes," the normal said. "We should be through with this man by then."

The truck arrived. Men debouched—and they were lobos. Suddenly control had shifted.

"Thank you for holding this man for us," the lobo leader said as the rifles of his new men covered the normals. "We really appreciate such interforce cooperation." He scribbled something on a sheet of paper. "Here is a receipt for him. You will be welcome to present it when you make your application for extradition through channels."

Knot did not like this. He knew what the lobos had in mind for him. They would lobotomize him, removing his psi power—and his knowledge of their plot against CC—and make him one of them. Like fabled vampires, converting their victims to their own kind. He would much prefer to be in the hands of the normals. But it seemed he had no choice. Extradition? It was a mockery!

They loaded him onto the truck and drove toward the volcano. A panel opened in the igneous face of its base, and they drove into a lighted tunnel. Deep in the mountain they debouched, and carried Knot on a litter to an elevator. It rose a considerable distance, smoothly.

What was this place? More than a villa, certainly! This was a considerable lobo stronghold, honeycombing the cone of the volcano, probably drawing power from what fading subterranean fires remained. Perhaps this was the center of the lobo operations on this planet, with the villa being only the visible tip of the berg. Innocent-seeming camouflage. CC should be really interested in this—if CC could get the report.

At the moment, this seemed unlikely. Knot should have gotten his report to CC first, instead of foolishly trying his rescue. Perhaps by this time there would have been a far more formidable rescue operation. . . .

In trying to be a hero, he had placed his whole mission in peril. Why hadn't he been able to see that before fouling things up?

The elevator stopped. They emerged into the villa.

Finesse stood there, poised and lovely. "Thank you, men," she said coolly. "Please store your rifles and enter that cell." She indicated a barred chamber where a number of other lobos stood. They were evidently prisoners.

"Take her!" the lobo leader cried.

The lobos started toward Finesse. Suddenly all of them hurled their rifles down and retreated with exclamations of dismay. "I have given them a fear of weapons," Finesse said to Knot. "How are you?"

"I'm afraid I need hospitalization," Knot said. With this abrupt rescue, he relaxed—and his injuries became overwhelming.

"We'll see that you get it." She looked at the disarmed lobos. "Now move into that cell!"

They hesitated. There were many of them, and only one of her. Then they seemed to become afraid of the open space outside the cell, and crowded into confinement.

Piebald had been wrong about Finesse's lack of positive control; she could force people into the desired actions by making all alternatives frightening. There seemed to be no limit to the number of phobias she could induce simultaneously, or to the number of people she could handle. What a psi-talent!

She closed the gate behind the lobos and locked it in place. Now at last she too could relax. "Oh, Knot, I was so worried! I couldn't remember when I'd seen you last, but I knew I must have sent you back for Hermine and Mit. Then I was picked up, and—" She touched her nose, which was still somewhat swollen. "That awful beast of a man! Did Hermine receive my thoughts?"

"She did," Knot said. "She guided me—"

"Hermine!" she exclaimed. "Where—?"

"On a mission outside. She's all right. I had a hard time getting here, and we decided—"

Finesse smiled, looking down at him as he lay on the pallet. "You surely did. But all's well now, or it will be, once I ransack the lobos' files and get you to competent medical care. Klisty's getting her things organized now. You don't know her; she's a little girl—"

"Hermine told me about her. Dowsing."

Finesse sobered. "One thing that monster turned out to be right about. I am not a normal after all. I am a psimutant, like you. I did not know it myself. Obviously CC knew—"

"I should have guessed. You made me afraid to leave, when I first interviewed CC, and you stopped those chickens from—"

"That was unconscious. No one knew—" Her brow furrowed. "Mit! *He* should have known!"

"CC put a block on him, preventing him from telling," Knot said. "So that no one could betray the secret prematurely. Until we were in the heart of the enemy camp, and needed your psi to escape. CC is ruthlessly disciplined about such things." He paused, thinking of another secret. "One other thing CC blotted from your memory—"

She kneeled beside him. "Oh, Knot—does it make a difference?"

"Of course it does!" he exclaimed. How could he steal a married woman from her family? "You—"

There were tears in her eyes. "I hardly remember our most recent contacts, but I think I love you, Knot. If you don't—"

"You can't love me! You have a—"

"I know you wanted a normal—"

In the midst of telling her about her husband, Knot

found he could not. She thought it was her psi that balked him. Knot knew he had no right to let her remain deceived—yet he wanted her so much, he had to let the lie stand. "I—feel the same," he said. "I love—" That much was no lie.

"Even though I'm not normal?"

"Let me find out. Kiss me."

She kissed him. He felt transported, as though he had just sipped milk of paradise. He seemed to rotate on his pallet, end over end as the two of them had in her dreams of love. His body tingled as if recovering from stun—which it was.

Knot moved his lips as though savoring fine wine. "I think I'm afraid of kisses," he said.

She raised her small normal fist as if to strike him, then dissolved into weak laughter. "You beast! Come on—we'll close down this place and co-opt a truck."

"I think not," Piebald's voice came from a speaker.

Finesse concentrated visibly, but the lobo only laughed. "I believe I am now beyond your range, psi-girl. I felt only the mildest apprehension just then, no real fear. You have fallen into a common trap for the novice, failing to ascertain the limits of your power. When you left me, your effect on me faded and then abated entirely—and I think you will not again get within range of me until I am ready for you."

There was the noise of doors slamming, all over the villa. "I have now secured the premises. You are confined to the region you are in. I have a master key that will allow me to pass freely between chambers, but you are not so fortunate. It is true you have a good many of my men in your power—but these are expendable. You, my dear, are the crucial one—now that we have uncovered your talent. Shall we negotiate?"

Knot made a signal to Finesse. She silenced the prisoners as she had Piebald, before, so that they could not yell warning. Then she dragged Knot on his pallet to the elevator door. It was closed, just as the others were, and locked, but it represented more access to a far larger portion of the establishment than any other door did.

Knot's wounds were weakening him, despite his effort to hold on. He had lost some blood, and could be bleeding internally, though probably most of the effect was from shock: the body's own withdrawal of blood from circulation. Laser wounds were normally clean, self-cauterized, with bleeding minimized, but holes in large muscles or gut were serious. "Tools," he murmured. "I know how to short—"

Finesse brought him a laser rifle. "Will this do?"

"Maybe." He squirmed painfully around, aimed the rifle, and fired at the lock. There was a bright splay of light, and metal dripped down. Knot squinted at it, aimed, and fired again. This time the lock released, and Finesse was able to get into the elevator.

"This gives access to everything, I believe," she said. "But I'm sure Piebald will have barricaded himself behind triple sets of locked doors. I wish we had Hermine and Mit to tell us for sure." She paused. "You're sure they're—?"

"The lobos don't know about them," he murmured. "They think I have all the psi."

"Oh." She was quiet, realizing that it remained unwise to yield any information at all to the lobos while the present issue remained in doubt. She took his hand.

Knot squeezed it, using the same code he used for the gross one. I DIDN'T WANT THEM TO GET CAPTURED.

To his gratified surprise, she squeezed back. She knew the code! SO WE'RE ON OUR OWN RESOURCES. I FEEL NAKED.

SEND TO HERMINE, AS YOU DID BEFORE. JUST SO SHE KNOWS.

YES. She concentrated a moment. THERE. JUST A SPOT SUMMARY. NOW WE MUST ACT.

The elevator operated. It was on a fail-safe circuit that could not be broken from Piebald's control unit. They dropped to the basement. Here the doors were not locked; it was more like a warehouse area.

"So you used the elevator," Piebald's voice came over another speaker. "Very intelligent. I hoped you would not be able to manage that, but am not surprised, given your assorted psi-talents. At least it freed your lobo hostages. But you cannot accomplish anything from the nether region."

"He's guessing; he doesn't know where we are," Finesse whispered. "Those speakers are all over the premises." She dragged Knot's pallet out of the elevator.

"You can't get anywhere like this," Knot said, keeping his own voice low so as to make pickup difficult. Squeeze-talk was much slower, and now that they were off the subject of Hermine and Mit it did not matter so much if they were overheard. If the system was so designed that the lobos could not pick them up, all the better.

And why *should* such an elaborate two-way system be installed here in the lobo headquarters? They could hardly have anticipated a situation like this! So it should be merely a variant public-address system. "Park me here and circle around. See if you can get within psi-range of him."

She considered. "I may have to. He'll have more armed lobos after us before long, searching all the rooms. But—"

"Put me near a circuit box. I'll create a diversion."

"You're almost unconscious already! Just relax and be inconspicuous."

"And be forgotten? I'm better off participating!"

"Um, yes." She checked quickly. "I wish—a certain party were here. We could locate a circuit box immediately. Ah—this should do it." She dragged him across to a terminal box. "I don't know what you can do from here, but—"

"You get on your way. I'll work out something."

She leaned down to kiss him again. She was in a plain flower-print dress, and the front fell away to give him a pleasant peek into her bosom. How sweet these fleeting glimpses became, when life threatened to be short! "Luck, Knot."

"Luck, Finesse. Don't bang your nose."

She was gone. His gut hurt, but his condition seemed to be stable. He refrained from looking at the wound, afraid it would be worse than it felt. Right now he had a job to do, if he could figure out how. He had to create a distraction.

Yet his concentration was diverted by his guilty conscience. Should he have told Finesse about her husband? Yes, of course he should have! He made himself a resolution: At the next opportunity, he *would* tell her. If things worked out so that one of them died, his silence would really have made no difference, but if they escaped the lobos, he would tell her. Yes.

Now he was able to focus on the problem. He used the rifle to melt off the box lock, and looked inside. There was a complex of connections and switches and several sophisticated fuses. His electrical expertise came into play; he didn't remember studying the subject, but he had certainly learned it well enough for this! This was a configuration typical of an access lead to heavy power outlets, such as miniature cyclotrons or heavy industrial lasers. But the layout was not right for that sort of operation. Where, then, did these lines lead?

Knot did more exploring, supporting his hurting body with increasing difficulty, drawing himself up to peer closely at the leads. In due course he found a schematic diagram, necessary to enable repair crews to correct damage, replace fuses and such without complicating the situation. He studied the diagram with the same mysterious expertise he had for locks and wiring. It seemed this power connected to the detonation mechanism for explosives set in a deep cave in the mountain. There was a fifteen-minute time-delay between commitment and execution, but the sequence, once initiated, was irreversible —assuming this setup were typical of its type.

Knot considered. Were they doing blasting for mining? In a volcano?

A volcano! Quiescent now—but surely titanic forces lurked below, and if these were triggered—

A self-destruct system! Naturally the paranoid lobos would include something like that. They didn't want the normals of CC prying into their sinister secrets. If there were any frontal attack on this fortress, and it seemed likely to be successful, the lobos would simply activate the detonator and take a hovercraft out of here within fifteen minutes, leaving the enemy to its fate amid seeming victory. A nasty trap, typical of this organization. But perhaps it could be made into just as nasty a counter-trap.

Knot worked carefully, pausing when he grew faint from pain and fatigue, willing consciousness to return. What use to save his immediate body, if the lobos won and lobotomized him? He used his fingers to pry key wires into a position for ready connection. Now the extra finger on his right hand was helpful; he could hold more wires safely separated, while moving new ones into place with his left hand. At length he was satisfied. He could short the mechanism in a moment, now, starting the destruct process.

If it turned out that he and Finesse could not escape, that they both faced torture and lobotomy, he would initiate the one-way sequence, taking Piebald and this whole fortress with him. Perhaps the resulting detonation would alert CC to the nature of the lobo threat. Even if not, it would still be a very satisfying way to die.

"Finesse," Piebald's voice came over the speaker, "you have tripped a signal beam, and we have located you. If you will glance at the ceiling, you will observe a laser weapon trained on you. I suggest you remain motionless until our police robot comes to apprehend you."

They had spotted Finesse! And a robot would not be vulnerable to her psi, any more than it would be to his own psi. They would recapture her in moments, or gas her unconscious, and that would be the end.

Knot had to act. He drew out the key wires and held them in his hands as he slumped down against the wall. His consciousness faded with every physical effort he made, but this had to be done. "Piebald!" he called, hoping that there were pickups here as well as speakers. He had grown dependent on Mit and Hermine for such information, and now felt inadequate. "I have shorted your station-destruct system, and I doubt you can bypass my connection before I can use it. Release Finesse, or I will blow up your mountain."

There was a pause. Then Piebald answered. That much had worked! "It seems we are at another impasse," the lobo said with seeming calmness. "My circuit sensors verify that there is an interruption in the destruct system. Yet if I release the woman, this station is surely doomed. If I do not—"

"Knot, he's stalling!" Finesse cried. "Don't trust him! Blow it up!"

But Knot hesitated, hoping for some better way to wrest control from the lobos. It seemed to him there was a missing element, a special key. Something they all had overlooked. But what was it? He concentrated—but instead felt his consciousness slipping away again. There was fresh blood on his thigh, leaking out, the injury aggravated by his activity. He had overextended himself, expending his last reserves of energy, losing too much blood; his brain was running dry, and was—

"Don't wait, Knot!" Finesse cried. "Do it!"

"You have foolish courage," Piebald said to her. "He hardly wants to destroy you, after coming all this way to rescue you. One can hardly blame him for hesitating."

Damn the man's insidious insight! That *was* a factor in Knot's hesitation. He had been led astray all along by his passion for Finesse, making wrong moves when he really knew better. The whole episode of the chasm enclave—

"He came to alleviate the threat to CC!" Finesse retorted. "By destroying you, he can accomplish that. The rest of us don't matter."

There was that. Knot's hand moved toward the critical connection. His mind and body were so numb that he could only master one impulse at a time. Destroy the villa, save CC. . . .

"It is obvious he loves you," Piebald said. "He could have attacked the villa by stealing a min-nuke from the Macho arsenal and crashing his aircraft into the mountain. He did not, because you were prisoner here. He will not destroy the mountain now, for the same reason. Love restrains him—and why not? You are eminently lovable."

"I love him too!" Finesse cried. "Knot, if you love me, activate that destruct system now!"

"How can you love him," Piebald asked, "when you are married to another man, and have a child by that husband?"

Piebald had known! He had done it! The demon!

"Oh, God, I—" Finesse choked off, remembering. The lobo's strike had been unerringly timed. Now her will, as well as Knot's, had been sapped. She had been caught expressing adulterous passion.

Better death than this dual shame! With abrupt determination Knot took the wires. But his head seemed to be reeling, his hands shaking. The wires drew out from his grasp as his hand fell. Piebald had been right; Knot did not really want to destroy Finesse, even to save CC, and that vitiated his imperative, sapped his strength, and denatured his will. The room shook and wavered as he struggled to retain volition. But he was too far gone. He slid ignominiously down the wall.

Men burst into the room. They grabbed Knot roughly and hauled him away from the box. He was barely conscious, unable to resist.

"We have secured the man,"' the lobo in charge announced. "The destruct system has not been activated."

"Excellent," Piebald replied. "Now, Finesse, you realize that you have no option except to—"

"Is that true, Knot?" she called. "Do they have you?"

Time for the lie. "No!" he exclaimed weakly. "I shorted the wires before they—"

"Then we must move," she said.

There was a sound, followed by a kind of scream and thud, as of a slight body hitting the floor.

"I'm sorry you did that," Piebald said. "That weapon was set on automatic, and I fear it has killed you. Your friend was bluffing, of course. Bring him here, men."

"Yes, sir," the lobo in charge of Knot's detail said. They hauled Knot into the elevator and began the ascent.

They had lasered Finesse! He should have known that a hardened criminal like Piebald would not be bluffed. What had he gained? Only her injury or death!

The doors were operative now. Piebald had released them, since his own men were in charge again. In this spot engagement the lobo had outplayed the psi-team. In a moment Knot was dragged before Piebald himself.

The lobo was exactly as Finesse's sendings had rendered him: a normally conformed man rendered grotesque by virtue of his striking coloration. But for that, he would have been handsome, for he was tall and robust with finely chiseled facial features.

"So you are the anonymous one we have labored so hard to apprehend," Piebald said. "I can see why you have been so formidable an opponent. You are, like me, a double mutant. A minimal physical distortion, and a major psi-ability—together with considerable determination and natural aptitude for espionage. I think we should have liked each other, had we met in other circumstances. I, like you, possessed the pride of the flesh."

There seemed to be little hope, but Knot decided to try to stall by drawing the lobo out in conversation. Maybe Finesse was not badly hurt, and would recover consciousness. He had to hope! "What kind of psi were you?"

"So good of you to inquire," Piebald said with pseudo-affability, and now Knot was sure he was not being fooled. He would stall precisely the length of time he chose to, then get on with his business, regardless of anything Knot might attempt. "I was an exploder. I could detonate virtually anything. I was not a pyro, able to set off only conventional explosives; I caused the nuclei of atoms to reverse their cohesion and fly apart. Nothing was safe from my power."

"I remember," Knot said. "I didn't realize you were that one. About ten years ago the news was all over the galaxy. The human detonator! They had to use a tele-pathic stunner to subdue you, and even so there was quite a blast—"

"Yes. I retain an affinity for explosives, though the chemical ones I am now restricted to are but a shadow of the psi ones of my former ability. You very nearly turned that against me, by shorting the detonator control circuit, as a worthy opponent should. I am exceedingly glad to have you in hand, though there would have been no way for you to have shorted my psi-control, in my better days." He frowned, and Knot knew he genuinely missed his old power.

Some strength was returning as Knot lay still on the pallet. "What do you want with psis?" Knot demanded. "Why go to all the trouble of capturing and evoking them, when all you do is kill or lobotomize such people?"

Piebald smiled. "That does appear counterproductive, doesn't it! Yet there is a rationale. We are not idly abolishing psi-talents; we are performing experiments. Our actual quest is for a mechanism to reverse the effect of lobotomy. You can appreciate that should we succeed in this, we would have at our disposal a tremendous reserve of devastating psi-talents, my own included. We might well be in a position to dominate the human galaxy."

"Yes," Knot agreed. All that psi, in criminal minds! The lobo thought such psis would take over the government of the galaxy, but the more likely result would be the opposite, as psi fought psi, knowing no sane limits. What devastation would ensue!

"We lobotomize under controlled conditions, then attempt surgically to reverse the operation, to restore the burned-out nerves while the loss is yet new. With minimal damage and immediate restoration, while the habit-patterns remain, we might achieve the key. But most important, we shall be free at last from the onus a cruel society unfairly placed on us. We shall be whole again! That is our grail, our ultimate objective. That unifies us, gives us courage to continue."

The man was serious. Knot still hated him, yet could see the point. If he himself should lose his psi, he would desperately want it back, just as the recent lobos Finesse had interviewed did. Still, this did not seem to account for the remarkable unity and discipline of the lobo movement. Success in restoring lobo-psi would only mean that men like Piebald had the ultimate power over lobos; any lobo wanting restoration would have to cater to Piebald, and become in effect a slave. Why strive so hard for that? Individual lobos should give up in disgust, start quarreling in the face of repeated failures, fighting each other, walking out. They were, after all, criminal types, and there was little honor among thieves. Instead they acted like truly responsible citizens, handling public services reliably, and organizing themselves efficiently. Again: How was this possible, in the absense of any psi ability among them?

"I see you do not entirely accept this thesis," Piebald said. "There is of course more to it than I have told you—but that is information we entrust only to committed lobos, and not to all of them. Perhaps the time will come, for you. As it happens, we now have two new, potent psis to experiment with. We value major talents, and especially the highly motivated individuals; these seem far more likely to achieve the breakthrough we are striving for. We had some lesser psis, now out of the picture, that were too weak to be good prospects. But Finesse, if she lives, is excellent; you are even better. You actually fought free of our solar power station and out of the chasm enclave—feats thought to be prohibitively difficult. You may be our most promising prospect to date." He raised his voice. "Status of the female psi?"

"Stable," a man answered over the speaker system. "The beam grazed her head and burned her left collarbone; no internal damage."

"That's a relief," Piebald said. "It would have been a shame to lose her, after I struggled so hard to evoke and classify her psi. Now—"

The lights went out.

"Who is responsible for this?" Piebald snapped. "We are in control of the situation; there is no need for—"

"I did it, Mr. Pie," a child's voice came. "I psied out the main illuminator circuit cable—and now I am using the console to release the poisonous snakes from the snake pit."

Klisty, the ten-year-old dowser-girl Finesse had saved when her psi was evoked! That was the missing element Knot had not been quite able to recall. The child, loose, on the side of the psis! Klisty could have no love for the lobos, after her ordeal.

"The child," Piebald muttered as if in pain. "I forgot the child!"

"You sure did, Mr. Pie!" Klisty's voice came. "Now all the snakes are crawling out. They're nice and warm now, very active, and sort of ornery. I'm up on a counter where they can't reach me, I hope, but I think they'll bite anyone walking around on the floor. So watch your step, Mr. Lobo-Pie; we wouldn't want you to get bit!" She sounded gleeful.

In the darkness and distraction, Knot summoned his remaining strength and dragged himself across the floor. He didn't know whether he would find Finesse or Klisty or a snake first, but at least he would get away from Piebald.

"You are bluffing," Piebald said. "You would be in as much danger from the reptiles as any of us."

The rigged circuit-box! If Knot could get back down there again—

"You just keep thinking that, Mr. Pie," the little girl cried. "Pretty soon you'll know for sure!"

Knot found the elevator and crawled inside. Already he had considerable respect for the little girl, who was taking the lobos' attention so well. Even if it were a bluff, it was tremendously helpful. But he found he couldn't reach the buttons to operate the elevator. If he tried too hard, climbing up the wall, not only would he risk fainting, but also the noise he made would alert the lobos. His escape was precarious on several grounds.

Someone screamed. "A snake! I've been bitten!" It was a man's voice—a lobo.

Knot heaved himself up and punched the first button he found. The elevator closed its door and began to move down, fortunately.

Now there was pandemonium in the villa. Knot could hear it over the speaker system. Lobos were encountering snakes all over, in the dark. Discipline had broken at last; the horror of fangs and deadly venom was too great. Klisty was having her fitting revenge.

Knot felt over the button panel, locating his floor by feel. He directed the elevator, and it stopped at the one he wanted. He crawled out, trusting that the snakes had not reached this level yet, and began casting about for his terminal box. This was not the same elevator he had used before, so his orientation was imperfect.

Meanwhile the babel in the speaker system continued. What a mess it must be up there! Klisty had acted with genius.

It took time, and pain, and iron will, but Knot kept crawling. His wounds were on the left side, which left his stronger right side intact; that helped some.

The elevator door behind him opened again. Oh no—someone was after him! Knot had hoped he had already been forgotten; that was his great asset, the fact that out of sight was usually out of mind. Knot lay still, suppressing his heavy breathing.

"I know you're there," a voice exclaimed. "I can sense the water in your body. Give up, or I'll shoot!"

"Klisty!" Knot exclaimed. "I give up! You don't know me, but—"

"Are you the one who was going to blow up the mountain?"

She had been beyond his psi-range, listening on the speaker system. Thus she had not forgotten this. "Yes. I'm still going to—if I can't rescue Finesse. How did you get down here? I thought you were perched on a cabinet, avoiding the snakes."

"I was. But I can tell where they are, in the main villa, because the floors don't match the conductivity of the snakes and people. So when the snakes went on by, I came down and caught a 'vator. I thought maybe that blowup circuit—I don't know anything about that sort of thing, but maybe if I wiggled the right wire—but I guess you had the same idea."

"Yes. But I am wounded. It's hard for me to get around. I have to crawl."

"I'll help you," she decided. "Where's the blowup place?" Childlike, she extended her trust too rapidly. But this was a blessing this time!

"On one of the walls of one of these rooms. If only Mit were here to locate it!"

"Who?"

"A friend of ours who happens to be clairvoyant. But he's on another errand at the moment. You can move better than I can; see if you can—"

"Yes. I'd better try for Finesse too." She took a breath. "Finesse? Are you awake?"

It seeemed unlikely that Finesse could hear the call over the babble, even if she were conscious. But she did. "Yes! Where are you, dear?"

"Down below with what's his name. I'm looking for the blowup box. Can you get down here fast?"

Now Piebald caught on. "The psis are escaping. Stop them!"

But no one responded to him. The snakes had terrorized the villa, so that no one was listening for orders.

Then the speaker system cut off. Piebald had gotten smart about that, realizing that it was benefiting his opposition more than his own side.

"I found the box!" Klisty cried. "Wires dangling loose and everything—"

Knot scrambled toward her voice. The lobos had set a barrier of sorts before it, a bench, evidently intending to work on it—but the pace of subsequent events had prevented them from doing that yet. Soon Knot had the wires in his hand. "I can set it off now," he said. "Foolish of them to leave it open—but I suppose they didn't dare fool with it. One wrong connection by an amateur could have destroyed them, literally! But if I start it going now, and Finesse can't make it down here in time—"

"I can go back up and look for her—"

"And get bitten by a snake or caught by the lobos! Don't risk it. If she's conscious, she's proof against those things, and you would only risk becoming a hostage. Better look for a truck instead. I think this is the vehicle level. I'll blow us up along with the mountain if I have to, but I'd much prefer to escape. Do you know how to drive?"

"No, I'm just a little girl."

He had to smile. He could not see her at all, in the dark, but she was definitely a little girl. "Well, see if you can find one anyway. I can drive if I can strap myself into the seat."

She was off again, invisibly. Knot sat propped against the wall again, with the wires in his hand. He knew his best course was probably to initiate the detonation sequence, to be sure of destroying the lobos, but the fear of trapping Finesse in it still held him back. She was married, she had a family; he still loved her and could not bring himself to kill her if there were any conceivable alternative. If she didn't make it down here—

"I found a truck!" Klisty called.

Knot, startled out of a developing reverie by her high voice, almost put the wires in his hand together for the detonation sequence. But perhaps that made no difference, now the decision was upon him. He could initiate the sequence, crawl to the truck and barge on out; at least he would destroy the lobos and save the little girl. Or he could wait for Finesse and risk losing everything. The snakes would not distract the lobos indefinitely. Once they got organized again—

Yet Finesse would be aware of the problem. She knew that Klisty, at least, was down here. Had Klisty mentioned Knot? Yes. So Finesse knew what he would be doing. She would use her psi to scare people away from her, perhaps generating the fear *of herself*—until she joined the child. If Finesse were up and about, she would make it—and she seemed to be up. So he had to have faith— and be alert for her approach.

Yet again, he missed Hermine the weasel. A little telepathy, or Mit's precognition . . . but no use to wish for what was not available. He had become too accustomed to leaning on the psi-talents of others; he had to lean on his own abilities now.

"Klisty—when she comes, we should feel some sort of fear, perhaps aversion. That will be the time to start the detonation countdown—and the truck."

"I guess so," she said hesitantly.

"Stay near the elevator. Let me know when you start getting frightened."

"I'm scared already!"

"Of Finesse, not lobos."

"But I'm not scared of Finesse!" Then she completed the connection. "Oh. Her psi!"

Knot heard the child move to the elevator. They waited. Klisty was right: He too was scared. So many things could go wrong, and if he passed out again, or the lobos charged in as they had before and stopped him . . . suppose Finesse didn't make it? If she got lost, or misunderstood what he was planning down here, or if the lobos somehow blocked her off . . . no, they would be afraid to do anything to interfere with her. It was him, Knot, they could approach most readily, and Piebald would surely realize—well, this time Knot would make sure to connect the detonation wires before he passed out. In fact, he could hold the wires so that even if he were lasered, they would come together. Even if they brought in vicious animals to launch themselves silently at him in the dark, or if a poisonous python slithered up and bit him . . .

Knot fidgeted. He was working himself into a state of unreasonable fear! He knew it was unreasonable, but still his breath quickened, his heartbeat accelerated, and he was frightened.

Suddenly Klisty's cry brought him alert. "Something awful's coming! I'm terrified!"

Her too! Something was associated with the elevator. The room remained dark, but he knew where that elevator was—and a deep and expanding horror emanated from it. The lobos must have set something truly horrendous on his trail! "We've got to get away from here!" he gasped.

Klisty was already retreating from the elevator. Then she stopped. "Finesse! It must be her psi, just as you said."

"That's it!" he exclaimed. "Now it's operating on us as well as the lobos, because she doesn't know who or what lies in her way. No wonder it's effective!"

All they had to do was meet her at the elevator and guide her through the dark to the truck. A terror explained was a terror abolished, wasn't it?

It was not. This was not the fear rising from ignorance; this was directly induced, nonpsychological emotion. No rational thoughts could abate it. It simply *was*. Knot found himself whimpering, drawing himself away from the source, though he had to desert his post by the switchbox.

As the door to the elevator opened, Klisty screamed and plunged out of the room. Knot's fear gave him strength to rise to his feet and lumber after her. Neither person could bear the proximity of that horror in the elevator.

"Klisty!" Finesse called. "Klisty, can you hear me? I'm losing control—"

"Turn it off!" Knot screamed, almost gagging in his terror. "We can't get close to you!"

"Oh." Her exclamation seemed hysterical. "Of course! I never thought—"

Suddenly the fear abated. She had turned it off. Klisty turned about and ran to her; Knot heard the footsteps.

"Oh Klisty! I'm so glad you're all right!" Finesse said as they met. "Now if only we can find what's his name—"

"I'm here," Knot called.

But now they heard the lobos closing in. They too had been released from the fear, and they too knew the stakes.

"We must get out of here," Finesse said. "I can drive them off, but in this dark I have to do it generally instead of specifically, which means I'll drive you off too. And—"

There was a series of sounds. "Finesse!" Klisty cried. "I've got you—what's the—oh, you're bleeding!"

"Her injury," Knot said. "Her effort drained her

strength!" He knew precisely how that operated. He started toward them.

"She's heavy!" Klisty cried. "I can't—"

"I can!" Knot said. The strength of fear was replaced by the strength of love. He lurched to his feet, reached the two, and got his hands around Finesse. He heaved her up over his right shoulder. "Lead me to the truck!" he gasped.

The child started off. "No, wait!" Knot cried. "The detonation system—I forgot to—we've got to—" He staggered back toward the box.

"We don't have time!" Klisty cried. "We don't even know whether the truck will run!"

But Knot was determined. He had to destroy Piebald. "All the more reason to be sure this place blows, before they recapture us." He reeled toward the wall, carrying his burden. They crashed; good, there was the wall. He slid along it until he came to the box, then let Finesse dangle across him as he felt for the wires. He connected them, hoping he had done it properly. "Fifteen minutes!" he puffed. "Now we *must* move out!" He wasn't sure whether he was making sense, but believed he was somewhere near it. He lumbered on.

"Over here!" Klisty called.

But Knot's brief splurge of strength, frittered away on inefficient movements, gave out. As he approached the truck, he stumbled, then collapsed to his knees and to the concrete floor, Finesse's limp weight bearing him down.

"Get up!" Klisty cried. "The lobos are coming!"

But Knot could not get up, and Finesse was unconscious. They could do nothing. They had stretched their resources as far as possible, and that had not been quite far enough. At least the lobo stronghold would go down with them.

The lights came on. Lobos burst into the room. In a moment Piebald himself appeared, looking down at them where they sprawled ignominiously on the floor.

"Congratulations on an excellent performance!" The lobo chief maintained his mannerisms, even at the height of conflict.

"Thanks," Knot gasped. "It is only fair to warn

you—" he paused for a labored breath—"that I have set the destruct mechanism. So we'll all go together."

Piebald strode across the room and checked the wiring. He never bluffed or counter-bluffed when he didn't have to. "Into the truck!" he ordered. "Bring the psis—all three of them."

What was the lobo up to? Knot felt himself being roughly lifted and dumped. Klisty screamed and fought, but was loaded anyway. "Spray them with knockout," Piebald called as he started the truck. "We don't want her waking and using her psi again."

There was the hiss of spray. Klisty's screaming stopped, and she collapsed on Knot. Finesse, beside him, never moved. The vapor drifted across, and Knot felt himself fading out.

They had lost. He knew that. They might have destroyed the lobo stronghold, but the three of them would still be fodder for the lobotomy testing program. Knot's sensible course was to let his pained consciousness pass, alleviating his mental and physical suffering. The forces of mutilation had, after all, prevailed.

Yet he could not. Knot hated Piebald and all he stood for. The lobo wanted domination of the galaxy by criminal psi-mutants. Knot saw again the torture and murder of the fat woman Lydia and the old man NFG, and the attempted killing of Klisty. Knot had fought so hard to avenge all this—and the mere destruction of the volcano villa was not enough. He had to destroy Piebald himself, and the lobo organization!

So Knot clung to consciousness as he had clung to the face of the sea cliff when emerging from the enclave chasm. He refused to yield to the knockout drug as the truck bumped out along the tunnel. Knot's body was frozen, but it still hurt, and that pain seemed to fight the drug. He had received a light dose; Klisty's body had taken the worst of it, and shielded him.

But mere consciousness was not enough. The truck was rushing onward. Piebald and a couple of lobos were in the cab. The trusses of the tunnel roof-support were shooting back blurringly. There was little hope that the detonation would occur before the truck cleared the mountain; Piebald well knew the danger, knew the time limit, and knew his fastest route out. He was perhaps the best fitted person present to get the truck clear in time. Knot felt mixed frustration and relief. His survival, for the moment, was linked to Piebald's, by unpleasant irony. How could Knot save himself and his friends, and destroy Piebald and his lobos and the nascent lobo empire —using nothing but his mind?

Finesse could have done it. She could have made the driver afraid of the road ahead, causing him to swerve into the tunnel wall. She could have made them all afraid of motion, so that they would stop and wait for the detonation. But Finesse was unconscious. Thoroughly so, since she had fainted before being touched by the spray.

Many other psis could have done the job—mind controllers or stunners or telekinetics or even a levitator, if he were strong enough to lift the truck's drive wheels clear of the ground and prevent the truck from traveling forward. But no such psis were here. Knot himself was the only conscious psi here—and his talent was passive. Alone, he might be forgotten, and have time to recover and escape—but Finesse and Klisty would be remembered. So psi was useless in this situation. It really had not served him awfully well, on this adventure; he had had the advantage of being unknown to the lobo network, but now they had him in their files, and would not forget him for long. CC had depended on too weak an ally, overestimating the usefulness of initial anonymity.

Of course, CC had to have known about Finesse's psiability, and had used her memory of an otherwise unmemorable person to trigger it at a critical moment; that had been a very clever ploy. So in that sense Knot had served his purpose. He had not been the weapon, but the trigger of the weapon. But CC had outsmarted itself, thinking the animals would be with them at the key moment, and they were not. Hermine and Mit were with the gross one, thanks to Knot's arrangement. Some help he had been there!

Light splashed down. They were clear of the mountain! Now the truck accelerated, putting distance between itself and the volcano. Piebald, cunning and ruthless, had saved them all, unfortunately. While leaving all his prior assistants and loyal supporters to perish without warning.

Hermine—Knot's thought looped back to that. Finesse could send to her, one-way, because the weasel was attuned. Finesse might get Hermine to summon the gross one. But Finesse was unconscious. No doubt Piebald was smart enough to keep all three of them sedated until they reached another lobo lobotomizing station. No chance there.

Could Knot do it himself? Hermine had been with him through a considerable adventure, and had known of him through Finesse too—which meant Hermine should remember him well enough. The intercession of a third party vitiated Knot's psi, just as a written note did, or a machine record. He and Hermine had linked minds closely during the weasel's engagement with the psi-rats of the solar power station; that was about as close together as two minds could get. They had been separated for a while now, but Hermine should be able to recall him, especially with Mit's reminder.

Was she close enough, in distance and emotion, to tune him in as she had Finesse? If so, he might send to Hermine, and let her arrange a rescue. She would need the power of a human mind to draw on—but if she were still with the gross one, that should do. The gross one actually had a good mind, when it was accessible.

He had to try. It was the only chance.

Hermine, he thought intensely. **Hermine, receive me. I am Knot, your companion of the chasm enclave. Hermine, I need help.** Was he getting through? He had no idea. Hermine was beyond her sending range; she could not answer him. Now he appreciated the extent of the faith Finesse had had, to keep making such detailed sendings, without response. He had to show something similar.

Light erupted behind them. Knot was facing partway back, his vision mostly obscured by Klisty's body. But the intense light had to be from the volcano. Even as he realized that, the sound came—a great, body-quivering boom. Then a series of lesser sounds, as of debris falling.

Would the detonation trigger the volcano? Knot didn't know. Perhaps it took time for the released lava to rise; the full process of eruption might take days or weeks.

It really didn't matter; that villa would no longer be usable. Its destruction was only a token; the lobo threat to CC continued. The lobos would keep on lobotomizing CC psi-agents, until either there were too few to function, or they achieved the lobotomy-reversal breakthrough—in which event they would pose twice the threat to CC as before. Only if someone exposed the nature of the threat before the point of no return—

It was like the villa-volcano destruction, he thought; once the key wires of the detonator sequence were crossed, the result was inevitable. Once the key lobo connections were made, CC was doomed, even though there would be a period of months or years before that became incontrovertible. Precognition had told the story —and Knot's mission was precognitively obscure. No one knew the outcome of this struggle, and perhaps that was because it was as yet undecided. The fate of the galaxy might hang on what he accomplished now.

Hermine! he thought desperately. **Finesse is with me and unconscious. She will perish if not rescued soon. You must bring help, somehow. We are near the volcano, in a truck, driving**—he paused to calculate his orientation—**driving roughly north now, at fairly high velocity. If you can intercept the truck—**

Of course she couldn't intercept the truck, he realized with dismay. Hermine was only a weasel. Unless Mit had an insight—

Hermine! If you are near, and Mit can tell where this truck will stop—if you can bring the gross one—

But it seemed to be useless. The weasel probably could not receive him, and could not act in time if she could. What could a little telepathic creature do? Even buttressed by Mit's clairvoyance and precognition, her resources were limited. She might be far away; he could be lobotomized before she reached him. Yet all he could do was try. **Hermine! Hermine!**

The truck continued north interminably, then made a turn west. Finesse stirred but did not revive. The lobos had made sure she was out for the duration, knowing she was the dangerous one. Knot himself seemed to be recovering some use of his limbs—but his injuries and fatigue kept him nonfunctional. **Hermine—we are turning west.**

Maybe near our destination. They will stop soon to drug us again, I'm sure, and I won't be able to send anymore. If you are receiving me, get help quickly. Any kind. We're desperate.

A loud buzzing fly came up and perched on the wooden side of the truck. Knot was afraid it would bite one of them, but it only waited.

The truck turned north again, then slowed and stopped. They were where they were going.

Piebald came around to the back. "I trust you three are comfortable?" he inquired. He swatted at a stinging fly. "I would have arranged better accommodation, had I had more warning about the necessity for this journey. We would not want you to wake too soon, now, would we!" He swatted again.

The other two lobos came around. "Ow!" one exclaimed. "Something stung me!"

Then all three of them were waving their arms about as a small swarm of large flies or small wasps attacked them. "What possesses these bugs?" Piebald demanded.

Possession! Hermine, is this your doing? Knot thought. **Did you send flies?**

A fly buzzed across to land near Knot's face. It seemed to be a cross between fly and bee, solid but fast, with yellow on its body. Its faceted eyes seemed to orient on him.

Bee, are you telepathic? Knot thought. **Can you receive me?**

The bee buzzed up as though brushed away, then settled back in the same place.

If you receive me, come sit on my head.

The bee buzzed across to perch on Knot's head.

So Hermine *was* responsible! The weasel herself might still be out of range, but the fast-flying bees had arrived in time. **I'm glad to see you. Try to stop the lobos from knocking us out again, and in due course we'll recover. Finesse can handle the lobos when she wakes, even if she can't move well.**

But now he heard the rumble of another truck. Oh no—more lobos? Piebald could have radioed for reinforcements from some other lobo station, gathering a new nucleus about him. Knot struggled to throw off his remaining paralysis, but his limbs only quivered; it was still too strong. The bee buzzed off.

The other truck slowed and stopped. Someone got out, thumping heavily on the ground.

"Look at that!" a lobo cried, pausing in his arm-waving to stare.

Then Knot heard the squeak of the gross one. **Hermine —you made it!** he thought.

Yes, Knot, the weasel's welcome thought returned. **I received you. We came as fast as we could. We had not gone far from the villa, for the gross one was having difficulty managing the truck, and also we hoped we could help you somehow. Mit thought we might succeed, if you got out of the mountain.**

Now the sounds of combat developed. The gross one was wading in.

Bless you! Knot thought with overflowing gratitude. Then, at last, he let himself lose consciousness.

Part III

MUTINY

CHAPTER 10

Knot woke in a comfortable bed. He had confused half memories of waking and hurting and lapsing out again several times; of nightfall, and bright day, and night again. This time, however, he was clear-minded.

Finesse was in a bed next to his. She was already awake. She raised an inquiring eyebrow at him. "Who are you?" she asked.

Laboriously, he began to explain, as he had so often before, with so many people. But she was smiling, then laughing. "Shut up, Knot! Hermine updated me!"

Knot smiled ruefully. "You know how it is."

"I forget," she said. She got out of bed and crossed to him. "But I have another reminder." She picked up a placard that hung at the foot of his bed, and turned it for him to read.

It said: THIS IS WHAT'S HIS NAME.

Knot tried to laugh, and felt his gut wound.

"I wasn't really badly injured; it was mostly shock," she said. She showed her left shoulder, covered by a bandage. "But you—it's a wonder you could move at all! You were in terrible pain, yet you did all that—"

"No, I just kept going because I had to."

"Hermine said she never felt such agony. It came through when you sent to her. You had minor surgery to put you back together, two days ago when we brought you here. You could have killed yourself!"

Knot smiled. "I thought I was trying to save my life."

She leaned down and kissed him. She had always had excellent technique in this sort of thing, and had not lost her touch. "You know, I wondered why CC would team high-powered psi-animals up with a normal person and a passive-psi double-mute. I found out about the normal —I really didn't know I was psi, Knot, you must believe that—"

"I believe," he said.

"But still it seemed that for this mission a more aggressive psi-power than yours would have been in order. But now I know; it wasn't just the insidious nature of your psi, which enables you to slip through the best enemy nets—and, incidentally, you performed some escape feats that would make the record books, if anybody could remember them—it was *you*. You've got courage and determination in adversity like none—"

"I was worried about you," he said defensively. "You were being tortured, and—"

She turned her lovely green eyes on him. "Yes?"

And what could he say? That he loved a married woman? Better to change the subject. "Where are we?"

She accepted the change readily. "At the alternate home of the gross one's brother. He has leased it to us for the nonce for a nominal fee—"

Knot came alert. "What fee?"

"Don't worry; it's been paid. He doesn't really believe the precog warning about the threat to him, but he's glad to see his brother again, and is humoring him by changing his itinerary so that he will not be anywhere near the place and time of his predicted death."

"That's the best course," Knot said. "I was a skeptic about precognition, but now I—" He shrugged. She was so pretty, and it was so nice talking with her, that he wanted to extend the conversation. That, at least, he could do without feeling guilty about her marital status. "I'm sure the gross one's brother is a good man."

"An excellent man. A true Macho, in the best sense. He doesn't think much of the present social system, doesn't like the enclave, is working for reform, and is trying to see that his brother doesn't have to go back."

"But the gross one wants to go back! It—uh, he—for

so long I didn't know whether it was male or female, but in the light of the third prediction—"

"The gross one is male," she assured him. "I had quite a conversation with him in squeeze-language. He has a high opinion of you, but says he tends to forget the details."

"Naturally."

"So he's a he, genetically. The physical appurtenances are mutilated, of course, like the rest of him."

"So that prediction can't come true."

"Wrong. He's marrying a rich normal this afternoon. That's one reason we took you off the sleep-heal drug; we knew you'd want to be awake for the occasion."

"Please don't make me laugh. My abdomen hurts."

"Remember that diamond? He delivered it to Strella's friend. She is now a rich normal, thanks to that gift. But she's getting on in years, and is frail, and doesn't quite know how to handle it. She's afraid someone will beat her up or kidnap her for the wealth. So—"

"She's marrying the gross one!" Knot exclaimed. "He can sure as hell protect her from physical violence!"

"Yes. She's well beyond the age where appearances or sex appeal count; she's almost blind herself. What she craves is loyalty and strength. She doesn't like idle chatter—"

"The gross one is virtually mute."

"Yes. So he's actually about right for her. And as the spouse of a normal, he cannot be deported to the enclave. So it's a marriage of convenience, and everyone knows it—but they'll both have better lives than before. She's the one who paid the nominal fee for this residence; she wants the gross one's friends to be taken care of."

"Oh." Knot had been on the verge of a dark suspicion, and was glad to have it relieved. "The gross one is not a bad person," he agreed. "He adapted well to the conditions of the enclave, but he remembers the gentler life before, and he's smart enough. There'll be problems, but—"

"They're being worked out," she assured him. "His brother has considerable clout in the Macho government." She stroked Knot's hair with her delicate fingers. "Now you just settle back and rest, and in a few hours

311

we'll put you in a wheelchair for the wedding." She began to rise.

"Hold!" he said, catching her arm. "What happened to the lobos? Are they under arrest, or still after us?"

"Neither. When the gross one arrived, Piebald got out of there, and we had to let the other two go. It was just a private altercation. We agreed on that, because I can't afford to advertise my real mission, and the lobos can't afford to advertise theirs. So it's mutual hands-off, for now."

"But—"

"Believe me, Knot, it's best. The Macho authorities are friends to neither side. So just relax."

After all that torture and killing, she was letting bygones go! But he was too weak to protest effectively at the moment.

"I like your company," he said after a pause. "Will you stay with me?"

"I thought you'd never ask!" And she made a place on the bed to join him. He was still too weak to do anything dramatic with her, but her presence was excellent medicine. Except—

This time he would do it, instead of stalling. "Finesse, do you remember that you are married?"

"I remember," she said, lying beside him. "When Piebald told me, it all came back. CC's erasures aren't permanent, which is one reason they won't do to curb criminals in lieu of lobotomy. I have a husband I love, and the sweetest little boy—"

"So what has been between us—I'm sorry. I didn't know, until we reached Chicken Itza. Since then there hasn't been anything. I know you can't remember, but I assure you—"

Her head turned to face him on the bed. "My memory was blanked by CC," she said. "I didn't know I was married, any more than I knew I was a psi-mutant. You were the only one I—"

"You knew originally," he said. "But CC didn't like my reaction to the news, so it erased the information from both our minds. But now we both know again. I only wanted to save you from the lobos, and now you're safe. So that ends it."

"In an oink's eye!" she snapped. "I forgot, but you remembered sometime back, didn't you?"

"Yes," he agreed faintly. "But I couldn't leave you in the hands of the lobos."

"And you fought your way out of the chasm enclave and tackled the lobo stronghold, to rescue me."

"It had to be done."

"Instead of reporting directly to CC the way you should have. You put the whole mission in peril."

Knot nodded, abashed.

"Admit it: You did it because you love me."

"I have no right to—"

"So now you're trying to do the noble thing, after all that danger and pain, and are ready to send me back home."

Knot remained silent. She made it sound both callous and ludicrous.

"Knot, you aren't the type. When the choice is between nobility and love, you love."

"Yes, usually."

"I would say," she said slowly, "that you have earned me."

"I didn't mean it that way!"

"Knot, I told you I remembered it all. That includes the pro-tem ad-hoc temporary convenient practical divorce, and his remarriage to another woman. I do love my husband, but I know he and my child will not be safe if they have anything to do with me during this period. I have a whole separate life here—a life with you. If I had remembered my marriage before, I would have told you this before. In two years I will be back with my family, and glad of it; right now I am with you."

"You don't have to—"

"And glad of it," she concluded, and kissed him. "You did so much, at such cost, selflessly, expecting not even to be remembered for it. You will be rewarded—"

"That's not—"

"And you have indeed won my heart. My eyes are open, I know where I'm going, and I know what is right for tomorrow and what is right for today."

"You—"

"Will you stop interrupting?" she exploded, and in

that instant her eyes reminded him of the volcanoes, novas and planet-buster bombs he had joked about with Hermine, so long ago. "I'm telling you I love you too!"

Knot was silent. She had pretty well destroyed his halfhearted attempt to do what he thought was right. Her definitions differed from his, and hers had become dominant.

She was correct about his nobility. It generally did lose out to expediency and sex appeal. But he also wondered: Was she doing this because, at heart, she did not really believe she would ever escape Planet Macho and rejoin her husband?

"And in a few days, when you can travel, we'll take a ship to CCC," she said. "You and I and Klisty. That should enable CC to handle the problem of its scheduled demise."

Knot could not believe it could be that easy. Not with the lobo Piebald out there loose. But Knot wasn't inclined to argue at the moment.

Planet Macho medicine was good, and Knot recovered nicely in days, physically. Klisty played cards and board games with him, and he found her just as likable a girl as Finesse did. Klisty seemed basically happy, whatever her situation; her thermostat was set for joy, and that made her a minor pleasure to be with.

But he also had time to think, while confined, and he was not at ease. This convenient resolution with the lobos—each side leaving the other alone. Finesse had expressed satisfaction, but Knot could not accept it. Neither Piebald as a person nor the lobos as a group were of the forgiving and forgetting persuasion. True, by this time they should have forgotten most of their interactions with Knot himself, because of his psi, and most of their notes on him should have been destroyed with the volcano villa. But they would remember Finesse, and correctly associate her with the destruction of their fortress. And Piebald probably had been canny enough to retain some note about Knot on his person. The lobos should be crazy for revenge. Just to let the known CC agents go, to report the lobos' secret and bring the emotionless wrath of CC down upon them—that did not compute. There should be an assassination squad on duty.

Surely Finesse was aware of this. Why did she so blithely ignore it? She was proceeding as if there were no threat at all.

He thought about it some more, between sleeps. Finesse was neither stupid nor cowardly. She could manipulate people in the most innocent-seeming manner, as she had when she recruited him for CC. Finesse—her very name advertised her nature! A potent psi, masquerading as a normal until the enemy showed its baleful hand.

The trouble was, Knot did not trust this. He wanted to know personally that he could get off this planet intact. He needed to form his own plan, in case whatever Finesse had in mind failed.

At night, when things were quiet, Knot quietly got out of bed and slipped out of the house. His psi would protect him here; anyone he encountered would soon forget the meeting.

Outside, he slunk into a convenient shadow and waited, watching. He did not spy any lobos—but of course they would be inconspicuous. Well, if they did not physically apprehend him, they would forget him, and he would slip through. That was the real advantage of his psi.

He moved on past an ornamental picket fence—and heard a motion in the night. It seemed to be a creature of moderate size, fast and sleek.

Knot stepped back and felt for the picket fence. Quickly he checked the pickets, locating one that was loose. He drew it carefully out of its frame, and ran his hand along its length; it was foam steel, light but strong, its nether end shaped into a formidable spike. It would do.

The animal moved close. Now its outline showed. Sure enough, it was a hound cat, the common local guard pet, a pleasing cross between canine and feline that suited the Macho mode. Assorted breeds were suited for racing, fighting or household duties. This one surely was a fighter.

Knot held the stake before him, its point toward the animal. He did not speak, and the hound cat did not growl; it was a silent confrontation. In this respect, Knot thought, it paralleled the one between lobo and CC agent.

A trained attack animal was deadly—but so was a trained man. Knot, in another of CC's little anonymous arrangements, had learned how to deal with the common animals. If this one pounced, it would meet the stake head-on. The thing had good night vision; it was not eager for that particular meeting. Knot was silently informing it that he had it under control. The thing prowled around, seeking an opening, finding none. Stalemate.

Then a second animal stirred. Quickly Knot felt for a second stake, keeping the first beast covered. He found another loose picket, drew it out, and got it oriented just in time. Silently he signaled the new animal: Attack at your peril.

Suddenly the second hound cat launched itself at the first. A terrific fight ensued—and Knot quietly got himself well away from the vicinity.

What had happened? Why would two trained animals turn from the hunt to an interpersonal quarrel like that, without provocation? It was as if psi were involved—

Of course! **Where are you, Hermine?** he thought.

There was a mental chuckle. **You took a long time to come out, naughty man.**

You put a mean thought into the limited mind of that houndcat.

It was fun. I could not approach the house while they roamed; they eat weasels.

Who sent them?

The lobos, of course. They are not pleased with you.

Knot smiled in the dark, knowing the weasel would pick up the expression from his mind. **They remember me?**

They have written a book about the mysterious party who routed the solar beam at the power station and blew up their party headquarters. They believe you are that party, though they don't remember directly. You have been constantly in their minds—which has enabled me to retain my memory of you.

That's nice. Knot glanced back, though it was his ears that were most useful now. The hound cat quarrel was abating, which could mean trouble for him. **Is there some place we can go to communicate at leisure?**

Yes. Mit says you must return within the hour, but that is time enough. Follow me.

Knot followed her, or rather her thought; the weasel herself was neither visible nor audible. Has Mit figured out how to get us off this planet intact?

Yes. During the mutiny.

Mutiny?

The mutant revolution.

How can the mutes revolt? They can't get out of the enclave.

The animal mutes.

Oh.

It will be easy to ship out during that distraction. But maybe we should not.

Oh? What is on your weasling little mind?

There was something in Piebald's mind, when the gross one brought us to rescue you. It was complex and unconscious, so I could not read it. But very sinister. And Mit has a distance premonition—

I thought he was a short-range precog.

He is. He is not reliable for distance or complex readings. But this one made him very nervous. He would not come out of his shell for a long time, even to eat. He does not want to leave this planet yet.

Knot did not like this. Does Mit often get timid without cause?

Never.

Yet if we don't leave the planet, we can't report to CC.

Yes. I wanted to tell you this, so your big brain could work on it. I cannot handle it; I do not know what is best.

I'll work on it. Have you told Finesse?

She has not emerged or sought to contact me. I think she is afraid the lobos will get us if she betrays our location.

She's more sensible than I.

Go down these steps.

Knot found the steps: grimy boards leading to a deserted cellar. Macho did have its derelict areas, its slums, if one knew where to find them. Certainly a good place to be inconspicuous. It was so good to be back with Hermine!

He pushed through a rickety wooden door and stepped into a cellar that was even darker than the outside night; his eyes could not adjust enough to make out any detail at all, but he trusted Hermine.

Mit says our chances are best if we make a treaty with the hive and its allies, Hermine thought. **You must negotiate, for you are a man.**

Hive? Knot thought questioningly.

Stand still, do not move, do not swat, and the hive will communicate.

Okay, Hermine. This was something unexpected.

There was a faint buzzing. It was as if a cloud of gnats were forming about his head, hovering near his face but not landing. Then a telepathic thought came, quite different from Hermine's, diffuse, fuzzy, yet strong. WE ARE THE HIVE.

Hello, hive, Knot thought. How am I to deal with you?

WE DO NOT TRUST MEN, BUT WE NEED SOME. THE WEASEL CLAIMS YOU CAN BE TRUSTED.

The weasel is almost as bad a liar as I am.

TRUSTED TO HONOR A DEAL WITH OUR KIND.

No. I have killed many bugs—

THAT YOUR LOYALTY, ONCE GIVEN, REMAINS FIRM THOUGH OTHERS FORGET.

That, maybe. I stand by my friends, and by the commitments I make, as well as I can. But my friends are not bugs.

SLAY THE WEASEL, OR WE SHALL STING YOU TO DEATH.

Bees! Flying softly, so he mistook them for lesser creatures. Of course the weasel had been in touch with the telepathic bees! Now they had betrayed her. **Get out of here, Hermine! This swarm means mischief!** Knot braced himself to do battle in the dark.

But no attack came. WE READ YOUR LOYALTY TO THE WEASEL, the hive thought came. YOU WILL ATTEMPT TO KILL US ALL, YOU WILL SACRIFICE YOUR OWN LIFE RATHER THAN BETRAY A FRIEND.

Yes! Knot thought. **That may not be anything you comprehend, but—**

CANCEL THREAT. IT WAS MERE EXAMPLE.

Mere example—and he had fallen for it. **Listen, hive: I don't like your example. I don't trust you, and I'm not about to make a deal with you.**

Knot, negotiate with the hive, Hermine's thought came, pleading. Mit says—

Knot forced himself to cool. **My friend whom you betrayed asks me to be polite to you. For her sake I will listen to your offer.**

WE MUST INFORM YOU WHAT WE ARE AND WHAT WE NEED.

I will listen; that's all I guarantee.

WE SHOULD NOT HAVE USED THAT EXAMPLE.

Is that the extent of your discourse?

Knot! Hermine seemed almost like Finesse, in thought. So ready to do the practical thing and forgive!

The hive presented its case. Knot, prejudiced against it, nevertheless found himself fascinated. This was an aspect of mutation he had never suspected—and it was extremely significant.

Human beings mutated when the sperm cells were exposed to the undefined radiation of space. Animals and insects mutated similarly. But unlike humans, some creatures such as flies, roaches and rats spent their whole lives aboard spaceships, and they had many more generations in a given period. As a result, their mutations were far more comprehensive, and had an impact on their species a hundred times as great as on humans. Natural selection operated savagely, with only 1 percent of each generation surviving.

But with that selection came extremely rapid adaptation to the new condition. Insects normally spread their eggs far more widely than mammals did, and were used to regenerating their populations from exceedingly small nuclei. Thus with only one egg of each hundred viable, this constituted merely a change in the environmental hazard. In a few years the species was surviving and stabilizing despite the horrendous rate of mutation. After a number of generations, variations evolved that could withstand the mutation effect. In addition, there were mutants that bred true, outside the ships. Evolution that in nature would have required millennia had occurred in years.

One such species was the hive: semitelepathic bee-flies who were in constant mental contact with each other. This group consciousness made every individual bee feel and suffer when any member was lost, and the aggregate was considerably more intelligent and disciplined than the individuals. Now the hive intellect was interested in eliminating threats to its welfare, such as the campaign against insects by the human population of Macho.

The hive needed, however, a human spokesman. A man to talk to other men and arrange a cessation of hostilities. Hermine had suggested that Knot was such a man.

But I am not a citizen of Macho, Knot protested. I can barely save my own skin.

WE WILL HELP YOU SAVE YOUR SKIN, IF YOU WILL SERVE AS OUR AGENT IN THIS MATTER.

But Knot remained angry about their "example." **No! I am already serving as agent to the Coordination Computer, whose policies I'm not sure I approve. I will not take on another dubious assignment.**

Knot! Hermine thought, upset. *It is no difficult thing the hive asks, only recognition and parity with man. And we need the hive's help against the lobos.*

The lobos are human, Knot responded. The hive is alien.

The hive has already helped us against the lobos. She flashed a picture of Piebald swatting at bees, while Knot and Finesse lay drugged in the truck. But for that interference, the lobos might have gone on before the gross one could catch up.

Damn! He did owe the hive a favor. But it appalled him, this notion of representing an alien cause.

WE OFFER ASSISTANCE, the hive continued. WE HAVE WORKED WITH OTHER CREATURES, SOME CLAIRVOYANT AND SOME PRECOGNITIVE, TO ASSEMBLE A COMPLETE CHART OF YOUR CO-ORDINATION COMPUTER CENTRAL. IT WOULD GREATLY FACILITATE YOUR MISSION THERE.

No, Knot responded. I have access to other clairvoyance and precognition, and need neither to make my report to CC.

OUR CHART IS UNIQUE. YOUR AIDES CANNOT MATCH IT.

Why did the hive think its chart was so important? Did the hive have an overrated opinion of its work? That hardly mattered to Knot at the moment. **Forget it.**

IF WE CANNOT NEGOTIATE WITH MAN, WE MUST MUTINY AGAINST MAN'S ORDER, the hive warned.

It was a bluff. Man and bugs had been fighting each other for centuries. **I expect you to fight man anyway. I will not help you do it. I don't trust you.**

Knot, you don't know what mischief you are making! Hermine thought. **Alone, I believed an alliance with the hive would help us escape the planet. Now with your human mind enhancing my intelligence, I understand that the stakes are far more important than that. The dominance of man in the galaxy may be at stake. We must come to terms with the psi-mutant animals.**

Why should a weasel care about the dominance of man? Knot inquired.

Man is a familiar master, she replied slowly, thinking it out with her present intelligence. **Man and weasel have come to terms. The hive is alien; it cares neither for man nor for weasel.**

The prosecution rests, he thought. **You can't use my brain better than I can.**

THEN IT SHALL BE WAR, the hive thought. **YET NOW THAT YOU KNOW OUR NATURE, WE MUST KEEP TRACK OF YOU, SO THAT YOU DO NOT BETRAY US.**

Of course I'll betray you!

Hermine's inchoate pleading moved him at last. The weasel was terrified, and not merely for herself. Knot decided to compromise. **I will remain neutral, neither helping you nor betraying you. That much I offer in return for the help you gave before.**

THAT IS INSUFFICIENT. WE CANNOT TRUST YOU, SINCE YOU MADE NO PACT WITH US.

True, Knot agreed reluctantly.

CARRY FIVE OF OUR NUMBER WITH YOU. TO-GETHER THEY WILL FORM A HIVELET CAPABLE

OF GRASPING YOUR SPECIFIC THOUGHTS. IF YOU BETRAY US, THEY WILL BEAR THE MESSAGE TO US. IF YOU JOIN US, THEY WILL PROVIDE YOU THE CHART.

Knot considered a moment. He didn't like the notion of tattletale bees, but was not unmindful that he was at the moment in the power of the hive. The bees probably could sting him to death here, or at least make him extremely uncomfortable. Probably five bees had been lost by swatting when they attacked the lobos; could he really object to five tagging along now? His headstrong actions had gotten him in trouble before; this time it would be better to listen to Hermine. **Agreed,** he thought.

The buzzing of the hive intensified about his head, then faded. The bees had departed.

Hermine was relieved though displeased. **At least you did not get us stung to death. But the hive could have helped us much. Now we still lack the means to escape the planet.**

Sorry about that, he thought penitently. **I just didn't like the way the hive tried to make me hurt you. If you have anything else in mind, I'll try to behave better.**

Without the hive, we need—she paused distastefully in her thought. **Mit says we need the rats. And roaches.**

The vermin, he realized. The other creatures who had sneaked aboard spaceships, mutated horrendously, and finally gotten to the point where they bred true—in mutated forms. The implications of that were slowly spreading through his awareness. Psi-powers that bred true without mutation! That—why, that could be the solution to the greatest problem man faced. If it were possible to have telepaths born to telepathic parents, and precogs to precog parents, with no negative mutations, no attendant decimation of the species—why then, galactic civilization could continue and flourish without the need for mutant enclaves. No mistreated minority class. The hive had it; man needed it. If the rats and roaches also had it, man could be in deep trouble.

Yes, Hermine agreed. **The mutiny means bad trouble for man. The vermin have been mutating and evolving much faster, and have made the breakthrough of nonmutant psi before man. If man does not catch up soon—**

Probably he should not have been so abrupt with the hive. Well, he could get in touch any time he chose, presumably. **Do you read me, spy flies?** he inquired.

There was a faint medley of replies. **Present—here—yes —affirmative—agreed.** They must be perching on his shoulders, and presumably they wouldn't sting him if he did nothing to them. Good enough.

Well, stand by, or whatever it is you do. He paused. **Let me know who you are, individually. Might as well make this companionable. Do you have names?**

There was a momentary mental buzz of consultation. Then: **For this mission, we are B_1, B_2, B_3, B_6 and B_{12}.**

Vitamins! Knot thought with a mental chuckle. **You are drawing from my subconscious imageries. I shall call you, respectively, Thiamin, Riboflavin, Niacin, Pyridoxine and Cobalamin. That's more personal than letters and numbers.**

There was an answering buzz that might have been humor. It was hard to tell how much was them and how much was merely a reflection of his own mind, but Knot began to like the bees better.

Here are the roaches, Hermine thought. **That species prospers because of its psi-talent for detecting incipient danger. When alarmed, they become undetectable.**

I can't detect them anyway, in this light, Knot thought distastefully.

Even in daylight, you could not. They turn invisible, inaudible, unsmellable, and unfeelable.

That's impossible! Knot protested.

It is a variant of your own psi. Living creatures cannot perceive them directly. In your case, living creatures forget what they have perceived. You are retroactively unperceivable.

Ah—but machines can perceive them?

Yes—and people who stand beyond the range of their psi. So they have not achieved ascendancy against man's instruments, yet. I am in mental touch with their representatives. If you will assist them in their quest to achieve safety from machines, they will accompany you and warn you of threats.

I can't tell them how to escape machines. I can't do that myself.

But you will be meeting with CC, who might be able to answer them.

Why should CC help the roaches to prevail against man?

CC is concerned with psi-mutants. These are advanced psi-mutants.

What about me? I don't want ineradicable roaches overrunning my premises.

If man does not deal with the roaches now, he will have to deal with their next generation of mutations. Then it may not be a matter of coexisting, but of man's survival.

She had quite a point. You reason like a human being.

Yes. It is exhilarating, drawing on your intelligence. I never conceived such grand notions alone.

They were certainly impressive notions. Man's survival? I will ask CC about the way for roaches to achieve safety from machines. That's all. I don't guarantee CC's answer. CC may refuse to respond, on grounds that it would be detrimental to CC's self-interest.

The roaches understand that. Their representatives will accompany you.

So now he had to carry the vermin with him! But what had to be, had to be; he could understand their need to have their kind meet CC. He had gone to a lot of trouble to present his own case personally to CC, back at the outset of this adventure. Where are they?

They are in your pocket, Hermine thought. They climbed up your leg just now.

But I never felt— But of course he would not have; nervous psi-roaches were imperceptible. Did that make it better, or worse?

Now the rats, Hermine thought.

How can you stand to deal with rats? They're your natural enemy!

Mit says I must, if I am to survive.

What rat would help you, personally?

I don't know. But I believe Mit. I shall perish without a rat.

Knot sighed. She kept coming up with compelling answers! If you can do it, so can I, I suppose. What is their talent?

They can find food. But more significant are the rat

fleas, who can nullify any poison their hosts assimilate.
But the fleas are vulnerable during their egg stage; then
heat can destroy them. They need help to safeguard that
portion of their life cycle.

Do you realize how ludicrous this is becoming? Knot
demanded.

Yes.

This is the ultimate limit. Why should I want to help
fleas? I would prefer to abolish them entirely!

I am not partial to fleas myself, Hermine admitted. But
they can help us. Drugs are a kind of poison—

Knot caught on. Such as stun gas and truth gas?

Yes.

All right. I will also ask CC how the mutant fleas can
protect their eggs. That's all.

Pick up the rats. They are hosts for the fleas.

I feel like a menagerie! But Knot reached down in the
dark and found two small furry creatures. He lifted them
and put them in a pocket. They were hardly larger than
mice. These assistants will enable us to escape the planet?

Mit thinks so. At least they will help us somehow. He
says the future becomes opaque soon.

You mean I'm picking up all these animals on speculation? Just because Mit thinks they may improve our
chances? No precognitive guarantee?

It is complex. CC could not read your future, even with
Drem the futurist. Now Mit is encountering the same difficulty. He feels it is best to recruit animals who can substitute for his powers and mine.

What's going to happen to you and Mit? Knot thought
with alarm.

Nothing—if we separate from you. We could survive on
this planet. The gross one would welcome us.

And if you stay with me?

Opaque.

I can't blame you for avoiding that risk, Knot thought
regretfully.

No. We are staying with you. We share your mission.

Knot was not even inclined to argue. He had felt naked
without Hermine and Mit, in the lobos' volcano villa.
Knot had been literally naked without noticing; it was
their psi he depended on. Thanks.

We like you. And Finesse. And Klisty.

Knot had not really thought about it before, but realized that Klisty could not be left on Planet Macho. The lobos would destroy her. She had become part of their mission involuntarily. But she was indeed a nice little girl, no burden to have along.

Knot breathed deeply. **Any more vermin to recruit? No.**

May I go home now?

Yes, immediately, Hermine agreed. **Mit says it is time.**

The master has spoken. Knot felt his way to the exit. **Do the rats have names?**

Yes. The male is Roto, the female is Rondl.

They are not telepathic?

Not. Only clairvoyant about food. Since they consume similar staples to men and weasels—

Yes, I understand. But I feel like a walking slum. Flies, roaches, rats, fleas—

Bees, not flies! the mini-hive interjected with buzzing annoyance.

Bees, Knot agreed. He didn't want to get stung.

The last three would be unnecessary as allies, if you agreed to represent the hive. Their chart—

According to Mit's guess—and Mit admits my future is opaque. Maybe no allies are necessary.

Maybe Mit and I are unnecessary too.

Mit did not respond. The weasel was getting as biting with her thoughts as she might be with her teeth. But she was right. He was forever complicating things by doing them his own way. Yet that was the way he was. Possibly that was why precognition was becoming inoperative in his vicinity. Well, what would be, would be—unless he was about to foul things up so badly that what would be would *not* be.

Funny man, Hermine thought. Her pique was abating.

Knot climbed the old steps and emerged to the partial gloom of night. The sky was overcast with no moonslight showing, but the city cast its own ambient radiance. His eyes had adjusted to the point where he could see well enough, and he made good progress toward his host's house.

I must leave you now, Hermine thought. **Mit says it will**

be bad if the lobos detect me with you. But the lobos do not know about the new animals. Take care of them, and we shall rejoin you when the time is right.

May I tell Finesse?

Yes. You must tell her everything. But not so the lobos perceive. They do have monitoring devices.

Right. Farewell for now, whiskerface. Thanks for all. Knot felt tight in the throat at this parting; the weasel had become important to his emotional equilibrium.

Mit had evidently timed things properly, because Knot slunk back inside the house and into bed without raising any alarm. He set his clothing on the floor beside the bed, trusting the creatures in it to make themselves comfortable. He lay awake for some time, wondering whether he had done the right thing. These tacit alliances with vermin —it was like a nightmare, a nonsensical development that would prove to be illusory in the morning. Yet—

Finesse came to his bed. She crawled under the sheet with him, and put her arms about him, and kissed him silently. Her legs clamped about one of his, and muscles twitched—and suddenly he recognized the standard squeeze-pulse code.

WHERE DID YOU GO? she demanded through thigh-pressure pulses. I ALMOST FORGOT YOU.

What a way to communicate! He had thought she wanted to make love. He kissed her, set his teeth in her lip, and gently bit: JEALOUS FEMALE!

She bit back. HAVE YOU BEEN SEEING THAT OTHER FEMALE?

Oops—she really did have the wrong idea! I MET HERMINE.

THAT'S THE ONE.

He started to laugh. She stifled him with another kiss. He drew her in tightly, his need for her bursting from its bonds. They proceeded in leisurely but intense fashion to lovemaking, all the time conversing by assorted pressures of contact. In the end they were in the most intimate stage —and communicating through meaningfully rhythmic genital contractions. Knot would rather have made simple love, but she insisted on having the whole story, and this was the best way to tell it without any spying lobos catching on. He told her everything.

ROACHES? she exclaimed in constrictions that became almost painful. FLEAS?

HERMINE SAYS MIT SAYS—

She relaxed. She had great faith in Hermine and Mit. Once she had the rationale, she accepted it more readily than Knot himself had. THIAMIN, RIBOFLAVIN, NIACIN, she pulsed. YOU AND YOUR INFERNAL HUMOR!

RIGHT NOW IT'S INTERNAL HUMOR.

She responded with a pulse that almost did him damage.

I DON'T LIKE DEPERSONALIZATION, he protested.

I LOVE YOU FOR THAT DISLIKE, she responded. Now at last she proceeded to the fulfillment he craved with proper enthusiasm.

Their reservation for interstellar travel was two days hence. They proceeded as if they had no inkling of the threat awaiting them. It seemed to Knot that some freak accident would happen while they were driving to the spaceport. Some other vehicle would suffer a mechanical failure and just happen to collide disastrously with their own. Yet if they acted too early to avoid such a calamity, such as changing their route, some other accident would be arranged. They would have to risk the accident—and escape at the latest moment, when no backup accident was available in time.

One thing was sure: The lobos did not intend to let them reach the sanctity of the space shuttle safely. Another thing was likely: Mit's precognition would not be able to anticipate the mishap far enough ahead for them to avoid it cleanly, without complication. The opacity of Knot's future was closing in, interfering with the crab's perception, decreasing its reliability. So they had no easy way to handle the threat.

They spent what time they could becoming acquainted with their new associates. Since all of these were secretive by nature, it was easy to conceal them; the problem was to interact with them without alerting any snooping lobos to their nature. Thus they tended to do it while indulging overtly in routine mundane chores like eating or bathing.

As it turned out, the new creatures were fairly good company. The roaches, by daylight, were pretty shades of red, green and yellow, and poked into things with cutely insatiable curiosity. Whenever anything happened that was out of the ordinary, or when even the mildest threat occurred, they faded to translucency. When the threat was strong, they vanished entirely. After the danger passed, they slowly became visible again. It was an intriguing process.

The rats, Roto and Rondl, were a neatly matched pair. He was glossy black, she rough-furred white. Both were insatiably hungry, and their noses were forever quivering. They had soon discovered every hiding place of food of any kind. Things the gross one's brother swore had been lost for years turned up, such as a can of genuine imported Earth brown beans; it had lodged behind a pipe below the sink. If anyone tried to eat a cracker in bed, a cute little rat was quickly there, whiskers vibrating expectantly. They also located garbage, for much of that, too, was edible—for a discerning rat. They were not tame; they bared their sharp little teeth and retreated when approached too brusquely. But a telepathic brother rat had evidently given them the word, and when Knot put down his hand they would come to it.

This bothered Finesse slightly, and she made a point of courting the rats with tidbits of food. They remained wary of her, until she started nudging them with spot phobias: fear of the wall behind them, fear of the doorway to the side, fear of being without human company. It gave her practice in the application of her psi, exploring its ramifications and limits. It was a major talent—and she was both thrilled with it and furious with CC for concealing it from her. She also continued to worry that Knot wouldn't like her as well, now that she wasn't normal, despite his efforts to reassure her. In the morning she woke and turned to him and inquired, "Are we still lovers?" and he assured her that nothing had happened to change that, and then offered to demonstrate, purely as a public service, and she accepted and they conversed in squeeze-language a lot more seriously than their actions suggested. That was when he learned of her experiments in psi, and she learned of his further thoughts and plans. He also reminded her of what he had told her before, which she had forgotten because of his own psi. She tended to remember the new creatures without recalling his part in it. It was an excellent session.

Klisty had a room of her own, and did not stir from it at night. She was old enough to realize that Knot and Finesse did not want any third party visiting at that time. In the day, however, she became quite useful, for Knot could tell her something, and she would tell Finesse—then Klisty would forget the matter because of Knot's psi, but Finesse would remember, because she had not received the news from Knot. A third party was invaluable, this way. What it was necessary for Klisty to remember, Finesse told her. Thus there was a lot of repeating of inconsequentials, but the disruptive effect of Knot's psi was minimized.

Klisty had the company of the animals in her room, however, so she was not really alone. The rats got to like her, and would settle down to snooze in her slippers. She made a sandbox for their function room; they were fastidious. She dubbed the three roaches Redbug, Greenbug and Yelbug, and made a cardboard box for them to hide in, and soon had them walking on her hands without fading. She held limited mental dialogues with the five bees, and arranged to leave a jar of honey open for them in an inconspicuous spot; Knot hadn't thought of that. At other times she contentedly watched the entertainment programs on the public holograph bands, which were pitched exactly to her level though labeled "Adult."

The five bee-flies buzzed out periodically, foraging in the garden, then generally returned to Knot's jacket, where they positioned themselves to merge with the pattern of the weave. They reported that hostile entities lurked outside; they picked up the lobos' minds. The fleas were not in evidence at all; they remained strictly on the rats.

None of the creatures was obnoxious. Even the roaches were careful about where they deposited their droppings. Knot's original aversion to dealing with vermin disappeared; in fact, they stopped being vermin in his mind. They became animal acquaintances—as were Hermine and Mit. Useful ones, too—for the roaches' sensitivity to danger would help a good deal as the group made its run for the space shuttle.

Hermine's worry, though, extended beyond that upcoming dash. Mit should be able to counter a purely local threat pretty well, by having Knot separate from the others so that they would be clear to precognition. Then Knot could use his own psi to sneak through alone. But there might also be a distance threat. How could bugs and rats, with their specialized little-species psi-powers, alleviate that? It was not, of course, their job to protect Knot—but if they did not help, and he and Finesse perished, these animals would lose their own quests too. So there was an atmosphere of cooperation.

Then the mutiny broke out. Suddenly the despised vermin of Planet Macho were rebelling against their inferior status. It was amazing what chaos this caused. The city's power failed and most commercial activity halted.

Actually, this was not as fortuitous or coincidental as it seemed. This mutiny had been gathering its power for some time, merely awaiting the appropriate trigger. Knot's damage to the solar power station had made it vulnerable; it had been operating at partial output while repairs were made, and any additional stress could knock it out again. When Knot had refused to participate in the mutiny, even as negotiator, there had been nothing to hold it back. Knot himself, he realized, had some responsibility here. Had he done wrong?

He mulled that over at odd intervals, and concluded that he was unlikely to be the critical key to the status of the planet. Others must have turned down the hive too, and in any event the hive might not have intended to negotiate in good faith, or might have presented demands that made acceptance impossible. The whole interview with him might have been merely for show, to delude human beings about the intent of the bees. Still, Knot did feel a certain mild guilt.

"Nothing to do but turn in early," Finesse said with a meaningful glance at Knot. "No telling when the power will return." It was late afternoon, but the light would soon fade; nothing much could be accomplished without electrical power, here amid the electrified society. How different this was from the chasm enclave!

Knot wanted to misinterpret Finesse's look, but he knew better. It was escape, not romance she had in mind. A day early, to fool the lobos.

They made no special preparations; that would have been a giveaway. They simply ate a good evening meal, closed up the house, and went to bed as the darkness closed in—exactly as many Macho citizens must be doing. Knot knew Finesse was sending to Hermine, arranging a rendezvous.

Knot thought to the bees: **Vitamins, we are about to go outside together. It is dangerous. Please ask your hive members not to harass us.**

The hive knows, the bees replied fuzzily. **You will encounter no bees at all. The vermin know you have joined the mutiny, and will spare you.**

I have not joined the mutiny! Knot protested, remembering how he had fought this battle with CC's minions before, and lost. How could he remain aloof from causes, when the causes had psi-information about his destiny? **I only agreed to consider—**

The bees did not argue. Their intelligence was evidently enhanced by his presence, as Hermine's was, but they lacked the mass of brain the weasel had, so could not respond as readily. Regardless, Knot was not about to turn against his own species. The revolt of the downtrodden vermin would have to proceed without him.

But as they were on their way to their rooms, in superficial innocence, a noise developed outside. Knot peered out the window, as any citizen would do. "There's a fire out there!" he exclaimed.

It is the mutiny, the bees explained.

Somehow Knot had not thought of it as a building-burning escapade. **I thought the hive was only showing its power, making a demonstration, not actually trying to kill people.**

We do not mean to kill people, only to get their attention so they will negotiate. We must show them our power, yes, but in a manner they cannot ignore. We must show them that we can destroy them. You would not present our case, so now war begins.

Knot shook that off. He still did not care to accept the blame for a war. Obviously he had underestimated the destructive potential of the hive. **Some of your bees are pyro-psis?**

No. We are a stable, superior species. We breed only telepaths. The rats are less advancd, less stable; they have pyros and other weed talents.

Weed talents. Add another major concept to the arsenal! By that definition, human beings were the weediest of all.

Still, bee definitions aside, it made sense. The rats were larger, longer-lived creatures; they would have had fewer generations aboard spaceships, and less chance to work into a stable mutant form. They would still have a tremendous number of deleterious mutations, and a few positive. They would have the wide range of psi-talents that man did. That had been evident when Hermine got caught by the rat trap in the solar station. That, in fact, had been Knot's first intimation that the animals were developing psi-powers comparable to those of man. So much had happened since that experience that he had not had occasion to dwell properly on the significance of that discovery. He really should have done so!

The rats cooperate with the bees? Knot inquired.

For now. We bees are better unified and disciplined. The hive coordinates.

The hive coordinated the talents of the other animals. It thus became their version of the Coordination Computer. This could certainly be a serious threat! The lobos represented one problem, but perhaps they were only one of a coincidental complex of problems, any of which could eventually destroy CC. Literal bugs in the governing machine could bring it down soon enough. CC would have to do some major overhauling of its policies, to survive the rise of the animal kingdoms. No wonder Hermine had been so anxious about his refusal to cooperate!

Of course it's serious, the bees agreed with a certain species pride. **If need be, we shall destroy your kind and govern the planet in your stead.**

That suggestion put it back into perspective. Bees running a planet? Ludicrous! **Oh, I think mankind will not be destroyed in one night,** Knot thought tolerantly. Still, he realized, incendiary rats could make a lot of mischief in a city. **What will happen when the rats and the hive start disputing for territory between themselves?**

We will destroy the rats, the bees thought.

Uh-huh. And soon the planet would be in chaos, as one species after another tried simplistic solutions to their problems. Man, at least, had been well broken in. No new species would gain, in the long run. Maybe he *should* have tried to negotiate a peaceful settlement; at least he could have educated the hive somewhat.

A flash of movement caught Knot's eye in the wan light. The colored roaches were running about nervously, and beginning to fade into translucency. That meant danger. Personal, immediate threat.

Knot put a hand down for one to climb on. It was the yellow one. "Hey, Yelbug—what's the matter?" he murmured. But the roach was unable to tell him.

The weasel is sending, the bees thought faintly. **The matter is urgent.**

Knot concentrated on Hermine, but read nothing. **Too far away for me to receive,** he thought back. **Can you bees read her?**

Yes. Then, in response to his prompting, they relayed the message: **Mit says the lobos will burn this house tonight. Hurry.**

So the roaches' fear was justified! How quickly a seeming vacation and recuperation period had become the familiar nightmare of combat and chase. The lobos intended to take advantage of the cover provided by the creature mutiny to eliminate their enemy without implicating themselves. Clever, ruthless, efficient; exactly what he should have anticipated from Piebald. Finesse had planned to trick the lobos by moving out a day early; Piebald planned to strike similarly early.

Tell Finesse, he thought to the bees. He had not joined the hive, but they were allies at the moment, since a fire would wipe them all out together.

Finesse had gone to the bedroom. The bees buzzed off in tight formation. Knot set down Yelbug, then ambled into the bedroom and lay down on his bed in his clothes, as though too lazy to undress properly yet. He wasn't sure what kind of observation the lobos might have operating now, with the failure of electricity, but he wasn't taking any chances. They were not unduly dependent on electrical tools anyway. Everything had to seem normal for the circumstance.

He lay there, rehearsing escape plans. He would have to gather the roaches and rats, coordinate with Finesse in the dark, and make early contact with Hermine. From that point, Mit's clairvoyance would govern. Once they got clear of the house, they merely had to keep Finesse and Klisty out of sight. Knot could walk openly, knowing he would soon be cleanly forgotten. Unless the lobos decided to shoot him with a laser, and blame the killing on looters.

Knot decided that he too had best remain hidden, as much as possible. Their preplanned route to the space shuttle should still be good; it existed only in their minds. If it was unsafe, Mit and the invisible roaches would advise him. Except how could he see that they were invisible—in the dark? And how could he be sure that he hadn't simply misplaced them? Be a shame to act precipitously because the roaches could not be detected in one pocket, only to discover them in another.

Certainly there was danger, but with the animal allies and Finesse's psi they should be able to navigate safely through. He hoped. Their formidable collection of psi-talents no longer seemed like such a perfect shield! He was concerned, but not really alarmed—or so he would convey to the others.

Finesse should have the message and be ready now. Knot rose silently, and found her waiting for him. Klisty stood in the hall; Finesse must have sent the bees to alert her too. Good.

This time they all left the house from the window, dropping silently behind bushes as Knot had the prior night. Again the hound cats were out—but this time they hesitated to approach the vicinity of the escapees. Finesse's psi was at work.

The lobos were out too. **Bear right,** the bees advised, relaying Hermine's directive. **There is a lobo behind the bush ahead of you. He hears you but will forget.**

They bore right, avoiding the lobo. They threaded their way through a gap in the hedge and stood outside the estate, looking back. The house was silhouetted be-

fore the light of fires in the near distance. There was no
sign of occupancy—but it was the same with the neighboring houses. All the residents were lying low, waiting
for the authorities to get the situation under control, as
they had been advised to do before the power failed.
Macho citizens weren't so macho at a time like this. Presumably many couples were passing the time by making
love, as was traditional in such situations.

A small breeze rose, carrying toward the house. "Stations ready?" a communicator box inquired. So they
had independently powered equipment; that made sense.
"Spread the ignitant; this has to burn fast and hot to
catch them before they can escape. Fire the adjacent
estates too; it has to look like random animal arson."

The nearest lobo went to work, spraying flammable
mist toward the house. Knot stood and watched, sorry
that the property of the gross one's brother, their bene-
factor, was about to be destroyed, but knowing that
any attempt to interfere would be foolish. It was best to
let the lobos believe that the three visitors had died in
the flames—for now.

Still, this galled him. Knot decided to exert his incon-
veniently individualistic nature again. Will the hive summon a real arson animal? he asked the bees. To fire the
terrain behind the lobos?

There was something like an insect chuckle as they assimilated his mental image. Agreed.

The roaches stirred in his pocket. We must move out,
he thought, and reached out to squeeze Finesse's arm in
warning.

They hurried away. The lobos, intent on their own mischief, were not aware of the escaping party. Even the
tightest of traps became pervious when clairvoyance was
involved.

Then the lobos fired the brush. Enhanced by the
ignitant, it burst into violent flame that the wind fanned
rapidly toward the house.

And behind the lobos, a rat ran—and fire blazed up
in its track, a line of it burning toward the lobos. In a
moment the closure was complete; the arsonists were
trapped in their own mischief. Knot smiled grimly and
turned away; he couldn't stay to watch the fun.

Naughty man! Hermine's faint, admiring thought came. He must have been projecting his mood.

"Problem," Finesse murmured. "The route I'd worked out goes through the lower-class housing region—and Mit says that is about to be torched."

"But the high-class neighborhoods won't be safe either," Knot pointed out. "The lobos will be watching them. They hate the Macho upper class and want to destroy it; they'll be concentrating on the best estates."

"Yes. So we have to hide elsewhere." She frowned; he could make out her expression more by the set of her body than by her shadowed face. "But fire is a danger anywhere, tonight."

"I could locate a water conduit," Klisty said eagerly. "That's the safest place, if there's fire—"

What does Mit say to that? Knot asked Hermine. He saw that Finesse was now carrying the weasel and crab, having picked them up when Knot wasn't paying attention. With their psi, rendezvous was easy.

He says it gets complicated, Hermine replied. **We should stay above ground as long as possible.**

So be it. They wended their way through the city, losing themselves in its streets. People were coming out in increasing numbers, becoming aware of the fires. Soon the limited reserve power failed, darkening the remaining buildings of the city: the hospitals, police stations, and transportation centers. More people came out, not understanding how a minor problem with animals could get this bad. The Macho citizens did not seem at all bold and mighty, now; they were disorganized, confused, frightened people.

The way is opening, Hermine advised Knot. **Mit has found a channel. We must move to the end of this street in fifteen minutes; then we shall be safe until ship time.**

Let's go! Knot thought with relief. They walked rapidly down the street. He had largely recovered from his wounds, thanks to the excellent medical care he had received, but his leg and abdomen still gave twinges as he exerted himself, and he was not strong. He would need to rest as soon as they were safe.

There was an explosion in a factory building nearby.

A column of fire shot slantingly into the night sky, bright smoke roiling from it. Then the dull boom came—an aftershock, as it were—shaking the pavement so that windows cracked and loose tiles dropped from the neighboring roofs.

There was a scream of hurt and terror that made them all freeze momentarily. But there was no sound to it. "That was a mental scream!" Finesse cried.

Do not pause, Hermine thought urgently. The opening is narrow, and will close off soon.

Oh, the fire—we are trapped! It was the anonymous person again, the thought seeming female. She was evidently caught in the building that had just been ignited. Knot exchanged glances with Finesse. They both knew it would be folly to ignore Mit's warning; they had to move.

Then Klisty ran toward the building. "We can't let her die in fire!" she cried.

Knot and Finesse followed. They knew it was foolish; they probably could not help, and would pay for it exorbitantly, but they had to try.

Stop! Hermine thought desperately. This is where precognition ends!

Knot hesitated. This was no minor delay, then; this was a significant turning point in the entire mission. Mit's ability would be crippled if—

A third time the scream came. Knot galloped on after the girls. If this was fate, so be it; he was human too.

They came to the building. It was a monstrous warehouse. Flames illuminated its upper interior, making the small windows stand out in stark brightness against the exterior gloom. An inferno in there, with the fire steadily eating downward.

The roaches in Knot's pocket were restless; it was dangerous here. As though he needed the aid of psi to tell that!

You are throwing away our chance! Hermine thought despairingly. Just as you did when we entered the enclave chasm.

Yet we did some good there, Knot reminded her.

Mit says we may survive, but probably won't catch our ship.

Our ship departs tomorrow, Knot responded. **We should have time.** But he knew time was not the question; the loss of half Mit's psi was the real issue. They faced a completely unknown future by following this course. They might be all right, or might all die instantly in another explosion of the building.

But he was really reacting on a gut level to a woman in distress, and playing a private hunch. He thought he could help, and still catch the shuttle. And how could the lobos suspect him of staying in the area this way, instead of fleeing? They would assume he had headed straight for the shuttle and try to cut him off there.

Yet Mit's precognition had not been speculation; it had fathomed a safe way through—that Knot was now giving up. Knot was no precog; his hunches and guesses were virtually worthless. So he could sum it all up: He was basically crazy.

Yet Finesse and Klisty had led the way. Why weren't *they* dashing for the shuttle? Did they share some sort of morbid wish to miss the ship? If so, why?

The mental scream came again. They had paused only an instant, assessing the situation, though to Knot it seemed like a long time. "All right, let's not dawdle while she burns," Knot snapped. **Bees: Can you safely fly in there and investigate?**

We can try, the bees buzzed, not even questioning the need. Theoretically they were here to make sure Knot did not betray the hive; now they had been co-opted to his purposes. Probably because the power of his human mind overwhelmed them, at this proximity. He had become their hive. They took off in their formation.

There was another explosion in the building, blasting them with heat and light. The flames dropped two stories, eating more rapidly toward the ground. **Come back, vitamin bees!** Knot called mentally. **This is too dangerous for you, after all.**

They straggled back, shaken by the blast but intact.

"I can help!" Klisty cried. "I can find a water pipe leading inside." She stretched out her arms and closed her eyes, concentrating. Knot knew Mit could probably do the job faster, but it was better to save the crab for more critical work. "Over there—slow water moving." She pointed.

"A sewer pipe," Knot said. "Is it possible to get in and out, quickly?"

Mit says there is an access conduit beside it, Hermine thought.

So Mit was back in action! Lead us to it, Knot thought. I don't like the way that building is blowing up.

It will destruct completely in thirteen minutes, she thought reassuringly. But Mit is not sure you can effect a rescue in that time.

I'll try, though. At least Mit and Hermine had stopped reminding him of the disaster of his course. They weren't nags! Knot followed directions and found the conduit entrance. He crawled in—and discovered he could not move efficiently. His body was wrong, and on hands and knees he found his injuries hampering him, and the cramped pipe prevented him from improving his lot.

"I'll do it!" Finesse cried. Knot peered up at her, and saw her face changing color in the fierce illumination of the flickering flames. At the moment she most resembled a creature of hell, but her mission was that of an angel. "I'm smaller, and in better health."

"You were lasered too," he reminded her.

"Minor—and I don't need my collarbone for this."

Knot yielded to common sense. "Make it fast!"

She wriggled past him, bestowing a kiss on the way, and disappeared down the smaller pipe. Hermine and Mit were with her, so he knew he should have confidence in her security. Still, the occasional shaking of the ground as the building disintegrated, and the inexorably approaching flames made him increasingly nervous. He also worried about Klisty, outside on the street. Check on her, he told the bees, and they set up a continuous circuit, buzzing from pipe to street, reporting: good . . . good . . . good. It was reassuring.

Then Hermine's thought came: It is a woman with a mutant baby. She is injured; we cannot bring her out.

Failure, after all! But he would not accept it. Then save the baby! Knot thought. If they could rescue the baby, they might also rescue the mother. He thought fleetingly of Thea the mermaid, longing for her baby. He hoped she would never be trapped in a burning building.

Mit says he can't see the baby's future—or ours, if the baby is with us.

A psi neutralizer? This could be a problem! Is Finesse's psi operable in the baby's presence?

A pause. Yes. Mit cannot answer, but Finesse was able to make me afraid of spider webs.

So the baby's psi-negation affected only Mit. That would be a grave liability—but suddenly the nature of the crab's reservations about this diversion mission was coming clear. No one liked having his psi blocked out.

Still, they wouldn't have to keep the baby; they just had to rescue it. Then they could separate from it, and Mit's talents would function properly again. Bring the baby out. Hurry. That fire is close, and any blast could put it down to the basement.

Mit doesn't foresee a blast.

Mit's precog is nulled.

Oh. The weasel had been set back by the realization. Then: Finesse wants to know: What about the mother?

You really can't rescue her?

She is mortally injured and will die within a hour anyway; only her concern for her baby sustains her now.

That seemed final. Put me in touch with the mother. Relay my thoughts to her: Woman, I am Knot, a psi-mutant. I will take your baby to safety. Give it to the woman. We have only a few minutes before the building destructs.

The woman's relayed thought came back. She was not a telepath; only the force of her fear and pain and concern for the baby had enabled her to broadcast her scream to nearby receptive minds. Probably the presence of Hermine and the bees had facilitated this, too. Can I trust you?

We would not endanger ourselves to make this rescue if we did not care, he assured her. We were passing, picked up your mental scream, and came to help. We cannot save you, but we can save your baby.

Yes . . . There was a pause while she passed the baby to Finesse. Thank you. I know I am dying anyway. But my little boy Harlan I hid here to protect him from CC registration. His father is a disk captain who doesn't even know. I feared my child would be taken from me if CC learned he was strong psi—

Does his psi cancel clairvoyance? Knot asked. We have experienced damping—

It confuses precognition. Harlan is a randomizer. No one can predict him. Because CC uses precog, and needs predictability, I feared—

That seemed a reasonable fear. Such a mutant could be a monkey wrench in CC's works. Mit's reservations might be tiny compared to CC's reservations! Best to keep Harlan well away from the computer. We are CC agents— but we are human too. We will give Harlan to some responsible agency so that CC will not know.

CC agents! she thought with horror. CC will know! My baby will be lobotomized!

No! Knot thought back. We will protect him—

Then a huge, authoritative explosion shook the conduit, followed by a continuing shudder as the building collapsed into leaping flames.

Finesse! Knot thought, horrified.

Safe, Hermine's thought came. Coughing in the conduit. Relief! And the mother?

She is gone. You should not have told her about CC.

Yes, he should have had more sense. How awful for the woman's last thought to be of betrayal and despair!

Finesse wriggled down the conduit, bearing the baby, who seemed too frightened to cry. "We must hide him from CC," Knot told her as he made room for her to pass.

"Where will this baby be safe, in this city?" she demanded

Knot had no immediate answer. They emerged at the street. The fire had spread to adjacent houses, and people were collecting outside. A number were injured. Mit says we may be trapped, Hermine thought. He can't tell while we have the baby, but his clairvoyance shows no likely escape right now.

"So we'll stay here and help," Knot decided. "We can't catch that ship until we find a home for the baby, and right now we have no safe place."

"Oh, let me hold him!" Klisty cried. She had the little girl's attraction to babies. Finesse considered momentarily, then passed Harlan over.

Now Knot became aware of the intermittent shower of fire, as refuse from the explosion and collapse descended. No wonder the fire was spreading!

They crowded under a metal canopy sheltering the doorway of an intact house. The shower was, in its awful fashion, rather pretty; fragments dropping like burning snowflakes, illuminating the night.

But people were hurting. Finesse went out to help, heedless of the drifting motes of flame. Knot joined her, drawing on his organizational expertise. "Is there a doctor, nurse or medic among you?" he bellowed. "Anyone with any training at all in first aid? No? Well, I'm not a medic either, but I have common sense. Get the wounded covered and under cover—in the doorways, away from the fire. Who has access to water? Salve? Blankets? Bandages? Any psis among you? Any strong men? Good—we need to carry the injured to safety."

"What's happening?" a woman cried. She was in night clothing, her hair and eyes wild.

"The animals have mutinied," Knot explained. "Pyrotechnic rats are setting fires in buildings, bees are deliberately stinging people, bugs are reading minds. The animals want parity with man. We'll have a bad time until the status of the animals is recognized." And here he was, inadvertently doing what he had refused to do for the hive: arguing its case.

"Rats? Bees? Bugs?" the woman demanded incredulously. "Recognize vermin? We'll exterminate them first!" She shuddered. "Bugs reading minds!"

There spoke the true Macho. Better to fight and die uselessly than to compromise sensibly. Knot found his own attitude toward the animals moderating as he perceived how narrow it looked in others. Psi-mutes were psi-mutes, whether human or animal.

Yes, Hermine agreed.

Knot held his peace, however, and went to a man with a broken leg, helping him to find cover.

It was the beginning of a long night. Knot and Finesse and Klisty did all they could, organizing the cadres of rescue workers and aides for the injured. As dawn came at last the rampaging animals retreated to the shadows, and the people were able to relax.

It was a sad morning. The city lay in ruins about them. A third of the houses in this vicinity had been gutted by fire, and a number of others were in bad shape. The streets were littered with people and belongings and debris. The central power remained off. It was the refuse of a war, and the war had only begun.

The hive had set out to make a demonstration of its power, one that could not be belittled or ignored. It had done so.

But the Macho government had responded bravely. Trucks arrived to take over, and Knot and his party faded into the woodwork of a deserted, damaged house, only allowing Klisty to go out with the baby to get milk and diapers if they were available. Knot and Finesse collapsed on a makeshift bed, holding hands.

"You are aware that this whole diversion was absolutely crazy," Finesse murmured. Her face was smudged by dirt and charcoal, and her clothing was on the way to being rags, but her inner spirit glowed through.

"Certainly." It felt so good to relax at last.

"We threw away our clear chance for escape, and now are mired in this war-torn slum."

"Perfect lunacy," he agreed.

"And now we have a baby to worry about too."

A baby. Now that assumed new significance. What he wouldn't have given to have a baby by her! Here, for the moment, in surrogate . . .

"I love you." She rolled over to kiss him, missed, and was too tired to correct the matter.

"I really don't feel right about—" he began.

"About my saying that, when I have a husband on another planet? Do you realize that CC will have blanked all memory of me from him, to prevent any possible betrayal of my mission? He does not know I exist, and my own son would not know me. That other woman probably loves him by now—he's a wonderful man, and I know exactly how it is—and when I go back I'll have to break up *their* good marriage, like an interloper—"

"But you were there first! You have priority!" Whose case was he arguing?

"To step in and mess up other people's lives? To destroy love and marriage on a technicality? To make the legal preempt the moral? I'm not even the same person I was then. I used to be normal, like my husband. Now I'm psi-mute, like you. I belong to a different reality. How can I return?"

How tempting just to agree. She was serving herself up to him on a platter; he had but to take. Yet he argued, from what atypical ethic he could not say. "If CC erases all your memories again—"

"Of course it is possible!" she flared. "CC can do anything, because CC is a machine without human feeling. But is it *right*?"

The questions were not getting easier! "Is *anything* right anymore?"

"How can we know? If we had done what Mit and Hermine felt was right, we would never have rescued that baby or helped all those people."

"We saved some lives," Knot agreed.

"So don't you start getting guilty about my prior status. Just accept what *is*, what is now. Maybe the present reality is our future. Would you like that?"

"A lifetime of exploding buildings, people injured and dying, war-torn societies?"

"A nova at you!" she exclaimed weakly. "You know what I mean!"

"I don't know," he said. "What would it be like, with a wife who could make a man afraid of his mistress?"

"*What* mistress?" she demanded.

He squeezed her hand, chuckling. "See—I'm already afraid!" But then he grew serious. "I'd like my future with you. If that's what seems right when the future arrives."

"Do you realize that I just proposed to you, and you accepted?"

"Help! There must be some loophole, some technicality—"

"Knot—" she said warningly.

"I'm afraid to say no—"

She finally got up the energy to kiss him properly. I

LOVE YOU, she repeated in squeeze, using her lips to make the pulses. DON'T LET ME FORGET.

I PROMISE, he agreed. Now, at last, he began to feel at peace with the decision. He had always wanted her and loved her, and because of that he had become exceedingly choosy about how he won her. He wanted no technicalities that could reverse it, even in the most hidden recesses of his conscience.

They lay together, too tired to work up to anything more, but it was a better fulfillment than any they had achieved during more vigorous times.

CHAPTER 11

In due course Klisty arrived. Not only had she obtained milk and diapers, she was weighed down with nutro tablets and antibiotic pills of assorted types. "They couldn't say no to a baby," she said, pleased.

"Or to a cute, bedraggled waif," Finesse agreed, stirring.

"I'll find water for these," Klisty said, depositing the baby with Finesse. Klisty had come through the night in better condition than either of them, perhaps because she had spent more time sitting and holding Harlan than running around the streets. She invoked her psi and soon located a functional pipe. Very shortly they had nutro drinks to go around, with shares put out in dishes for the rats, roaches and bees.

Hermine did not deign to join these creatures; she went out hunting for herself. Finesse found a flavor Mit liked and fed him by hand.

"They were asking who organized this," Klisty said. "The government people said a lot of lives had been saved. But nobody could remember very well. I started to forget, too, until Hermine reminded me."

"What are we going to do with the baby?" Finesse asked, her strength returning as she ate. "I had forgotten how much fun babies were, but we can't keep him with us. Mit can't help us much while Harlan is fouling up his precog, and we can't take him to CC."

"Oh, why can't we?" Klisty demanded. "You got me a ticket; couldn't you get him one? He can sit in my lap if there isn't room—"

"It's not the ticket or the room," Knot said. "I promised his dying mother we would protect him from CC."

Klisty's brow furrowed. "Does CC hurt babies?"

"Well, Harlan has disruptive psi-power. CC's precogs wouldn't be much good with him around."

"Oh." The girl considered as she chewed on a pill. "Does his psi mess up all precognition near him, or just precognition about him and his companions?"

It was an excellent question. "It could be some of both," Knot said. "Mit can't precog at all when Harlan's near, and that upsets Mit. But he wasn't able to tell anything at all about Harlan when they were separate, or about us after we joined Harlan. Our future perception ended at that point. Even CC was unable to discover what I would do on this mission, and it is now evident that that was because I joined Harlan and blocked off any precognition relating to that. So I would say it is a generalized local effect narrowing to a specific distance effect. So you can see we wouldn't want him near CC's high-powered precogs."

"Why not?" she persisted. "Isn't he like you, covering up information about himself, not harming anyone else? CC works with you."

That seemed reassuring on the surface, but as Knot thought about it he suffered the opposite emotion. "I wonder. You know, we have not been entirely at ease about returning to CC. The lobos know something we don't, and Mit himself was nervous about that, before. Once we make our report, our job for CC will be done. Is it possible—" He paused.

Finesse's voice became sharp. "Whatever are you hinting at, Knot?"

Knot sighed. "Now you know I don't really like all of CC's policies. I realize that was part of what made CC select me for this mission, so I could make contact with CC's *real* enemies. But still, my doubts are valid. CC doesn't seem to care about the misery of the enclaves. I realize CC is only a machine, never intended to care in the human fashion; it just wants to get its job done. But that being the case, how do I know CC cares about *us?* Once we report that the lobos are behind its present problems, so it knows what to do, will it have any further use for us?'

"I've worked for CC for years!" Finesse snapped.

"Then why didn't it send someone to rescue you, when you disappeared on this planet? It had to know you were gone; it didn't need my report for that."

"That would have tipped off the lobos that I was more than a routine investigator. As you said, CC is a machine. It doesn't care about individuals. It cares about the job."

"Precisely. How do we know we won't all become inconvenient to CC, once our report is done? Our mission would be finished, but we would know an embarrassing amount about CC's vulnerability. Could that have been what was bothering Mit? The fact that we're all expendable the moment our mission's done?"

"How does this relate to the baby?" Finesse demanded.

"Two ways. First, if we take Harlan with us, he will share our fate. Second, if I should find myself slated for disposition, I'd like to be able to make a run for it without being boxed in by high-powered precogs. Harlan could protect me from that.'

"You're paranoid!"

"Yes. Recent events have sharpened that personality trait."

"No one else would even think CC could—would—"

"Maybe we should ask." He addressed Hermine mentally. **Should we take Harlan with us to CC? Please answer for yourself and for the other animals.**

There was a delay while the weasel surveyed the animals. **We are unanimous,** she announced. **We all want to take Harlan along, and hide him from CC.**

"Unanimous!" Knot exclaimed. "You can't all be so attached to a human baby!"

Even Mit thinks it is best, now. Something is wrong, and this confuses the wrongness, and maybe helps put it right.

Finesse, a party to this discussion, relented. "I didn't really want to ditch Harlan," she confessed. "But after the promise we made to his mother—"

"We promised to protect the baby," Knot said. "We still propose to do that, and perhaps protect ourselves as well. We can take him along, but not yield him or knowledge of him to CC. It seems as good a choice as leaving him here on this mutiny-torn planet."

"Yes," she agreed, with a certain relieved misgiving.

At last they slept. They knew it would be foolish to go near the spaceport by day; the lobos should have caught on by this time that the party hadn't perished in the flames of the house, and another assassination squad would be lurking near the spaceport. Maybe, Knot thought with dubious hope, the lobos would give up the watch after noting that no one showed up for that shuttlelift this afternoon. The lobos could assume that Knot and his party had gotten wiped out in the violence of the night. And it was a nice pretext to avoid making a decision immediately.

Harlan woke several times, loudly, as babies tended to. Each time Klisty got up and tended to him, feeding him, changing his diaper, crooning him back to sleep. She was thrilled to be entrusted with this chore. The girl was definitely an asset. Knot did not know how to tend to babies, and Finesse was so tired she never woke at all, despite her prior experience with her own child. Obviously if they had to park Harlan somewhere while they reported to CC, they would leave him in Klisty's care.

In the evening, after some discussion, they commenced another quest: for a family of four with pets, departing for the far galaxy. In this effort the hive helped, providing information to its five bee-minions. Knot still had not agreed to represent the hive, but he was impressed by the power it had shown, and by the justice in its position. It was indeed a planetary power! It wanted parity for animals, and it preferred to obtain this by negotiation. Knot had a tacit sympathy for both the desire and the method. As with CC before, he was being gradually converted despite his resistance, and knew it, but still had to play out the full skein before making an overt decision.

They located the family. It had died in the ravage of the night, trapped in a collapsing building. The reservations were now open. Mit had only to find a safe way across the city to the spaceport access road. Shorn of his precognition, he was having trouble; a road that was open one moment might be clogged the next, and he lacked the brain to integrate the entire pattern at once. Again the hive assisted; bees were apt at patterns, and there were many bees, and the hive also had access to some precognition beyond Harlan's interference-range. The bees indicated the open route, though they could not foretell whether the party would actually use that route.

"You said you made no deal with the hive," Finesse muttered darkly. "Why are they helping so much?"

Knot explained his thinking about the tacit progress of his agreement with the hive. "I seem to be vulnerable to that sort of encroachment, as you well know. It also seems the bees feel I may do some good for them anyway, if they help me now, even without any formal agreement. And—I may. They just don't seem so much like vermin to me, anymore; they seem more like—" He fumbled for the appropriate concept.

"Like mutants," she finished for him. "People in alternate shapes, and people with psi-powers. You have a soft heart for that kind."

"Don't you?"

She smiled. Her face was clean now, and her nose no longer swollen. "I lost that battle when I met Hermine."

"I guess psi is the great leveler," he said.

They found a deserted car in running condition. Its owner, Mit assured them, was dead; this was not really stealing. "It's not really honest, either," Klisty muttered, but did not make more of an issue of it.

They drove carefully to the spaceport, arriving shortly before the shuttle's departure time. The connection was with a diskship, but not one destined for CCC or Chicken Itza; the lobos were not watching it closely.

They trooped to the embarkation gate. The electric power remained off; the CC readout machine had been replaced by human clerks. Knot held out his arm, which Finesse had carefully taped over with a new code-pattern: that of the Fosfor family. It would not have fooled the computer scan a moment, since it did not match the bone imprint—but these were inexperienced, harried clerks, in a hurry. They hardly even looked at the pattern; they had him call out the number from memory while they checked it against the fare tally.

The process was similar for Finesse—now Mrs. Fosfor—and their two children and container of animal pets. The line was already being swelled by other late arrivals. "Three miniature kittypups," the final clerk said, peering into the homemade box.

"Actually, they're tame rats," Knot said, to abate the man's surprise. "The kids wanted kittypups, but they were too expensive, so we just called them that." He winked.

Tame rats! Hermine thought, affronted.

He can see you're not a kittypup, Knot responded. **The lobos will be alert for a weasel. So try to merge with Roto and Rondl for now.**

I'd love to merge with them! she thought, with a mental picture of a weasel consuming a rat carcass. But she huddled dutifully between the two rats so that her different nature was not particularly evident, and projected a mental impression of ratness to the clerk to enhance the illusion.

They passed inspection, as Mit had thought they would—without being sure. The baby Harlan still bothered the hermit crab because of the way Harlan interfered with even the simplest acts of precognition. But even Mit now believed it was necessary to have this cover. He was in Knot's pocket, making a halfhearted attempt to sulk.

Knot saw a man who might be a lobo, but he couldn't be sure. Odd how all the lobos he had met had been males; where were all the lobo females? There might be fewer of them, since women tended to be more docile, more law-abiding, but still there should be more than one. Piebald had claimed to have a wife, yet she had never manifested at the villa.

But this was irrelevant at the moment. Knot placed his trust in his psi, sure no lobo would remember his face or form directly, and marched boldly on by. The man glanced, but did not challenge him.

Then Finesse—and she had made up her face and hair to deviate from her norm, so that she really looked like a different woman. She did not have the forgetting protection. But Hermine was helping her, projecting a general impression of greater age. She got by too. Finally Klisty—who had been made up as a boy, to match the Fosfor son. She passed readily.

At last they were aboard the shuttle. Knot began to

relax as the ship sealed, and would have breathed a sigh of relief when the stasis came—had the stasis itself not made that impossible. They were on their way.

Still, he checked. **Hermine, are there any lobos aboard? No. All normals except us.**

Very good. Of course they still had to get through the pretravel distance precog verification while the ship remained parked in orbit—

Oh no! How could they get Harlan through that? **Hermine, I just thought of a snag. Harlan will foul up the voyage precog. We won't be able to go until Harlan is removed from the ship. We can't take him along.**

I will ask Mit. She paused. **Oopsy, that's no good! He can't procog it either.**

It will also expose us to the lobos, Knot continued. **They will investigate the return.**

I will ask Finesse.

The stasis released. Finesse looked at him, startled. "I never thought of that! We're in trouble!" She glanced at the baby, now peacefully sleeping in Klisty's arms.

"I think we'll just have to break up our party at the orbiting station," Knot said regretfully. "You can take Hermine and Mit on to report to CC, and I'll stay here to take care of the rest."

"No! I'm not separating from you again," she said firmly. "I've worked too hard remembering you, to forget you now. CC might erase what memory your absence didn't. I don't want to lose another man that way!"

"But we can't leave Klisty alone! She's only a child."

Finesse glanced obliquely at him. "You like her, don't you."

"Yes." He smiled. "Now don't get jealous. I like her, but I love you. It's just that I feel responsible—"

"So do I. We'll all go together, or stay together."

"You realize that probably means we'll never leave Planet Macho?"

"Oh, we might hire a private ship for a short hop to a neighboring system, bypassing the precog check."

"If the lobos don't get us first," he said. Still, it was not a bad notion. Many small individual-passenger and two-passenger ships existed; travel in them was risky, but feasible for people in their situation. "There's also the matter of our mission."

"I'll send a message to CC, asking that another agent be sent. We can give our report to that agent, who can take it to CC. It's workable, if slow."

And safer for them all, in the event CC was finished with them. Yes—rejection for this present voyage would not be a complete disaster. "And we can settle down peacefully amid the Planet Macho mutiny and breed normal children," Knot said.

"You will simply have to compromise with the hive, and put a stop to the war. The rest will not be too onerous."

"Which reminds me: How could you have been born mutant, and your folks never know it?"

"Obviously they did not want to believe it, and since it was subtle it may not have manifested until Piebald—" She stopped, disliking the memory, momentarily touching her nose.

Knot, of course, knew her talent had been operative before. "When I interviewed CC and started to get balky, I began to experience a phobia. You must have been responsible."

She concentrated. "I did seem to live a charmed life. No one ever caused much trouble for me. As a child I thought a dog was going to attack me, but something frightened it away. Still, there were many other times I was bothered or frightened, and nothing like that happened."

"So you had the psi all along, but suppressed knowledge of it, and used it only in unguarded moments, unconsciously. So there was never any obvious connection to you."

"I suppose I just wanted to be normal," she agreed, a trifle wistfully. "When I started working for CC—honestly, I thought it was my expertise as an interviewer that qualified me for that job, plus the fact that CC had taken care of me so long—remember, I really did not have much of a human family life—and when I associated with so many psi-mutants, I began to wish I had power like that too. But I knew I didn't. If any of the clairvoyants caught on, CC must have erased that knowledge from them, keeping the secret."

"CC is good at keeping secrets," Knot agreed ruefully.

"But now that I have experienced psi myself, I never want to lose it. The very notion of lobotomy—" She grasped Knot's hand tightly. "Knot, suddenly I'm afraid to go back to Macho. The lobos—their experiments—like the historical Nazi ones—I have so much more to lose than I knew before! Let's make a try for the disk flight!"

Knot didn't have the heart to remind her how hopeless that was, or that the effort could only raise a commotion that would pinpoint them for the lobos; she was well aware of this. What use to dwell on the negative aspects of the situation, when they could do nothing to ameliorate them?

How did the roaches feel about it? If the human party was headed for trouble, so were they. Knot glanced down into his pocket where they hid. All three were visible and peaceful. They weren't worried—and that was odd. They should have the most sensitive awareness of danger —unless their psi, too, was nulled by Harlan's presence.

Is it? he asked Hermine. **Can Mit answer that?**

Mit says yes, he can answer. No, the roaches are not affected. They are not really precognitive; they just know when danger becomes more likely.

Isn't trouble becoming more likely now?

The roaches don't think so. Of course, their range is limited.

Limited range—that could explain it. Still, the moment of crisis was not far removed. "You were tuned in?" Knot asked Finesse. "Which do you think is correct —our logic or the roaches' unworry?"

"Redbug, Greenbug and Yelbug, of course. What is logic compared to psi?"

"No comparison," he agreed faintly.

Nevertheless, they awaited the docking and verification with trepidation that they tried not to communicate to Klisty or the other travelers. Knot remembered his first trip in space, seemingly so long ago, when he had been precipitously falling in love with Finesse. Much had changed, but not his feeling. He took her small fine hand again and squeezed it reassuringly. WISH US LUCK.

SO WISHED, she squeezed back.

The docking and checking routine proceeded without a hitch. The orbiting ship was not affected by the turmoil on the surface of the planet; the mutiny was a matter of local curiosity here, rather than life and death. No challenge was made. Soon they were seated in the diskship, under way.

Knot hardly dared believe it. He squeezed Finesse's hand in communication again. WHAT HAPPENED?

NOTHING HAPPENED, she responded, as mystified as he. MAYBE THIS IS AN ILLUSION, A SWEET DREAM. LET'S NOT WAKE SOON.

They went into stasis. No doubt about it: The ship was traveling. It was not going directly to CC, but they would transfer later to one that was. Once they were certain they were free of the menace of the lobos, they could change their itinerary openly. The important thing was that they were safely in space, despite Harlan's presence.

What could account for it? It behooved him to find out. He was not the kind to accept an illusion unquestioningly. **Hermine, does Mit know why we had no precog trouble?**

No. Mit says the ship's procog could not have operated.

Could Harlan's power be intermittent? Maybe it does not operate when he sleeps, or is distracted.

No, it is constant, like yours. His future cannot be anticipated whether he sleeps or wakes.

They would not have permitted the ship to launch without a positive report. Yet obviously they had. What could account for this? No ship launched without a report by an accredited CC precog. Credentials were rigorously verified. The ship's telepath would detect any substitution of personnel, or any prevarication by the precog. It was a tight system, virtually foolproof, as it had to be. So the reading couldn't have been faked—yet it couldn't have been accurate, either.

Klisty wants to know whether precogs are always right, Hermine thought.

Tell her I'm not sure, Knot replied. He didn't want to alarm the girls. **If a precog sees an accident coming, he**

makes the ship wait, so that there will be no accident. So in that sense he is wrong, because the accident never happens. Yet he is also right, because if he hadn't seen it and given warning—

Suddenly Knot, listening to his own thoughts, had it. The voyage precog had seen no accident, therefore had approved the voyage routinely. He had not been verifying the ship's safe arrival, but had taken the shortcut of checking for a problem. Since Harlan's psi interfered with precognition, the precog had drawn a blank—and assumed it was all right.

Tell Finesse and Klisty, Knot thought grimly, that we owe our own security to the insecurity of the ship. Like the game of finding the pea under the cup: One way to win is to find the pea. Another way is to call out which cups do not have the pea. If the gamemaster is cheating, and has no pea under any cup, the second system is effective for the player. In this case, if the pea is disaster, the precog looked at the voyage, found no disaster, so assumed all was well. But the reason he did not find it—

Was because Harlan blanked it out, Klisty's relayed thought concluded.

Which means we're traveling blind, Finesse added. We don't know this ship will arrive safely.

It's a fair gamble, Knot thought. Better than returning to Planet Macho. If we get bounced from the next ship by a more alert precog, we're still out of range of the lobos.

Unless the lobos on other planets have been given the word, Finesse thought.

But the pilot will be most upset if the ship cracks up and we all die in one big gooey squish, Klisty thought. Then she started laughing mentally, a bit hysterically, knowing that her image was ludicrous but that there was indeed some risk of ship malfunction.

Soon they were all laughing, though frozen in stasis. Hermine relayed the cacophony as well as she could.

But as it happened, there was no disaster. Few ships these days had serious trouble; the odds had been well in this ship's favor. They docked in orbit about Planet Gumbo where, after a few hours' delay, they transferred to a ship going to CCC, refueling at Chicken Itza.

Knot, as usual, had to reintroduce himself to people,

and remind his companions of his recent interactions with them. "Oh, now I remember!" Klisty exclaimed. "You're fun to keep meeting for the first time!"

When at length they orbited Chicken Itza they took the shuttle down openly; no one cared where they were going. Knot remembered the warehouse where the fighting cocks were parked. He would not go wandering and releasing any chickens this time!

No one challenged them as they made their way to the hay room where CC's terminal was hidden. But Hermine and Mit were tense, the latter unable to precog but quite worried about what he might have seen had he been able to. The colored roaches became nervous, too.

Knot caught Finesse's eye and gestured to his pocket; she nodded, understanding. The roaches had anticipated no threat in the diskship, and had been correct; they had been aware of no problem in the shuttle's descent, and had been right again. Now they felt trouble. They became more agitated as the party approached the terminal.

"Use your psi," Knot murmured to Finesse. "Scare away all people and creatures from our vicinity. Just to be sure."

She nodded agreement. Still the roaches reacted, beginning to fade out of sight. Knot paused. He did not want to use telepathy here; CC might have a monitor on such communication, and it would not be expedient to advertise that they no longer quite trusted CC. He put his hand on Finesse's arm: WE HAD BETTER GIVE HERMINE AND MIT TO KLISTY, AND MEET CC ALONE.

Addressing Klisty, he pointed down the hall where he remembered the fighting cocks being caged. He knew Hermine would warn her against releasing any of those, should Klisty be so foolish as to try it.

Then he lifted Harlan from Klisty's arms. With luck, Mit's psi would be able to protect the child, if she got far enough away from the precog-nullifying baby. But now Finesse objected, silently. She didn't want Harlan going into CC's presence. Belatedly Knot remembered that aspect; of course he couldn't do that! Reluctantly he passed the baby back. At least Mit's clairvoyance would still function, and that was worth considerable.

Suddenly the five bees buzzed across from Knot to Klisty too. It seemed they did not want to be on hand for the CC interview after all. The rats became restless, and the roaches had disappeared entirely. This was a microcosmic animal mutiny!

All perceivable creatures transferred to the girl. "I feel like a sinking ship," Knot muttered.

Then Knot and Finesse braced themselves and walked on to meet CC. They might be rendering themselves expendable, but they felt duty-bound to make their report to the machine.

The terminal was there amid the hay, exactly as before. No one not in the know would suspect its nature without the aid of clairvoyance. Finese fooled with wisps of straw projecting from the hay-bale table, and the mother-robot hologaph formed. "You have completed your mission?" Mombot inquired with mechanical yet dulcet tone.

"Yes," Knot replied. "We know who is attacking you. Prompt action should eliminate this particular menace and make it possible for you to survive and maintain the human empire. However, there is another complication."

"What is this?" the machine asked.

"There is mutiny among the animals of Planet Macho —and perhaps elsewhere. The planet is being ravaged. The animals desire parity with man, and wish you to assist them in obtaining it. There are also specialized requests—"

"This is of no special concern," CC replied. "We have means to subdue the hive intellect."

"You already know of the hive?" Knot asked, surprised. He remembered how the hive had offered him a complete chart of CCC; had the two forces already encountered each other? "Some other agent reported?"

"My master reported."

Knot felt a chill. Had someone else managed to use the override code? That could mean serious trouble! He began to tap his foot—but could not recollect the complex pattern Mit had picked up before.

"Desist," CC said. "I am not to be overridden again; I am already on override."

Bad news! "Who is your master?"

The holograph dissolved, then reformed—into the image of the lobo Piebald.

"No!" Knot cried, and Finesse made a little scream.

Now Piebald spoke for himself. "As you know, the odds were against your success. As it happened, you actually facilitated our victory over the machine. We now govern the Coordination Computer."

Numbed by the extent of this disaster, Knot could only ask, "How?"

"You obtained the secret override code."

"But I never gave it to you!" Knot protested. "I don't even remember it myself!"

"Naturally not. CC erased it from your memory, and from the memories of the weasel and crab. But Finesse overheard it as you tapped it out. It was in her subconscious memory, available to our drug interrogation at the Macho station because she was not aware of its significance. All we had to do was reach a key CC terminal."

So the great machine that governed the galaxy had overlooked a single human detail, much as the psi-precog had overlooked Harlan's influence, and brought defeat upon itself. Mit and Hermine had been afraid of something like this, without being able to define it. Yet—

"If the lobos got to CC—why didn't they destroy it?" Knot asked Finesse.

"Why destroy it—when you gave us the tool to make it ours?" Piebald queried in return. "When I realized what we had, I moved right in. I never expected to convert CC to our purpose, but when the chance came—"

The opportunist had scored. Cunning man! "But we left you at Planet Macho," Finesse protested weakly.

"I took your ship."

"You were not on the ship with us!" she argued. "Hermine would have been aware of you instantly!"

"Your scheduled ship, that proceeded directly here. It seemed there were vacancies."

Piebald had taken Knot's reservation, just as Knot had taken Fosfor's reservation! "CC would never have admitted you; there are guards—"

"I used your identity, of course. Gloves with six fingers and four fingers. A crooked manner of walking. Facemask. The confusion caused by the animal mutiny assisted, and once I was aboard ship no one questioned me. CC, of course, was expecting you; you are distinctive enough in your way."

"But still, the futures mutant, Drem, would have been watching, playing through an advance report. CC would have known before you arrived that—"

"Do you suppose you are the only one adept at foiling such precautions? It seems there is now a randomizing psi associated with you, that prevents recognition of your activities and of events in your presence. I landed on this planet, hid, and waited two days until you arrived. Then, under cover of your null-precog, I slipped in just ahead of you and tapped out the code. Now I am emperor."

Finesse was crestfallen. "We did it ourselves!" she said. "We opened the gate to the enemy. While we passed animals and babies back and forth, he was in here using the override code!"

"No wonder the animals were nervous!" Knot agreed. "We should have checked out their concern more specifically. We assumed the threat was to us personally, when actually it was to CC, to our mission."

"But I made a phobia!" Finesse said. "You should not have been able to approach!"

"Indeed, I could not approach *you*," Piebald agreed. "But you were not yet at the terminal. I was able to fight off the fear long enough, though it was no pleasant exercise. Once I had control, I was able to go elsewhere. My holo, of course, is not affected by your power. I admit it was a ticklish maneuver—but worthwhile."

Knot realized that the lobo was indeed as cunning and determined as Knot himself. Piebald was right: There were others who could do amazing things, when they had motive and opportunity. He had badly underestimated Piebald.

"Now I believe your usefulness has ended," Piebald said. "I thank you most sincerely for the service you inadvertently rendered my cause, but now I need time to implement my program. So—"

Knot made a dive for the lobo, but passed right through

the image. Knot had acted without thinking, and made a fool of himself. Yet the lobo seemed annoyed. "Damner!" he cried out. Was he swearing?

Then something seemed to take hold of Knot's willpower. He righted himself and came to stand at attention. Then he advanced on Finesse.

"Knot!" she cried. "You look funny! What—?"

He grabbed her by the shoulder and shoved her back against the wall of hay. His small left hand closed into a fist and drew back at shoulder elevation. He punched brutally forward at her nose—

And his fist shied away, as a sudden phobia inhibited him. He was afraid of her skin! He dared not let his hand touch it!

Then the compulsion left him. Now Finesse's eyes glazed. Knot fell back, knowing her psi was about to attack him more devastatingly. What was happening?

As he moved, he saw a man standing in the doorway. He had the look of a psi about him.

"Damner, hold on to her," the Piebald holo said. "She's the dangerous one."

So this was Damner—a mind-control psi. Probably posted here to protect CC—and now at the service of CC's enemy. Knot lurched into the man, distracting him.

Immediately the control shifted back to Knot. He flung himself away from the controller.

But that released Finesse. Having experienced the psi-compulsion herself, she now knew what it was. She concentrated—and suddenly Damner was in terror. His eyes turned round and white and he cried out incoherently. She had given him a phobia, perhaps a fear of hay.

"Shift to her, I said!" Piebald shouted. "Stop her from using her psi on you!"

Damner made a visible effort—and Finesse stiffened, as Knot was released again. The man could only handle one person at a time.

Knot started forward again. "Marie! Nancy!" Piebald yelled.

Two grown female hound cats appeared in the doorway. Knot realized that Piebald must have brought them with him, his own guardians. This was trouble compounded.

Hermine! he thought. **Loose the fighting cocks. Send them after the hound cats!**

The holograph man pointed at Knot. "Attack!" Piebald ordered.

As one, the two sprang. They were impressive creatures by daylight, with large feline muscles and projecting canine snouts. They had grace and power and endurance, and were not to be balked long by a mere man. Not in fair combat.

Knot turned, grabbed a bale of hay by its two strings, and heaved it up. It was bulky and heavy, but desperation gave him strength. He used it clumsily to balk the two animals, then shoved it on top of them. Their teeth and claws dug into the hay, accomplishing nothing. They snarled and spat around mouthfuls of hay. Knot hauled out another bale, trying to bury them, but they writhed about and drew themselves free.

"Make her attack him!" Piebald yelled. "Cancel them both out!"

Knot heaved up a third bale, trying to score on Damner—but suddenly he, Knot, was deathly afraid of hay. The controller had done it, establishing the chain, making Finesse fight Knot. That, combined with the two hound cats, spelled doom.

Knot dropped the bale, backed away, banged into a wall of hay, recoiled in horror, charged forward, saw the bale on which the holograph image stood, froze in panic, would have fallen except that there was hay littering the floor, and realized that his only real escape lay outside this chamber, beyond Damner. Knot launched himself at the doorway with the strength of madness. In his urgency he trod on a hound cat, hardly noticing or caring; the creature snarled and tried to bite, and Knot kicked it fiercely on the snout, not in self-defense but just to get it out of his path of escape. He shoved past Damner, still heedless of all opposition other than hay. In that instant he could have hurled the man into a wall, perhaps hard enough to break the control—but Knot could take no time for that while he was near hay. In the back of his mind—buried under hay, as it were—he realized that this was a way Finesse could make a devastating weapon of any person, making a berserker that could seriously disrupt an army. Suddenly he was out of the chamber, panting his relief—

And encountered a phalanx of elegant fighting cocks. These had bright spiked red combs, elongated daggerlike beaks, and feathers that most resembled protective padding against missiles. Their claws were so stout and sharp that their feet did not rest flat on the floor; instead they walked with a kind of springiness, the claw points curving into the ground and gripping there. Their manner, too, was in no way reminiscent of flighty or timid creatures; their cruel little eyes peered at him aggressively from beneath visorlike ridges of headfeathers. Devastating birds!

Then he spied Hermine. She had brought the cocks; they were under her guidance! **A man-mutant!** he thought at her. **Compulsion—he's controlling Finesse. And two hound cats—**

The weasel did not reply mentally; she was too busy directing the traffic. The cocks dwarfed her; any one of them could have destroyed her in seconds by peck and slash. But the birds charged past Knot and into the chamber—just as the two hound cats were charging out in pursuit of him.

Knot flattened himself against the wooden wall as the two forces met in instant combat. Each hound massed quadruple what any cock did, but there were a dozen cocks whose fighting spirit was matchless. They met the hound cats not with fear or challenge but with scream-squawks of savage joy. Wings spread, revealing sharp little hookfeathers that helped them hold on to their prey; beaks plunged forward, and talons swiped the air.

The hound cats were no less eager to fight. Their long saberteeth flashed, their own claws flexed out, and their bodies hurtled into the fray. A cock was flung up toward the ceiling rafters, to descend bleeding, one wing broken, but still a crowing ball of ferocity. A hound cat screamed in pain as a beak caught her eye, making the fluids squirt; then she rolled on her back and caught the cock with all four feet, ripping it apart. The battle spilled out into the hall, fur and feathers flying, so violent and vicious it was impossible to tell which forces were prevailing.

Damner had been abraded by Knot's precipitous passage. Damner leaned against the wall, gathering his will. Knot found himself no longer afraid of hay. He charged into the man, hitting him with his left shoulder, trying to knock the wind from him, then whirling into a combat throw. But Knot's left side was small, and the leverage was wrong; he could not complete his throw effectively. He struggled to force the man over—

And froze, then let go. Damner's will was on him again, forcing him to relax. The mutant's psi was irresistible!

Then Damner screamed. Finesse, released, had struck with her own psi, invoking another terror. Damner fled down the hall, heedless of the fighting animals. Three cocks and a hound cat were hurled to the side to clear his way. He was berserk, as Knot had been. Then Damner was gone.

"I gave him claustrophobia—the most intense case," Finesse said breathlessly as she came to Knot.

"Keep on him! Don't let him recover equilibrium until we can set the cocks on him!"

She nodded and ran after Damner, keeping him in range. Should the controller's range be larger than Finesse's he might otherwise control her from beyond her ability to affect him, and he would surely not let her go again. She had to stay close. She was no longer needed here; the cocks had countered the hound cats.

That left one job for Knot. It was possible that Piebald had forgotten him now, at least for the moment, and that set up a critical opportunity. He thought to Hermine: **Get the override code for me again. I've got to change CC back before Piebald realizes what I'm doing.**

Mit says it won't work—

But Knot moved on inside. He was glad he was no longer afraid of hay, and found it hard to imagine how he could have been, a moment ago. Finesse was right: She was not the same woman she had been. She would not be able to settle down with a normal man. Suppose she got mad and used her psi on him? It would not require many episodes of that to damage his love for her. She belonged with another psi-mutant, who would respect her talent and understand her situation. She had used her psi on Knot, devastatingly; he still loved her. Would always love her. But he hoped she wouldn't tease him with any more hay phobias.

Just give me the data, he thought to Hermine. **Mit's precog isn't operating, is it? He doesn't know whether this will work.**

Hermine relayed the data reluctantly. Knot walked up to the terminal. The holograph of Piebald still stood above, watching him. No chance to be forgotten, then, but still it could work. As he understood it, the override code was preemptive; the most recent application of it would be the one in force. As with a chess piece taking over a square from the opponent's piece occupying it.

"You're one tough opponent," the lobo said. "But I have already summoned reinforcements."

Naturally Piebald would try to distract him, to prevent him from applying the code. Knot ignored him, and began tapping out the code pattern that Mit and Hermine provided.

"You will not be able to complete that override command," Piebald said. The holo could do nothing now except talk; he could not interfere physically.

Knot kept tapping. "Why not? It takes time for reinforcements to arrive—several minutes, I happen to know —and there are a lot of aggressive birds in the way." He was rather enjoying the lobo's discomfiture. Once Knot achieved control of CC, he would act against Piebald immediately, to prevent any recurrence of this mutiny.

"Because I shall stop you." The image raised its fist.

Knot laughed, almost losing his code-beat. "Strike, holo-lobo! You can't touch me!"

Piebald took impressively careful aim, bracing himself exactly as though he expected substance to meet substance, putting on an excellent dramatic show. But Knot refused to be bluffed; he kept tapping, smiling.

The lobo struck—and the blow connected to the side of Knot's face. It was no knock-out strike, but its surprise made it devastating. Knot reeled back. "You're real!" he gasped.

"I stepped onto the platform while you were occupied," Piebald said, stepping down. "I thought you might try something cunning, like this; that's the way my own mind works. I never depend on others to do my job for me; I use them only as front-line diversion. I don't remember exactly how you got here, but I certainly know of you through my researches, and have been careful not to underrate you. Sure enough, you nullified both the psi-mutant and the animals, and came here to finish the job. So I anticipated you, and acted to prevent it. You acted exactly as I would have acted, in your situation."

So the lobo had begun to forget, when he had removed himself from Knot's vicinity—but had come prepared for that. Knot's code recital was forgotten; the unexpected blow had entirely disrupted that. His head was hurting. Had he realized—but the fact was, the lobo had outsmarted him, this time. To be lobotomized was not to lose intelligence or force of will; that was becoming clearer the longer he interacted with Piebald.

Knot realized that his dream had abruptly been realized: he was alone with his archenemy, indulging in fair individual combat. Knot's prior wounds still weakened him somewhat, but he knew he could do what he had to.

Knot launched himself into Piebald. Knot caught the man by the arm and swung him around. "I will refresh your memory," Knot said, pausing before making his heave. "I blew up your volcano redoubt on Planet Macho. I set the bees on you, and burned up your arsonists and put your solar power plant on the blink."

Then he heaved—but Piebald counterbalanced, dropping low and sticking out his hard stomach, making the throw impossible. Now his arm closed about Knot's neck as he went into a stranglehold. The man knew combat technique!

"I appreciate that information," the lobo said. "Now I shall destroy you and your girl and your two animals here; you are all too dangerous to allow to live, handy as you might otherwise be for our research program." He tightened his grip, drawing Knot off balance.

Knot struggled, but was helpless. He could not get his feet under him to restore his balance, and could not reach any part of the lobo's body. It was a fundamental principle: Break a man's balance, and you control him. Piebald had applied it expertly.

Knot's consciousness was already fading, as the pressure on his neck transmitted to his carotid arteries. The sharp bones of Piebald's arm pressed against the muscles of Knot's neck, forcing them aside, making the arteries beneath vulnerable. Some people thought the jugular vein was the key spot, but it was not; the hidden carotids were the targets of choice. The flow of blood to his brain was being cut off. In moments he would pass out.

Knot's struggling feet hit something. A pitchfork, brought down by his prior manhandling of the bales. He hooked his feet about its handle and heaved up with all his remaining strength. Piebald was drawn slightly off balance himself, and had to let Knot lower to the floor. The strangle remained tight, however, and Knot's head was being shoved forward cruelly. Not only was he losing consciousness, but also his neck was getting near the breaking point—or so it felt.

Yet he had a slight advantage. His body was uneven, and this made the strangle less tight than it should have been. Thus he had a few extra seconds to fight. His flailing, long-armed right hand found the shaft. He grasped the pitchfork, hauled it up, and wrestled the tines upward toward his enemy's face. His grip on the weapon was awkward, but both Piebald's hands were occupied with the stranglehold, and the man could not block those long, sharp points. Knot shoved—

Piebald let go, avoiding the menace. Knot was free— but unable to rise. His consciousness was still too faint. The lobo snatched the pitchfork from his weakened, grasp, lifted it high—

Cocks burst into the chamber, half winging, half running toward the lobo. Hermine had directed them to victory in the hall, and now was coming to Knot's rescue.

Piebald drew back, swinging the pitchfork around to cover the cocks. "Terminal self-destruct!" he yelled.

The CC terminal, obedient to the command of the override master, exploded. The flash and concussion blinded and deafened Knot, and he relinquished consciousness at last.

Knot was roused in only a few minutes. "We won the battle, lost the war," Finesse said sadly as she stroked his hair. "I made Damner so scared he knocked himself out against a wall. The two hound cats are dead. But Piebald escaped. There's an access passage for CC service-men. . . ."

"Yes," Knot agreed. "Piebald's just as slippery as I am. He hid there, then came out. He must really have done his homework on CC before he came here. The lobos always make sure to know their enemy. He played every card on cue."

"That means he's still emperor. He didn't destroy CC, just this terminal. We can't override through this termi-nal, now, and it's the only critical one on Planet Chicken Itza. Unless we can trap Piebald on this planet—"

"Monstrously fat chance of that!" Knot muttered.

"True," Finesse agreed morosely. "He's the master, as far as CC is concerned. Any lesser CC outlet will honor his personal code, and there are plenty of those termi-nals around. So he can communicate with CC, and so can we, but we can't override him. Not from this planet. In fact, he'll soon have us arrested. We have to hide—again."

"With all the resources of CC after us, this time," Knot finished. "The lobos have really taken the advantage."

"Yes. CC is now our enemy. We support the ousted program." She lifted her head, her small chin firm. "But we're not entirely helpless. CC does not yet know about our extended animal alliances. Klisty had the sense to keep all the creatures except Hermine and Mit clear of the action. Maybe it was Mit's advice that was responsi-ble. Piebald either knows or will soon learn about Her-mine and Mit through CC, anyway."

"He knows about Klisty and Harlan," Knot said. "He used the null-precog effect to get through to CC him-self."

"Oh no!" she cried, chagrined. "Then we'll have to make that alliance with the hive."

"Exchanging one evil for another," Knot said. "The hive is just as much mutinous as the lobos." He climbed to his feet, still feeling light-headed. "Let's not make that deal yet. Maybe the lobos and animals will cancel each other out."

"I still have the feeling there's something important we don't know," she said. "I wish we could get hold of a power-clairvoyant, one who grasps fundamental social forces—"

"I know what you mean. I've had the feeling for days. There is some force operating that we have not perceived directly." He shrugged. "For the moment, let's gather what we have and get out of here. This is unsafe territory for us."

Mit directed them to Klisty and the other animals. The little girl was cleaning away tears. "I wanted to help, but Hermine and the bees told me we all had to stay out of it, no matter what. They didn't know if you'd survive—"

Finesse put her arm around the girl's shoulders. "They were right, dear. We are playing in an extremely rough league now. It was essential that no person or machine see those animals. That may save all our lives in the next few days."

"But I thought the animals had questions to ask CC, to get their status—"

"The Coordination Computer has turned against us," Finesse explained. "The lobos got to it and changed its basic directive. Everything it knows about us is now our liability—but it doesn't know about the bees, roaches or rats—we hope."

"Then it's not over," Klisty said grimly.

"No—it may never be over," Finesse agreed. There was a pause while they all considered that. How could they fight the full resources of CC? The single-compulsion psi-mutant, Damner, had been almost more than they could handle.

"We have to get out of here before the CC forces seal off this barn," Knot said. "And we'd better get off this planet before they ship in a good clairvoyant or broadscan telepath."

"Yes," Finesse said. "Before we were up against nonpsis; now we must overcome the whole of the psi-forces CC can bring to bear against us. We've got some of the best available psi-mutes in our own group, right here, but let's not fool ourselves. We're grossly overmatched."

"We need more," Knot said grimly. "We need enough psi to put up a decent front against CC—and that's virtually impossible."

More animal psis? the bees inquired, buzzing back to his shoulder.

Animal psis! He had been thinking human, for no good reason. **Yes. We need psi-powers to oppose the human psis that will be brought to bear against us. Psi-blocks against clairvoyance, telekinetic attack, telepathy, compulsion—the only defense we have now is against precognition.**

We have read the minds of some chickens, the bees thought. **We had to do this, to be sure they were not going to eat us. We learned they are hiding psi-mutes.**

Real hope flared. Of course! On an experimental chicken-breeding world there would be many unsuccessful mutants—and many successes the breeders weren't looking for. CC did not register chickens the way it did people; comparatively few psi-animals came to its attention, such as Hermine and Mit, while the rats and roaches escaped its attention. Who would interview a chicken for its mental powers? Simple, rapid inspection by handlers sufficed. Chickens that looked normal to such handlers, that seemed fit for laying or eating or combat—such birds could have all manner of psi-talents, unregistered. If the chickens themselves quietly acted to preserve these psi-mutants, there could be a considerable collection now. And the chickens *would* act—for the first chicken precog who saw the fate of those who did not act would react automatically. This did not require intelligence, any more than fleeing from a wolf did; it was simple gut-level survival.

"I think this planet too may be ripe for mutiny," Knot murmured. "This may be the mutiny we want to join."

Finesse looked at him, surprised, grasping it. "If they can use psi the way they fight—"

Lead us to the head chicken, Knot thought.

There is no head, the bees thought back.

There must be a group whose purpose is to save the psis. Yes—the Clucks Clan.

Aloud, Knot said: "Yes, we may have discovered a major psi-ally. The bees will show the way."

Are you near to joining us? the bees inquired.

Nearer than I was, Knot admitted.

They moved out. No CC forces intercepted them;

Knot suspected this was because the fighting cocks patrolled the barn, attacking any intruders. Klisty had released them all, with Hermine's mental proviso that they leave her party alone. The weasel was still keeping track of all those warriors, keeping them on duty and clear of the human party; that was why she was not available for this quest for the psi-chickens. If Hermine lost her concentration, Doublegross Bladewings could turn on Knot's party and do the lobos' job for them.

But Knot knew that before long the humans would bring up sedative gas dispensers and knock the cocks out. In fact, the humans would probably flood the whole barn with gas.

The hidden psi-chickens were not in the barn, however. A tunnel had been scratched out of the deep dirt, leading to the old burrows of some large native creatures. Here a collection of motley chickens met them, of all three varieties: fighting, laying and meat birds. From them came strong telepathy.

We are members of the Clucks Clan. We know your purpose. We do not trust you. Humans are smart while we are stupid. Now we shall be slaughtered.

Knot had had to do a lot of compromising, especially with animals. Yet they were, in their fashion, quite similar to human mutants; that came through more and more strongly. What significant difference was there between a man whose arms were feathered like wings, and whose mind was feeble—and a chicken whose telepathy enabled it to draw on Knot's own intelligence during its interaction with him? He had dealt all his life with variations of the former; why not now deal with the latter? Surely the chickens had the greatest need of help, as they had been bred only to serve and feed man without regard for their own preference or species welfare.

Hermine, I believe we are safe from the fighting cocks here, Knot thought. **Keep the others of this party informed, human and animal. I am going to negotiate with the chickens.**

It's about time, the weasel thought back.

Chickens—I mean, honorable Clucks Clan, he thought. **I know you lack intelligence and organization. Otherwise you would have used your psi-powers long ago to gain**

your freedom from exploitation. If you will lend us your psi to accomplish our purpose, we will give this planet to you. No longer will you serve man.

There was a flutter of excitement and doubt. We Clucks are not smart—concept too big—cannot trust man. Our main Clan is far away—

Then take us to your leaders! Knot thought impatiently. This region is hardly safe anyway. Not for us, not for you.

A local threat: that they grasped. Still the chickens hesitated, uncertain what course if any to pursue. They would never get anything done! This inability to make a decision was of course the very thing that had prevented them from acting effectively before.

"Gee, Mr. Knot," Klisty said. "I like chickens. Last year I raised a flock of pullets for the eggs. Nice pink eggs. I never mistreated them, honest! They would feed from my hand and sit on my arm. I bet if I could talk to these ones—"

Hermine, interpret for her, Knot thought, conscious of the brevity of time. They had to accomplish something positive rapidly.

"No, they're afraid of weasels and things," Klisty demurred. "The cocks aren't afraid of anything, so Hermine could think to them, but these ones—"

"But Hermine's our telepath," Knot said. "The chickens have telepaths, but for delicate negotiations I prefer to use our own telepath. Their telepaths can verify our dialogue."

"They don't much trust people or weasels," Klisty said. "We aren't going to make much progress unless we meet their people halfway."

"The bees," Finesse murmured.

Perfect! Bees, will you interpret for Klisty? Knot thought.

There was a buzz of dismay. We don't like chickens.

Naturally not. They eat your kind. But by that token, they will not fear you, and may speak plainly. If you stay close to Klisty for protection—

CC forces are closing in, Hermine thought urgently. Mit says they are gassing the outer chambers of the barn.

The bees rose in a group and went to the girl. A dialogue began, to which the others were not party.

"They say men are coming," Klisty said, worried. "They can't concentrate on negotiation right now. This cave is not far enough away from the barn—"

"We'll have to run out of the barn—" Knot began.

Mit says they have already closed off our exit.

Knot thought fast. "These are birds. They must have some strong fliers among their mutants. Klisty, ask their telepaths to summon hundreds of flying chickens and carry us all away from here. Then we can continue negotiations."

Klisty shook her head. "They say no. The only way out of here is through the barn, and the gas is flooding it. They are about to teleport out—"

Teleportation! "But *we* can't—" Finesse began.

"Then teleport us too!" Knot cried. "They must have birds who can teleport others. If they can handle the load—"

Klisty consulted. "For a short hop, yes. Then the fliers take over."

"Then *do* it! Get us all away from here! The animals too. I promise we won't hurt any chickens!" **This means you, Hermine!**

The weasel responded with a miniature nova, no more than a flash of light: token defiance.

More consultation. Then four fat hens sidled cautiously up to Klisty, surrounding her, clucking. "Bawk-bawk-bawk-CAWK!"

And the child and baby were gone—along with one hen. And the five bees.

"Your turn next," Knot told Finesse. "You take Hermine and the rats with you."

Finesse took the three animals and went to stand amid the three hens, who clucked nervously but finally decided to do it. "Bawk-bawk-bawk-ba-CAWK!" And Finesse was gone, with her animals and the second hen.

Finally Knot himself went. He was the most massive package, and the roaches in his pocket were fidgeting nervously. But now he could hear the hissing of gas in the barn, and knew he did not have much time. "Let's go!" he said.

The two remaining hens sized him up. They clucked back and forth between themselves, as though deciding which one should assume this chore. Knot thought he smelled the first whiff of gas. "Move it! Move it!" he exclaimed.

At last the larger hen squawked in the code—and Knot was wrenched from his physical and mental moorings. He suffered vertigo as he saw an inverted world shoot past him. The barn seemed transparent, while the air seemed opaque. Then he landed heavily on the ground, the hen panting beside him. He hadn't realized that hens could pant, but of course she had carried quite a load.

He was in a field of grain, alone except for the roaches and his teleporter. He could guess what had happened: His larger mass had interfered with the hen's aim or control, and he had landed somewhat apart from the others. Probably Klisty and Finesse had been separated too.

At least they were well away from the barn. All they had to do was find each other; then—

Man, where are you? a thought came. It had the feel of a chicken-sending. Knot did not know how he distinguished one telepathic thought from another, but he did.

Here, he thought back dutifully.

Almost immediately, he saw shapes appear over the horizon. They looked like vultures—no, they were giant fowl, with monstrously spreading wings. Specially bred for carrying burdens, no doubt. On a planet like this, they would have racing fliers, and swimmers, and other specialties, and some of these would escape to the open range. Excellent!

The giant fowl spotted him and glided down like eagles. Knot suffered sudden concern; if these were fighting birds—but evidently they were under telepathic direction, and had come prepared. They had a woven-string litter, like a hammock. Knot hung himself in its framework, and the birds hauled up on the diverging extremities. There were a score or so of them, each flapping violently. Soon he was lifted up, to swing somewhat perilously above the waving seed heads of the field. The teleport hen clucked and disappeared, traveling in her fashion to a more secure roost. Her job was done.

Once they had achieved suitable elevation, the birds caught an obliging draft and winged more rapidly across the surface of the planet. The terrain shifted from flat field to rolling hills and gullies dotted with trees. This was a rather pleasant way to travel, once he got used to it. When they passed higher escarpments, Knot became conscious of the associated updrafts that affected the birds' flight. At one point they swung low over a ridge, and he feared his posterior would scrape; but in fact the clearance was a good two meters. This reminded him of childhood dreams of flying, with vicious animals in pursuit on the ground, leaping up to snap at his extremities while he flapped his arms desperately to gain altitude, never quite getting up there. Now it was the chickens flapping—but fortunately they did make headway, and as the ground slanted into another valley the elevation became comfortably high again. Phew!

In due course other flying flocks converged: those bearing Finesse and Klisty. The child waved happily; she was enjoying this. "Whee!" her high voice came faintly. What a change of pace and style from their prior travels!

It was a long trip, and the birds evidently could not maintain this energy output indefinitely. Even Knot, who was glad for the rest, found the strings of the sling chafing and digging into his backside, and he needed to urinate. He was sure his companions were no more comfortable. What was fun for a few minutes was tedious for a few hours.

As the day waned they landed by a wilderness stream. Edible tubers grew along its banks; the hungry rats were quick to sniff these out. Their party would never go hungry as long as these psi-talents were operating.

It was dusk. The chickens wandered off, foraging amid bushes and turf, happily filling their crops with the wild seeds available and incidentally serving as an area guard force. Though these were not fighting cocks, they were very large fowl with strong muscles in wings and legs; they were not noticeably shy. Knot was sure wilderness predators would keep clear of this locale tonight.

It was evidently intended by the Clucks Clan that they spend the night here, since they had to wait on their litter bearers, who seemed reluctant to fly in the dark. The humans found fine brush and ferns and formed beds. They washed in the stream, exclaiming over the chill of it. The air was warm and the sky clear; they needed no shelter.

"Was this the way it was in the enclave chasm?" Klisty inquired idly.

"Yes," Knot said. "Except that this is like heaven, while that was more like hell."

"Was the mermaid like hell too?" Finesse inquired.

"Did the weasel blab about her?" Knot asked, dismayed.

"Of course not; I know nothing about Thea or her quest."

"That's a relief," Knot said weakly.

"Did she really have a bigger bosom than—"

"I'm going to feed that weasel to a Bladewing!"

They lay looking up at the bright stars, tracing constellations that were unknown on Knot's home planet of Nelson, or Klisty's home planet of Macho. They argued about which star was which: whether Nelson lay in the region of the sky resembling a five-armed mutant man, or in the one that looked like a human brain with a dagger projecting from it: lobotomy in progress. Klisty was happily ensconced with assorted animals. She delighted in having the bees, formerly objects of considerable apprehension, now buzzing about her hair. She was trying to talk them into making some honey for her.

Knot and Finesse made love, somewhat awkwardly because they did not want to disturb their fernbed or make their activity too obvious, but pleasantly enough. Knot heard the child's patter as a background to his exertions in the dark.

"Gee, it's fun out here with everyone. In the orphan camp we always had curfew and stripes on the hands if we were late. And not much psi; I sort of had to hide my talent so I wouldn't get teased. But you animals know about psi, don't you! I wish I could stay with you forever. Right here on this planet, maybe; it's so nice."

She was interrupted by a cry from the baby. "Oh no, Harlan—your bottle's empty, and we're out of formula powder. Here, I'll see if we can get you some more."

Knot and Finesse lay silently beside each other, listening. What did Klisty have in mind?

Fortunately the child liked voicing her thoughts.

"Okay, you telepathic clucks. Where are the teleporters? Can you reach them? Good—bring them here. Right. Now tell them to 'port over some formula powder. From where? Look, there must be lots of it in the storehouses, for mixing with chicken food or starter mash. Powdered milk, you know. Just move a bag—oops! That must weigh as much as I do! Well, I'll take it, and we can all have milk for breakfast tomorrow when the old folks wake up."

Old folks? Knot squeezed Finesse's hand. The young folks could manage!

In the morning a half-familiar figure was tending a fire. He was crippled, sitting in a chair that floated a handspan above the ground. His head was bald on top, hairy from eyebrows down, his eyes glittering out from their bushy sockets. Behind him stood a middle-aged woman, evidently an attendant. When the man leaned forward to lay a stick of wood on the fire, she watched him—and his chair floated conveniently close.

"I don't recall it, but we have met before," the man said as Knot stirred. Since Knot and Finesse were naked, this encounter was awkward, and he hastened to don his clothing. Finesse was slower; she had too good a body to hide as though it were indecent. "I am Drem, the futures psi. Perhaps you remember me better than I remember you."

Now Knot recognized him. Knot was alarmed, for this suggested that CC had already located them—yet the roaches were at ease. "Yes," he agreed somewhat noncommittally.

Drem indicated his attendant. "This is Essene, a levitation psi-mute who is helping me get around." The woman nodded.

"You work for CC," Knot said. "I thought we were hidden from CC's minions."

"This is a special situation. Let me explain—and you put your telepath on me, to verify my sincerity."

I'm on, Hermine thought, appearing momentarily from the brush where she had been hunting. **This is important.**

"The Coordination Computer has been corrupted by the enemy it sought to eliminate," Drem said. "We knew this was the moment it happened, though we were unable to anticipate it. This puts the psis who are employees of CC in an awkward position."

"I should think so," Knot agreed wryly.

"To oppose CC would be mutiny, and this would be a most serious step. We would all be subject to the penalty of lobotomy, as nonsocial psi-mutants, unless we took it farther and took over CC ourselves and established a new order. We do not like to think in this manner. Yet to support CC against the civilization of man would be treason, for which the penalty is the same."

"We had no difficulty deciding," Knot said. "We support the original order—the one to whom we made our commitments, even though we have some reservations about details of that order."

"That is simplistic. Had I done that before, I would have refused to cooperate with your explorations of the futures, since I had never sworn allegiance to you as emperor. Or so CC's record assures me. We psi-mutes have generally stayed clear of CC's politics, and not passed judgment on those who issue CC's directives, regardless of the manner in which they achieved the ability to do so. Not all the members of the Galactic Concord came to power in ways we approve, yet we acknowledge the validity of their offices."

"He's got a point," Finesse said. "If the employees start deciding the policies of their employer, anarchy soon results."

"Um," Knot agreed. "Yet to follow the employer blindly, even when everyone knows his authority has been usurped—that's disaster."

"Some of our number share that view," Drem said. "Already there has been strife. The controller Damner, isolated from the rest of us, decided to maintain loyalty to CC. As a result he found himself fighting those he would have preferred to align with. The rest of us face a similar decision."

"I have another simplistic solution," Knot said. "Since you face the same penalty either way, for mutiny or for treason, do what you know is right."

"We are not certain what is right."

"Use a clairvoyant," Finesse put in, somewhat acidly.

The psi smiled. "As you are surely aware, ethics are not subject to clairvoyance." He spread his hands. "And as you must also know, we cannot at present read the future through precognition. You are intimately associated with that future, and one of your number is a null-precog. My own psi also becomes valueless in that connection. We simply do not know the outcome of this confrontation. Therefore we are at a loss. We cannot even put ethical considerations aside and side with the winning group."

"Be pragmatic," Finesse said. "Declare for the original order, fight the lobos, help us restore the prior mandate, and then there will be no further conflict. You don't know what to expect from a new order, but with the old you will be secure."

Drem shook his head. "We psis are not agreed whether the old order should be restored."

"Not agreed!" she exploded.

"There are substantial evils in that system," Drem said. "For every successful psi-mutant, there are perhaps a hundred unsuccessful ones. Even some of the successes are like me." He made a gesture to include himself, grimacing. His voice was strong, but his body was a wreck; now Knot saw that he even had straps to hold him upright in the floating chair. Apparently he had always been physically decrepit. "A great deal of grief underpins the existing order. The failures, the bereaved families, the antimutant discrimination, the enclaves, the necessity of subverting human concerns to machine arbitration—the lobos represent a reform movement of sorts. They will certainly bring change, possibly even improvement."

Knot nodded. "I have reason to hate the lobos, but that thought has crossed my mind too."

"Oh, has it?" Finesse demanded. "I could never accept the domination of the galaxy by that ilk!"

"So the two of you differ between yourselves," Drem said. "Thus you are familiar with our problem. We psis are not united on this matter. Some of us want to fight the lobos, while others are in favor of supporting them. We are split down the middle. Yet we do not wish to fight each other. When psi opposes psi, civilization suffers.

Being unable to choose, yet agreeing on the need to remain united, we have elected to remain neutral, as a group."

"Neutral!" Finesse cried indignantly. "How can there be neutrality in a situation like this? A torturer and murderer has perverted CC's prime directive and usurped power, and you know it!"

"Yes," Drem agreed. "But as I clarified before, we cannot presume to issue directives of policy to CC. We may privately disagree, as individual soldiers in an army may disagree with the overall policy, but it is beyond our province to oppose it overtly."

"I'll directly oppose it!" she said. She whirled on Knot, still with only half her clothing on, lovely in her animation and dishabille. "And you, you temporizer—where do you stand?"

Knot thought about the things Piebald had done. He had killed two innocent people in extremely brutal fashion and brutalized a third: Finesse herself. There were probably many other similar crimes Knot had not been witness to. Yet Knot himself had killed; he was not of superior moral fiber in this respect. Perhaps not in *any* respect. No decision—there. If he should side with the lobos, he would lose Finesse; if he sided with her—

"I oppose the lobos," he said, hoping that the mechanism of his decision had been less shallow and self-serving than it seemed to himself. Surely there was a sensible body of belief he was drawing on. . . .

"And your associated psis?" Drem asked.

We are with you and Finesse, Hermine thought. All the animals are against the lobos. It might be different in the case of the animal mutiny—

"They are with us," Knot said.

"So you will be attempting to depose the lobos from power," Drem concluded. "We surmised as much, and this is why I came here. We feel it is essential for you to understand our position. We are going to remain aloof, supporting neither side, interfering with neither. When the issue has been decided we will serve the party in power—whoever controls CC. Another member of our group is at this moment informing the lobo commander."

"You are standing aside, just watching?" Finesse demanded. "Not doing a single thing to promote justice?"

"Yes," Drem agreed. "That is the nature of noninvolvement. Because not all of us are prepared to abide by such a compromise, we have arranged a modification. Each side may enlist two of our number for assistance."

"Do you think this is some stupid game?" Finesse demanded. "That you are the spectators, handing out little prizes to encourage better mayhem?"

"No game at all," Drem assured her, seeming oblivious to her cutting edge. "Our lives and the future of civilization itself may depend on the outcome. It is really a power struggle, and any psis who commit themselves to the losing side will share the fate of that side. We are vitally interested in the outcome of this struggle—but can neither foresee it nor participate, beyond the limit we have set."

"Well, we won't use any of your psis!" Finesse said.

"You do not have to. The lobos may select two, though, putting you at a disadvantage if—"

"Get out of here!" Finesse screamed.

"As you wish. Naturally we shall not reveal your location to the lobo chief, and will not reveal his location to you." The chair floated swiftly away, the woman following.

"Do you think that was wise?" Knot asked. "A couple of good, experienced psi-talents complementing our own could really help us."

"We don't know what side Drem is on," she said. "*He* could be working for Piebald!

No, Hermine thought. He spoke only truth.

"Still," she grumbled, "we're better off on our own."

With that Knot could not entirely disagree. "At least we know we don't have to fight the entire psi-complement of CC," he said. "That reduces the odds against us from prohibitive to merely adverse."

"We'll have to fight two of those psis," she reminded him grimly. "Along with all the mechanical resources of CC. We don't even know which two psis."

"We can find out, when we get within range."

"And they'll find out about us!"

"Meanwhile, we can make a pretty good guess. Piebald

will go for a clairvoyant, almost certainly. And something to counter your phobias—"

"The controller!" she cried.

"That must be it." He hesitated. "Though I understood that the arrangement was starting only now."

"Could they set it at two psis after the fact, once they started figuring things out? To make up for the psi Piebald already used against us?"

"Could," he agreed uncertainly.

"Does it make a difference?"

"I suppose not. We have to deal with the fact, not with the way the fact might have come about. We'll be on guard against clairvoyance—and whatever else. Let's get on with our present mission."

Klisty served up milk for all, then had the surplus teleported back to the warehouse. The flying chickens returned, took up the litters, and resumed the journey. In a few hours they all arrived at the island redoubt of the Clucks Clan, the leadership of the free chickens.

Here the birds were smarter, but also more careful. **How can you give us this planet,** their telepath asked, **when you are fugitive yourself?**

This planet is governed directly by CC, Knot replied. It is used as a refueling station for diskships, and for experimental breeding of chickens. I don't approve of excessive mutation in humans, and doubt that it can be good for chickens either. So it should be stopped. CC is the one who can stop it, by discontinuing the breeding program. The breeding of mutations, I mean. Then this world would revert to normal, with many stable breeds of a great many chickens. If chicken and egg imports were halted, man would have little use for this planet. Chickens could govern it themselves, in peace.

We are not smart, the leaders repeated. **We lack the human capacity for foresight and organization. We could not manage a planet.**

The bees have organizational talent, Knot pointed out. With the help of the hive—

We will not help chickens! the bees protested. We abhor all species who prey on bees!

The animals, too, would have problems, Knot saw. If their mutiny were successful on a galactic basis, they would soon be fighting each other. They might be better off under the control of man, as they had been for centuries.

No! the bees protested.

And how could we trust your promise? the suspicious chicken continued. Once you depart this planet, we shall have no hold over you.

There was that. Knot remembered that historically the normal procedure, when warring factions made alliances, was to exchange hostages. We might leave one of our number, he thought reluctantly.

"I'll stay!" Klisty cried, "I like it here!"

Knot was marshaling a protest, but the chickens were already pouncing on this as they might on a juicy bug. Would the girl organize us? Would she fathom our problems, so we could approach them with intelligence?

Did the chickens seek a hostage, or a ruler? The issue was becoming confused.

"Oh sure," Klisty said. "I like solving problems. I never had much responsibility before."

"I'm not sure—" Finesse said, dubious for the same unspecified reasons Knot was.

She is young, Knot cautioned the chickens. She would require much help from your telepaths and clairvoyants to gather information, and from your teleports to distribute feed properly in winter. You would have to answer all her questions, and take good care of her. She would make some mistakes, and would need companionship of some other human beings her own age. That should set them back!

All this is easily accomplished.

It was? Knot had thought he was raising insuperable objections. "Well, maybe in that case—" he said aloud.

"Knot!" Finesse protested. "You're selling her into slavery!"

"No. I'm making her queen of the chickens. It's just a larger coop, with more responsibility."

Startled, Finesse was silent. Klisty clapped her hands girlishly. "You mean I can stay?"

What would happen to the child if they took her to CCC to fight the lobos? Knot did not like the alternatives that offered, but this one seemed best. Even if it did not work out well, it should be better than torture or death at the hands of the lobos. "If you really want to," he said benignly. "If the chickens help us reverse CC's setting. If we don't accomplish that, nothing else counts; the lobos will be in power."

We will provide you with psi-birds, the chickens promised eagerly. **We have telepaths, teleports, clairvoyants, eggspoilers—**

What we really need are counters to these talents, Knot thought. **We have a good counter-precog, but CC's psis have other ways to detect us.**

We have no psi-counters, the chickens responded apologetically. **We did not realize they were valuable, so did not salvage them. We do have one who can amplify psi in others.**

Pieces clicked together in Knot's mind. **May we try your psi-amplifier?**

Finesse looked at him. "Amplification is the opposite of what we need! With most of the psi on the other side, it'll just increase the odds against us."

"Maybe not," Knot said.

After a pause, a somewhat homely rooster arrived. **Can you amplify any psi selectively?** Knot asked it via the chicken telepaths.

Yes, the rooster's thought was relayed back.

Then amplify the psi of the roaches in my pocket.

Roaches? the rooster inquired with interest.

Not to eat! Knot clarified quickly. **These are allies, sacrosanct.**

The rooster strutted about, not pleased. He eyed Knot, trying to discover where the roaches were. The roaches were aware of the danger, and became increasingly nervous.

Finally the rooster crowed. Nothing happened to Knot but there was commotion in the group. "He's gone!" Klisty exclaimed, looking right at Knot.

"Yeah, sure," Knot said, not finding this failure humorous.

But Finesse too seemed alarmed. "Did you teleport him out?" she demanded of the chickens.

We have not interfered, the chickens assured her. **Were your bugs teleporters?**

"You mean you really can't perceive me?" Knot demanded, still suspecting a joke. No one reacted.

"The roaches!" Finesse said. "When they get frightened, as they would when a rooster eyes them, they become invisible, inaudible, probably telepathically undetectable too!"

So now *he* was unperceivable, being in the ambience of the roaches' amplified psi. That was what he had hoped for, but he still wasn't sure it was so. For one thing, how was it that he could perceive all of them so readily, if there was a perception shield between them? He decided to test this properly.

"I'm going to goose you again," he announced, striding over to Finesse. When she did not react, he moved his hand suggestively—but decided to kiss her instead. No sense in living *too* dangerously!

Her lips were mushy, unprepared. Her eyes stared through him. She did not perceive him at all! He was not a ghost; when he pushed her, she was solid, and had to catch her balance. But she was not aware of the reason for it.

"That is what I call amplification," Knot said. "You roaches disappear only when frightened, and you can't have stayed that scared all this time, but I have disappeared regardless. Yet I am not in a shell that blocks the outside world off from me. This is the perfect protection."

"This is making me nervous," Finesse said. "Release the amplification. I want to see if he's still here." And she did look nervous; evidently she feared something more sinister had occurred.

The rooster clucked—all the chickens seemed to accompany their efforts with sound—and suddenly everyone was looking at Knot.

"So it worked," he said, feeling awkward, onstage.

"Could you see us?" Finesse demanded, hardly relaxing.

"I saw you, heard you, felt you, and picked up the telepathy," Knot said.

They were impressed. "Could that rooster amplify a teleport?" Klisty asked. "You could jump right to another world!"

But some discussion convinced them that it would be foolish to try such a thing. The vagaries of interstellar motion were such that jumping directly between worlds would not be safe. Amplification could enable more people to be moved longer distances on the surface of a planet, but that was the practical limit. Considering the way three people had been spread across the terrain when teleported the relatively short distance from the barn to the open field, accuracy was a prime consideration.

"Still," Knot concluded, "we could use a teleport. And the amplifier. I think with these psi-tools we have a fair chance against CC."

They discussed it some more, and the agreement was made. Klisty would remain as hostage-queen, while the rest of them would travel to CC with the two chickens. If they succeeded in reversing the program, they would send the news through CC channels; Chicken Itza would belong to the birds by fiat. If they failed—

They did not dwell on that. The chickens provided a henhouse nicely furnished with roosts, nesting boxes and hay for their lodging, and left them to work out their campaign. Klisty started in on her duties immediately, learning how to organize and govern a planetful of chickens. It was a busy time.

CHAPTER 12

Making plans to counter the lobos was no simple matter. "Knot," Finesse said, "I'm not sure what you have in mind. If we reach a CC control terminal—what then?"

"Why, we reverse it, of course. We wipe out Piebald's dictate, and set up our own."

"What is our own dictate?" she asked.

Now that the question had been put to him, he was uncertain of his answer. He had served the existing order before, albeit with certain reservations. But if he had to take over control of CC to restore the program, was the old order the best he could implement? "First we honor any outstanding commitments. Chicken Itza to be freed—"

"Yes, of course. But what of the fundamental system? Are we going to leave everything as it was before, including the lobos?"

"I suppose a modified program, to eliminate the worst of the present evils—"

"Evils!" she exclaimed. "What evils?"

"As you said, the lobos. We cannot allow them to continue lobotomizing law-abiding psi-mutes—"

"That does not require modification of the program. Just enforcement of the original program."

"And abolition of the slum enclaves. And cessation of the shameless exploitation of animals—"

"Animals aren't people!"

"Communicate with Hermine and tell me that." He was

trying to be reasonable, but wondered what she was getting at.

"Hermine's special. She's psi."

"So are these chickens. So are the rats and roaches and flies. Maybe in times past they were beneath man's serious notice. That is true no longer. They have achieved parity in psi, and are moving ahead. They deserve recognition now. That's what this mutiny is all about. This is the age of psi."

"The mutiny is the turning of CC against the welfare of mankind!" she insisted. "We have to turn it back."

"Or make it serve the interests of civilization more perfectly than it has before."

"You can't direct it to any better course! We established that before."

"I didn't have enough information before," he said. "Neither did CC. The old program may have been best suited to the needs of a single species, man—but now we know that civilization will comprise multiple species, including chickens, rats, roaches, and bees. Only a new program can represent their best interests."

"That's what I suspected. If you get control of CC, you may after all betray the program you came to restore."

He had to concede that. "I would not term it betrayal, though. Now the crisis is upon us. We were unable to prevent it—that was what we established before. My proposed policies never received proper examination. A new situation is opening up. So if we can improve things by changing the setting on CC, maybe we should do it."

"No! The old system was functional. It has been proven by experience. It is the only proper one."

Knot thought about the chasm enclave of Planet Macho. Had Finesse been there, she might have found new insights. His own perspective had evidently broadened more than he had been aware of, there. Finesse, instead, had been tortured by the lobos, so she was much more aware of the lobo evil. The two of them had grown apart without realizing it, because of the traumatic differences in their experiences. It behooved him to seek ways to mend that rift before it became more significant. But at the moment, there was a more pressing concern.

"Let's not argue," he said. "We don't even know if we

can get to a suitable CC terminal for override, so it is as yet academic. We agree that the lobos should not remain in charge; that's enough for now."

She was silent, but he knew that the argument, if such it was, was not over. It had merely been postponed. A split was developing between them, and that was uncomfortable even though he believed he understood it. Already he felt the beginning coolness in her attitude toward him.

There was also the problem of strategy. They had a fine nucleus of psi-mutant talents now, several of which CC and the lobos did not know about. With the limits set by the CC psi-employees this gave Knot's party the psi-advantage—maybe. But CC had vast resources, and well understood how to deal with psi. The overall advantage had to remain with the machine. The lobos themselves had a most dedicated and efficient organization, backed by that ineffable power that Knot had never been able to pinpoint. There seemed to be some advantage in being lobotomized, paradoxical as that might appear—and Knot would have felt a lot better if he could have fathomed its precise nature.

"We can't just march to CCC and take over," Knot said. "We need more than we have, or our effort will be futile."

"More what?" Finesse asked, still cool. "More commitment from the animal kingdoms?"

He elected to ignore that. She could be very cutting, but he would simply have to live with it. "More information. CC we know, but the lobos we don't know."

"Don't know!" she exclaimed. "I know them better than I ever want to remember!"

And how could he blame her for that? "They're too disciplined, for criminal types. They shouldn't obey a leader like Piebald with so little question. He has no loyalty to them; he let all the ones remaining in the volcano villa die without warning or help. He's been pushing a program of experimentation that is dangerous—as in your case, where you almost wrapped up the lobos right there—and is unlikely to be productive. There should be deep rumblings of discontent, even open rebellion—yet the lobos remain unified, like the hive. The hive is unified by telepathy, so that's explicable; bees are social insects anyway. Men are less amenable to that sort of unity, especially the criminal types. There has to be some overwhelming cohesive force —and that must be what CC has really been fighting. If we could only understand the nature of that force, and locate its source, we might destroy the lobo unity. *Then* we could go after Piebald and CC."

"There may be something to that," she agreed slowly. "Considering that the lobos have used neither psi nor advanced electronics—until now—they have been suspiciously effective opponents. Your psi enables you to hide from almost anyone or anything except CC itself, yet they chased you down quite handily. With no hive-psi and no computer communication—they must have something that the normals don't. But it's intangible. We have never seen it, only its effect. How could we find out what it is, at this late date, if CC itself was unable to do so before it was too late for it?"

"I've been mulling that over. CC didn't know that the lobos were its enemies; had it known in time, it might have divined their weapon. We do know about the lobos, and maybe with the help of psi we can work it out. A couple of things Piebald said may be a key to how his mind works. I don't know; it's really not much at all—"

"Get on with it!"

"Well, he tried to use your husband against you, restoring your memory when you were at a crucial pass. It didn't work—"

"It was a hard strike, though," she admitted.

"But if he felt it would be more effective than it was, maybe that means it would have been effective—if he had been the one struck. And the other thing—"

"His wife!" she exclaimed. "He has a wife! He mentioned it—"

"Yes. You were sending, then. You said something about his raping you, and he said his wife would object. And he never did—" Knot paused.

Finesse smiled, warming despite the subject. "No, he never did rape me. I'm sure it wasn't any sensitivity about my feelings that restrained him. Had he thought rape would make me evoke my psi—" She shrugged. "Of course, he simply may not have found me attractive—"

"You're attractive," Knot assured her. "Unless you made him dislike you, through psi, unconsciously—"

"That would have made him fear me, not dislike me. He never feared me, until my psi manifested openly. *I* must have been the one afraid, or I would have given him a phobia about blood or something—"

"No, your psi was keyed to me. When the Doublegross Bladewings threatened me, then your psi acted. You never used it to help yourself, until—"

"Yes. I'm not too pleased with the way CC set that up."

"So Piebald's wife must have some real power over him," Knot concluded. "If something happened to her—"

Finesse shook her head. "He's tough. He'd just bluff it through—or even write her off, as he did the lobos at the villa."

"Still, if we could get to her, maybe we could learn something. If she knows what unifies lobos—"

"She may not even know what Piebald's doing! He suggested as much."

"In which case, perhaps we ought to tell her. If she does happen to have any clout—"

Finesse smiled. "Your diabolic way of thinking grows on me. But CC supervises the diskships; if we try to travel there—and we don't even know where she is. Or even if she exists; he might have made her up."

"Yes. Traveling is going to be a problem. But I wonder—with all the psi we can borrow here, whether—you know, amplification—"

"Interplanetary teleportation? You know that's too dangerous!"

"Well, what about psychic projection? Like a holograph, only psi-generated. If we could arrange something like that—"

"Suddenly I'm with you!" she said. "That would be safe to do, and safer to confront the lobos with, too. Such a projection could not be captured and tortured."

The details took several hours, and represented Klisty's first organizational test. It was necessary to locate the proper psi-fowl and acquaint them with the nature of the task. Since this was complicated, and the birds were not bright, it took some explaining. Finally Knot made the excursion, while Finesse remained behind to keep the psi-chickens on the job and plan the forthcoming approach to Coordination Computer Central. They knew it would come to a direct confrontation eventually, and the sooner the better, before the lobos got well entrenched. Knot's effort was merely to improve their own chances.

They had determined by amplified distance clairvoyance that Piebald did have a lobo wife, that she resided in another villa on Planet Macho, and that her name was Hulda. That was as much detail as they could get with the preliminary setup, and probably a good deal more than would have been possible to other psis, since clairvoyance across galactic distances was a phenomenal effort. Psi-holo projection at this range—about fifteen thousand light-years —was virtually unheard of. But with the resources of a planetful of unregistered psi-mutants to draw from, unusual efforts became possible.

Knot appeared—he could not call it materialization, since he had no material reality here—at the edge of a lake. The villa sat just beyond a pretty deep-gold beach: old-fashioned stucco with a roof of large red tiles. Flowers bloomed beneath its windows, and spreading trees shaded it. A pleasant place, surely the habitat of someone who had aesthetic sensitivity.

He approached. His body seemed real even to him; he could see his arms and legs, and they moved properly as he walked. He came to the door, marveling that there were no guards here. Perhaps there were devices set to detect physical intrusions—or maybe this place was so well hidden that there was no fear of intrusion. Piebald had said that his wife knew nothing of his activities. Still, if the chicken-psi could find it, CC could have found it. What prevented such disclosure? That was the mystery he had come to investigate. Among other things.

He stepped up to the door and knocked. That didn't work; his hand passed through the panel without impact. So he walked on through it, as a ghost might. Perhaps he *was* a ghost. Who could say how much of the great supernatural heritage of mankind derived from unrecognized psi? But he had speculated on this before, and no doubt would again; now was not the time.

He heard sounds, and moved toward them. This was a complete projection, sonic as well as visual. Several chickens had had to be coordinated for it. He had no physical ears to receive sound or eyes to see, yet through psi he could function as though he did. Not only could he perceive sounds, he also could make them. Not by knocking on doors here, but by making sounds with his real body, on Chicken Itza, which sounds would be projected here.

He found a handsome woman doing her laundry. She was of middle age, but well preserved and possessed of a certain sex appeal. Her dark hair was swept into a bun and covered by a tasteful kerchief. She wore slacks and a flower-print blouse and open sandals. She was reclining by the washing robot, her fingers resting on its hand-held control unit.

"You are Piebald's wife?" Knot inquired.

"And you are the anonymous min-mute who has caused so much trouble, visiting in astral projection," she responded.

Knot was taken aback. "You know of me?" Silly question. "Piebald said you knew nothing of his activities—"

"Spare yourself that hope. My husband is acting under my instructions. You will not influence him through me."

Knot, off balance, reacted by attacking—as he was prone to do. "You are aware that he has been torturing psi-mutes? Lobotomizing innocent people? Perverting the Coordination Computer's program?"

"I am aware that he has been performing essential experiments, trying to unriddle the secrets of psi, and now will turn the big machine to that vital research. The ignorant might term that torture and perversion." She changed a setting, and the robot went into a new cycle of washing.

No ameliorative influence here! Piebald had not lied about having a wife, but about her connection to his machinations. "You know that his last subject was a very pretty woman, younger than you, and that the subject of sex came up?" A half truth . . .

"That phobia-psi-mute? He might have raped her as an object lesson, but he would never develop any personal interest in her. Not until she became a lobo herself. You are attached to her? You are aware she is married?"

This was one tough woman! He could not provoke her at all; she only responded with disquieting information about himself and his associates. If the lobos knew about Finesse's husband, they could abduct him at any time, thereby putting very painful pressure on Finesse. They would surely do it—when they thought it would be effective. Unless CC had hidden him where they could not find him—and of course now they could find him through CC itself. All Knot could do now was try a direct question; Hulda just might contemptuously answer it. "What is the secret of the lobos' power?"

She smiled. "You don't expect me to answer, but I shall surprise you, min-mute. The secret is lopsi. Lobo-psionic power—a force neither you nor CC can combat, because it is intangible."

"Lobo psi? But lobos, by definition, have no psi!"

"Not in our bodies, no. I was a distance precog, condemned because I foresaw the mutiny against the existing order, and knew that it would be successful. But though my brain was cut, my power remains—for lopsi speaks through me. All the psi powers of all the lobos, cut off from their former moorings, seeking some avenue of expression, find it through me. I direct all the lobos, and all obey me, because of the immense power I represent. Through that power I shall soon be empress of the galaxy."

"A disembodied psi-power?" Knot asked, bemused. "*That's* what organizes the lobos?"

She seemed not to be aware of his skepticism. "Let me give you a capsule history lesson, min-mute. Many psi-societies have existed before man, and many creatures before us have dominated the galaxy. *All* space-faring species developed psi, because of the genetic radiation of deep space. All had a problem dealing with psi-criminals and psi-misfits. Most turned to ghettoization of unsuccessful phys-mutes and lobotomy of unsuccessful psi-mutes—and thereby destroyed themselves. For inevitably both the exiles and lobotomy punishment were turned to political purposes, and great numbers of noncriminals were exiled or lobed, and their psi was added to the reservoir. Psi, once evoked, cannot be suppressed; it can only be severed from its moorings. Gradually it builds into a pool that is greater than any other, and its force invades the so-called normals, and turns them against their society, and violence erupts and continues until those cultures are destroyed. Many, many have fallen unwittingly into this trap. But I—I know this, now, for lopsi has told me, has vouchsafed to me the secret of its nature, and so I am directing the campaign to salvage our kind and our species."

She was of course deluded, perhaps insane. Obviously Piebald had ensconced her here in this pleasant retreat, where she could do no harm, and let her spin her fantasies unchecked. No wonder there were no guards; who would bother to attack Hulda? Probably Piebald visited her every so often, and gave her all the news, and let her interpret it as she wished, and agreed that he and the other lobos were doing it all for her, so that she could be empress. He might love her, if he happened to be capable of that emotion, and not want to hurt her; hence his belief that Finesse would be more profoundly affected by knowledge of her own spouse than she was. This might be the best way to handle Hulda's aberration. But by the same token, Knot would not be able to gain much leverage on Piebald through Hulda.

"I too am trying to salvage our kind," Knot said. "But my kind is not lobo; it is mute."

"You oppose us; you represent the force of species destruction. You must be destroyed."

Uh-huh. The inability to tolerate dissent: another signal of unbalance. She had seemed quite balanced originally, but now was revealed as the opposite. "So you lobos are taking over the galaxy, closing down civilization?"

"Putting CC to better use than lobotomizing those who oppose it, yes."

Her sentiment was so like his own that he was shaken. Had he been premature in judging her? Better to argue the case further, and see what developed. "But you bring anarchy!"

"We do. But it is better than total destruction."

She seemed sincere, and he agreed. He had no special fear of anarchy, and would gladly risk it rather than suffer the curse of unrestrained mutancy to continue. But if she were actually sane, despite appearances, how was he to account for her embracement of the concept of this "lopsi," the disembodied psi force? This was akin to belief in the supernatural. "How do you communicate with lopsi?"

"I don't. It communicates with me. I study the signals of its will—the patterns of leaves floating upon the waters of the lake, the motes of dust in the slanting sunbeams, the configurations of the clouds in the sky, and I interpret the will of lopsi. I tell my husband, and he directs our kind to the necessary actions—and lopsi confirms their actions and punishes those who disobey."

A pattern here—but how much was rationalization, how much delusion? "Punishes? How?"

"They die in accidents, in fighting, in explosions such as the one at headquarters. Only the chosen survive, the ones who remain in lopsi's favor, such as my husband. He is an ugly man, but hideously smart. He listens to me, therefore he succeeds. If he did not listen, he too would perish."

Knot decided he had it straight now. The blessed survived, the damned died—by retroactive definition. There was no way to refute such a philosophy; it was insulated from reality. Religions, in the past, had prospered on it.

The truth was that Piebald was indeed ugly, and indeed smart. He might listen to her, but his success had to do with his intelligence, not her advice. He would simply tell her he had done what she directed, regardless of the truth. "I thank you for the insight, Hulda. I shall relay it to my associates—but I doubt they'll join your side."

"Suit yourself. Our side will prevail. You may join it and survive, or oppose it and perish. I foresaw the outcome when I had my psi, and I am confirmed in that vision now as the realization is upon us. Join or die: That is the extent of your free will. Consider carefully."

"I shall." And Knot faded out.

Back on Chicken Itza amid his friends and the tired chickens, Knot made a full report. "Does she sound sane to you?" he asked.

"She's a conniving woman," Finesse said. "I know the type. She may be partway crazy, but canny too. Piebald probably pays more attention to her than you think. And perhaps it does explain the unity of the lobos: They're all a little bit crazy in the same way. Lobotomy must have some adverse effect on sanity; a prop the brain normally depends on has been removed, leaving at least a token imbalance, and need for compensation. A lobo is *not* a created normal; it's a surgically corrected abnormal. The lobos could honor her as a prophetess, and so Piebald could indeed draw his authority from her, just as any cultist leader draws his authority from the god or demon he purports to serve. The lobos want to believe in this force she describes, this lopsi, and so they honor her, trying to make it true. Lopsi may be nonsense, as all the other oracular pronouncements and cults in human history have been, but to the right clientele, the one with inherent will-to-believe, that sort of thing can be extremely compelling. The lobos are tailor-made for exploitation by a salvation movement; they all want so desperately to recover what they have lost. If they don't convince themselves there is hope, they have no reason to keep on living."

"A salvation cult," Knot echoed. "Of course! We have been looking for something rational. You're right; some of the greatest movements in human history have been cultist, the ones that survived despite persecution, in fact seemed to thrive on it. Like mutation, most of those cults are nonsurvival, but the few that do endure can become great movements . . ."

It was as though his agreement caused her to reverse. "Still, the lobos have had remarkable success, and it's hard to believe it can all be the product of fanaticism. CC has dealt with cultists before, and CC knows history better than anyone. If there really *were* a discorporate lobo psi, subtly making all lobos perform its will, or at least motivating them to accept its imperatives, that could account for a lot."

"The supernatural can always account for a lot!" Knot said. "Let's write this effort off as a wrong lead, and get on with our task. *We* are not blind fanatics."

Finesse smiled, agreeing. "Not blind, anyway. Let's just call this a lesson in the psychology of our opponent; maybe it will come in handy. To whatever extent the lobos believe in divine will, they won't worry about our efforts, and that will help us."

"Hulda will tell Piebald of my visit to her," Knot said. "So Piebald will know we have psi-projection. He'll expect us to explore CCC that way first. He won't be so alert for a physical visit."

And a physical visit was necessary. Even if they could use the override code by psi-projection, it wouldn't stick; Piebald would simply reoverride. They had to go there and take out Piebald himself.

The problems of travel required some planning. "Even amplified psi won't stop the CC detectors," Finesse pointed out. "And we'll have to sleep at some point, and that includes the amplifier rooster. What happens to our cover then?"

What, indeed? It was a relatively short hop from Chicken Itza to CCC, but their mission had no time limit. In addition, the CC readouts were operating on this planet, as there was as yet no overt mutiny here, no power cutoff. That meant they could not sneak aboard any ship under assumed identities. Passengers' baggage was routinely rayed to check for contraband; that would not do either. How, then, were they to board?

At last they found the way. They donned cold-suits raided from little-used emergency supplies, fitted themselves with powdered-oxygen capsules, and had themselves sealed into crates of chicken carcasses being shipped to CCC. There should be no machine inspection of this lot, since it was only routine meat.

There were interminable delays. Knot slept—and worried that he would have trouble reminding the others of their mission, after the effects of sleep and stasis made them forget. Then he reminded himself that they would remember the mission; it was only Knot they would forget. In the context they would discover themselves in, it would be easy enough to accept the reminder that he was part of the mission too. He was keenly aware of the loading process, as his crate got thumped into the hold by the conveyor system, and other crates were piled on top. He was buried under frozen meat. Suppose something happened, and it couldn't be unloaded? How long before the cold penetrated his suit and made him become what he claimed to be? He tried to shiver, but the stasis closed in, freezing him in another way.

Mit says all is well, Hermine's thought came.

Thank you. It was immensely comforting—not merely

Mit's relayed assurance, which was at least slightly suspect while baby Harlan was with them, but also the fact of Hermine's presence. From the start of this adventure, she had been Knot's most constant companion and useful aide. Perhaps this was what was now inclining him toward the cause of the animals. Once one knew an animal like her, how could one not appreciate animal nature?

I like the way you think, Hermine thought.

What about bees? an insect-thought came.

ALL animals! Knot answered. And let himself sleep.

The journey, apart from their unusual mode of embarkation, was routine. There was never any turnabout outside the galactic disk, because CCC was only a few hundred light-years distant. Chicken Itza was the main food supplier for the personnel who serviced the Coordination Computer; it had to be conveniently close.

Hermine, her telepathy amplified by the chicken, extended it to the mind of a passenger in the ship. She fed the images to Knot on a continuous basis, so that their minds merged as they had while they fought the rats of the Macho power plant. Thus it was as if Knot looked out of other eyes.

The disk approach was nothing special; stasis pre-empted it. But the shuttle dropped down onto a small but phenomenal planet whose entire surface was burnished metal. There was no vegetation visible, no mountains, no seas or wilderness. Everything was artificial, measured and clean. The externals of the Coordination Computer. The passenger looking was highly impressed; he found it hard to imagine a single computer as big as a full planet. Why, he wore on his wrist a device two centimeters in diameter that gave him the precise time in any of fifty planetary systems, recorded stray notes that might occur to him, monitored his vital signs constantly and gave warning if any declined, and displayed the picture from any of several galactic news broadcasts. If all this could be handled by this small, feather-light chip, how much more could be handled by the similar chips of the Coordination Computer—amounting to planetary mass!

Then the stasis came, and the vision cut off. Hermine's perception spread about the ship, extending to the minds of the animals aboard. There were flies, roaches and rats here, too, stowaways that man's ingenuity had not been able to eradicate, and their psi-development and species stability were similar to what Knot had encountered on Planet Macho. They could not effectively mutiny on the ship; man had too firm control here. If necessary, in an extreme case, the human crew could evacuate the ship and open the air locks, allowing the cold and vacuum to decontaminate it. Except for protected insect eggs, perhaps. But for generations the vermin had been quietly spreading their breeds and mutations to all the planets the ship orbited, transferring to the shuttles with the passengers and spreading out from the spaceports. The vermin also remained on the shuttles until able to transfer to other diskships, in this way forming a galactic network. It had been a mindless thing, before; now, with the enhanced perceptions of psi, it was becoming conscious. Rats were becoming exogamous, preferring to breed with those of other ships; thus there was an imperative for crossing from vessel to vessel. The animal mutiny had been quietly building for many animal generations.

In fact, Knot realized, the mutiny of animals would continue as long as their psi kept advancing—and that would be as long as spaceships roamed the galaxy. The situation was already virtually out of control: How could man eradicate roaches he could not perceive? He had to stop both the mutation of animals and the travel of such mutes about the galaxy—and that could be effected at this stage only by the complete cessation of galactic travel itself. Which would abolish man's own galactic empire. Thus his only real choice was to come to a reasonable accommodation with the psi-animals.

Yes, of course, Hermine agreed. *That has been obvious for some time.*

Then if we recapture CC, we must take action. But he knew Finesse was not ready for that. She still believed in the old program, and could not perceive the necessity for change.

You must see that you take over CC, not Finesse, Hermine agreed. *She is wonderful and we love her, but she represents disaster too.*

Thus his problem of the microcosm became a matter of galactic import. Knot knew Finesse would not be easily persuaded, and not easily mollified at such time as he countered her will.

Then the shuttle landed. The crates were unloaded, bumped onto another conveyor, and stacked in another refrigerated warehouse. Step I had been completed: the approach to CCC.

All they had to do now was reach a key terminal, tap out the override code, and put CC back on course—assuming they could agree on the course. After eliminating Piebald and getting through the CC psi-defenses that had successfully repulsed the attempts of a battery of enemies for decades—until Knot's own party had enabled the lobos to take over.

First they had to get out of the frozen crates. The teleporting chicken could not move them out; he had to have freedom of motion himself, to flap his wings and crow, in order to enable his psi to function. This was a liability Knot didn't like—but a chicken was a chicken, not the smartest or most versatile of creatures. He had to function as he functioned. Hermine, with her telepathy operating even during stasis, was much superior that way.

There lay the answer. *Put a thought in the mind of the warehouse supervisor that our crates should be stored separately,* Knot directed. *Near some noisemaker, if possible.*

Hermine reached out—and in due course their crates were moved near the main freezer unit, which made the floor vibrate with the effort of its exertions. Under the cover of that noise Knot exerted leverage and burst out of his crate, which had been modified at key spots to permit this.

Good—this was deep in the storage area, with no human personnel in evidence. Knot freed Finesse and Harlan and the animals, and he and Finesse reassembled their crates as well as they could to make them appear untouched.

The CC telepaths are aware of us, Hermine thought. *They are neutral, so are making no response. They are not even avoiding us, because Piebald is watching them, and* will know we are here through their actions if they deviate from their normal routine.

That tells us Piebald has not selected a telepath to work with him, Knot thought. I suspected he would not, because he doesn't trust psi. He may, like us, wait to select his psi allies until he has a better notion of the challenge.

They held a quick council of war. "Piebald should be here in CCC," Knot said, keeping his voice low so that the freezer noise would drown it out at any distance. "He knows we're coming; he just doesn't know when or how. Hundreds of ships orbit CCC every day, so it's hard to watch them all."

"But how many come each day from Chicken Itza?" Finesse asked.

There was that. They could not afford to assume they had arrived unobserved; the lobos might be biding their time, making sure this was not a feint. "Our best course is to strike before Piebald is prepared. We must locate a priority terminal and use the override code—in the next few minutes, if possible."

"We went over all this before," Finesse reminded him. She was right; he was rehashing the matter unnecessarily, in his anxiety. "The main things we have to beware of are CCC's psi-detectors. The machines aren't like human psis, but they can give a bleep when psi is close. One bleep out of place, and the lobos will swarm down on it. CC keeps track of every employee."

This, too, was a rehearsal. They knew they could not walk blithely about the premises; that was why they had brought a teleporter chicken. Hermine, Knot thought, have Mit locate—

Mit says there is a master terminal twelve levels down. It is sealed in a locked vault, but we can teleport in.

Is it safe? This was almost too good to be true, so it could be a trap.

Mit cannot tell, without precognition. There is no person near, and no machine sensor.

That was the penalty for having baby Harlan along. But without Harlan, they would have been vulnerable to CC's many precogs before they arrived, and Piebald would surely have used one of them to nail Knot's party. So he had to operate blind, for now, trusting that this

gave him a sufficient advantage over CC. So far this
seemed to be working. If, by chance, Piebald *had* selected a precog, he had wasted one choice.

"Let's gamble," Knot said. "We can move our whole
party in—"

"Let me go first," Finesse said. "I can stand guard and
scare the lobos off, if we trigger an alarm."

Knot knew there should be no alarm, or Mit would not
have reassured them. Finesse just didn't want to be left
behind. But this would give her first try at the terminal—
unless he kept Mit with him. Stay with me, he thought to
Hermine. You know why.

There was a nudge of agreement from the weasel.
Then Knot kissed Finesse and let her go. She carried
Harlan; he had the other animals.

This would be the first test. If Piebald was using a
telepath, despite indications, he might be waiting for
them to separate, so he could tackle them singly. The
controller might overcome Finesse, in Knot's absence, if
the controller was indeed one of Piebald's selected psis.
But they both knew this was the kind of risk they took,
in this preliminary game of strategy. Each side had to be
cautious, for premature action could lead to disaster. Yet
failure to take such risks could be just as disastrous. The
trick was to take risks and win.

Hermine relayed precise instructions to the chicken—
and Finesse popped out of the room.

They are there, Hermine thought. No alarm. But Mit is
uneasy. He wants his precog ability. He believes something
is lurking, but he cannot focus on it.

The roaches are uneasy too, Knot agreed. The three were
fidgeting and turning translucent. But we know this mission is perilous. The moment we start the override code,
CC will advise Piebald, and his minions will converge.

The chicken returned, alone. Knot made sure everyone was with him, picked up the other rooster, and stood
ready. "Okay, Cocksure," he murmured.

The wrenching came. He and the animals were in the
chamber with Finesse. There was the terminal, as accessible as he could want. "It's not a fake, a decoy?"

"It's real," Finesse said. "Either Piebald didn't figure
on teleportation—this room would be inaccessible to

us any other way—or he has some other plot in mind."

"Bless his presumed oversight." But Knot noted that the three roaches had now disappeared. They were aware of incipient danger, and that could not be ignored.

Yet they had to try the terminal; otherwise their mission was pointless. If this were a trap, it would have to be sprung. Knot positioned himself before the terminal. **Have Mit give me the code, as before.**

A pause, then: **Mit says he can't.**

Can't? He did it before.

Another pause. **He says he used precog for part of it before. It isn't a simple linear code; it has a temporal component. That's why no clairvoyant ever snuck in and got it before we did; only a clair-precog combination could do that, and by the time any intruders discovered that, CC would capture the clair or precog who tried. Mit is one of the very few who possesses the right combination—and he can't get that code while Harlan is with us. No wonder he was upset!**

And Piebald must have discovered that very soon after he took over, and realized that if they blocked out precognition, they would not succeed in this. So he could have chosen a precog to help him—by making sure that that precog remained nonfunctional. Piebald needed to take no other steps, with that reassurance. He had ignored Knot's intrusion because Knot represented no present threat.

Meanwhile, Hermine was explaining the situation to Finesse. "Of course!" she agreed. "A good code is not static; it changes with the times, so only people with contemporary authority can use it. Mit would have to precog the time factor—and now he can't."

"But if we move Harlan far enough away to free Mit's precog, we'll also be opening ourselves up to Piebald's precog," Knot said. "I'm sure that's the nature of this trap. Precognition is much more dangerous to us than clairvoyance, because Piebald can't be checking on us continuously. He needs to precog our time and nature of arrival, and trap us then and there. We've been continuously covered by Harlan's psi. If we make even a small opening, they'll nab us."

"Of course we can't separate from Harlan," she

agreed. "It's bad enough having to bring him here when we promised to protect him from CC. We'll just have to risk using the old code. After all, it was still current a few days ago, when Piebald used it."

"But I don't remember it!"

"Obviously I do," Finesse said. "Piebald got it from me. Maybe Hermine can—"

I shall try, Hermine thought. But after a pause she added: I cannot. I can read only surface thoughts, and this is deep.

"Try enhancement," Knot suggested urgently, indicating Henny, the amplification hen. They had brought her instead of the original amplification rooster because the latter had been too interested in the psi-insects.

Hermine tried it—and this time she was able to read it. Knot began tapping it out as she relayed the code.

An alarm sounded. Suddenly a holograph of Piebald appeared, looking around. "So it is you!" he exclaimed. "You must have chosen a teleport to assist you."

So the lobo didn't know about the chickens, yet. Good. Knot continued tapping, hoping to complete the override before the lobo could stop it. Then CC would be neutralized, and it would be just the two sides fighting it out.

"That's no good," Piebald said. "I changed the code. Did you suppose I was so stupid as to neglect such a detail, after the trouble I had with you on Chicken Itza? I made sure I would not be vulnerable to that again. The old code only calls my attention to its use; CC notified me instantly."

"We've got to get out of here," Finesse said. "The lobo suckered us. We've lost this round."

"You cannot get out; the trap has been sprung. I have a lot more than a single will-controller psi working for me now."

Yes; Piebald had all of CC. But CC was to a great extent helpless without its great battery of psi-mutes.

Finesse and Cocksure disappeared. "Catch us if you can," Knot said.

Piebald snapped an order to someone off-projection. "Flood the chamber with stun gas!"

Immediately the gas hissed from concealed nozzles.

But already Cocksure was back, and Knot and his party were being wrenched back to the freezer compartment. Cocksure was a powerful teleport; he could handle more mass than the first hen-teleporters they had encountered, and take it farther. And he could, it now developed, do it without crowing. That helped!

"So it's a chicken teleport!" Piebald was exclaiming as they left. "Not a CC psi!"

"We're in trouble now," Finesse said grimly as Knot arrived. "Piebald will be out after our rooster, to pin us down. He won't come within range of my phobia psi until—"

"Don't I know it! If he has a clairvoyant, he'll locate us in minutes, now that we have so kindly informed him of our presence. He no longer needs a precog."

"But we'd better keep blanking out precognition, or he'll anticipate our next move," she pointed out.

"We can't go back to Chicken Itza in the crates. That ship is already on its way to other ports. But without having the current override code, we can't—"

"We'll have to go for our backup plan," she decided. "Make for the master switch—the one that turns CC off completely. But I don't know where it is."

Hermine, can Mit tell—?

No. It is hidden in too-complex wiring, and is not within his range. If we get closer to it, he might locate it.

"We'll just have to keep jumping around, avoiding Piebald, until we find that switch," Knot said. "We have to depend on chance to get Mit in range of it."

"We could jump right into trouble," she pointed out.

"Worse trouble than if we stand still? Who jumps first?"

"I do," she said firmly. "I can scare off anyone I come upon, and protect your arrival."

Knot remained uncertain of that. She was spearheading their motion, protecting him from danger, and might find herself in trouble before she could use her psi. But he didn't argue; at this point, everywhere was dangerous. "Get going!"

She popped out. **Do they have a psi-detector operating?** he asked Hermine while they waited.

The machines are operating, but there are so many neu-

tral psis they can't distinguish us yet. CC is still isolating our pattern.

That was a help! The neutrals were neutral, yet really assisting Knot's party—at the moment.

The rooster popped back. Teleportation intrigued Knot; there was never any problem about air displacement. People and things were moved instantly from one place to another without any atmospheric consequence. The psi handled it, obviously—but how? His private theory was that the air was exchanged with the object, so precisely that there was nothing more than that slight noise.

And he was with Finesse again. They were in a storeroom, but not a freezer. Squared-off beams of genuine wood were stacked to the low ceiling.

"What does CC need wood for?" Knot asked.

Mit says for paneling conference rooms.

"Don't distract Mit and Hermine for minor things," Finesse snapped "We're trying to locate the master switch. Mit is having trouble orienting on it."

"Probably because CC was not constructed to have that particular switch easy to get at. We can be sure it will be a challenge to reach it, even when we pinpoint it exactly. Check out-of-the-way-places."

"What do you think we're doing?" She popped out.

A CC sensor has located us, Hermine thought urgently. **Trouble!**

Already the chase was heating up! Knot couldn't wait for Cocksure's return. He dived for the door.

The bees flew up from his shoulder, startled. At the same time, a stasis unit came on. The air behind him seemed to freeze. Knot was clear of it, barely; he righted himself and looked back.

Two bees had not made it out in time; they hung suspended in air, motionless.

Maybe they'll escape unnoticed when the stasis is switched off, Knot thought without great hope. **Bye, Pyridoxine. Bye, Thiamin.**

Bye, the two bees thought back. They did not seem unduly alarmed.

Then Cocksure teleported back. "No!" Knot cried, realizing the danger. **Hermine—warn him away!**

But it was too late, even before he formulated the protest. The rooster had landed in the stasis field, and now was frozen there. The party had lost its teleporter.

Can you locate Finesse? Knot asked Hermine. *Can we get to her?*

Uncertain, Hermine replied. *She is near the master switch.*

Which meant she would try to take over the switch and reprogram CC her way. Which was perhaps why she wanted to travel first: to be sure it was Finesse, not Knot, who did it. Their split in intentions might be manifesting overtly now. If she could locate it by herself, and act before he arrived, she would be in control.

Wait—what was he thinking of? This was not the override code, it was the master switch. It did not matter who turned off CC; the result would be the same. Civilization would grind to a halt until CC was turned on again. The tension of this mission was making Knot paranoid, and he couldn't afford that.

The more Knot thought about the old order, CC's prior program, the less he liked it. The lobos represented disaster, surely—but so, to his way of thinking, did the status quo. The horrors of the chasm enclave—

But the first priority was to stop the lobos. So—no more suspicious thoughts about his associates! *We'll go to her,* he thought. *Have Mit show the way.*

There is an alarm barrier between us.

And they could no longer teleport safely past it. Yes, the game was getting harder! *What alternative route offers?*

A human search party approaches. We must pass it.

Knot worked it out: While that search party went through the machine checkpoint, the press of people would conceal Knot from detection. The machines could not readily tell people apart in a crowd. The trick would be to do this without being noticed by the people. Time to draw on his other assets. *Tell Henny to amplify the roaches' psi.* For the roaches were nervous now, fading out. *And stay close to me!*

The search party arrived. Sure enough, these were lobos, the only people Piebald really trusted. Knot stood still, hoping the psi was working. He could see the chicken at his feet, and the three bees on his shoulder, and Hermine and the rats in his pockets—but the party paid no attention. His whole group was imperceptible.

He still had not discovered how to make the roaches imperceptible to machine surveillance, though. They were helping him now, but he had not been able to help them. How could psi work on something that was not affected by psi?

Satisfied that he could not be seen, he picked up Henny and merged with the group of lobos. He would have to stay with the lobos until they crossed the machine checkpoint, which might be a little while. Had he been quite certain this would work, he could have dived across the checkpoint as they came in—but that would have been chancy. The machine might recognize the motion as being contrary to that of the rest of them, and sound another alarm. So Knot walked in step with the man at the end as they moved toward the room that remained in stasis.

"All right, spread out, in case there's trouble when I turn off the stasis," the group leader said. "Probably a false alarm, but you never know." He glanced about. "Jol and Ent, you go around to the far side—" He cast about. Ent? Where are you?"

Knot hastily stepped away from the man he stood beside. "What do you mean, where am I?" Ent was saying. "You blind, all of a sudden?"

The leader blinked. "Must be. I looked right at you and didn't see you. Get on around."

Knot knew he would have to be more careful. The fringe of the amplified psi had fogged out the other man, and that could have called attention to Knot—especially if Ent had happened to turn while inside the field and seen Knot.

The leader waited until all were in their place, then touched a hand control. The stasis abated. Cocksure squawked and fluttered for the nearest exit, and the two bees zoomed in confused circles. **Fools!** Knot thought. **Get out of there! Hermine, tell Cocksure to teleport himself out—**

One of the lobos sprayed a jet of stun gas from a portable tank he carried, and the rooster fell unconscious. The bees escaped, but did not know where to go.

We cannot help them, the three who remained with Knot thought. **They cannot perceive our thoughts.**

We can't emerge from hiding until we get through the machine checkpoint, Knot reminded them.

The party of lobos re-formed and carried the unconscious rooster with them. When they passed the checkpoint, Mit let Hermine know, and Knot dropped back. One hurdle navigated.

All right—tell Henny to ease off. But he suspected they were already returning to visibility, because the roaches were no longer alarmed. It was hard to be sure, when they were all in the roaches' amplified psi-field.

Now it was fairly simple to rejoin Finesse and Harlan. Mit guided them through unerringly. There were other checkpoints, but it was possible to avoid them, and Mit did; it made their route circuitous, but delayed them only slightly.

The others were on a lower level. Knot descended a spiral access-staircase and turned right, knowing he was getting close. He took several steps—

"So good to meet you again, unmemorable one," Piebald said.

Knot whirled. The lobo stood there with two uniformed men behind him, each wearing the CC insignia. Piebald held a box in his hands.

For a moment Knot just stood there, chagrined. "How—?"

"You are so psi-conscious, you overlook the physical," Piebald said, gesturing behind him. There was the open door to a private passage. The door had been closed; Knot simply had not thought to have Mit check behind it.

"Meet Gwant, my clairvoyant, and Hoscow, my tele-kinetic," Piebald said, gesturing to the two men with him. He set down the box. "Hoscow, dispose of this man."

Suddenly objects floated out from the passage: small metallic stars with flashing edges and points. The ancient *Shurken*, or throwing stars, in this case wielded by the mind.

We need help, Knot thought to Hermine. **Summon one of the psis we have coming to us. A fighting talent. A—a pyro, maybe.**

I shall try.

And tell Henny to amplify the roaches' psi. We can confuse them awhile—

But already the stars were flying toward him. "The chicken!" Piebald cried as Knot began to fade. "Get the chicken first!"

"It's faded out!" Hoscow complained. But his barrage of stars swerved in air to cut through the space where Henny had been visible. One struck. The hen squawked in pain. The amplification stopped, and they became visible again.

"That did it!" Piebald cried. "Now they can't hide."

Knot, in a rage, launched himself at Piebald. The three bees lifted from his shoulder and shot forward to sting the telekinetic.

But Piebald, no slouch at combat, dodged, and Knot crashed into the wall. Dull pain gathered in his right shoulder as the instant numbness of the shock abated. For a moment all Knot could do was lean against the wall, recovering.

The kinetic was slapping at bees. One bee dropped, then two, then the third. Then the stars lifted again, spinning in the air like malevolent powered flight-toys, orienting.

The mental knockout! Knot thought, and felt the weasel's assent. He framed an imaginative supernova, and detonated it, and saw the stars drop as Hoscow reeled from the mental blast. Even in this strife, Knot appreciated the irony: a nova to abolish stars.

"The weasel!" Piebald yelled. "She's the telepath! Get her next!" And he jumped at Hermine, who had dropped from Knot before the collision with the wall, and was standing a short distance away. Piebald's booted foot came down in a stomp, and Hermine scooted away.

"We know how to deal with the weasel," Piebald shouted. "Release the vipers!"

Oh no! Knot thought. **Not snakes again!** The lobos seemed to have an affinity for poisonous things.

The clairvoyant, who had stood inactive after the nova, now recovered enough to reach to the box. He unsnapped the catch and jumped back. Immediately snakes boiled out—small, fast, evil-looking serpents, surely poisonous species from assorted regions. They ignored the people and slithered rapidly after Hermine. They seemed to have no difficulty with the smooth floor.

Knot knew there was no place the weasel could go where these predators could not follow. It would be extremely risky for Hermine to turn and fight even one of them; any scratch could be fatal to her. It might take time, but she was probably doomed. **Come to me!** Knot thought. **I can lift you up—**

But the snakes were already between them. **They will kill me,** Hermine thought. **They are trained to hunt small animals. I must flee.** She disappeared.

Now the kinetic was back in shape. A swelling was rising below his right eye where he had been stung, but that was discomfort, not incapacity. The deadly stars lifted again. They wobbled, showing that he had not yet thrown off the effect of the nova, but in moments he would be in fighting fettle.

Another person arrived. An old woman, with gray hair floating out like a ragged mop. She looked faintly like a witch, but wore the CC emblem. "Desist, Hoscow," she snapped.

"My pyro!" Knot cried with desperate hope.

"The same. Nostra, at your service." She looked again at the telekinetic. "You know me, Hoscow. I shall not warn you again."

"Throw your stars!" Piebald shouted. "Wipe them both out!"

The stars began to move—and a sheet of fire appeared. All three men on that side of the hall burst into flame. Their clothing and hair were burning. They danced in agony, trying to put out the flames.

"Sorry I had to do that," Nostra said calmly. "But I did give fair warning."

"You certainly did!" Knot agreed, moving in on Piebald. All he needed to do now was overpower or kill the man, and the issue should be settled. The lobo had made a mistake, confronting Knot personally; he might be able to make Knot look like a fool in physical combat three times out of four, but the odds were worse than if he had his lobo minions do it for him.

Then the CCC fire-extinguishing system came on. Fog

sprayed out of nozzles, chokingly. Knot had to retreat, knowing that if Piebald recovered, the war was not yet over. But the chemical was irritating Knot's eyes and lungs; he could not accomplish much in its midst, and might only be handicapped so that Piebald would kill him instead. Piebald was tough, though; he would surely be able to fight well in this medium, and would surely recover quickly from his burns. What harm could fire and chemicals do to his complexion, anyway?

At least Knot could use the fog as cover for his own getaway. He charged down the hall in the direction he had been going when intercepted. Finesse was somewhere ahead.

The encounter had been a draw. But Knot had lost his teleporter and psi-amplifier and three remaining bees and, effectively, Hermine. She could not come within psi-range of him without encountering the snakes. Which meant he could not utilize Mit's clairvoyance either. He had to rejoin Finesse and get to that master switch before Piebald got back into action.

He slowed to a walk, letting Nostra the lady pyro catch up. She had really pulled him out!

But Piebald was already back in action. "Just so you know, forgettable one," the intercom system said. "I am burned but not out. My telekinetic will be out for the duration, and my clairvoyant is in difficulty, but now that I have you pinpointed I do not need them. I have my loyal lobos, and you have, I think, very little to stop them. Gird yourself!"

"That is one nasty man," Nostra observed. She seemed not too badly winded from the run. "But clever—extremely clever. He postures as though a stagestruck idiot, but do not be deceived."

"Thank you, woman," Piebald said, and Nostra put her hand to her mouth. Her voice had given away their present position. Her very expression of concern for the enemy's intelligence had proved that intelligence. "You echo the sentiments of my wife. She lacks my propensity for violence, but endorses its results."

"The intercom can pick up our footsteps anyway," Knot said. "Stay close to me; I need you to keep those lobos at bay."

"Be careful," she warned. "There are limits. I cannot project fire more than a few meters."

Knot lifted Mit to his face and tapped quickly on the shell. WHERE IS FINESSE? LEAD US TO HER. TELL ME HOT OR COLD.

Mit tapped his own shell with his large pincers, once. The pyro looked perplexed, but said nothing. Knot walked rapidly down the hall, while the crab clicked in single beats. This was not as effective as telepathic communication, but it would do.

Then the beats became double. Knot halted, backtracked to a cross-passage, and started down it. The single clicks resumed.

Suddenly Mit made a flurry of clicks. Knot looked at the roaches. They were invisible—unless he had lost them during the melee. He didn't gamble on that; he ducked into the nearest opening, drawing Nostra with him and gesturing her to silence. He flattened himself against the wall. Sure enough, a group of lobos was hurrying down the hall, turning a corner into Knot's former path; he heard their walking and talking. Had Mit precogged them? No, Harlan's damping power evidently extended widely, stopping precognition throughout CCC. Mit had simply used his clairvoyance to pick up the lobos at a reasonable distance.

"He says they're in this area, somewhere," a lobo was saying. "Block off all passages here, then make a room-by-room search. Don't handle anything you don't understand."

Good—the lobos weren't any more familiar with these premises than he was. They had to feel their way around. That greatly increased his chance to avoid them. It would be best to have no direct contact with them; then he would be that much harder to pinpoint.

The lobos passed. Quickly Knot sidled out, following Mit's clicks, Nostra following silently. Soon they had to hide again, but got through without real difficulty. It was obvious that the crab's specific clairvoyance was more potent than the enemy's perception. Piebald's clairvoyant had been burned in that sheet of flame and was not too sharp at the moment. What was his name? Gwant. Probably Gwant's information would be somewhat fuzzy for the

duration, yielding only a very general notion of Knot's
whereabouts that had to be verified by details of lobos. Unless Piebald was tricking him again . . .

Then Mit's clicks warned him; they were approaching
a CC checkpoint. There was no safe, fast way around it,
and without Hermine to translate, Knot could not obtain
a swift alternate route. The hot-cold method of following
clicks was too cumbersome, in this case. They would
simply have to touch off the alarm and move quickly. It
might make no real difference, at this stage.

Nostra put her hand on his arm. "Let me trigger it, and
mount rearguard," she whispered. "You go on."

With luck, the lobos would be distracted by her formidable opposition and forget him. That was another thing
that was probably fouling up Gwant's clairvoyance. How
could a person orient on something he kept forgetting?
Knot's own psi was surely helping him in subtle but effective fashion, giving him much longer breathing spells than
another person would have had. Yet Nostra's aid was
welcome. Knot thanked her with a squeeze, and moved on.

The alarm sounded. Nostra stood beside the bell,
emitting little flying flickers of flame. Knot put his ear to
Mit's shell and hurried.

They took a small conveyor belt down through a factory
area, then opened a warehouse door. And came face to
face with two more lobos.

Knot reacted in his usual fashion. He charged them.
His right shoulder caught one in the midsection—and pain
flared, for that was the shoulder he had cracked into the
wall when fighting Piebald so recently. Knot drew back,
and drove his left fist at the other lobo's gut. The man
gasped, but shrank back, hitting Knot's left jacket pocket.

There was a squeal. Oh no! The rats had been struck!
He had forgotten them, since they couldn't help in this
struggle.

Knot bulled into the lobo, shoved him back against the
wall, grabbed the hair of his head with his right hand,
and cracked that head into the wall. Once, twice, hard.
The man sagged.

Knot ran on, following the clicks again. He ducked
around another corner, then stopped to check on his

pursuit. While waiting, he checked his pocket, half afraid of what he would find.

The rats were in sorry shape. The blow had pressed them against Knot's ribs, and he feared there were internal injuries. Roto's nose showed a drop of blood. THEIR CONDITION? he tapped to Mit. ARE THEY IN PAIN?

A single, affirmative tap: bad news.

ARE THEY BLEEDING INSIDE?

They were. And growing weaker.

WILL THEY SURVIVE?

That required precognition, and Mit could not answer. Knot feared he knew the answer, though: They would die unless properly treated, soon.

"I'm sorry, rats," he murmured. He knew their fleas could nullify poisons, but this was sheer physical damage. "If I could heal you—"

Then he realized that he could do this, in his fashion. There had to be a psi-healer here, and he had one more psi coming to him. "I choose my second psi," he announced loudly, for the benefit of the nearest intercom pickup. "I want a healer, now."

"A healer will join you," Drem's voice came. The CC psis knew precisely where he was, of course, even if Piebald didn't. "Lobos, you must give the healer safe passage."

"I know!" Piebald snapped. "If the anony-mute is fool enough to choose a healer instead of a killer, I'll not interfere!"

Probably the lobo was right, Knot thought. Who but a fool would squander his vital resources for the welfare of a couple of hungry rats?

In a moment the healer arrived: a small, thin young man with a large nose—not at all what Knot had expected. His image had been of a tall, benign, long-bearded man, vaguely Christlike, with an almost inaudibly gentle voice.

The healer checked the rats, his sensitive hands passing over them. Immediately the suffering creatures relaxed, their pain alleviating. "Yes, I can heal them," he said, his voice somewhat nasal. "They will sleep several hours, and wake restored. And very hungry. My power guides the restoration, but their bodies do the work."

"They can find food," Knot said, smiling briefly. "Come with me; I may need you to restore me, soon."

The man put his hand on Knot's sore shoulder. Healing warmth seemed to flow from that hand, and the pain faded. What a massage this man might give! "I can do it—but you, too, would sleep while the restorative forces of your body mobilized. I don't think you can afford that at the moment. My name is Auler."

"Auler," Knot repeated, fixing it in his mind.

"And is this an associate of yours?" the healer inquired. He lifted a finger to show a bee-fly perching on it. "I found it injured in the hall, and healed it, and it seems to be a telepathic creature, though its broadcast is too weak to be intelligible to me."

"Pyridoxine—Bee Six!" Knot exclaimed. "I thought you were lost after the stasis!"

The bee flitted across to his shoulder. Nearly, she agreed.

Your thought is very strong, Knot thought, surprised. Aloud, he said: "The telepathy of a single bee may seem weak to you, but the telepathy of a hive of them becomes very, er, commanding. Thank you for rescuing this one."

The healer made it well. I slept and recovered.

So your strength is as the strength of ten, because your honey is pure.

The humor was lost on the bee. I have made no honey on this mission, because there are no flowers—

Never mind. If we survive this, I'll find you a whole field of flowers.

I would prefer to return to my hive.

You will. Save your new strength, B₆. I may need it soon. Aloud again, he said: "I value my friends, Auler, and this is one."

"And the rat is another," the healer said gravely. "I could use a few friends like you—but I fear you require more than a telepathic bee at the moment."

Mit clicked warning. More lobos were coming, having granted the healer his safe passage with a reasonable margin. The war was on again. Knot made a mental note: Piebald was a torturer and murderer, but he had honored the deal. For what that token was worth.

Knot drew Auler to cover. "I do have more than the bee—but probably not enough. I'm afraid I have drawn you into an awkward situation. When it becomes too obviously hazardous to your own health, get away from me and save yourself."

"As you wish." The healer actually seemed to be enjoying this. Perhaps he had not had experience with opponents like the lobos before. He would learn.

Mit clicked another warning, and they retreated farther. Without Mit, things would certainly be more complicated!

They came to another CC checkpoint. This time Knot barged on through, letting the alarm go off. He followed Mit's directions, and finally caught up to the subcomplex where Finesse was supposed to be.

And Knot experienced abrupt and awful fear of what lay ahead. Auler, beside him, seemed to suffer similarly.

He had found Finesse, almost—and couldn't get close to her!

Knot steeled himself, held his ground, and tapped the floor with his heel: KNOT in beat-code. Did she know that variant? It was not identical to squeeze-code, because it had no holds, but it was similar.

She did. Abruptly the fear subsided. Finesse appeared, visibly relaxing as she verified his identity. Then she was in his arms—and while they kissed, they conversed in squeeze.

WHAT HAPPENED TO YOU? she asked.

STASIS FIELD CAUGHT COCKSURE. WE FOUGHT PIEBALD. LOST BOTH CHICKENS AND FOUR BEES. RATS ARE HURT AND HERMINE IS FLEEING SNAKES. HAD PYROTECHNIC PSI FROM CC POOL, WHO IS NOW SERVING AS DISTRACTION. MAN WITH ME IS A HEALER. WHERE IS HARLAN?

SLEEPING AROUND CORNER, she kissed back. YOU WERE VERY CARELESS WITH THE WELFARE OF OUR FRIENDS. I THINK WE'RE CLOSE TO THE MASTER SWITCH. IS MIT STILL WITH YOU?

Knot broke the contact at last and brought the little crab from his pocket. WHERE IS THE MASTER SWITCH? he tapped on the shell.

Mit clicked, and Knot started walking, with a meaningful glance at Finesse. She would have to guard them from the lobos. She fetched Harlan and followed.

The hot-cold trail led to a massive, locked door. "Just like that," Finesse fumed. "A physical barrier!"

Now the lobos showed, just beyond the range of her psi. "It is sealed off," Piebald's voice came. "You are trapped at a dead end."

"You have a clairvoyant animal," Auler said. "Perhaps he can divine the combination."

"We'll try," Knot said. "Here, healer, you hold the baby while Finesse protects us. I'll see if Mit can work this out."

Mit inspected the door, tapping it with his pincer as Knot carried him close. He became agitated. YOU CAN'T DIVINE THE COMBINATION? Knot asked with a sinking sensation.

NO—YES, the crab tapped.

YOU COULD—IN OTHER CIRCUMSTANCES?

YES.

Now it was the guessing game, perforce. Finesse stood glaring at the lobos down the hall, whose activity suggested they were preparing something unpleasant. Auler, looking concerned, was murmuring to the baby. Knot knew he had to solve this riddle quickly. But he was at a loss how to proceed. What circumstances would affect the perception of a clairvoyant?

The question brought the answer. Harlan! He cut off Mit's precognition, limiting his ability. HARLAN PREVENTS?

YES.

THIS COMBINATION HAS A TEMPORAL COMPONENT?

YES.

IS IT THE SAME AS THE CC OVERRIDE CODE? Knot asked with abrupt insight.

YES.

So they could no more pass this door that blocked the way to the master switch than they could take over mastery of the Coordination Computer. Piebald must have known it.

"Why don't you kill your baby?" Piebald's mocking voice came. "*I* would."

The awful thing was, that would do it. With his full powers restored, Mit could grasp the current code. They knew it, Piebald knew it—and they all knew that they would not take that step. Their lives and the welfare of the galaxy might depend on it, but they would not harm the baby. Piebald, in a similar situation, would have done anything he needed to, to win. On a purely rational basis, they were inadequate; they let their feelings interfere with their mission. The irony was, Harlan himself might suffer more as the result of their refusal to hurt him—but still they balked.

"Oh no!" Finesse exclaimed. "They're setting up a stasis projector!"

Which spelled doom. Most projectile and heat weapons were banned from CCC because they could damage valuable machine components, but stasis hurt nothing—and was quite effective. They would be unable to avoid it this time.

"There may be one other way," Knot said slowly. "I refused to join the bee hive, but they left me with an option. I had forgotten it."

Finesse glanced at him suspiciously. "What option?" Then she concentrated on the lobos down the hall, and they moved away from the projector. She had, for the moment, made them afraid of it—but that was at the limit of her range, and she could not delay them long this way.

"A chart of CCC, perhaps including access codes. They used precognition to assemble it; I did not understand why, before, or why they thought it was such a significant achievement. They must have had power in their mass-mind to penetrate Harlan's null-precog. We could get that chart from Pyridoxine, here—but I would have to align myself with the hive."

"Does the hive's interest conflict with the original CC program?"

"The hive wants autonomy for the psi-animals. I would be supporting the animal mutiny. Now that I've come to know so many animals so well, I respect their motives more. Animals have died to forward our cause here. I don't think CC cares one way or the other about animals, so there should be no great conflict."

"I think I could pick gaping holes in your argument— if I had the time," she said. "But I think we need that chart. Very well. You join the hive—but I remain true to CC. If you betray the computer, I'll fight you."

He believed her, though what she really meant was that she would fight him if he opposed her view of CC, her dedication to the prior program. There was that split again. He was more ready to compromise than she —and they might have to compromise, to beat the lobos. "Let's hope it doesn't come to that."

She looked nervously down the hall. "Whatever you do, make it fast. I'm weakening, and they're getting stronger. I think we have less than a minute."

I join you, Knot thought to Pyridoxine. **Give me the code, if you have it. The combination to this lock.**

Immediately it flowed into his mind. Knot tapped on the metal of the door, following the complex pattern. He worried that the stasis would catch them before he completed the code. But the lobos were taking their time, sure that he had no escape. Suddenly the door clicked, unlocked, and swung inward.

"They must have killed the baby after all!" Piebald cried, amazed. "Activate the stasis immediately!"

Knot and Finesse and Auler piled through and pushed the portal closed behind them. They had beaten the stasis!

They were in the chamber of the master switch. The switch turned out, to Knot's surprise, to be a simple massive red-handled knife lever, a make-or-break connection in the main power line. Knot did not know what the power source was, but evidently all of it channeled through here.

"Now we have a problem," he said. "If we pull that switch, we'll cut off all power on this planet. The heating will fail, the air regeneration, the elevators, lights— everything. We'll probably die ourselves. But if we don't pull it, the lobos remain in control of CC."

"Little do you know the art of hard-nosed bargaining," Finesse said grimly. She strode forward.

The door behind them opened. Piebald charged in. He held a translucent ball in his hand.

Finesse, hearing him, turned. Suddenly fear filled the room. Knot, Piebald, and Auler scrambled for the door. But in their haste they crashed against it, pushing it closed. There was a click as it locked.

Finesse stood with her hand on the switch. "Yield, Piebald," she said. "Or we all shall die, and all your minions with you. You know I will do it."

Baby Harlan, who had been sleeping in Auler's arms, woke and started crying. With that sound, the fear abated, though it did not entirely fade. Piebald straightened up and cocked his arm to throw the ball. Knot lurched toward him.

The arm moved. Knot, seeing that he would be too late, grabbed instead for the ball. He knew it had to represent a threat. He missed; it struck him on the side of the head, exploding into gas. Immediately volition left him; he collapsed beside Auler, unable to move. The gas surrounded them both.

Piebald staggered forward. He had had a whiff of gas himself, but not enough to put him down. He also showed signs of weakness from the effect of the burning he had received before; his mottled complexion was augmented by red blisters. But he refused to allow such trifles to restrain him.

Finesse concentrated—but could not seem to make the lobo retreat. "Don't you know what happened?" Piebald gasped. "Your anti-precog baby, who has been such a thorn—he's more than that. He's anti-psi. He was improperly raised, unhealthy—but now better feeding and the healer have restored some of his vitality. His full ability is beginning to manifest, and now it is blocking your psi too. Your own ally is betraying you! You have become like me. Your psi is gone!"

Finesse reacted immediately. She jerked on the red handle. A fat spark jumped as the connection broke. "CC is gone too!" she cried.

"No, not yet," Piebald said, continuing toward her. "It will take several minutes for CC's circuits to fade out. That computer is planet-sized, remember! There is considerable current in the wiring. I can restore it—"

She attacked him, her hands clawing at his face. But Piebald, even weakened by burns and stun gas, could handle himself physically. He blocked her arms aside, then delivered a savage right-hand blow to her face. Again Finesse's nose was smashed. She fell back, blood pouring out. It was the most devastating strike he could have made, physically and psychologically.

Knot, his face on the floor, saw it all; he happened to be pointed the right way. He winced, but his body did not respond. He could do nothing.

Piebald reached for the switch, to close it and restore power to the computer—but Finesse tackled him from behind. He had made the error of assuming that the smashed nose would send her into crying helplessness. But underneath, she was as tough as any man. Now she was a blood-smeared demoness, intent only on victory. Any notion she might have had of feminine wile or helplessness had been vanquished with her nose. Her hands passed around his head, nails going to his face, gouging his eyes. She hated this man every bit as much as Knot did, and with reason.

It was an awful struggle. Knot, immobilized, caught only snatches of it, mostly by ear. The woman he loved, against the man he loathed, both reduced to animalistic level in this terrible conflict—and still Knot could do nothing. He was forgotten—of course. Though perhaps not primarily because of his psi, now; if Piebald's theory was true, Harlan was canceling out Knot's psi too.

Aahh, you bit me!

For a moment Knot thought it was a cry from one of the visible combatants. Then he recognized Hermine's thought. The weasel had been caught by one of the poisonous snakes! And still he, Knot, could do nothing. He could not even send the healer. Hermine, perhaps his closest friend, dying—

Knot concentrated in a fury of helpless anger. There had to be some way!

He saw one of the rats, Rondl, crawling across the floor, partially incapacitated by the drug, but getting stronger. Of course—the drug was a form of poison, and the psi-fleas neutralized it in the rat's body. That was their symbiotic service. Too bad Knot himself did not have such a resource—

Didn't he? **Pyridoxine!** he thought to the bee. **Summon Rondl here.**

The bee remained immobilized physically, but aware mentally. She concentrated.

Nothing happened. Her power was too small, by itself. Knot realized that she needed a boost. **Relay!** he ordered her. **Rondl, come here!**

Now the rat responded. In a moment she changed course and came to him, as though he had put his hand down for her.

Tell the fleas to bite me, Knot thought urgently. **Many of them, now! To nullify the poison—**

He felt the minute stings of several bites. Never had he been so glad to be attacked by insects! The immobility of his body began to abate. The effect spread outward from the sites of the bites, until he had control again. His rage at what was happening to Finesse and Hermine had accelerated it; he really wanted to recover!

Knot climbed to his feet. Piebald was choking Finesse —and had been for some seconds. Her face was purple under the mask of blood. Still she fought, her fingers like claws, reaching for his face. He shifted his grip quickly, grabbed her hair on either side, lifted her head, and rammed it down against the metallic floor. He was trying to kill her—and this would accomplish that very soon.

In these few seconds Knot was lurching forward, his strength resurging. He knew his own eyeballs were turning bloodshot with the effort, for the view before him was blurring. Only Piebald showed clearly, like a figure hung on the cross-hairs of a gunsight. There was his target!

Knot came up behind the man. Knot took careful, almost gentle hold of the lobo's own mottled hair. Knot held the head firm—then lifted his large right knee in a savage blow to the side of his enemy's face.

Once again Knot had underestimated his opponent. Piebald yanked his head aside as Knot moved, drawing him off balance. The knee only grazed the lobo. Piebald let go of Finesse and caught at Knot's uplifted leg.

Then it was elemental savagery again—only this time the lobo faced a man, not a woman. Knot, his scruples damped by shock and hate, attacked with insane fury.

Fists, feet, teeth—anything. Piebald, at first taken aback by the sheer ferocity of it, soon began to exert his calculating strategy. He countered Knot's strokes, tied up his limbs so that they could move only ineffectively, and maneuvered him gradually from the offensive to the defensive. He entangled Knot's left arm in a bruising armlock and started working toward a strangle with his legs. Knot resisted, but was unfamiliar with this particular mode of combat; it had not been covered in his brief course. As it turned out, legs were more clumsy than arms, but had far more power, and they could indeed be tightened about the neck in a strangle—if a person knew how to do it. Piebald knew how, and the lobo had the leverage. When Knot's strength expired, as it had to, Piebald would have him helpless. Once again, the lobo was winning.

Finesse remained unconscious, perhaps in coma. Blood pooled on the floor by her face, and there was a pallor to the rest of her visible skin that boded ill. That terrible strike of her head on the floor: concussion—or death?

Knot knew he needed help. But where could it come from? The room was sealed—and if it weren't, the lobos would be charging in to help Piebald. The healer Auler was unable to heal himself, while stunned. Harlan—was only a baby. The rats—

Bee Six—tell the rats to attack Piebald!

But Roto and Rondl were too timid. They hung back. They were not like the tough rats of the Macho solar station; they were gentle white-collar rats, harmless. They had done all they were psychologically capable of when they lent the use of their fleas to rouse Knot.

Then Mit the hermit crab emerged from Knot's pocket. His shell had protected him from most of the battering, and his clairvoyance told him what to do. Perhaps it wasn't psi, now, in the ambience of Harlan's null-psi, but elementary crab sense. He was little, but he had fighting spirit.

Mit scrambled up the lobo's arm, going for the face. Piebald could not deal with the crab, because then he would have to let go of Knot and lose his advantage. But they both knew that Mit knew exactly where to pinch to do the most damage. Perhaps a key nerve complex in the neck; perhaps an eyeball—

Piebald's nerve broke. He had lost his psi long ago; he did not want to lose his sight too. He grabbed for the crab—but Mit was already dropping to the floor, knowing precisely when to make his move. Clairvoyance could not be readily surprised, even when largely nulled out. Knot wrenched his right arm free, grabbed the lobo's hair again, and jerked Piebald's head around. Now the initiative was Knot's!

He went for a strangle of his own, but the lobo blocked it. They fell into a position of impasse, neither man having an immediate advantage, neither being able to initiate a new sequence without putting himself at a disadvantage. Had this been a polite competition match, the referee would have separated them, setting up for a new round. But this was real, and there was no way out.

But the master switch was down. CC was dying, as its residual power inevitably drained. The longer the impasse held, the closer Knot came to victory—and death; for once the computer passed below a certain stage, its electronic banks would suffer, like brain cells dying in a man, and then even the reversal of the master switch would not restore its full function. There would have to be extensive replacement of units, and reprogramming, before it functioned again—and without CC's directives to bring the supply ships, it might be years or decades before such repair was possible. Civilization could collapse in that interim. CC was the brain; cutting off its power was like cutting off the supply of blood to the human brain. Certainly the lobos would not benefit. Already the illumination was dimming, and the air was becoming close.

"This is pointless!" Piebald gasped. "No one gains if we all die!"

"How true," Knot agreed, hanging on. He reveled in the fading light, knowing it spelled his victory, of a sort. CC was shutting off every nonessential power drain, conserving its rapidly dwindling resources for its key units, clinging to the facsimile of life it knew. But, like Finesse, it would soon be unconscious.

"You are a mutant," Piebald argued. "A double mute,

like me. You know the horrors of the present system. Ninety-nine failures for every successful mutation. Death for many, enclaves for the rest. All this is known—and deliberately fostered by the present CC program. Those mutations have to be stopped!"

"What do you care?" Knot demanded. "When you got control of CC, you didn't turn it off. Now you're fighting to preserve it—program and all."

"I care! I am a mutilated mutant—a mute-mute—as all lobos are. I, unlike you, have lost the redeeming part of my mutancy. I know, even better than you do, the evils of the system."

"So why didn't you turn CC off?" Knot demanded, bothered by the appeal of Piebald's statement. It disturbed Knot deeply, this superficial similarity between them. Both had been born min-mutes physically, max-mutes psionically.

"Because the answer is not to destroy CC. Only the ignorant believe that. Many of those ignorant are lobos; we know that. We tell them what they are capable of grasping. But we leaders know better."

"Like your wife?" Knot demanded, remembering her blithe insanity.

"Her most of all. She speaks for lopsi, our ultimate authority."

Knot was astonished. "You believe that?"

"Of course I believe in lopsi! That belief motivates my whole life's work! Everything I do is for the furthering of that reality!"

Was Piebald crazy too? "Yet you want to convert CC to your own aggrandizement! Why change the system, when suddenly it serves your selfish interests?"

"Our interests are close to your interests, if only you realized!"

"Oh sure. I love to smash the noses of beautiful women, torture old men to death, burn down houses with sleeping people in them, feed women to monsters, kill people freely when—"

"We have tried to kill you," Piebald said evenly. "You have been our most dangerous opponent, as the present crisis indicates. You destroyed our Macho headquarters, killing many of our people. I radioed a general evacuation, but not all could escape in time. I regard those losses as your responsibility, not mine. Just as you killed many mutants in the chasm enclave, in order to effect your escape. When balked you attack, always. Do you consider your own hands clean?"

That set Knot back. He had, indeed, killed many people in the course of this mission, and he was not proud of it. And Piebald had not, after all, callously left the lobos of the volcano villa to die; he had warned them from the truck, and saved many. Knot had been too ready to believe too much evil of his enemy. Piebald was bad, very bad—but not as bad as Knot had thought. "No, my hands are dirty, soiled with blood. I am not fit to govern. I'm fit only to stop monsters like you. The present system may not be perfect, but it is surely better than what your kind offers. If you will simply admit that, and let one of our number apply the new override code to make CC ours, your people on this planet may survive. Otherwise—"

"The present system is far from perfect—but it can be vastly improved," Piebald said. "This is our intent. First we must cut off the generation of mutants. Then—"

"I tried that, in an alternate future sequence. It only led to the collapse of galactic civilization, and chaos."

"Because you were equating civilization with empire. Like the ancient Romans, you thought the only future lay with the organization in power. But the Roman Empire fell—"

"And led to the Dark Ages—"

"And thence to modern Europe, and on into the space age. Even in the depths of darkness, it was only Europe that suffered; the Arabian sphere and the Chinese sphere flourished in golden ages. This must happen again. The old CC program, like the decadent Romans, actually stands in the way of progress. It offers temporary political stability, at the price of ruinous mutation and grief. A mutiny against that order is essential. As the dinosaurs had to be eliminated before the superior mammals could rise—"

"You're quite a scholar," Knot said. "You should be happy CC has been turned off. There will certainly be chaos, and an end to mutation, and successful mutinies all over the galaxy!"

"But the chaos can be greatly lessened if CC is *not* destroyed!" Piebald cried, and he seemed amazingly sincere. "If CC is used to direct the new order, shaping it sensibly, with long-range human history in mind, instead of allowing a crash—"

"We've been through that!" Knot said. "I have seen how you lobos direct things. I'd rather let there be chaos."

"You have seen us doing research—"

"Research! I call it torture of innocents!"

"We use coercion to force psi-talents to manifest—"

"Which you then extirpate by lobotomy!"

"And try to correct immediately by remedial surgery! Had we been successful, we would have had the key to restore all lobotomized psi-talents. But we have had no success with long-established lobos; our psi-connections are permanently gone, as far as present technology is concerned. So we had to go to new lobos, with strong wills, who might—"

"That's what you had in mind for Finesse," Knot rated.

"Yes, and for you. But how much better it would be to replace our necessarily crude methods with the sophistication only CC could employ. We could solve the problem of lobotomy—"

"So that's your special interest! The death penalty was eliminated in favor of lobotomy, and now you want even that to be undone so criminals can get off entirely free! No restraint at all for crime!"

"We do not condone crime," Piebald said evenly. "Lobos are the most law-abiding citizens. On many planets, we are the police force itself, and our record is excellent. Lopsi keeps us disciplined."

Knot had to concede the discipline of the lobos; he had marveled at this himself. "But criminals who are not lobotomized will have no deterrent, no restraint; is that what you seek?"

"There will be restraint. A telekinetic who uses his power to kill a man by stopping his heart from pumping is a murderer who deserves punishment. I too abused my psi, and had to be restrained; I too deserved retribution. But they should not have abolished my valuable psi-talent; they should instead have abolished *my criminal drive!* They did it backward, preserving the criminal while sacrificing the psi."

Knot, startled, almost lost his leverage. Eliminate the criminal aspect of man, not the psi! So obvious!

"We lobos seek a better way—for us and for everyone," Piebald continued. "Research—not only to cure lobotomy and criminality, but also to penetrate the mystery of mutation itself. So that man will be able to control mutation. To produce given psi-powers at will, with *no* failures. Only the tremendous resources of the Coordination Computer can do this effectively. But that means removing CC from its present, unsound program, even if chaos results for a time."

"I know. The dinosaurs and the mammals. I simply believe—" But the lobo leader's vision of the failure threatened to overwhelm his doubt. The answer to the whole mutation problem—including the developing mutinies by the animals. Because this would put human mutation on a par with that of the more psi-evolved animals. Humans too would have controlled psi for every individual. Not the cessation of all mutation, with its attendant disruptions and further loss of power to the animals, but domination of mutation. All the good with none of the evil. Yet how could he believe that this murderer would really usher in such a miracle?

"Then believe this," Piebald said. "Our prime initial ambition is to eliminate lopsi."

Knot laughed. "To destroy the alleged source of your power? That disembodied alien force that makes all lobos cooperate? I doubt that."

"It is a dangerous force. The only way to preserve civilization long-term is to control mutancy and psi, lest they multiply cancerously and destroy the parent body. Mutancy we can cut off only at the source, preventing mutant births. Lopsi we can drain away, like releasing the sluices of a dam about to burst from flooding. By restoring the individual psi-powers to decriminalized lobos, making them complete and useful citizens again. What a golden age it could be, once mutancy in all its forms has been tamed to serve instead of to chasten man!"

Knot hated this ruthless lobo. But Piebald's words were making a lot of sense. Suppose—

Then he looked at Finesse, lying still and bloodied, and his unbelief hardened. He knew that she, if she lived, would never be deluded by this glib package of promises. And if she died—

"I do not trust you or your dream. I can meet most of my commitments to the animals and to myself by letting CC die. This way is painful but sure."

Piebald, seeing his persuasion fail, struggled desperately. But he could not free himself from the balk position they shared. "You are deluded! It's such a waste!"

"Yes, isn't it?" Knot agreed, smiling as the wan light faded to darkness. The air was almost unbreathable now, too. They would die when CC did.

Suddenly the light brightened, and a fresh draft of air wafted across the room. Both Knot and Piebald looked up, blinking, startled.

A man stood by the master switch. He had just closed it, restoring power to CC, and the response had been almost instantaneous. He was a CC teleport.

Then the chamber door opened and other CC psi-mutes entered. Damner the controller strode toward Knot and Piebald, closely followed by a mature woman.

Knot's will left him. He released the lobo and stood up. Piebald did the same. They were in the power of two psi-controllers.

Now Drem the futurist was carried up. "Yes, we are interfering, when we had agreed not to," he said without preamble. "Did either of you actually think we would stand idly by and watch our employer be pointlessly destroyed? We agreed to serve the winner—but there is not to be any winner, just two losers, and we all will perish, your way. We did not agree to that. So we are taking necessary action to break the deadlock. Now we shall release your bodies—but whoever makes an untoward move will be subjected to will control again. Understood?"

Knot, released, nodded. So did Piebald. This was a new aspect of the situation; neither of them knew what it meant.

Behind Drem, other psi-mutants were reviving the healer and Harlan, and attending to Finesse. "How did you get in?" Knot asked. "We had most psi blocked out."

"It took a concentrated effort to neutralize the psi of the baby," Drem said. "We had to use our psi to neutralize the neutralizer, as it were. Once we accomplished that, we were able to act, and we have done so, before it was too late. It was no easy chore, but it had to be done."

"So you psis are taking over CC?" Piebald asked.

"Not so. Our compromise stands," Drem continued. "We shall serve the victor. But to ensure that there *be* a victor, we are now requiring that this matter be settled by arbitration rather than physical combat. Each of you will select an arbiter, and these arbiters will review the facts of the case, discuss the issue, and come to an agreement, perhaps a compromise. Do you agree to abide by their decision?"

"No!" Knot said.

Piebald, after a moment, said, "Yes."

"Why do you decline?" Drem asked Knot. "Do you feel the procedure is unfair?"

"I fear it is a trick to give the lobos control," Knot said. "Or if not, that the lobos will violate the terms of the settlement and usurp control."

"Rest assured: we shall not serve any usurper. Neither you nor the lobos will be able to penetrate CC's defenses again, after this. Winner and loser will be protected from each other."

Still Knot did not accede. He knew Finesse would not agree to anything less than complete restoration of the original program, regardless what any arbiter might decide.

"Do you fear an objective review of your case would defeat it?" Piebald asked.

That stung; that was exactly what Knot feared. How could anyone who had not experienced the horrors of the lobo villa understand how superficial Piebald's logic was? Incalculable harm could be done in the name of objectivity—as the entire history of CC demonstrated. But how could he explain that—to these employees of CC?

"We prefer to have your agreement on this," Drem said. "But we shall have a decision, which we shall enforce, regardless. If you will not choose an arbiter, we shall select one for you."

Knot saw he had no choice. He would have to accede to this superficially reasonable disaster. "It is duress, but I will participate."

"That suffices," Drem said. He looked tired. The futures psi was physically weak anyway, and this event had not strengthened him. Knot could sympathize. "We have all made decisions under duress—the duress of events." He turned to Piebald. "The arbiter for the lobos?"

"My wife," Piebald said promptly. "The lady Hulda the Prophetess."

A group of CC psis assembled and concentrated, reminding Knot fleetingly of the psi-chickens. Suddenly a projection of the lady lobo formed.

Hulda looked about, startled. "You are here as our arbiter," Piebald said. "The issue is at impasse; you must speak for the lobos."

She nodded, grasping the situation with astonishing rapidity. "I always have."

"Your arbiter," Drem asked Knot.

Whom should he choose? So few understood the situation, or were in any position to argue the case if they did. Whom would Finesse trust? Hermine the weasel? But Hermine drew her intelligence from the one she communicated with, and might be unduly influenced by Piebald, whose mind was devious and unscrupulous. And Hermine—how could he have forgotten!—had been bitten by a poisonous viper. She could be dead by now.

It needed to be a human being. "I prefer to argue my own case," Knot said.

"No. You attempted to forward your own case, and failed. It must be another party, one not involved in this present action."

That reduced the options still more. So few had any inkling—

The child, a thought came. It was the bee, Pyridoxine. **She knows.**

She would have to do. Knot had joined the hive, and partaken of its benefit in the form of the precognitive chart of CCC; he had to respect the judgment of the representative of the hive. "Klisty, on Planet Chicken Itza," he said.

There was no argument. In a moment the girl also appeared in image, as startled as Hulda had been. These CC psis could do marvelous things!

"Klisty," Knot said quickly, "we fought to a draw, here on CCC. Now we are in arbitration. That's when representatives of the parties get together and work it out. You must talk with the lobo lady here, and decide who shall govern the Coordination Computer and what the policy of CC shall be henceforth."

"Oh, I couldn't!" she cried, abashed.

"If you do not, we lose by default. The bees believe you are suitable, and I daresay the chickens do. You must discuss it, and whatever the two of you agree on, that will be done."

"Oh—I see. I guess. All right. But suppose we can't agree?"

"There will be a third arbiter, to eliminate the chance of a tie vote," Drem said. "This must be from the number of the CC psis, agreed upon by the two of you."

"The healer," Piebald said immediately.

The quickness of the lobo's mind! Knot tried to find some reason to oppose the choice, and could not; Auler the healer seemed ideal. If he leaned at all, it should be in Knot's direction. "Agreed."

But Auler objected. He had just been brought out of stun and was working on Finesse. "I have a patient here."

"We do have other healers," Drem reminded him. A young woman came forward.

Auler spread his hands. "So it must be. I'm sure Jan can manage."

All three arbiters vanished—the two images and Auler. "What?" Knot asked, nonplused.

"The arbitration is private, free of coercive influences," Drem said. "They can affect each other only by reason. They will reappear to announce the decision."

"But I haven't finished acquainting Klisty with the facts!"

"Our telepaths will acquaint her with everything she wishes to know."

435

"But she's only a child! She doesn't know what to ask!"

Drem did not answer. Knot knew why: He had selected his arbiter; now he had to let her function. He had serious misgivings, but the decision was now out of his hands.

Auler the healer and Harlan had been brought out of stun together. The baby was now fully alert, being held by one of the psis. Three other psis stood watching: Evidently these were the ones suppressing Harlan's psi. A tricky business!

Jan, the lady healer, was now working on Finesse. She looked grave. "If there is brain damage, my psi won't reverse it," she warned.

Knot knelt beside Finesse. All this time he had been debating the fine points of arbitration, while she lay here bleeding! "She is alive?"

"Yes. And will survive, physically." The psi glanced across at him. She looked disturbingly like Finesse herself; perhaps his fatigued mind was manufacturing similarities where none existed. Of course the two did *not* resemble each other; Finesse was leaking blood from her smashed nose, and though her face had been wiped clean, it was nervously pale. "But she may suffer mentally or psychically, depending—"

"Psychically?"

"She has been injured in the head, the site of psi."

"Like a lobotomy?" Knot demanded, horrified.

Jan nodded. Now she looked less like Finesse. She was not as pretty, for one thing, and her eyes were brown. "Very crudely, yes. It's not a good analogy—"

"Oh Finesse!" Knot whispered, stroking her damp hair. The healer's psi had started the tissues and cartilage along their restoration, but her face was still a ruin. What of the mind behind it?

Knot looked up at Piebald, and saw the lobo watching, unconcerned. Damn the man!

"I would give up the galaxy for you," Knot said to the still figure, taking Finesse's limp hand. "Don't leave me now!" But he knew that was not enough. She could not hear him.

"It might help if you could reach her mind," Drem said. "We can relay your message telepathically—"

"No. She would not listen." Knot paused, not liking any of this. "The only person who could reach her would be Hermine, the weasel. But Hermine—" Was that the last nail in this coffin?

The psis checked. They located Hermine and brought her to him. Knot took the little furry body in his hands, cradling it, feeling its warmth. She lived! **Hermine,** he thought. **How glad I am you made it!**

Then he spied the set of punctures on her tiny shoulder. So it was true, he thought, horrified. **You were bitten!**

The viper is dead now, she thought with satisfaction. She was physically exhausted, her fur ruffled and specked with blood, but otherwise seemed sound. **I broke her neck.**

But the poison—

I exchanged some fleas with Rondl, she admitted. **Just in case. I thought they might be useful.**

The psi-fleas—counteracting the snake's poison! Smart weasel! She had been in far less danger than Piebald had imagined. **I know you are tired, but I must ask of you one more effort. All is not well here; we may lose our mission. But Finesse—you must think to her, try to give her will to recover even if—**

I know, Hermine agreed. **Finesse is my friend too.** Hermine focused on the unconscious woman.

After a moment, the weasel reported. **She is there—but does not wish to return. She fears the war is lost.**

Tell her it is being arbitrated! Knot thought urgently. **We have an even chance.**

There was another pause. **She will fight. She is coming back to help—**

Hulda and Klisty and Auler reappeared. "We—we decided," Klisty said, while the others stood soberly beside her. "It didn't take long at all. We discussed it all, about the enclaves and the animals and lopsi, and—and the animals get autonomy, each with its own planet, and—"

So the hive would have its desire, and the chickens, and the rats and the roaches, who would be protected in their egg stage by having a planet free of roach-predators.

Knot was glad for them. But— "CC!" he cried. "Who controls CC?"

"The lobos," Klisty said. "I'm sorry, but that's what's right. They'll stop the mutations. Their research—lopsi —they really need CC real bad, and—"

Do I tell Finesse? Hermine asked.

"And this is really what's right," Klisty concluded. "We all agreed. It'll stop the mutiny."

Knot made a futile gesture. **I will not lie to her, though I lose her. Tell her the lobos and the animals won. It is no bad thing, really—** He hesitated. **No, that won't do. Put me in direct touch—can you link our minds, as you did with you and me against the rats?**

I can try. Will yourself to me, as hard as you can, and I will relay—

He willed, and she tried. Suddenly Knot was with Hermine, seeing Finesse through weasel eyes, sniffing her through a weasel nose. Then that faded and they were plunging through nebulosity toward Finesse's hidden mind.

Finesse was a vortex of awareness, deep in the chaos of her own unconscious: a buried dream; Knot was another, and Hermine a third. He could not exactly talk to either of them now; there was no voice. But he could signal.

He intersected his vortex with Finesse's, impinging on her sense of identity. FINESSE, he communicated in diffuse squeeze.

KNOT! she replied with a swirl of gladness. YOU LIVE? HOW GOES IT IN THE CONSCIOUS WORLD?

BADLY. THE LOBOS HAVE CC, THE ANIMALS HAVE AUTONOMY. THERE WILL BE CHAOS IN THE HUMAN REALM.

THEN YOU AND I ARE DEAD. She seemed relieved that it was over.

NO. WE LIVE. THERE WAS ARBITRATION, AND KLISTY DECIDED. THE LOBOS HAD THE STRONGER CASE, OBJECTIVELY.

THEN I PREFER TO DIE, she thought, and plunged downward through roiling clouds of emotion.

Knot plunged after her. IF YOU GO, I GO WITH YOU.

NO! She shot down faster. He did not know what might lie in the nethermost reaches of her mind, but it seemed to be growing hotter, and the clouds were coming to resemble smoke.

I LOVE YOU! he thought despairingly, trying to retain his perception of her despite the obscuring mists and currents. THERE CAN BE LIFE FOR US, AMONG THE ANIMALS AND PEOPLES OF THE NEW ORDER. MANKIND IS NOT LOST, ONLY SET ON A NEW PATH, LIKE THE EUROPEANS AFTER THE ROMANS—

NEVER! I AM AT HEART A ROMAN! She shot away so swiftly she was only a blur.

Knot followed again, knowing they were both flirting with death or insanity, inverting their own minds and Hermine's toward schizophrenia. LIKE THE MAMMALS AFTER THE DINOSAURS—

I AM A DINOSAUR! She passed through grotesque streamers of semisubstance, foul-smelling.

Knot followed determinedly, though he did not like this region at all. YOU ARE A MAMMAL, NO QUESTION OF IT! He ought to know!

Suddenly a monstrous flux of sinister power loomed, dark and evil. A malignant storm, part fire and part acid, it extended toward them, sending out flanking tendrils.

Finesse halted, appalled. NO—HELL IS TOO AWFUL! she thought.

THAT IS NOT HELL, Hermine thought. I HAVE SEEN IT BEFORE, IN THE MINDS OF THE LOBOS. IT IS LOPSI.

Knot understood. BECAUSE WE ARE LOBOTOMIZING OURSELVES! WE ARE RETREATING FROM OUR LIVING BODIES, FOLLOWING OUR PSI TO LIMBO. WE ARE JOINING THE DISEMBODIED LOBO PSI, BECOMING PART OF ITS POOL.

NO! Finesse thought with sheerest horror. THAT IS WORST OF ALL! I WOULD RATHER LIVE IN CHAOS.

SO WOULD THE LOBOS, Knot thought. THEY SERVE THIS DEVIL FORCE, AND WISH TO BE FREE, FOR THEY BELIEVE IT WILL DESTROY MANKIND, AS IT HAS DESTROYED OTHER CIVILIZATIONS BEFORE OURS. THEY MEAN TO USE CC TO ABOLISH IT.

A NOVA AT YOU! Finesse thought furiously. YOU ARE TRYING TO PERSUADE ME TO GO BACK. IT WON'T WORK!

THEN I SUPPOSE WE'LL HAVE TO LET KLISTY RAISE BABY HARLAN AMONG THE CHICKENS.

THE BABY! she thought, shocked. KLISTY'S ONLY A CHILD! SHE CAN'T—

NAUGHTY MAN! Hermine agreed gleefully.

YOU'RE NO BETTER, WEASEL! Finesse thought furiously. I'LL MAKE YOU BOTH SORRY! Yet beyond her anger was a certain humor and relief.

And Knot, knowing she would return now with him and Hermine to fight it out among the living, to abate chaos and live life and love love with vigor and dispatch, was mute.

THE FALL OF WORLDS TRILOGY
BY FRANCINE MEZO

The FALL OF WORLDS trilogy follows the daring galactic adventures of Captain Areia Darenga, a beautiful starship commander bred for limitless courage as a clone, but destined to discover love as a human.

THE FALL OF WORLDS   75564 $2.50

Captain Areia Darenga is brave, beautiful, intelligent and without passion. She is no ordinary human but part of a special race bred for a higher purpose—to protect the universe from those who would destroy it. For without the blinding shackles of human emotions, Areia can guard her world without earthly temptations. But when she leads a battle against a foe, Areia finds her invisible control shattered—her shocking transformation can only lead to one thing—love.

UNLESS SHE BURN   76968 $2.25

A tragic battle in space has transformed Captain Areia Darenga into a human and leads her to a death she would have never known. Exiled to the hostile planet of M'dia she lives in the desolate reaches of a desert, struggling for a bleak survival. But then she is rescued by M'landan, a handsome alien priest who awakens in her a disturbing passion and mystical visions of a new and tempting world.

NO EARTHLY SHORE   77347 $2.50

Captain Areia Darenga has found life-giving passions in the arms of M'landan, high priest for the M'dia people. Forced from their planet, M'landan and his people are threatened by an alien race who seek their total destruction. As they are mercilessly tracked across the universe by their enemies, Captain Areia, M'landan and his people search for a world where the race may be reborn.

Available wherever paperbacks are sold, or directly from the publisher. Include 50¢ per copy for postage and handling; allow 4-6 weeks for delivery. Avon Books, Mail Order Dept., 224 West 57th St., N.Y., N.Y. 10019

AVON Paperback   Mezo 2-81 (5-2)

**FOR THE FIRST TIME IN PAPERBACK, FOUR
SPACED-OUT FANTASIES OF CHILLING SATIRE
AND MIND-BENDING FUTURISM FROM THE
MODERN MASTER OF SCIENCE FICTION:**

THE CYBERIAD — 51557 $2.50
The intergalactic capers of two "cosmic constructors"
as they vie to out-invent each other building gargan-
tuan cybernetic monsters all across the universe.

THE FUTUROLOGICAL CONGRESS — 52332 $2.25
A traveler from outer space comes to Earth for a conference, but a revolution catapults him into a syn-
thetic future paradise created by hallucinogenic
drugs.

THE INVESTIGATION — 29314 $1.50
When dead bodies inexplicably resurrect themselves, a shrewd detective and an adroit statistician
match metaphysical wits in a case that lies beyond
mind, beyond this world.

MEMOIRS FOUND IN A BATHTUB — 29959 $1.50
Far in the future a man wanders pointlessly in the
designed destiny of a vast underground labyrinth,
the final stronghold of the American Pentagon.

*"A major figure who just happens to be a
science fiction writer ... very likely, he is also the
bestselling SF writer in the world."*
Fantasy and Science Fiction

LEM 2-81

THE BEST IN SCIENCE FICTION
AND FANTASY FROM
AVON ◆ BOOKS

URSULA K. LE GUIN

The Lathe of Heaven	43547	1.95
The Dispossessed	51284	2.50

ISAAC ASIMOV

Foundation	50963	2.25
Foundation and Empire	52357	2.25
Second Foundation	52290	2.25
The Foundation Trilogy (Large Format)	50856	6.95

ROGER ZELAZNY

Doorways in the Sand	49510	1.75
Creatures of Light and Darkness	35956	1.50
Lord of Light	44834	2.25
The Doors of His Face The Lamps of His Mouth	38182	1.50
The Guns of Avalon	31112	1.50
Nine Princes in Amber	51755	1.95
Sign of the Unicorn	53132	1.95
The Hand of Oberon	51318	1.75
The Courts of Chaos	47175	1.75

Include 50¢ per copy for postage and handling,
allow 4-6 weeks for delivery.

Avon Books, Mail Order Dept.
224 W. 57th St., N.Y., N.Y. 10019

SF 2-81